FOCUS

by

Sallie Lowenstein

Sallie Lowenstein

Lion Stone Books
Kensington, Maryland

Published by
LION STONE BOOKS
4921 Aurora Drive
Kensington, MD 20895
tel: 301-949-3204
fax:301-949-3860
e-mail: lionstone@juno.com

Cataloging-in-Publication Data
Lowenstein, Sallie
Focus/Sallie Lowenstein
p.cm.

Summary: When Andrew Haldran decides not to follow the
traditional pattern of being genetically Augmented to be
focused on one profession, his father takes a job on
another world to try and earn enough money to
suppport his son's decision.

ISBN 0-9658486-3-9
[1. Science Fiction 2. Mystery 3. Young Adult Novel]

Library of Congress Catalog Card Number: 00-093207

First Edition
Manufactured in the United States

FOCUS

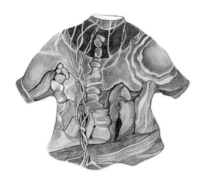

This book is dedicated to
my son, John, who has
always loved knowledge!

Many thanks to
Robert Kenney,
Rachel Kenney,
Frank Lowenstein
and M.A. Harper
for their support, input
and encouragement

Sallie Lowenstein writes, makes art
and lives outside of Washington,
DC. Behind her house sits a 400
square foot garage that she and her
husband converted to a studio
where she sculpts and paints and
sometimes teaches. In their house
is a computer, a desk, lots of different dictionaries and thesauruses
and lots of paper and notebooks for
writing. Ms. Lowenstein welcomes
her readers to send letters to her at
lionstone@juno.com, and she pro-
mises to write back.

Other Books by Sallie Lowenstein:
Daniel the Medusa Hunter
The Mt. Olympus Zoo
Evan's Voice
*The Festival of Lights, A Family
Hanukkah Service*

I

"Focus," my father had said to me for the first time when I was six. "Just focus, Andrew. It's the key to everything."

My mind had immediately wandered off to wonder about the trees, the meanings of dreams, and the stars and the moons.

"Andrew, pay attention, son," my dad had said when I was nine. "It's never too early to begin to focus on your future." My mind had wandered off to speculate on dinosaurs and history, on wars fought and peacetimes brought to fruition.

When I was fourteen, my father declared, "Andrew, you can't put this off much longer. You only have until your seventeenth birthday to decide what you want to do with the rest of your life. You must focus soon."

My mind skipped gently past the ultimatum to a place where I had always been able to go, where my dreams came together, where I made up heroic stories in which I starred: Andrew, a man who used his knowledge to solve mysteries, crimes and injustices. If I made up a plot for which I lacked the knowledge to resolve the conflict, I attacked the problem in the real world. My parents often found me immersed in a book or making lists and charts on topics obscure and useless to everyone but me. I never told anyone what I was doing and even at fourteen I still craved the excitement of the worlds I carried in my head.

Slowly as my fourteenth year passed, disturbing villains and dilemmas began to poke their heads into my stories. A computer chip crawled into the brains of hapless children and turned them into robots; an evil succubus drained the consciousness of revolutionaries and left them shells of their former selves who could no longer fight for justice. At first I tried to ignore the intruders by starting the plots again and eliminating the irritants from my story lines. I turned fifteen, and one night as I went to bed, Hero Andrew was in line for the movies and found himself prohibited from entering. The movie was rated *F*, for the Focused only. Masked people in dark capes threw tomatoes and eggs at the hapless, unfocused hero. I shuddered and closed down the story. That year I carefully kept Hero Andrew swimming under the seas, or scaling the Himalayas, floating on a raft across an algae-covered, alien ocean or exploring an ice planet. He never rested, and I was determined not to think about anything except my lists and stories. I kept Hero Andrew away from evil, and myself away from facing the decision my father advocated more and more as he repeated like a litany, "Andrew, it's time to focus."

The more he said it, the more I tried to reject the idea, but no matter how much I wanted to, I couldn't stop time from rolling through my fifteenth year. I knew that my parents were still expecting, perhaps hoping against hope, that I would focus and be able to make a choice about what I would be. As for me, the faster the year sped by, the more I longed for an era when people studied how things fit together and interlocked; where generalists were still needed in the world and precise choices were not the norm.

"I can't decide," I told my mom. "I'm not ready."

"You keep saying that, Andrew," she said in frustration. "When will you be ready? When are you going to commit?"

"I don't know," I said.

"Your time to decide is running out! Be careful you don't miss your chance to be Augmented."

My friends were already declaring right and left: James to be a pilot, Martin a doctor, Abe a merchant chief. Mary decided to be a tailor and Shirley a mechanic. They fearlessly filled in and filed their forms, and went home to proud and smiling parents.

"I heard Miriam is going to be an astronomer," Dad announced one morning as he fried eggs for Cindra and Louisa.

"Yeah," I answered glumly.

"Why so sad?" Dad asked.

"I dunno," I said.

"Still undecided?"

"Yes and no."

"Do you want to look at the List of Occupation Choices again?"

"No, Dad, I don't need to, because I'm not going for Augmentation."

"Andrew, we've told you over and over, there's nothing to be afraid of. The gene manipulation just enables you to do your job better."

"Better than I would have naturally, right, Dad?" I interrupted. "I know the mantra. Augmentation focuses you so you can pursue one topic really well, exclusively, in fact. Well, thanks, but no thanks. I like me the way I am."

"Andrew, you're a great kid. We like you the way you are too, but without Augmentation you won't be able to compete. Certain levels of training will be out of reach for you. There must be something on the List of Occupations that you would like to be. I hope you'll reconsider."

"Dad, that's exactly the problem! I want to be most of the things on the List, not just one of them. So I've decided. I'm staying general. I know the consequences, but I'm not going to change my mind. I already filed the papers," I burst out and held my breath.

My father lifted his large bulk, shaking a head that should have belonged to a wrestler instead of a diplomat, and stalked out of the room. "Rebecca," he growled. "I can't do a thing with him."

Of course, my father had expected to win me over. That was his job, winning people over, coaxing them into reasonableness. I smiled to myself. I had practiced being defiant, winning impossible battles against all odds and pressures, standing firm and cool in my dreams, and I had won against an Augmented master.

Cindra looked up from her eggs. "Whatcha gonna do when we leave, Andy?"

"Leave?" I asked. "Does Dad have another posting?"

She nodded, bobbing her corkscrewed hair around.

"When?" I asked.

"I don't know. I'm only six," she said. "Ask Louisa, she's already eight."

"Louisa?" I said.

"Soon. Maybe tomorrow," she said.

"Louisa," I shouted, "that's dumb!"

"Yeah, maybe, but you're dumber and you're gonna stay that way cause you don't wanna be smart.

"You don't know anything! Augmentation doesn't make you smart. You're too young to understand," I fumed.

"I do too understand. If you don't get Augmented, Andrew, you aren't going to do anything good."

"I want to be good at a bunch of things. If I focus, I'll only be able to do one thing well, Louisa!" I practically yelled at her.

"Mommy and Daddy do lots of things good," she protested.

"Like what?"

"Read to us, help us with our homework, play with us."

"Daddy makes bad eggs," Cindra said. "I'm gonna be a chef when I grow up so my kids will eat good."

"Fine," I said, throwing up my hands. "I'm going out. Tell Mom and Dad I'll be back."

Trying not to panic, I slipped out into the corridors of the city that hung suspended above vehicle lanes. Far below the clear-cast tubes through which I walked, frenetic wall to wall traffic clogged the roads. I ignored it just as I ignored the symphony of raindrops that suddenly drummed down onto the tubes.

My father's postings were always for several years. If I went along, a year-and-a-half from now I'd be an adult and my father would no longer get an allowance for me unless I was in school, and I couldn't go on in school unless I was Augmented. The Corps would send me home alone, without a place to live or a job. The best I might get was a hard-labor, low-paying, little hope job.

"Andrew," my mother called, catching up to me, her easy glide-and-stride gait bringing her quickly to my side. She reached up to pat my shoulder. "You heard about Dad's new job, sweetie?"

"Sort of. I heard you were going from Cindra and Louisa."

"We're all going. We are not deserting you."

"And a year from now, how are you going to afford me? I'll just have to come back. I might as well stay."

"Andrew, your father and I were pretty sure what you were going to decide, so he has taken a job with a private company that isn't one of these underpaid, government diplomacy tours-of-duty."

"But Mom, Dad loves his job. He got Augmented to be a diplomat in the Space Corps. He can't give it up."

"Andrew, we may be disappointed, but we love you. You're more important to your Dad than a career in the Corps. It'll be fine. We should have done it long ago." She reached up, kissed my cheek and turned on her heel back towards home.

II

Despite my parents' reassurances, late at night I could hear their whisperings. Their words were indistinguishable, but the tones of irritation and worry were sharp and clear. Some nights, in the dark I could hear my father lumber into the great room at the center of our apartment and pace up and back, stopping, pacing. I could picture him staring out the huge, glass-paneled wall, his big face reflected against the night on the other side. Would a tear trickle down the side of his nose?

"Don't worry Dad, I'm tough. I've got places to go," I would whisper in those wee hours and slip into a Hero Andrew story.

Three weeks before the packers were to come, I awoke in the night, but no one was up. My father wasn't lumbering across squeaky floorboards; my mother's mouse-light tread was absent. I rolled over seeking the trailings of a dream. In it I had closed my eyes, twirled my finger about and punched it down onto the List of Augmentation Options right onto what I would be. I fumbled about for a pencil and paper to write the answer down, but I couldn't remember what my finger had landed on. Had it been naturalist or physician, historian or biologist or even stand-up comedian? I had considered each one at some time, but whatever my choice had been, it was as elusive as the waking end of the dream. My eyelids drifted together and within a few moments, the image was mixed and whipped back into a stew of sleepy specters.

Morning in the city sent sunlight gliding through the oval leaded-glass of our apartment windows as pre-timed alarm shutters snapped open. Eye-shaped sun dappled the rugs and walls and landed on my face.

My parents were insisting I continue school until we left. Excitement and anxiety reigned high among my friends as they talked about their futures. I listened and smiled, but volunteered nothing. I had nothing to tell. The tension rose until the annual Futures Assembly was held. Names and further educational institutions were announced. My classmates sat up straight, smiled, rose, centered their bodies as they walked with pride to receive their assignments. The best students still got into the best schools, but everyone knew they all had a shot at success. Sometimes Augmentation changed people in unexpected ways. Not often, but sometimes, a Sonny O'Connir came along. Ten years ago, Sonny had gotten smarter, much smarter, so much smarter that kids still rumored his parents had bought more than Career Augmentation. Or, sometimes a Martel Arronson came along and crashed. Martel had fallen so low that kids said it had been malpractice.

Martel made everyone anxious. Sonny made everyone dream.

"Your name wasn't called," Marcia said, looking up into my height. She was a tiny wisp, almost childlike. I had always liked her. Her choice of Toy Designer seemed made to order.

"I'm still undecided."

"Really?"

"No, not really," I said, surprising myself in a wave of relief. "I'm not going for the A."

"Oh, Andrew, I'm sorry!"

"Why? Because I'm not willing to give up everything else to be really good at only one thing?"

"But, Andrew," she said softly, "you may end up losing everything."

"Maybe," I said, knowing all too well she might be right.

She reached for my hand and squeezed it. "I wish you luck, lots of it."

She walked slowly down the hall, before turning and calling back, "You've got courage, Andrew. Guts!" She vanished behind a crowd of chattering girls.

I cut classes. I didn't want to say good-bye. I didn't want to explain. I didn't want to be pressured. I stumped back through the plastic tubes, dreaming a new story, wishing I had my mini-comp to type it into, but the little computer was already packed. We had spent hours sorting to storage, to shipping, to hand carrying. I knew from past postings that half the things we stored would be outgrown or outdated when we returned, and half the things we shipped wouldn't return with us at all. Usually, it was what we hand carried that was really important to us.

I stopped at the entrance to a bookstore, checked my money and went in. I ignored disks and perused hard-bound books. Most were used. I ran my fingers across bindings and flipped through volumes of history and myth, science, ecology, philosophy and finally some novels. I eagerly added ten hard bound writing notebooks which were on sale for practically nothing. I had started writing stories down in the last few weeks, and even though almost no one wrote anything by hand anymore, I liked the way my mind moved when I was writing with a pen. So I bought up the notebooks.

The stack of books was high, as the clerk bagged them. She was probably twenty-one and had on an Un-Augmented, U-A badge, as required by law to notify unsuspecting customers she wasn't a knowledgeable specialist. If we weren't going on a posting, I'd be wearing one of those badges the day I turned seventeen. I'd heard tales of U-A's who had beaten the system, pretending to be Augmented, and making it good in a professional field. Only recently a great con-artist had been caught practicing medicine. Indignation had been so great, his patients' families had beaten him near to death, even though they admitted at the trial that he had saved several of their lives. The con-man was quoted as saying, "It was worth it!"

I was surprised the U-A clerk was reading a thin volume by Marcusin and Dover on the possibility of genetic connections between sentient races. Most people thought Marcusin and Dover were quacks. I wasn't sure. Why couldn't base DNA be common to human and alien sentients? There were similarities. Why couldn't there be a common beginning to sentient races? If so, Dover and Marcusin wondered if the sentients could cross conceive. Most scientists said that even if there was some distant connection, it was too removed to make gene mixing viable.

"What do you think about Marcusin and Dover?" I asked her.

"Huh? Oh, I'm no specialist," she stuttered.

"I know, but you can still think."

"Yes, but others can do it better," she replied, giving the standardized response along with my change.

"Why? Cause they got Augmented? Maybe their vision is too narrow to let them see patterns," I suggested.

"What are you, some radical Philosophy Augment?" she asked.

"No, I'm not," I said, gathering my purchases into my arms. "So what do you think?"

"I'm busy. I'm not allowed to discuss things with customers," she said handing me the receipt.

Her answer left me dazed. Even though the hard corners and edges of my books cut into my hands, I felt disturbingly detached from reality as I walked home.

III

The movers came and did their job, passing swiftly through lifetimes of belongings without so much as a double take. They wrapped and packed and sorted with indifference. When they left, we faced a forlorn flat, empty of everything but trash and bits and pieces of packing equipment, broken accumulations of household junk and incomplete toys and games. Stripped of everything else, we moved about in a packing-day-daze, bagging and carting the remains to the trash receptacles, trotting back for second, third, fourth loads until the apartment was bare except for dust motes floating lazily in stripes of sunlight.

"Come on Andy," Cindra said, tugging on my arm. "Mom says to stop dreaming and get a move on it. We've got two hours til our shuttle takes off."

"Okay, I heard."

"But, you didn't answer. Why don't you answer people, Andy?"

I mumbled and said, "I think I've answered, Cindra. I hear myself answering."

"Louisa says you're peculiar," she said, having trouble pronouncing the last word.

The girls were probably right. Dad was always assuring Mom I'd grow out of it. And Mom was always asking Dad, "When?"

"When he gets a girlfriend," Dad would laugh sometimes.

"Maybe he should become a TelePrompTer," Mom would joke back. "He'd never have to answer anyone, just type in what other people needed to say."

I hoped that wasn't what I ended up with as an option. I shook my head as my stomach fell, questioning if I'd made the right choice, knowing at that moment I no longer had an alternative.

The shuttle stood boarding-ready. We trooped on, the girls each holding one of Mom's hands, my dad shouldering a large bag that cradled a battery driven minicomputer and a hand-held holocorder. Everywhere Dad went, he carried that holocorder, accumulating archives of family events, that presently filled eight storage boxes, despite the micro-sized mini-discs. His brother and he were notorious holo-shooters, arriving like twins, holocorders strung awkwardly around their necks, prowling parties, sticking people together into poses that satisfied their mania for records.

I had to admit, it was fun to run through the holographic memories Dad had recorded. And, I had to admit, Dad was a pretty good holographer. The only problem was his passion for quantity. Just before we boarded the shuttle, Dad lined us up and shot a picture, just for the record.

We settled into our seats, Mom, Dad, Cindra and Louisa on one side of the aisle, me trapped against a portal next to a startlingly blue-eyed, flaccid-faced man without a single hair on his head.

"Well now, young man," the guy said to me as he struggled to squeeze his long legs into a comfortable position. "Where you off to?"

"My Dad has a new posting," I said as I flipped open one of my books.

"Whatcha reading?" the man persisted, I suppose trying to be friendly.

"*The Rise and Fall of the Old Millennium,*" I told him.

"Geez, you must be a History Augment."

I smiled and dug into the words.

"Never knew one of you before," the man said loudly to get my attention.

"You don't now," I said quietly, hoping to get him to stop talking so I could read.

"Aw, come on. No one else would read that stuff."

"I'm unaugmented."

The man visibly shifted away as far as he could get in his seat. "Nobody unaugmented would read that stuff," he insisted.

"Sorry," I said. I concentrated on my book.

The man gulped a drink and said, "Hey mister, why don't you trade places with your kid?"

Dad looked up. "Pardon me? Is there a problem?" he asked from across the aisle.

"Yeah!"

"Andrew?" Dad asked.

I shrugged.

"You bet, there's a problem. I ain't sitting next to some U-A! And where's his badge?"

"He isn't seventeen yet," Mom snapped.

"Yeah? He's awful tall not to be seventeen, lady!"

"And what were you Augmented for?" Mom asked the man, a slow red streak creeping down from her hairline which told me she hadn't really ignored that he had accused her of lying.

"I'm a ship-side-technician," he said proudly. "Best in the fleet."

"I cannot testify to your technical ability," Dad said, "but I can say with authority that you are well versed in bigotry."

The man's smile vanished. "Hey, I got a right. Ain't you ever heard the saying: Put U for unseen with an A for addled, and whatcha get is that," he said pointing at me.

The red slid to Mom's nose. Not a good sign.

"Mom," I intervened. "Forget it. It doesn't matter. He'll survive. I'll survive. It's only a couple of hours. The worst that can happen is one of us will get a few cooties from the other."

Cindra and Louisa giggled.

"I ain't got no cooties or nothin'," the man growled.

I smiled at the man and returned my attention to the pages of my book. He inched as far away from me as his size allowed, twisting until he actually leaned into the aisle to avoid me. When we finally left the shuttle and boarded the passenger ship, I saw him carefully brush himself off, and for just a split second it made me want to check myself for his cooties, too.

The actual space trip was peaceful for the first week until Cindra and Louisa trashed the cabin with toys. Dad grumbled about it and Mom tried to tidy up after them, only to have each advance repulsed by a new onslaught of game pieces and stuffed animals.

"Do you think they'll have elephants where we're going?" Louisa asked hugging her stuffed pachyderm.

"No," Mom said. "The only Earth-side creatures, other than man, are cats."

"What do they call this world again?" Cindra asked.

"Miners World," I answered

"Why?" Cindra asked.

"She keeps asking and forgetting," Louisa complained.

"So do you," Cindra accused.

"Stop, before you start," Dad commanded. "We've got two-and-a-half months to go in this cabin and no one, not anyone is going to fight! Got it?"

Two small heads went up and down.

After two weeks there had been thirty-one fights. I kept track between reading my books and writing stories. Mom started to pace the corridors constantly and Dad's growls and grumbles came more frequently, and more loudly.

"Please, Andrew, play with us," my sisters begged.

"Please, Andrew, play with them," my parents begged.

"Okay, okay, I'll tell you two a story, if you quit fighting."

"A long one?" Cindra asked.

"I think it better be," I said.

"Do you tell good stories?" Louisa asked.

"You guys tell me when I finish the story. It's called *Beautiful Silence*."

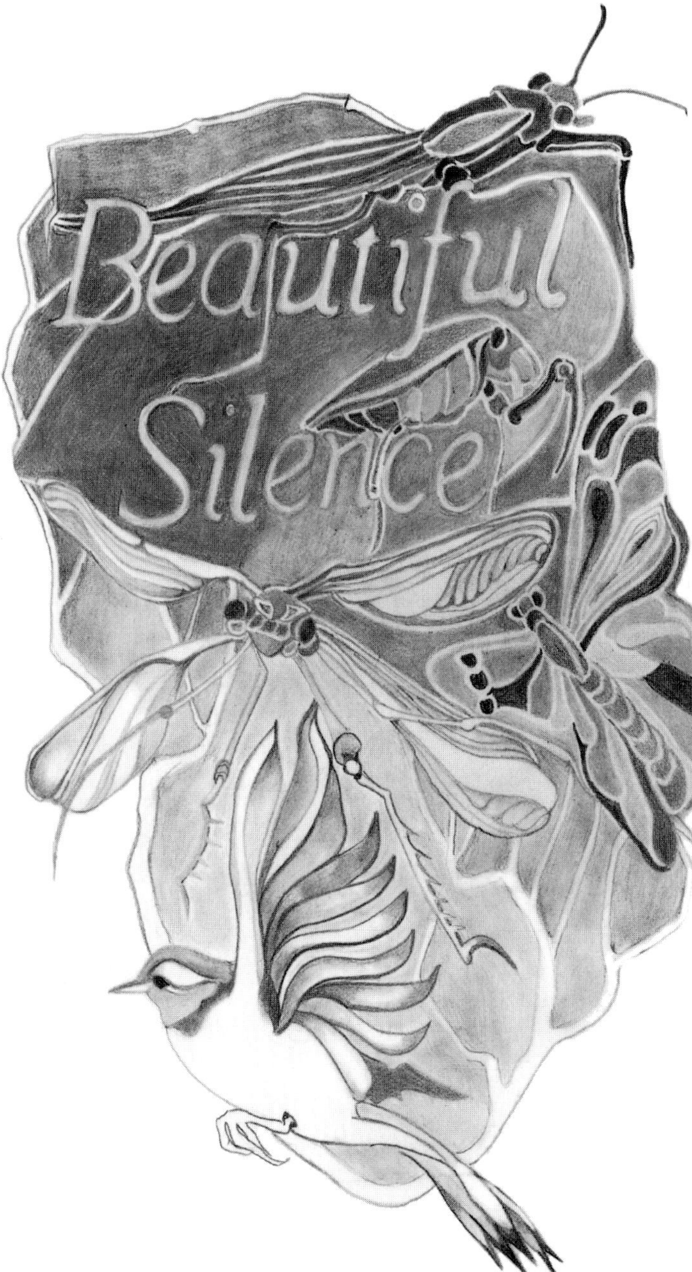
Beautiful
Silence

Not so long ago, but also not so close to now, lived a boy named . . .

[Uh, what do you two think we should call him?]

[Peter.]

[No, no. Alvin.]

[Okay.]

The boy's name was Alvin Peter Pooterbax.

[*Giggles*]

And Alvin Peter Pooterbax was, as you can imagine, a little bit poofy, a little bit puffy and a lot chattery. His chubby little face looked like it had a hole in it because he was always, always, always talking.

It drove his mom and his dad, his sister Heather Hope, his brother Arnold Nathan and his cousins Marvella Lila, Pontifax Harold, Marvin Mitchell and Miranda Celia, and his Uncle Calvin Aloysius and Aunt Patricia Paula nuts.

[Those are silly names. *Big toothless smiles*]

It didn't drive them nuts because he talked too much. It drove them nuts because they couldn't get a word in edgewise, or upside down or sideways either, and they all loved to talk.

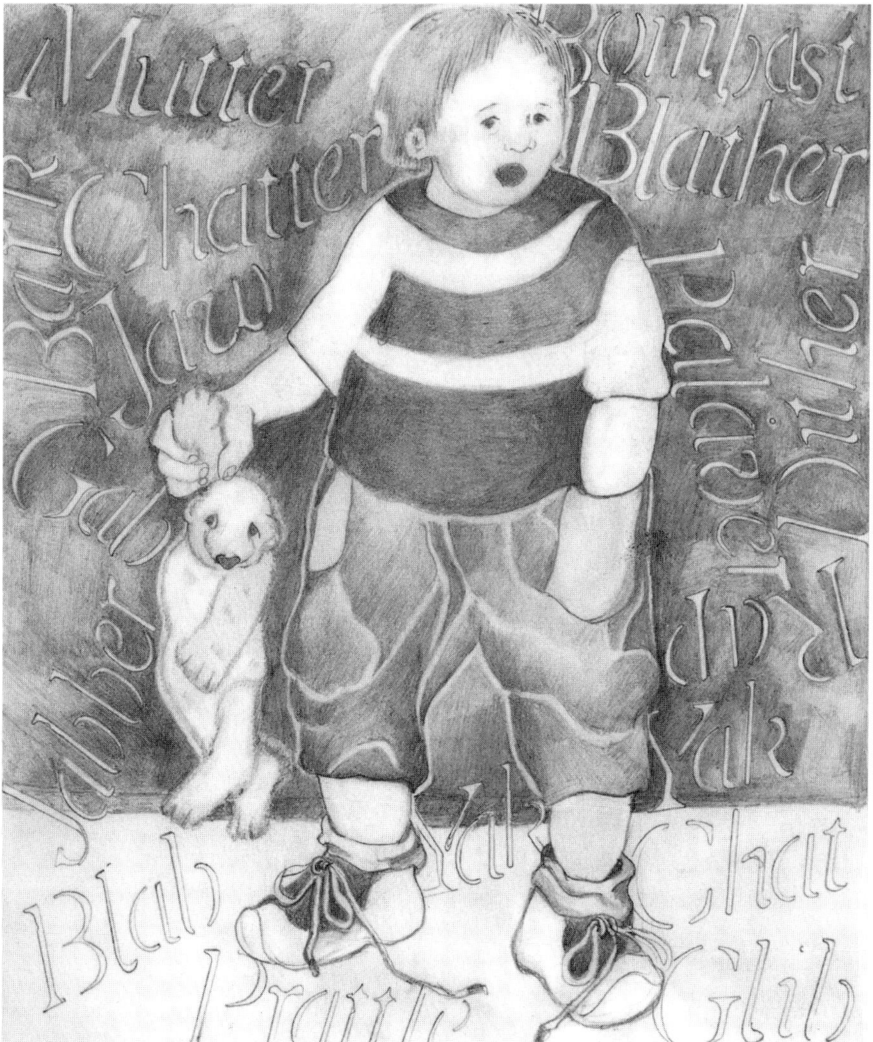
Mutter
Bombast
Chatter
Blather
Jaw
Yak
Yak
Blah
Chat
Prattle
Glib

Now, Alvin Peter Pooterbax lived in a place where there was only one real rule in school!

[Wow, only one?]

[Yes, as I said, one rule in school.]

It was their golden-encrusted rule! Everyone got to talk as much as they wanted, but no one could talk when anyone else was.

It worked perfectly until Alvin Peter came to school. No one, not anyone, ever, had been able to talk as long as Alvin Peter Pooterbax without taking a breath. Faces began to turn red as the class waited for a pause; kids began to fidget as they waited for their chance; and one kid even burst out in song, which wasn't exactly talking, but Alvin Peter Pooterbax still kept speaking.

After several days, every single child hoped that Alvin Peter would get really, really sick and stay home for a long, long time. Then they began to pray he would get sick and stay home even one whole day. But, Alvin Peter was very healthy. Now, then, everyone got very anxious, even the teacher, and what do you think happened?

[The kids got tired of waiting and poisoned him?]

[No, no, someone beat him up!]

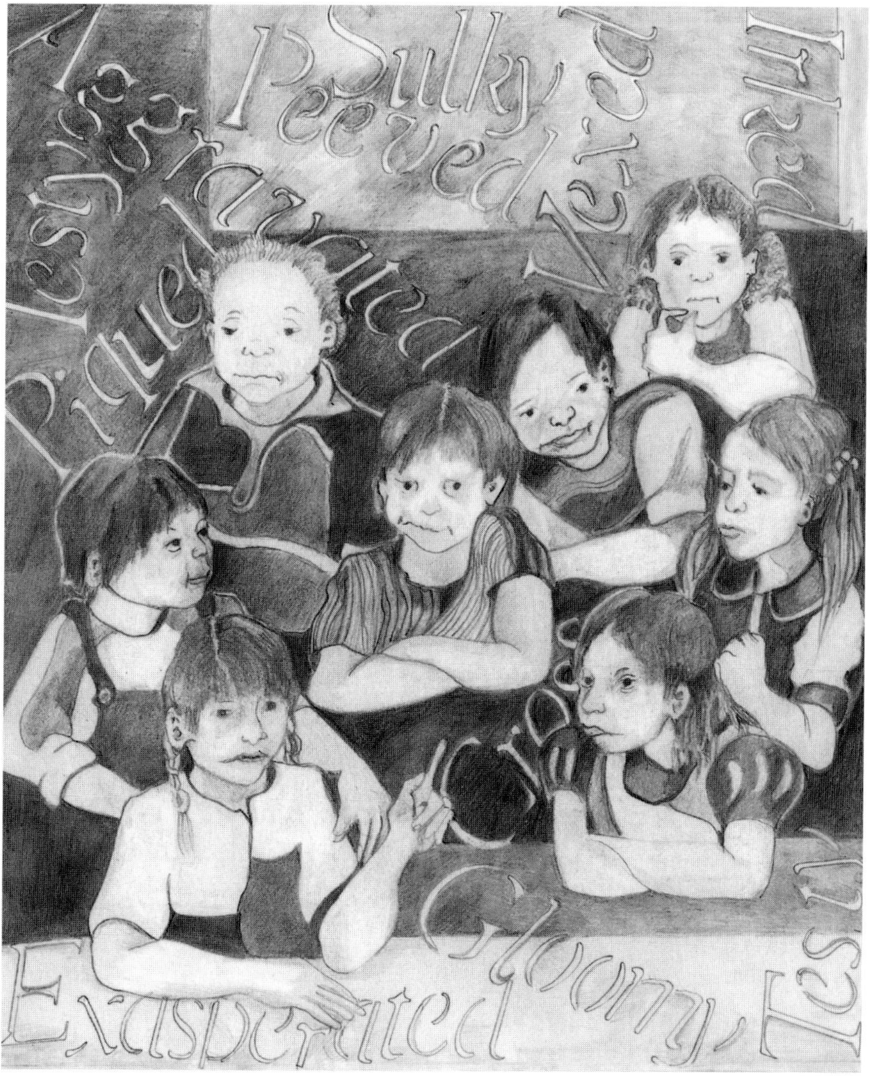
Sulky
Peeved
Exasperated
Gloomy

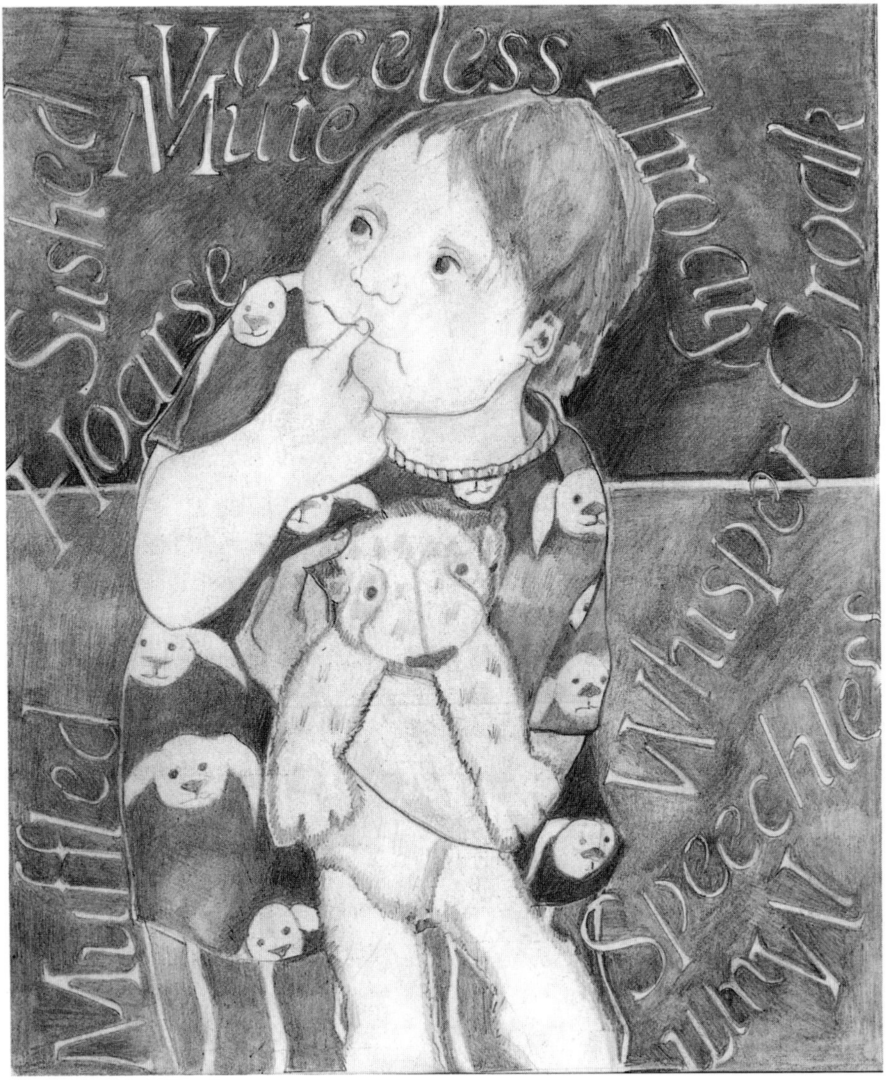
Voiceless
Mute
Hushed
Hoarse
Muffled
Throat
Croak
Whisper
Speechless
Mum

It happened early, one morning. Alvin Peter woke up with laryngitis. His mother smiled and his father smiled broadly. His little brother chattered merrily in the silence and his big sister laughed out loud at Alvin Peter. Then, his parents sent him off to school.

[But, he was sick!]

They probably weren't very good parents, but they knew this was just what the doctor had ordered for the school. Alvin Peter sat at his desk not saying a word.

—What's wrong with Alvin Peter, the class asked their teacher.

—His note says he has lost his voice, said his teacher with a big, smiling sigh.

—Really, truly? Oh boy, and a hip, hip, hip HOORAY, everyone hooted in delight, and then sat down with quiet plops at their seats and began the first normal day since Alvin Peter had begun school. Everyone had a chance to speak.

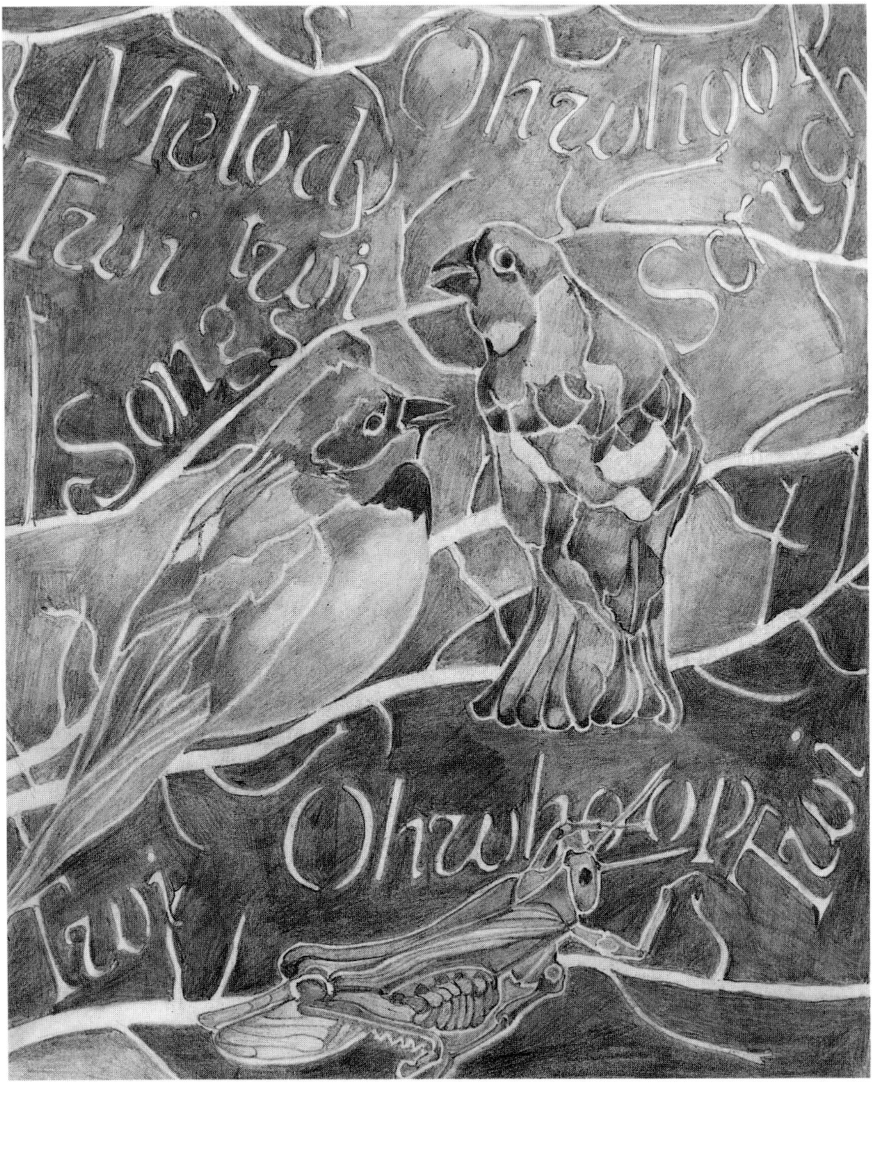

Melody
Ohwhoop
Tui tui
Songs
Tui

Alvin Peter Pooterbax could not say one word. He listened to the other children's answers and conversations and when he got bored with that, he listened to the birds outside the windows and heard the one that said ohwoop, ohwoop, ohwoop, and the crickets' constant, shrill twi, twi, twi, twi, twi and even the dry crack of the fall leaves still on the trees as the breeze brushed them.

At eleven a.m. the teacher asked everyone to write a story. Alvin Peter put his pencil on the paper and heard the scratch of the point writing his name. He looked up and heard the breathing of the girl next to him and the faint notes of a piano down the hall.

Alvin Peter smiled. He cleared his throat and felt his voice return, but he didn't say anything. He listened. And when he finally spoke again three days later, it was softly and he ended quickly.

Alvin Peter Pooterbax had finally learned to hear and not just to speak.

[*Pause.* That's it, that's the end]

[Aw, is that all? What happens to him now?]

[That's all of the Alvin Peter Pooterbax tale. I don't know what happens to him, but I've got other stories.}

[Tell, tell, Andy! Please, tell us another.]

[I'll read one later, if you guys don't fight.]

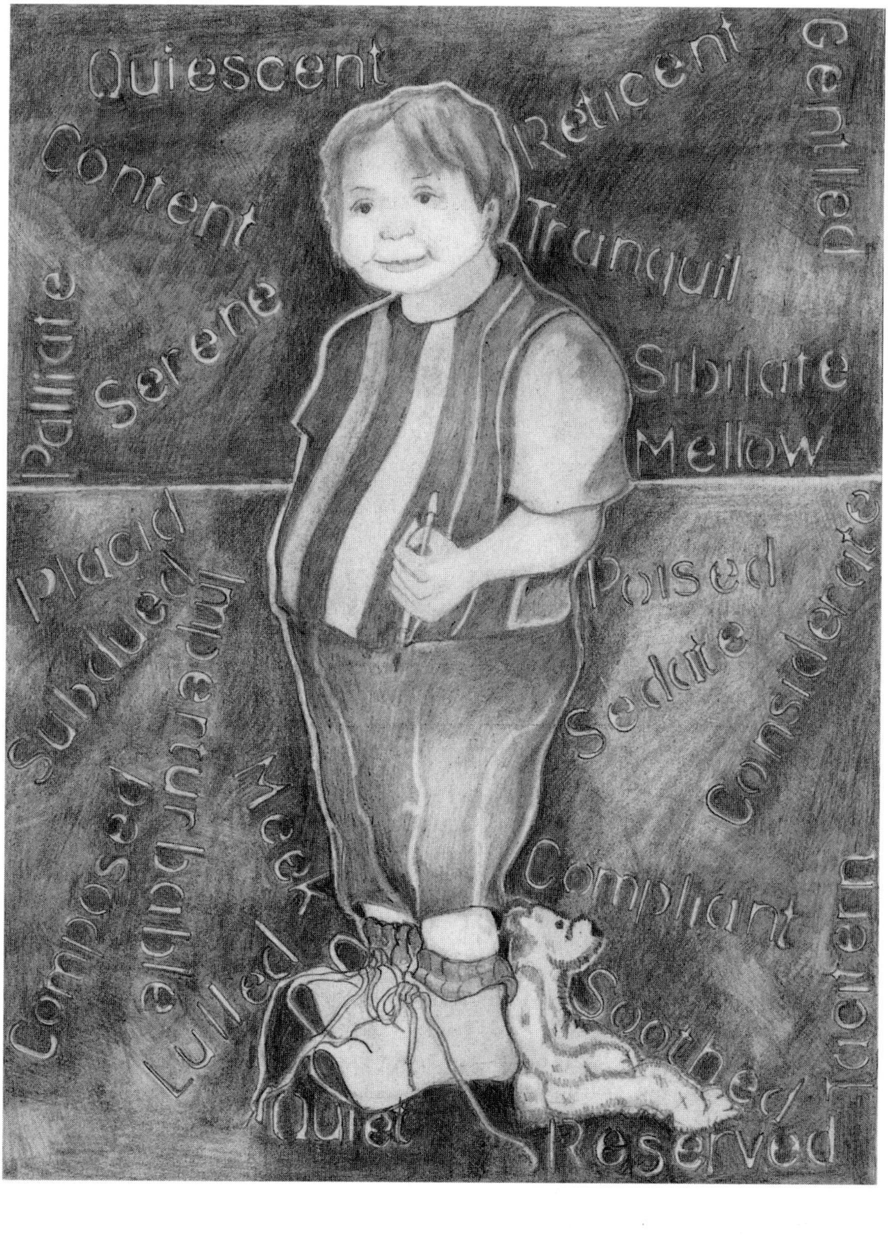
Quiescent
Reticent
Content
Tranquil
Palliate
Serene
Sibilate
Mellow
Placid
Subdued
Imperturbable
Poised
Sedate
Considerate
Meek
Compliant
Composed
Lulled
Soothed
Taciturn
Quiet
Reserved

IV

When we came back, Dad was studying the planet-side info documents. He rubbed his brow and shook his head, then calmly stretched, picked up the documents and threw them all in the trash.

"Darn blasted, most useless information I ever read. Doesn't say one specific iota of anything. Doesn't have language disks, doesn't even have a photo of a native, barely mentions anything cultural. Junk! Useless!" he pronounced and stalked as far away from the trash can as he could get.

"I wonder why," Mom said. "Usually these things are precise, if for no other reason than security."

"Hmfmp," my father replied. "I guess private companies out for profit don't have the same standards as the Corps."

"I guess not," Mom said.

"Uh, Mom, Dad, how come no Negotiator-Diplomats from the Corps have been assigned to Miners World?" I asked.

"From what the companies claim, there's no one to negotiate with," Dad said.

Mom shook her head. "That's not possible. The companies are dealing with someone."

"Well, that may be so, but all that trash I just threw away doesn't mention any government. It doesn't mention anything useful, period, the end."

"Maybe you're looking at it from the wrong point of view," I suggested.

"And what point of view do you suggest, Andrew?" he asked in a quiet, practiced, polite tone, but I knew he was annoyed.

Mom scratched her cheek, one of her signals of professional discomfort. She liked to know how to prepare, to be ready. It was part of her makeup as an Augmented Bodyguard. My mother's choice was one of a number of Augmented professions that brought with it obvious physical changes as well as focus. Young pictures just before Augmentation showed her as a delicate teen with soft-ened edges to her face. The wiry hardness had come after, and with it a sharp-eyed alertness that made her a canny bodyguard, and when occasion called for it, a savvy hunter. Mom's very first assignment had been to protect a recently Augmented, particularly headstrong, young diplomat named Stephen Haldran. It had become a lifelong assignment.

"When we land," she said, "everyone will have to be very careful and everyone is going to obey me the first time I speak. Got that, Andrew? You hop when I snap."

I nodded.

"No daydreaming," she said, emphasizing her seriousness with what I called her evil-eye-look.

"I promise, Mom, but that's a ways off, so be sure to remind me again."

"Don't worry, I'll be reminding everyone frequently for the next month or more."

And she did. She spent her time trying to ingrain safety rules in us and teaching us self-defense. The exercise was probably a good idea because the girls stopped bickering and actually played quietly while Dad reread the info docs he had retrieved from the trash, and tapped into the data banks on the ship to see what else he could find out.

Miners World was populated with sentients, but sentients who seemed to be unorganized and without a government. Normally that meant the sentients were primitive, but the aliens of Miners World held secrets to the highest forms of technology yet discovered. Ironically, none of the said technology was visibly in place on the planet. In fact, only tidbits of information had become available to the companies whose representatives were planet-side, and those bits and pieces were being pulled out in fragments from the aliens in what the companies called Mining. The company employees were sent to mine for glimmers of information and technology worth billions, but scarce and difficult to obtain. The process had given the planet its name: Miners World. And the lack of any organized leadership had prevented the Corps from sending any true diplomats.

"Okay," Mom said. "That still doesn't tell us what kind of conditions to expect. Except for the company's promise of a peaceful environment, there is no evidence as to the security status of the world. How could the Corps allow citizens to go there and not check out the security risks?"

"Got me, it's a real anomaly," Dad admitted.

"Aw gee, I think it's pretty evident," I said sarcastically. "The Companies don't want any interference. They bought the Corps off."

Dad turned on me like a bear protecting its cub. "Andrew, that is completely uncalled for. The Corps has not been bought off!"

"Then what's the scoop?"

"The scoop is, young man, that the Corps probably didn't see any significant reason to invest resources in Miners World. With all the real crises, they don't have spare diplomats. Okay?"

"Sure," I said skeptically, "sure, Dad."

The trip finally came to an end. We decelerated and descended in the late afternoon in a small ship-to-planet shuttle. As we slid into the atmosphere, we caught glimpses of tree covered mountains. The shadows of clouds fell across the slopes and played on the surfaces of twisted ravines. As the sun began to set, the little ship slipped between the verdant mountain sides, and into valleys of yellow clay and cracked earth.

We were cast out of the shuttle into the moment between twilight and full nightfall and then the day closed down on us the rest of the way, drowning us in darkness. I thought we were alone until a hunched figure detached itself from a puddle of shadow and stepped into the newborn moonlight.

"Best to hurry," the figure said without so much as a greeting or introduction. "About to storm bloody-murder. Storm here is not pretty."

The man barely waited as we gathered our bundles and bags. He was off at an irritatingly quick pace. We could barely keep our belongings in hand and keep him in sight. We were tipped by the luggage this way and that, reminding me of drunks on the deck of a boat, but the guide scuttled along lickety-split like a large beetle, ignoring our awkward struggle.

"Attention, stay alert," Mom grumbled as a bag slipped out of her hand and she grabbed for it.

I brought up the rear of our mangled line of five, which spread further and further apart until we coalesced abruptly in front of a wooden affair that looked vaguely house-like.

"This is it?" Dad asked.

"Quarters, yes," the Beetle announced, then added almost sympathetically, "not too bad within." He pushed through the door and stepped back as we struggled inside and dropped our bags and bundles. "Well timed your arrival. Market day tomorrow. Bring shopping bags," he called from the door before he turned and scurried away.

"Who was that, Daddy?" Cindra asked.

"I'm not sure. He didn't exactly introduce himself," Dad said.

"Is he who you're replacing, Dad?" I asked.

"I doubt it, but if so, I'd say he's been here a little too long. What an odd duck!"

"I just hope he isn't typical of the people on this posting," Mom said as we looked about.

The house was only two, unusually large rooms without any windows, but when we looked up, the stars were visible through a myriad of fist-sized holes stabbed into the ceilings. The only sign of civilization in the outer room was an earth-side propane stove in a corner and four crates which sat both immovably and irrationally in the middle of the room. The walls between the two rooms didn't line up so that the doorway was very narrow, and when Dad tried to pass from one room to the other, he had to squeeze through sideways. Except for five raised platforms built against the walls, the second room was empty, too.

"Must be beds," I guessed from the naked pillows and pale green sheets placed neatly at the end of each platform.

Cindra and Louisa were poking their heads and hands into an assortment of niches and cubbies built into the walls of the rooms. One ran from the floor to the ceiling, but was about two inches wide, while others were squat and filled with little nodules of wood growing from the walls of the house. A human-style door hung lopsidedly over a toilet closet, which also sported a hole punched through the roof.

I peered up at the hole and said glumly, "What do you think it's for? A shower when it rains?"

"Then where's the drain?" Louisa asked, looking down.

"Come out of there you two," Mom said.

I sat down on the floor with my back against a crate. Circles of dim phosphorescence set into the walls softly lit the rooms. I chose one and ran a finger tentatively over the glow. It felt like rubbery, stretched skin.

"I wonder how you turn off the lights?" Mom mumbled, voicing my own question, as she looked about for a switch.

"Well, at least there are actually clean sheets, even it the applicability of the word 'bed' is questionable," Dad said with a deep frown.

"In all our postings, we've never been in such a minimal circumstance," Mom commented.

"I'm sorry, Mom," I said. "If it weren't for me, you wouldn't have come here."

Mom and Dad glanced at each other. "It's going to be fine, son," Dad said. "I'll put the girls to bed. Why don't you help Mom see if there's a discernible way to secure the house and compound."

"Sure," I said.

My mother and I stepped outside under an ashen sky shaded slightly orange around its lower levels. A huge moon cast out golden light, but even with the illumination, it was hard to see our new home as more than a pile of wood with a small porch hanging off the front. A low, ineffectual fence stood guard about a hundred feet away, circling around, but never meeting itself. The gate was just an open space without any means of securing it.

"Mom," I said. "Do you think we have neighbors, or are we just out here all by ourselves?"

She shook her head. "I don't know, but I think I'll keep watch until it's light. Go back inside, Andrew."

"This is quite a change from our other postings," I said. "I really am sorry."

"Andrew, if things go well here, your dad will earn enough money for all of us to be rich forever. All he has to do is make a couple of finds, and that's it, we can go home. And with your father's diplomatic skills, that should be a cinch."

I nodded and slipped inside. I hoped Mom was right, but it was strange, just too strange, here. Our diplomatic postings had always provided luxurious, carefully secured environments, but here, we were in a wasteland, in an isolated and empty house. Even after our personal freight arrived, the house was going to be minimal at best. And yet my parents thought they could leave here rich. It didn't fit.

I crawled into bed and my mind fuzzed over until I found myself embroiled in my continuing saga of Hero Andrew riding to the rescue across deserts, escaping from the wrath of dreadful dragons, running before ice slides, always fighting for justice and fairness. I fell asleep and lost myself in my dreams.

V

Dad roused me from sleep, finger on his lips, pointing to Mom curled on a bed. She looked so vulnerable, her dark hair spread on the pale sheets, her thin hands relaxed around the stuffed bear she always slept with. Dad used to tease her about Bernie the Bear, but whenever he could, he would tuck the little ursus under his arm and fall asleep. As big as Dad was it made us laugh to see him hugging beady-eyed Bernie. If the people Dad intimidated during negotiations with his basso voice and barrel-chested height had seen him with his arms wrapped around Bernie the Bear, they would have laughed, too. In any case, it was truly Mom, deceptively gentle Mom, Mom who could be viper deadly when and if she needed to be, Mom, whom they should have feared. While Dad and the girls lined up for the toilet closet, I slipped outside again. The pale yellow sky was clean and crisp, just tinged with warmth. Apparently the storm had missed us. Tiny blue flowers and fingers of leaves clung between the cracks in the clay yard. The center gate-posts were a flat red, unadorned and ugly. Beyond them roseated clay stretched endlessly, until it met with the purples and greys of the distant mountains. I followed the wall around the house. The land changed in contour depending on the direction I looked in. Hillocks rose and fell in quick succession. If I turned my head I could see a geological formation that stood isolated, sculpted by the wind into a clay obelisk. Another turn and the dry land was broken by lumpy earthen humps. And always, there was the clay that coated everything.

"Hope we're not going to stay here all day," I said to Dad as he came out and gave a great, wrenching stretch, his huge arms reaching towards the sky.

"Nope," he said, breathing in heavily. "We'll find our way into town, search out the Miner's Club, and find out what happened to the furnishings for the house. We'll look for a restaurant, too, since there's no food here, even though there is kitchen equipment in some of the cubbies."

"Do you know how to get to this Club, Dad?"

"Well, I've got a map."

"Oh," I said trying to be noncommittal. Dad's lack of success with maps on foreign worlds was the stuff of family legend and story. "I think I'll go pack a few supplies, Dad."

He frowned and shook his head. "No trust, Andrew. That's your problem. I've studied the map carefully this time."

I was about to remind him of "the time that . . ." when much to my relief the Beetle scuttled through the red gate clad in an eye-popping chartreuse tunic.

"Ready? Time to go," the Beetle announced.

"My wife is asleep. I'll wake her in a minute. By the way, I'm Steven Haldran," Dad said, offering his hand.

The Beetle wiped his hands down the sides of his tunic before he offered his hand back. "Pardon. I am Tomas Chalder. Clerk to the Miner's Club."

"It's nice to formally meet you, Mr. Chalder. This is my son, Andrew. Now, if you'll excuse me, I'll awaken Rebecca."

Dad left me standing awkwardly with Tomas Chalder.

"Hey, Mr. Chalder, what happened to the storm last night?" I asked, trying to make conversation.

"Miscalculation. Later today, so I am here early."

"Say, listen, the house is fine except there's no furniture in it."

"Really? Oh. Yes. All gone."

"Yeah, but where do we get some?"

"Ask at the Club. Lots there."

"Okay," I said uneasily. "Uh, well, uh, oh yeah, what are the holes in the roof for? And how do you turn off the glow spots in the walls?"

"Sun comes, lights out. Holes? Let your soul out when you die? Or the rain in when it comes? Sun in for plants?"

"What plants? You've got no idea why they are there, do you?"

"Maybe," the Beetle said, his lips smacking as he spoke.

"Well, if there's no furniture, no way to turn off the lights, and holes in the roof, why have a house?"

He shrugged. "Your father did not want to stay at the Miner's Club. Not much better there, except for no holes." He snapped his mouth shut.

"Geez, don't you ever elaborate."

He didn't even bother to answer. Cindra and Louisa came out hand in hand, with Mom and Dad close behind. Mom looked a bit frazzled and her hair was still in flying curls, but her eyes were already alert and searching. Dad had a mini-holocorder dangling from his hand.

"Just a short walk. Not too far. Clay is firm. Not bad today," Mr. Chalder clipped.

I noticed the air was heating up a bit and tied my jacket around my waist.

"The sky, see the edges orange?" Chalder asked.

"Yeah?" I said.

"Storm," the Beetle predicted again.

"What kind of storm, Mr. Chalder?" Mom asked.

"Howlings. Always come with orange sky."

"Howlings?" Louisa repeated questioningly.

"Will it come through the holes in the roof and get our things wet?" Cindra asked.

"Wet? Never heard howlings make things wet. Only crazy ones," Tomas Chalder said incoherently.

"Dad," I said softly, "this guy is already crazy."

"Perhaps," Mom whispered back, "but he presumably knows the way to town. Let's be diplomatic."

After that we walked quietly. Every once in a while, Dad clicked the holocorder and then returned it to his pocket. It got hotter, and what was a short walk to Tomas Chalder was a long one to my little sisters. All too soon they were begging to be carried. Dad scooped Louisa up and Cindra got a piggyback from me. Mom kept her hands free and her eyes roving.

"Not used to children hereabouts," Chalder said. "Just little bit. There!" He pointed triumphantly to the top of a sheer hill. A cluster of ramshackle alien buildings clung to the edge of the slope. They balanced so precariously they looked ready to tumble down into the waiting embrace of a solid stand of barren and twisted trees.

"They make quite a good defensive wall," Mom commented.

"What does, Madam?" the Beetle asked.

"The trees and the hill, Mr. Chalder."

"Protection? Against the worries?" He looked puzzled.

"Worries?" Mom asked, her professional antenna on the alert. "About what? Are you having problems here?"

"Problems? No. Worries, a bit." Tomas Chalder pointed the way through the door of the Miner's Club.

It was a dark establishment of rambling rooms, made in the same disconnected way as our house, except it didn't have the holes in the roof, which made it very dark. A group of people sat in over-stuffed chairs which were clearly refugee furniture from home. They greeted Dad and Mom, fixed in their seats, a few slightly waving their fingers at us.

"Welcome, welcome," a darkly mustached fellow said, his teeth catching on the hair on his lip. Someone's fingers tapped out a nervous rhythm. "Sit, sit. We heard you were coming. Haldrans, isn't it? Nice to have some new blood to talk to. Gets quite boring sometimes."

"Really?" Dad said.

"Not the work, mind you, just the limited community. The work makes it all worth while, but we do have an unwritten law. No work talk."

"Why?" I chimed in.

"Well, well, and what's your name?"

"I'm Andrew Haldran."

"Oh my, funny coincidence. I'm Hal Andrews."

"Yeah, that is strange. Why no work talk?"

"Persistent aren't you? Because, we're all competing for the same prizes and obviously we don't want to help each other."

"Then what do you talk about?" I asked.

"We speculate constantly about home, and occasionally about who will make the next, big discovery."

"Any worries?" Mom asked, and I knew, even though she was being casual, she was trying to find out what the Beetle had been referring to.

"Worries? Other than work? Hardly. The Natives are all far too passive, and we far too diplomatic for anything very worrisome to surface," a lanky, gray-haired man who introduced himself as Petersenes said rather snidely.

"What about storms?" I asked.

"Storms?" Mr. Andrews replied. "Sometimes we get quite a lot of rain, and up in the high mountains it storms even more."

"What about howlings?" I insisted.

"Howlings? Oh yes, Chalder, poor man! Interchanges the words howlings and storms, doesn't he? He's a bit over the edge you see. He was one of the first negotiators they sent. He coined the term Miner. Somewhere along the way, he lost it, but he wouldn't go home and he wouldn't, or couldn't, say why. He is really harmless and sometimes useful, so he was dubbed clerk, and paid a small fee into his account back home."

"And, you have an errand boy," I finished out loud

"I can see you have not been Augmented for diplomacy," Mr. Andrews commented dryly.

"But so cute," said a very tiny, elderly lady whom I had missed noticing she was so ensconced in a particularly over-stuffed chair.

"Geez, she's old," I whispered to Mom. "What's she doing here?"

"Don't be so judgmental, Andrew," was all she answered.

"But, my, my haven't we all lost our manners? Nobody has been properly introduced at all. I am Mrs. Jane Pattison. Let me welcome you and say how nice it is to have some more children in the community again. There has been a scarcity."

"Well, this is Andrew, Louisa and Cindra. I'm Stephen and this is Rebecca," my father said graciously.

Introductions went around the room, but I could only re-member a few names.

"Are there any native kids to play with?" Louisa asked.

"No one has ever seen one, that we know about," Mrs. Pattison said. "Now, what would you like to eat. I'll bet you're starved. Our menu is decent sized, but not huge. Chalder harvests a selec-tion of wild fruits for us, which are quite interesting. He has also baked some breads this morning. Tea, Mr. and Mrs. Haldran?"

"Sure, thank you," Mom answered, while Dad nodded in agreement.

"Me too, please, tea," I put in.

"Good, good," Mrs. Pattison said. She got up with a litheness that belied her apparent age and vanished into the nether rooms of the Club.

"How many rooms are there in the Club?" Mom asked, trying to add to her sense of security.

"They are hardly rooms. We call them spaces. You see, they're not clearly enough defined to be rooms. There are no truly defined halls, rather space after space each opening into another. None of the rooms are the same size, and none of their doors open fully into the next room. Some doorways are almost completely blocked by another wall. The only way we've been able to count the rooms or keep any kind of track of them has been by marking them with numbers, but even that is not thoroughly satisfactory," Mr. Andrews remarked.

"Why not?" Mom asked, a wariness coming into her voice.

"Because, there always seems to be some little cubby we've missed, some slender closet that pops up we haven't noticed before. The first week I was here, I couldn't find my way to my own room. Had to rely on Chalder."

"I take it you didn't build this structure," Dad said.

"Of course not. It was here. It was empty. We occupied it."

"Why not build one more to your liking?" I asked.

"For heavens sake, isn't it obvious. No materials, no labor."

"Well, why not pick a smaller structure, a less complicated one, then?" Mom asked.

"This is one of the smaller empty ones. The first Miners appropriated it, and since no one has objected, or come up with a better location, the Miners stay," said a short, soft-spoken woman of about thirty who had just joined us. "By the way, I'm Caroline. Let me know if I can help you in any way." Her face was open and smiling and she was the only one who seemed truly friendly. I liked her immediately.

"Hi, Caroline," Mom said.

"How big do the buildings get?" I asked her curiously.

"The largest ones anyone has surveyed to date are about one hundred kilometers west of here," Caroline said. "They are three to five times as large as this one, even though there only seem to be scatterings of aliens occupying them."

"So, you mean, that on a planet with an extensive community of the most highly knowledgeable beings humans have come across, this is the highest level of architecture they have developed?" Dad asked incredulously.

"That's about it," Mr. Andrews agreed.

"As far as we know," Caroline added.

"Makes absolutely no sense," Mom muttered.

"No," Mrs. Pattison agreed, returning with Chalder right behind her, "which is why we constantly speculate on the alien population, to absolutely no avail."

"Me, not," Chalder stated quietly at my elbow, then nudged past me carrying a tray of richly colored fruits. "Breakfast here," he said clearly. He gave out plates to the Miners where they sat and then passed the fruits. There were only two extra chairs in the room, so Louisa and Cindra and I sat down on the floor to eat.

Everyone stopped talking as they devoured the fruits and breads. I was hypnotized by the way the fruits were constructed. All were asymmetrical shapes, no two alike. Only color repeated itself, so I assumed the colors marked different species. Chalder had broken them into sections, which the Miners deftly pulled apart and swallowed in neat little gulps. I examined the large lavendar ball on my plate suspiciously before I pulled a piece from it. Inside it were smaller shapes, each composed of more, even smaller identical shapes.

"Don't dissect it my boy," Mr. Andrews chimed in. "Just pop it in. Quite delicious really."

I followed his advice and a tangy sweetness filled my mouth, spreading down the back of my throat. I popped another and sipped some tea.

"Like it?" Chalder asked me right by my ear.

I nodded, feeling like a conspirator for no reason.

"Bio-engineered," he whispered. "So think they."

I tried to look at him, but he was already moving on with another tray of breads.

"Uh, you said these grow wild. They're great. Why don't you ship some home?" I asked.

"No seeds, didn't you notice? And Chalder won't say where

they grow, if they grow. We have certainly never seen them growing anywhere," Mrs. Pattison said.

"Everyone knows, Chalder is incapable of telling anything coherently," a small man said.

"Maybe he just doesn't want to give the secret to us," Caroline suggested. "That's actually pretty straightforward."

"Caroline, you have such a good heart," Mrs. Pattison said with a twinge of sarcasm in her voice. "Why can't you accept that Tomas is irredeemably incomprehensible?"

"Because," Caroline said simply, "I think you all underestimate him."

"Sure, sure," Hal Andrews said. "I just think you have a crush on the stupid freak."

"Have you tried searching for the fruits yourself?" Dad intervened before the conversation got any uglier.

"Now, Haldran, we hardly have either the time or the know-how," Mr. Petersenes said nasally.

"You don't try to resolve many of the inconsistencies here do you?" Mom noted.

"We are truly too busy, Mrs. Haldran. I dare say you won't see much of your hubby. You'll see."

"Uh huh, well, maybe the kids and I will look into these little mysteries. It'll give us something to do."

"Splendid. Good luck, my dear," Mrs. Pattison nodded. "That is what we were hoping you'd say."

Mom looked surprised as she realized they'd manipulated her. I could tell she was mad, but Dad stepped in and said with a smile, "Well, they're better at their jobs than I thought at first glance, Rebecca."

She opened her mouth to say something, but before she could, the sound reached us.

VI

It started slowly, like a wind tickling at the edges of chimes, added a gentle thumping rhythm and grew into a howling storm.

"Oh, good grief," someone shouted.

"Howlings," Chalder said, smiling broadly while everyone else covered their ears.

Dad had Cindra and Louisa in a bear hug, and Mom headed for the door.

"Mom," I screamed catching her arm. "It's a storm, where are you going?"

"It doesn't sound like a storm, Andrew. Listen."

I listened and behind the noise I could still hear the chime-like sound or maybe it was a song. "What is that?"

"Howlings," Chalder beamed at us. "Beautiful. No?"

"I'm not sure, Mr. Chalder," Mom yelled. "How long does it go on?"

"Until the changes," Chalder answered and began dancing in a circle.

"He's crazy," Andrews called. "This could go on for hours. Would you like a tranquilizer?"

Mom whipped around and glared at the man. "It's against my profession, Mr. Andrews."

"How about the children?"

"I said no," Mom repeated icily.

"You'll change your minds," Mr. Petersenes said confidently.

We stood together as we watched everyone but our family and Chalder doze off into a woozy sleep, still seated in their chairs of choice.

"Stephen," Mom said. "What have we stepped into here?"

"Howlings," Chalder said, sticking his face between Mom and Dad before taking up the dance again, maneuvering between chairs of sleeping Miners.

"Can you take us home?" Dad asked him, or tried to as Chalder danced.

"Dance," he said or answered. "Do you not hear the music?"

He swayed to a rhythmic beat. His body shifted subtly and an almost-grace overtook him. I watched and listened. I could feel myself beginning to respond to the chiming, as if it was a hidden call under the thunderings.

"I wanna go home," Louisa wailed.

"Howlings everywhere," Chalder remarked. "Home no good, little girl."

"Stephen," Mom appealed as the girls added their own cries to the noise.

On a whim I took Louisa from Dad and set her on the floor. "Dance, Louisa. Let's have fun, okay?"

She wiped at her tears and nodded.

"Here, let's do what Mr. Chalder does?" I said into her ear.

We watched, but couldn't follow the Beetle's steps. Cindra joined us and wasn't any better at it than Louisa and I were.

"Mr. Chalder," I called to him, "show us how."

He turned and I saw his eyes were clear, burning brightly. He stopped briefly, began again, but slower. Cindra picked it up, then Louisa, and lastly me. At first we just had the steps, then we heard the rhythm and finally, twinkling in the background, I could hear what had to be song. I was trying so hard to hear it like words or notes, that when the howlings stopped, my mind went blank. I looked up, startled.

Mom said quietly, "It's over, Andrew."

"Wow, Mom, I . . ."

"It's okay," she said and began moving from snoring person in the room to snoring person. "They're fine, if you can call being drugged fine. Let's get out of here!"

Outside, the air was bright and full of strange smells, as if it had been a real storm. The light was blinding after the gloom of the Club and we tripped and stumbled for a bit.

"I wanna go back to the house," Cindra whined.

"No," Chalder said, appearing beside us and pulling at Dad's sleeve. "Market day. Now. Not again, not for two months."

"Now, after that? After the howlings?" Mom asked.

"Now," the Beetle insisted.

We followed him for probably a mile along a wide path and into a huddle of collapsing structures that looked more like stacks of roughly hewn and gouged boards than buildings. There were no signs of a market. It wasn't even possible to be sure if this was a village.

"There," Chalder pointed. "Water People."

"Where?" I asked, looking for someone selling water.

"He means that alien over there," Dad said. "See, son?"

What I saw was wafer thin, with long arms ending in lengthy fingers. The face was distorted and flattened, the skin drawn, almost translucent. The figure was so flat, all I could think of was a slice of a specimen for a slide.

"It's yucky," Louisa squealed.

"Where is this market?" Mom asked.

"Come, Chalder said. "Stare not."

We hurried after him, as best we could, but our shoes stuck in mud, pulling up with a sucking sound. The Beetle didn't seem to stick at all and I wondered if his scuttling gait was an adaptation to the terrain. Then again, he wore no shoes.

We were breathless from freeing our feet by the time we got to an open square of buffed and polished clay. There were no vendors, no other takers, no signs of a town, a store, a building, not even a tree, yet piles of unattended fruits and foods were laid out on the sienna earth in a flourishing of colors like an exclamation point in all the emptiness.

"Into your bags, what you want." Chalder's tongue flicked in and out moistening his lips.

Dad turned about, looking from side to side, but there was no one else there but us. "Don't we pay anyone?"

Chalder shook his head. "Here for the Miners to take, but I only come." He pulled some net bags from a pocket and began filling them.

"I'm going to take pictures of this," Dad said, patting his shirt pocket for his holocorder. "Oh, my!"

"What's the matter?" Mom asked.

"My 'corder, it's gone!" Dad said, patting his pants pockets this time.

"You must have left it at the Club," Mom said.

"I guess so. Too bad. Okay, let's gather up some of this food," Dad instructed us. As the rest of us began, his hands searched his pockets one more time to be sure the little 'corder wasn't with him. Finally he bent down and plucked some food out of the piles on the ground.

"Did we bring bags, Mom?" I asked, as I picked up fruits and vegetables.

"Of course. What self-respecting mom comes to a market unprepared?" She pulled a hefty roll of plastic bags out of her pack. "Here you go. Fill them up, gang. How long will the food keep without refrigeration, Mr. Chalder?"

"In chill rooms, a long time. Show you will I."

"We must leave some sort of payment," Dad said.

"Why?" the Beetle asked.

"Could you explain please, Mr. Chalder, who arranges this market?"

"Know you not?" he asked back quickly.

"I had assumed it was the Club."

The Beetle raised his head and smiled, actually smiled. For the first time I saw his eyes, a pale brown, flecked with yellow. We waited for a response, but there was none. "Home," was the only word he uttered. He pointed a finger to direct us.

We scooped up our bags and started to leave, but when I looked back, the Beetle wasn't behind us. He was gone.

"We're on our own," Dad noted.

"Do you have that map, Dad?" I asked with a grin.

VII

I awoke that night to whispering and hissing. When you're living in two rooms, it's hard to argue without waking anyone, which was what Mom and Dad were trying to do.

"Stephen," Mom whispered, "I'm telling you, these Miners are. . ." Her voice vanished as Dad's hiss interrupted her.

"Rebecca, I came to do a job. You know what's at stake. Give it a chance."

"It'd be okay for you and me, but we have three kids with us. And, I'm telling you, something is awry here."

"For goodness sake, Rebecca, what? Isn't your famous sixth sense working overtime?"

"Maybe, or maybe yours is defunct, turned off."

This was a favorite joke in the family. Dad and Mom each claimed to have an extra sense, but they rarely sensed the same thing.

"Listen, Stephen, stop and think. The Miners have all been here for some years, yet they seem to know virtually nothing about the planet, and the only person who may actually be able to tell us anything useful is a certified nut case who can barely form a four word sentence."

"He may not be much at talking, but Chalder can dance and he didn't need to be drugged to get through the howlings." I could hear Dad's smile. Mom must have frowned or something because of what Dad said next. His voice was a tone louder as he forgot to whisper quite as softly. "Okay, okay, Rebecca. Seriously, the Miners are the best negotiators in their fields that some very powerful, private firms can buy. Some of those men and women are world renowned in their specialties. Thirty-four of the best Augmented professionals available sent to collect the technological treasures of this world! Despite appearances, I promise you, they know what they're doing."

"Be that as it may, they seem to be hiding in the Club."

"From what? There doesn't appear to be anything threatening here. There are no reports of anything out of the ordinary."

"Except for Chalder's 'worries'," Mom reminded him.

"Now really, Rebecca, you can hardly give that credence. Give me a chance to see what's going on when I go tomorrow to the mines, appraise the other Miners as best I can and get a look at the Natives."

"All right, all right, Stephen. Just be honest with yourself."

"Okay. Promise. Goo' night."

Morning came up fast again, golden and yellow, without a trace of orange. Outside the little blue flowers were everywhere now. I hurried through breakfast and grabbed Dad as he was about to leave.

"Let me come, please! I want to see the Natives," I begged.

"Not today, son. You have to be approved to enter the mines. Give me a little time and I'll try to arrange it."

"Please, Dad. Besides, who would approve me?"

He shook his head. Mom came up and patted me. "Another day. I wouldn't let you go even if your father would take you, Andrew. Too many questions and not enough answers for my taste."

I slumped out into the yard. Louisa came up with a jump rope.

"Wanna help turn?" she asked.

"Sure, why not? There's nothing else to do."

"He said yes. Come on, Cindra," she shouted inside.

The rope whizzed up, over, up, over, boring, but the girls were having a great time.

"Oh," Chalder said with delight as he came through the gate, garbed in deep purple. "Oh, oh! Jump rope! Can I?"

Cindra and Louisa looked at me.

"Sure, why not?" I said. "Do you know how to jump rope?"

"Goody," the Beetle answered, hesitating barely a moment before he jumped right into the middle. I blinked. He was stretching out of his beetle-likeness as he bobbed up and down on his toes. I could hear him chortling happily under his breath until he finally missed on the forty-third swish of the rope.

"Want some water, Mr. Chalder?"

"Please." I blinked again. He had shrunk back into the beetle.

I threw my end to Louisa and took Mr. Chalder into the house.

"Mom, Mr. Chalder needs a drink and the girls need a turner."

She went out while I put some water in a cup.

"Nice your Mom. Gentle."

"Yeah, well sometimes. My dad went to work today."

"To the caves? To exchange?"

"Is that what they do? Exchange? What's it like there?"

"Like it should be."

"How's that?"

"You, Andrew, wish to see it?"

"Of course, but Dad said not today."

"I will show you now," he offered.

"Dad wouldn't like that."

"Stephen Haldran will never know." I noticed it was a full sentence.

"Really?" I asked.

"First, I'll show Mrs. Rebecca where the cool rooms are. Rush not. Exchange is slow. It is the way."

I was noting a change in the Beetle. I wondered if it was a sign of some growing trust in us.

"How did you come here originally, Mr. Chalder?"

"Me, came I to negotiate, but I got lost."

"Lost?"

"Here, lost in exchange."

It was confusing how he constructed his sentences so ambiguously, as if English wasn't his native language.

The Beetle went to one of the crates and twisted it. It moved aside to reveal rickety steps.

"Neat," I said.

"Cool room. Food keeps nice."

"Can I go down?" I asked starting for the steps.

"No, first I. Stuff may be in old cool rooms."

"Stuff?"

"Old stuff," he repeated. "Smelly stuff," he added and went down. His head came back up and he said. "It is clean. Now bring food."

I carried the bags of fruit and foods to the opening and handed them through. He disappeared and before I could follow, he was up and swinging the crate back into place.

"You show mother later, Andrew. We go now."

"Where?"

"To the exchange."

I couldn't tell if it was a place or something that happened, but I decided it didn't matter all that much. "Now?" I asked.

"Follow if you can."

"Gee, thanks," I said, but he was already scuttling off.

I raced after him. In order to keep up, I had to run. At first the ground was mucky and I thought I'd lose him as my feet stuck over and over. The Beetle did his strange little steps that barely left time for him to sink and I wondered if I could do the same, though Mom and Dad would have a fit if I became a barefoot Beetle as a profession.

The muddy ground gave way to a wide track of inlaid glass that caught the morning sun in a glitter of color. Even though the Beetle straightened his body as we hit the road and his gait became longer in the stride, it was easier for me to keep abreast of him on the hard surface.

"Hey," I said breathlessly. "Who made this road."

"The aliens."

"Which ones? The Natives or the Water People?"

"The aliens."

"I didn't think either of them made anything."

"The aliens," he repeated. "Who else?"

"But nobody seems to think they make anything."

"Miners are wrong."

I shook my head and shut up for a moment. "How much longer to the exchange?"

"There," he said, directing his head towards a cave entrance.

"That?" I asked, but he was already scuttling into a gap in the side of an earthy, orange cliff.

The smell of clay was overwhelming, wet and clawing, but Chalder entered without pause and it was either follow or wait for someone to come out who could get me home.

"Is this the way my Dad got here?" I whispered.

"Ask him," was the taciturn reply, as he pushed into a passage barely wide enough for us to traverse. For two hundred feet, our shoulders brushed the walls. Dampness filled my nose. Finally we burst into a wider channel of tunnel, filled with spotty light from holes that had been bored into the roof of the cave. Chalder squeezed sideways through a narrow slit and I followed to find myself looking through twelve inch fissures in a rocky wall. Fifty feet below us was an immense grotto.

"There is Stephen Haldran," the Beetle whispered breathily, pointing out my father.

Dad was standing silently, very quietly watching a Native who sat in the middle of the barren chamber. Unlike the Water Person we had seen, this Native was well proportioned. Its face was marked by orange and brown designs as if painted. Even from this far away, its eyes burned yellow. It lacked hair of any kind and although it was clothing-less, I could see no indication of sex. Its torso, arms and legs were decorated with thin shiny lines, and as far as I could see or hear, it was doing and saying absolutely nothing.

Finger to his lips, Chalder indicated for me not to speak. I watched a few more minutes. Nothing, except that Dad sat down on the floor to wait, folding his large legs beneath him. I tapped my guide and pointed to the exit.

He shook his head. I thought he didn't want to go, but instead he pulled me out in the other direction. We squeezed back through a tunnel and popped out into the open air where we'd come in.

"You were going wrong," Chalder said.

"I guess I got turned around. How many ways to get out are there?" I asked.

He raised his hands to me, palms up.

"Gee, it'd be really easy to get lost in there."

He smiled and his eyes came alive. "In lots of ways, lost."

"Why didn't my dad ask anything?"

"He was waiting."

"How long will he have to wait, Mr. Chalder?"

"He will not get an answer."

"Why not?" I asked.

"Trust me, Andrew. Come."

I trotted behind him like a puppy. "Want a swim?" he asked.

"Sure, but where?"

He turned off the main road and scuttled along a mucky path, but not as fast as before. The sun got hotter and the terrain changed The ground was covered in mossy-soft, lavender flowers. I reached to pick one and Chalder grabbed my hand.

"These belong here," he said gently and clearly.

"How long have you been here?" I asked.

"Long enough, not too long," Chalder said obtusely.

"So, do you want to leave?"

"Leave cannot. Wait I must," the Beetle said plainly.

"For what?"

"For it to be completed."

I was sorry I had asked. The conversation had been truly disjointed, not all there, not complete. Complete? Hadn't Chalder just said he was waiting to be completed? Was there some convoluted logic to his chatter that I was missing?

"Andrew, what will you grow to be?" Mr. Chalder asked as we walked along the mossy ground.

"Confused," I answered. "I haven't got a focus. I decided against Augmentation."

"Mine focus, gone, changed, changing."

"That's not possible. You can't lose focus."

"No?"

"Not if you were Augmented. It's forever, final, irreversible and it can't change!"

"Mine vanished. Vanished, old Augment did."

"Then what does that make you now?" I asked him.

Chalder cocked his head. "Lost."

Maybe the Beetle was lost, maybe crazy, but my intuition told me that if we wanted to understand Miners World we needed to know more about him.

Without really thinking, I asked, "How old are you?"

The Beetle looked startled before he answered. "Thirty-seven standard. Old, eh?"

"Not too old," I said sheepishly. "Don't you have family back home whom you want to see?"

"Back home," Chalder repeated wistfully, and for the first time sounded human. "Gone," he reverted to the Beetle. "I left."

"You sure don't give out much info, do you? And then a fella has to figure it all out cause there's something there all the same."

"You are mining me, Andrew," Chalder smiled, again seeming more human. "There. The swimming hole."

He pointed at a murky water hole with a purple under-glow. Something yellow and stringy was moving beneath the surface.

"Woops," he said. "No longer can we swim here. Home now."

VIII

Mom was waiting by the gate, hands on hips, lips clenched. I braced myself.

"Oh, oh, mad madam," the Beetle concluded.

"Oh, yeah," I agreed.

"Well, Andrew, where have you been?"

"Mr. Chalder gave me a tour."

"A tour? Of what?"

"You know, local stuff." That didn't seem to dilute her anger so I whispered to her, "Mom, there's something about him, something mysterious. I was just trying to get to the bottom of it." It was partly true.

"Andrew, this is not one of your stories. Stop this. Do not create a mystery where there isn't one."

"I'm not Mom!" Who knew if I was or wasn't creating it. It was perfectly possible that Tomas Chalder was just demented.

"Mr. Chalder," Mom said, turning to him. "You mentioned worries yesterday. Come have some tea and tell me about them."

"Worries? None. Bye now," he said and scurried off, returning to his huddled shell.

"Well, so much for answers, at least from him," Mom muttered under her breath.

"I thought you didn't put any stock in Mr. Chalder."

"Mr. Chalder, I believe, is the one thing I can totally agree with the Miners about. He's not all there and not very reliable. Even if he were, he probably couldn't tell us anything about Miners World because there probably isn't anything to be told."

I shook my head. Mom was wrong. I was suddenly and absolutely sure mysteries abounded on Miners World. For once I wouldn't have to make up an adventure for Hero Andrew. I just had to figure out what was really going on, and so far the only possible source was the Beetle.

Cindra and Louisa were playing jacks on the floor of the house. Cindra was pretty good at it, but no one was better than Mom. She sat down with them, and threw the ten stars which scattered in a perfect pattern. I left them to it, plopped down on the porch steps, and watched the sky as I tossed an Andrtrian coin, catching the eight-sided unit to see how many points I could accumulate. Each side was worth a different amount. On Andrtri you tossed it, and whatever landed up was what you paid for goods, no matter what you were buying. It meant every toss of the coin was a chance to be ripped off or to get a terrific bargain. Andrtri had one of the most successful and peaceful economies known to man. It had been one of my favorite postings. I flipped the coin again. The landscape and yard were painfully empty.

"Mom, can I go for a walk if I take the trusty map?"

"Where?" she called back.

"I don't know. I'm bored. I just want to explore."

"Why don't we all go?" she said, coming to the door. "Tell the girls a story while I get ready?"

"Sure. Do you two want to hear a story I just wrote?"

"Is it as good as Alvin Peter?" Cindra asked.

"I hope so."

"Did you write our Alvin Peter story down?'

"Not yet, Cindra, but I will."

"I like Alvin Peter. Why didn't you write another story about him?"

"Maybe I will, but see if you like this one, okay?"

"Okay," they said. "What's it about?"

"You'll see."

I flipped open a gold-edged notebook I had filled with neat purple letters and began to read.

Retirement

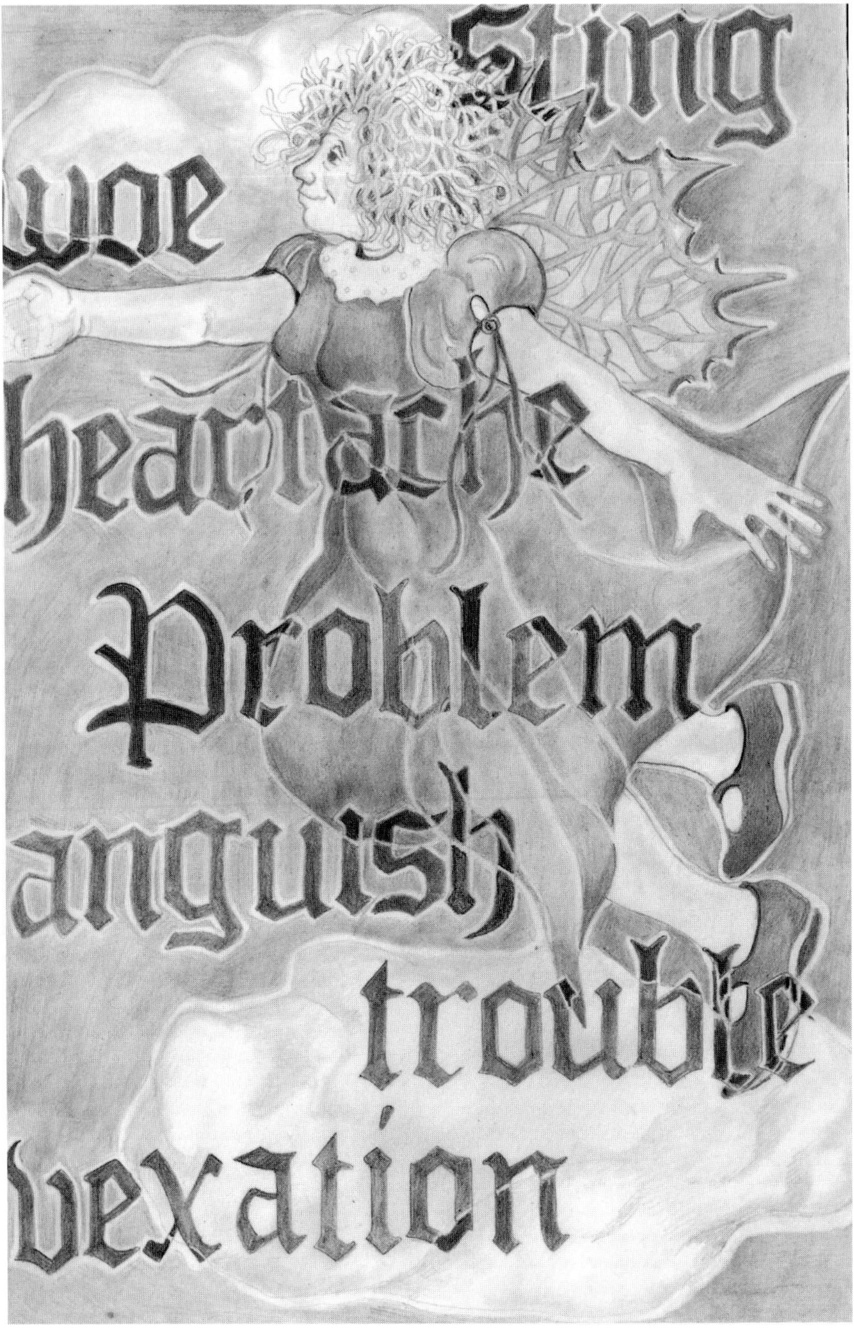
woe
Sting
heartache
Problem
anguish
trouble
vexation

It ended up that the problem with being Cinderella's Fairy Godmother was that everyone knew what Cinderella looked like and that she had married a prince, but no one knew what the Fairy Godmother had looked like, or what her name had been, or whether she had lived happily ever after or not.

[You both know the story of Cinderella, don't you?]

[*Nods up and down.*]

To make matters worse, fairy godmothers lived forever, but people stopped believing in them.

[I believe in them.]

[No you don't, Cindra.]

[Yes, I do, Louisa.]

[Quiet or you'll never hear the story, you two.]

peanut-butter
Cookies &
brownies
green Tea
oolong
snickerdoodle

There she was, jobless, homeless and anonymous. So, the Fairy Godmother did what all old folks do. She went to live in a retirement home and made cookies for her neighbors and had everyone in to tea. She was the old lady on the twenty-first floor named Gloriosa.

[I don't like that name, Andrew.]

[I'm sorry. Did you know it means glorious?]

[Then I guess it's okay.]

Anyway, everything was tolerable until old Mrs. Pantia moved into apartment twenty-one-fifty-three. Mrs. Pantia wasn't as old as she was depressed, and even Gloriosa's cookies didn't do much for her mood. Looking at Mrs. Pantia depressed everybody else and disrupted the good-feeling spells that Gloriosa's cookies were always loaded with.

[I wish Mommy could make magic cookies.]

[She can't even make good cookies, Cindra.]

[You're right, Louisa. Anyway . . .]

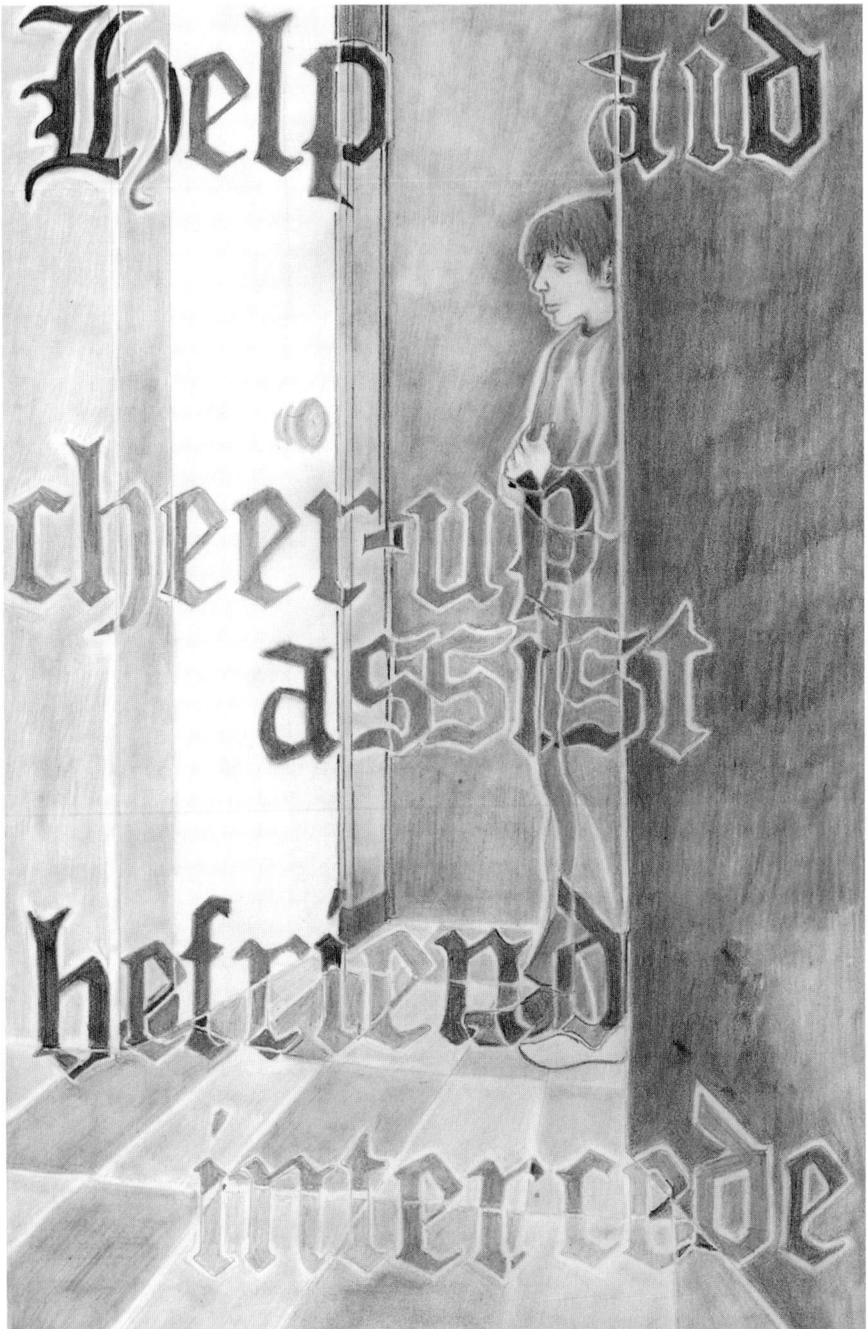
Help
aid
cheer-up
assist
befriend
intercede

Pretty soon everyone was going out of their way to avoid Mrs. Pantia. If she was in the laundry room, no one else was. If there was a place by her in the dining room, no one ever sat there. If she came into the exercise room, everybody left. They all felt bad about it, but they didn't know what else to do.

[Why didn't they take her to a doctor?]

[*Sigh*. Just listen.]

It was approaching the Winter Solstice when Gloriosa noticed the kid hanging around the twenty-first floor. He was scrawny, with straggly brown hair and big green eyes. Every time Gloriosa walked down the hall when no one else was around, there was the kid.

Finally one day he said, "Why don't you help her?"

"Who?" Gloriosa asked. "Help who?"

"Mrs. Pantia. She isn't so bad, not really," the kid said.

"Oh? Well, she doesn't like my cookies and there isn't much else I can do for her."

[She could take her to the doctor.]

[Will you quit with the doctor, Louisa!]

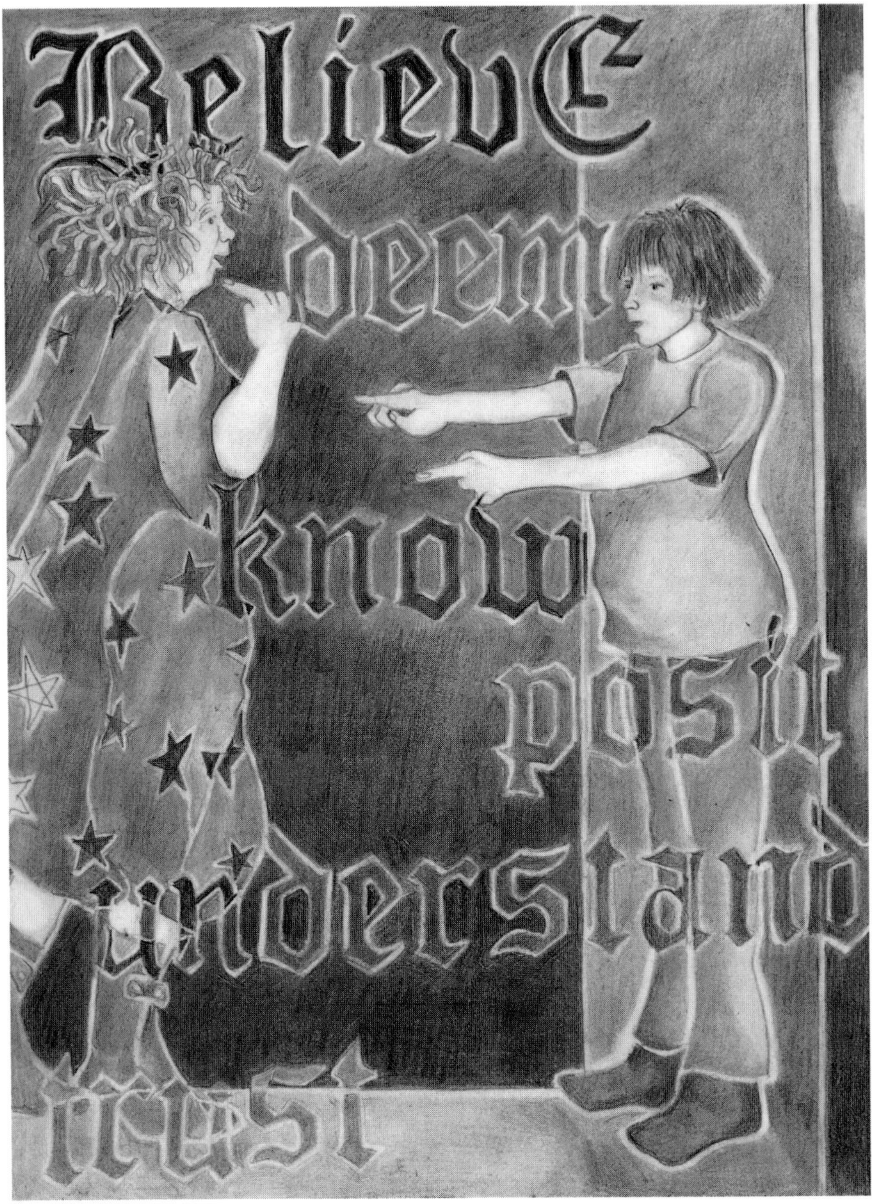
Believe
deem
know
posit
understand
trust

"Sure there's something you can do." the kid insisted as Gloriosa started in her door. "After all. you're a fairy godmother."

Gloriosa stopped short and froze in mid-stride. "Nobody believes in fairy godmothers anymore."

[I do.]

[That's stupid, Cindra.]

[I'm not stupid, Louisa.]

[Shssh. Quiet. Please!]

"I believe in fairy godmothers." the kid said very seriously.

"You're crazy. What gave you such a crazy idea? Look at me. Do I look like a fairy godmother?" Gloriosa asked. hoping to divert the kid.

"I saw you in a book ." he said with calm assurance.

"Me? You saw me?" Gloriosa asked. more and more surprised and more than a little skeptical. "If you saw me in a book. what's my name?"

"Gloriosa Eloise Marina G. Mother." he answered without hesitation.

[That's a silly name.]

[I thought you two liked silly names.]

[We do. Yes, we do!]

Gloriosa sat right down on the threshold of her open door with her mouth dropped wide and her eyes popped open.

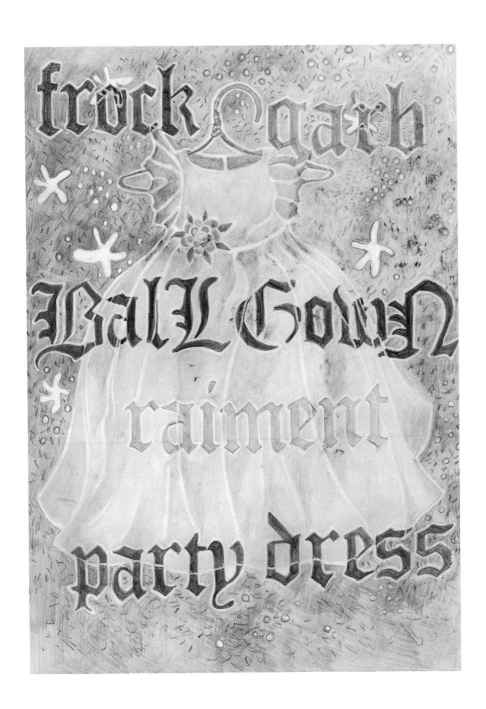

frock garb

Ball Gown

raiment

party dress

"What's your name?" she finally stammered.

"Arthur Pantia. She's my grandma, you see."

"Oh! Well, Arthur, what do you think I should do to help your grandma?"

[Wait, Andrew. I want his name to be Peter.]

[This isn't an Alvin Peter story, Louisa. His name is Arthur. I'm the author and that's what I chose.]

[Oh, okay. *Pouty lip*]

"You could send her to the Retirees Solstice Ball on Saturday. You know, all dressed real pretty. And maybe you could be sure some handsome guy meets her, or something like that."

"Oh, I could, could I? Arthur, I haven't cast a spell in years, other than Happy Cookies. I'm rusty! Not a little rusty. Hundreds of years worth of rusty!"

[*Giggles.*]

[She isn't really a fairy godmother, is she Andrew?]

[Wait and see, Louisa.]

"But you could still change yourself into something glittery and just magically appear or some such. Then you could wave your magic wand and poof . . ."

"That again. Tell me, Arthur, why does everyone think fairy godmothers have wands?"

"All the ones in cartoons do. Don't you?"

"Never, but I guess I could at least say a few words over your grandma and get her some tickets to the ball."

[Told you she wasn't a real fairy godmother, Cindra.]

[Andy, couldn't you let her have a wand?]

[Sorry, Cindra.]

[See, no wand. She isn't really a fairy godmother.]

[Oh no, Louisa? You may be surprised.]

[Hurry up and read some more.]

[So you like the story, guys?]

[Come on, more, now!]

[Mom is ready to go. I'll read some more when we get home.]

[Promise?]

[Yeah, I promise!]

IX

The girls skipped happily along, big-brimmed, straw hats balanced on their little heads. Mom had her mop of tangled curls pulled out of her face in a head band, her defensive glances already up and running. Sometimes my mom reminded me of a primeval hunter. Sometimes she was the ultimate mommy. That meant she really did do more than one thing well.

She and the girls danced a few steps ahead of me. A moment, a step, a dance, another step and mud engulfed their feet, suctioned them instantly up to their ankles.

"Stop, Andrew," Mom barked at me.

I halted, still on dry ground, my mouth open. The mud seemed to be bubbling out of the ground.

"Was there a pond on the map?" I called to Mom.

"Nowhere we were going," she said, shaking her head.

"Either the map was wrong or we took a wrong turn," I called back.

She stretched over and yanked on Louisa who was closest to her. She pulled so hard I could see her wiry muscles knot against the strain. With a sudden suck, she unearthed Louisa's feet and called to me, "Catch her!" She swiftly tossed Louisa into the air, sending the silly straw hat flying along like a saucer. I caught her as the hat landed with a soft pop in the mud. A moment later the mud gulped and the hat vanished. Cindra was crying. Mom reached for her, just barely able to grab her under the arms. She pulled, but Cindra was a tiny bit too far away. Louisa clung to me, arms and legs still wrapped around me as we watched. Mom pulled again and Cindra inched towards her. As she moved, flat yellow flowers on stringy pale stems began to spring up along the edges of the muddy surface. Mom glanced their way and gave a mighty tug. I saw Cindra slide towards her, while more yellow flowers budded in the mud, only now, little tendrils were wiggling out of the flower centers.

"Mom," I called nervously as she gave an immense wrench and freed Cindra. She didn't answer, but I could see beads of water standing on her arms and dripping down her face.

"Catch again," she called, telling Cindra to hold onto her hat and to help by jumping.

Cindra was crying as she landed in my arms.

"Are you hurt?" I asked.

"No," she sniffled. I patted her head and turned back to Mom. She stood perfectly still watching the flowers as the mud rose higher on her legs. If she moved, more tendrils popped up.

"Mom, I don't like this."

She didn't answer, but Louisa and Cindra were both sniffling loudly now.

"What should I do?" I called, feeling completely inadequate despite my daily dreams of heroic daring.

She remained silent and immobile, as the mud inched up her legs. I began to panic.

"Mister Andrew," I heard, and there was the Beetle. "How got you to this place?"

"Help her," I cried, not bothering to answer.

"Not to worry," he said and disappeared.

The sun got more intense and Cindra popped her hat back on. I pulled a cap out of my belt and wished I had a hat like hers, no matter how silly it would have looked. I could almost feel my skin peeling. I glanced at Louisa, tears streaming down her cheeks, and popped my cap onto her little head.

"It'll be okay," I said more to myself than to my mother or my sisters.

"Where did Tomas go?" Louisa sobbed.

"He'll be back. Mom, hold on, Tomas will help us!"

The hunched and withdrawn Beetle hardly looked like a hero riding to the rescue as he scurried back. He dropped a twisted tree branch out over the mud and stepped gingerly onto it. He straightened his body, and then, suprisingly lean and tall, he walked with easy grace and perfect balance, along it to my mom.

"Stuck," he stated directly.

She just stared at him.

"Quick now," he said. He reached under her arms and pulled her from the mud without so much as a strained muscle. He didn't even put her down, just walked easily back, only slightly hurried and at the last minute, with Mom still in his arms, took a flying leap. They landed in a heap at my feet, as tendrils of yellow flowers sucked the branch into the bog with a gulping sound.

"Thank you, Mr. Chalder," Mom said hoarsely, untangling herself and standing up rather awkwardly.

"Smart woman, didn't move," he said. "Nasty are bog vines."

She nodded. "I'd say dangerous."

Now the Beetle nodded. "You were lost. Want to go somewhere, next time, wait. I come."

"Okay, but how do we contact you?" I asked.

He didn't answer me as he helped my mother to her feet.

"Home now, wash off all mud," he said.

"I couldn't agree more," Mom answered. "Home we go."

"This way," Mr. Chalder said and picked a direction I wouldn't have chosen. I decided the landscape was confusing. All the landmarks looked the same. I was relieved when I caught sight of our ugly, red gate.

While Mom and the girls washed, I watched Mr. Chalder pluck the little blue flowers from the cracks in our yard. He carried them delicately in the palm of his hand.

"Makes good, safe tea. Calms nerves."

He took the flowers inside and Cindra came out, sparkling clean.

"Mommy wants you to come inside," she said.

Light was pouring through the holes in the ceiling. I went to wash, returning to the Beetle's clipped voice. He was actually speaking more than a word or two at a time as he sipped a cup of blue tea. Each time he took a sip, he began speaking again.

"No, no, Madam Haldran. Not so. Aliens all are useful. All!"

"My name is Rebecca, by the way," she said. "Are you saying that even the Water People we saw in the village are useful in some way?"

"Even those."

"What do they do?" Mom persisted.

He stared at her and I held my breath for his answer.

"Go mine for the answer," he finally said. "See what is learned."

"I don't think the Miners will look for the answer to that," Mom said.

"Ask then yourself," Tomas Chalder suggested. The Beetle took a last gulp of tea and turned to me. "Take you tomorrow, young Andrew," he said, stood abruptly, and left.

Take me where? To do my own mining?

Dad passed him in the yard, greeted him and came in. "Well," Dad sighed, "I hope your day was more successful than mine, or as far as I could tell, anyone else's. Once you ask a question, no one speaks for hours, not native, not human. Marshal told me this could go on for months, longer than normal because a new Miner, that's me, has entered the negotiation areas." He sat down on a crate. "This is already frustrating and it's only the first day."

"What did you ask?" Mom inquired, not mentioning our mud bath.

"Nothing spectacular. I asked about a computer program application for development of viral vaccines. The company knows a lot. They just need one little piece of information to have a real breakthrough."

"Couldn't that be hoping for the needle in the haystack, Dad?" I asked.

"Sure, it could be, but no one ever seems to know when they'll hit pay dirt with the Natives. It's pretty random. I gather the most important part is keeping contact and recognizing the value of whatever they offer. Hal Andrews and Marshal say the Natives are just ornery, toying with us."

"Maybe you should ask a less specific question, Dad," I said.

"Andrew, it takes so long to get any answer that it would be a waste to ask something general, if they even actually, eventually answer it."

"But, Dad, Mr. Chalder suggested . . ."

He cut me off before I could finish. "I appreciate your efforts, Andrew, but I do not think suggestions from a half-demented man are going to solve this."

"Maybe you should listen to us, Dad," I said defensively.

"Andrew," he said, his voice with a warning tone now, "I'm afraid that neither of you could know enough to help."

"Sorry," I said, clamping my mouth shut and compressing my own anger.

I left them and went to sit outside again. This was looking like a long and boring post. No one my age, a father who was likely to be frustrated a lot of the time, a hostile environment that was supposed to be safe, no bookstores and limited mobility. At least Cindra and Louisa had each other and their lessons, but me, I didn't have anyone, unless you counted a thirty-seven-year-old Beetle.

X

The next day dawned as boring as I had feared. Cindra and Louisa woke me before Dad and Mom had stirred.

"Go away! I'm still asleep."

They stood at the foot of my bed with their fingers to their lips and beckoned to me without saying a word until I padded barefooted into the other room.

"What do you guys want?"

"Come on, Andrew, please read some more about Cinderella's Fairy Godmother. We're so bored!"

"Please, please, please, Andrew," they whined in chorus.

"Okay, okay, let me brush my teeth and I'll meet you on the porch."

When I got there they were sitting on the step in their little nightgowns, their hair awry and their small faces still sleepy. Louisa squeezed her elephant tightly.

"Okay you two, starting where we left off. Remember, Arthur wants Gloriosa to cast a spell on his grandmother?"

"I still don't think Gloriosa can cast a spell cause she doesn't have a wand," Louisa said.

I ignored her.

"Do you think someone could have cast a spell on Mr. Chalder?" Cindra asked.

"You could kiss him and see if he turns into a Prince," Louisa said, sticking her tongue out at Cindra.

"Why don't you kiss him, Louisa?"

"Do you guys always have to fight? Let's just start the story, okay?" I said.

I opened my notebook.

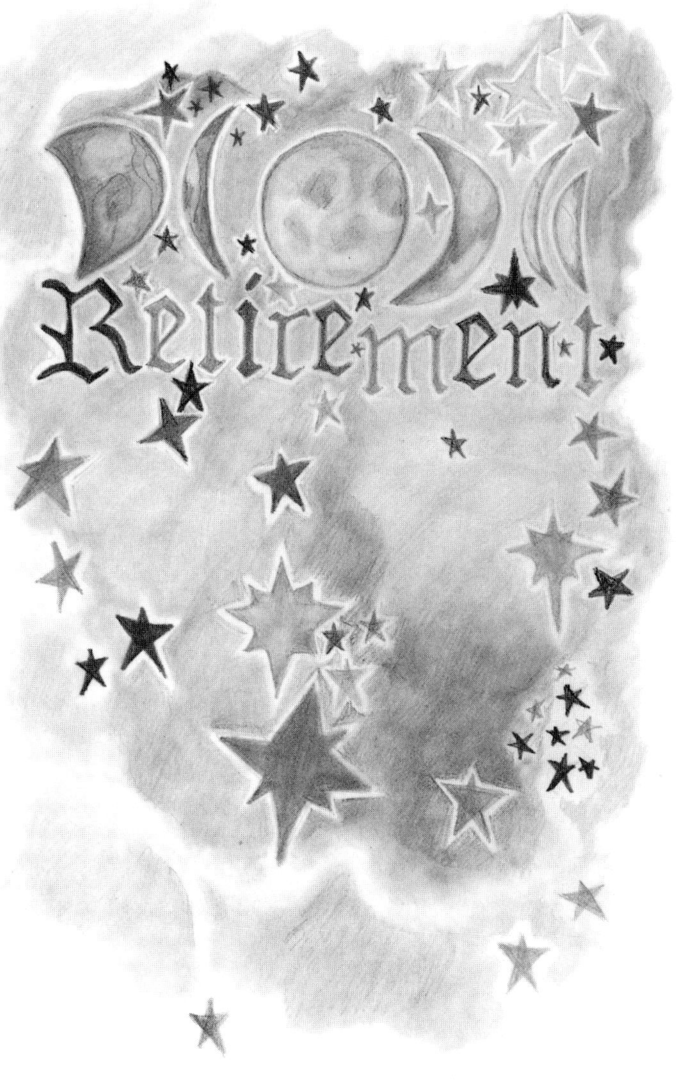
Retirement

"What about a carriage and some footmen?"

"Arthur!" Gloriosa screamed. "Stop! You're in the wrong century. She can take a cab. I'll send a gorgeous dress over, I'll throw some magic dust, I'll be sure an eligible, good looking, older gent meets her, but that is it, okay?"

"Is that the best you can do?"

"Yes, the very best I can do."

"Then it will have to be acceptable. But do it right," he warned, backing down the hallway. "Or I'll be back," he threatened, his voice fading away as he turned a corner.

Gloriosa was too relieved he was gone to do anything except close the door, throw the bolt and take two headache pills.

She tried all night to conjure up stuff. It took her twelve hours, but she managed the tickets and the gent. The next afternoon she had to buy a dress at a fancy boutique because Mrs. Pantia wasn't the right age, size, shape or era for any of the dresses Gloriosa could still conjure. Gloriosa had it delivered and hoped it would satisfy Arthur.

[What did it look like, Andrew?]

[I don't know.]

[You gotta tell. Can we make up that part?]

[Okay, go for it.]

[It was silvery with little pink roses sewn on.]

[And it had real silver buttons with blue-Tritan stones in them.]

enchantress

sprite

charmed

fair fay

Godmother

71

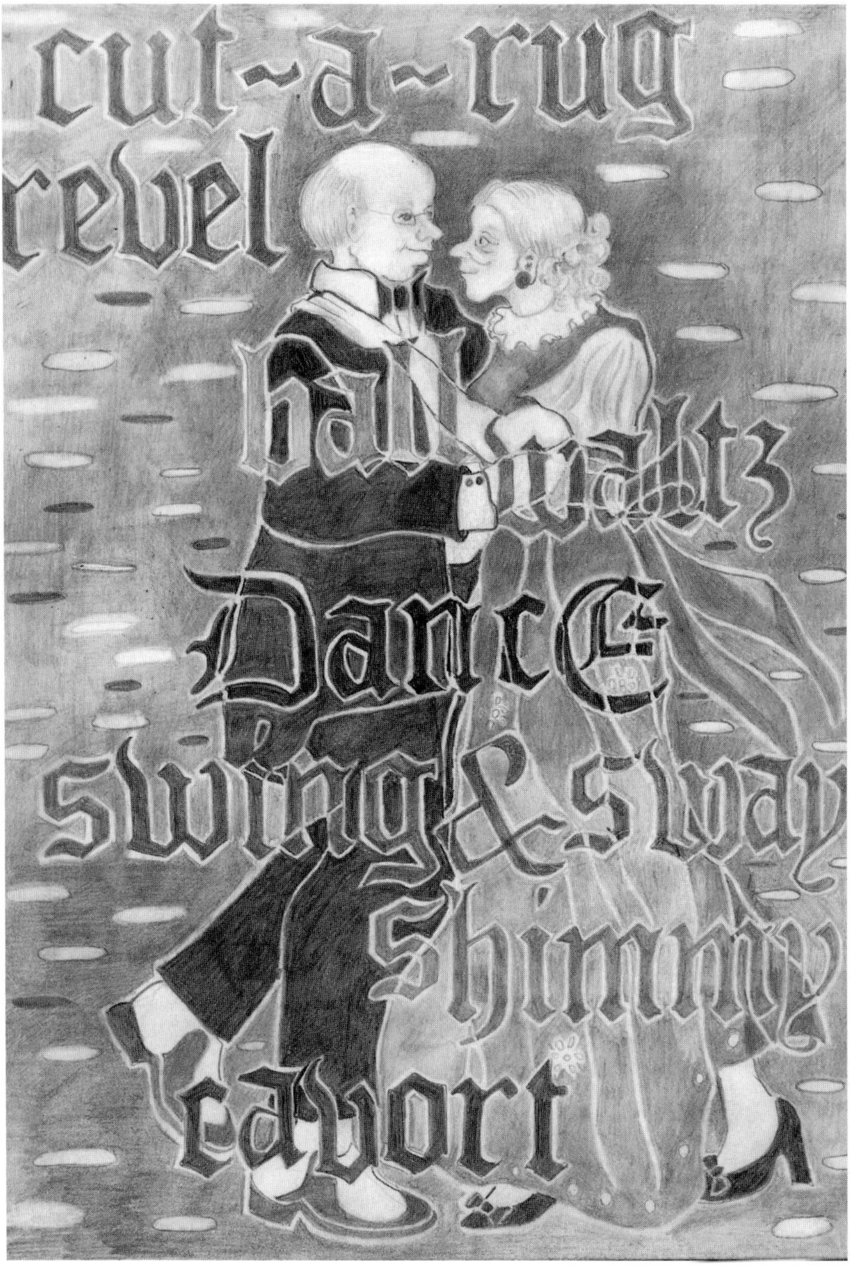
cut~a~rug
revel
waltz
Dance
swing & sway
shimmy
cavort

[And she had a silver shawl to match and a long bow down the back of the dress.]

[That's great, guys, I'll put that in the story!]

With a stroke of genius, Gloriosa sent Mrs. Pantia a free coupon she had cut out of the community news-paper to get her hair done at Betty's Beauty Salon, downstairs.

The night of the dance, Gloriosa's curiosity got the best of her. After a few tries, she managed to cast an invisibility spell on herself. It was worth the effort to be able to peek in on the ball and see Mrs. Pantia laugh-ing and smiling and dancing with a dapper old man, although it wasn't the one Gloriosa had planned on. Mrs. Pantia really looked lovely and Gloriosa could even imagine her as a beautiful, young thing, sur-rounded by admirers and friends .

[And princes and kings and knights, right?]

[Well, maybe, Cindra.]

When the clock struck eleven, there was one last dance and everybody went home exhausted. The old gentleman escorted Mrs. Pantia to her building, and Gloriosa just happened to be getting on the elevator at the same moment as Mrs. Pantia.

"Mrs. Pantia, you look gorgeous," Gloriosa said, pretending surprise.

"Thank you, Gloriosa, I had a wonderful evening," she said radiantly.

"Who was the gentleman who brought you home?"

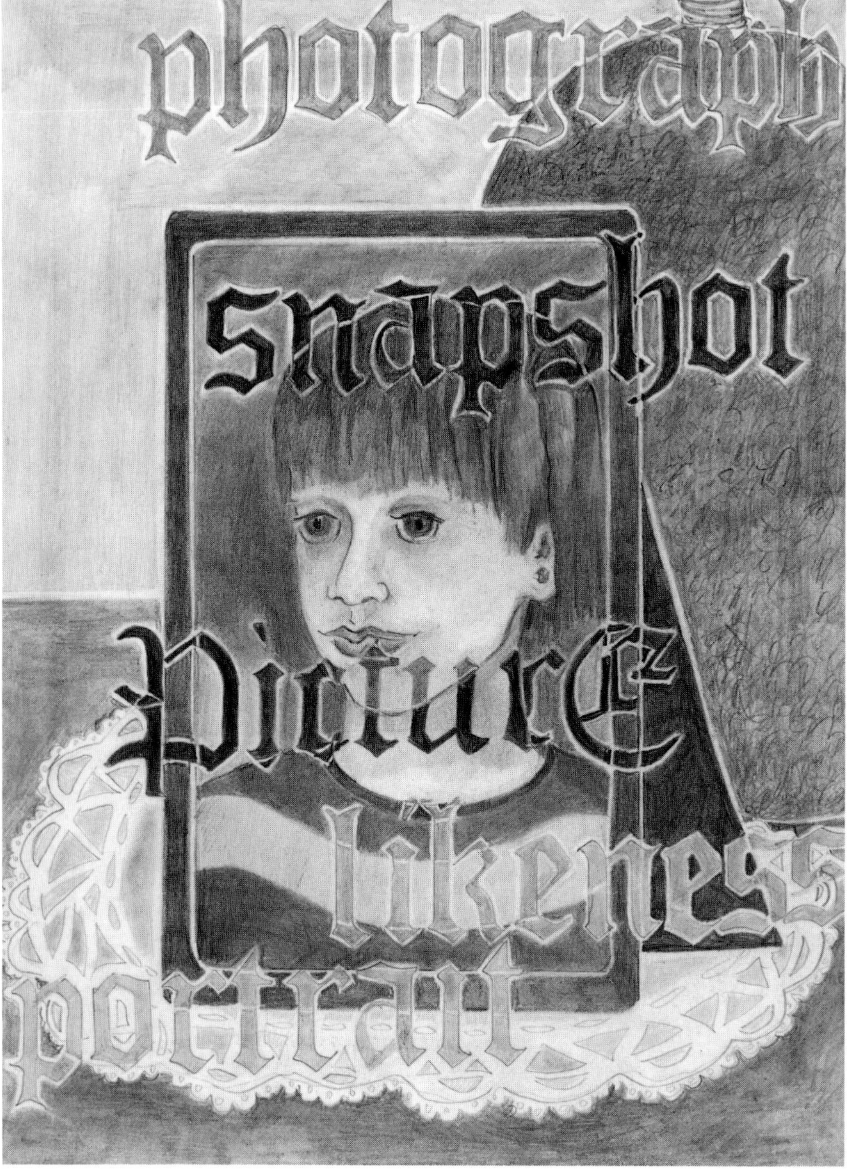
photograph
snapshot
picture
likeness
portrait

"He's just a marvelous man! His name is Mr. Harry Prince. And he has asked me to a picnic with him next week," she added, smiling broadly.

[See, he is a prince!]

After that, Mrs. Pantia always joined everyone for tea when she wasn't with Mr. Prince. She chatted with everybody about the weather, recommended good books to read and baked bread for the homeless. One day, when everyone was in Mr. Raines' apartment for coffee and cookies, Mrs. Pantia announced she would be moving out because she and Mr. Prince were to be married.

[She's getting her prince!]

[Of course she is. That's a fairy godmother's job.]

[I thought you didn't believe in fairy godmothers, Louisa.]

[Humph.]

[There's only a little more now.]

"How wonderful! I'm so happy for you," Gloriosa said, thinking how pleased Arthur would be.
    "Gloriosa dear, please, be my matron of honor."
    "I'd be delighted," Gloriosa said, smiling.
    "Good," Mrs. Pantia sighed. "I have so little family left, you see, and Harry comes from a huge family."
    "But, of course, Arthur will be there," Gloriosa said consolingly.

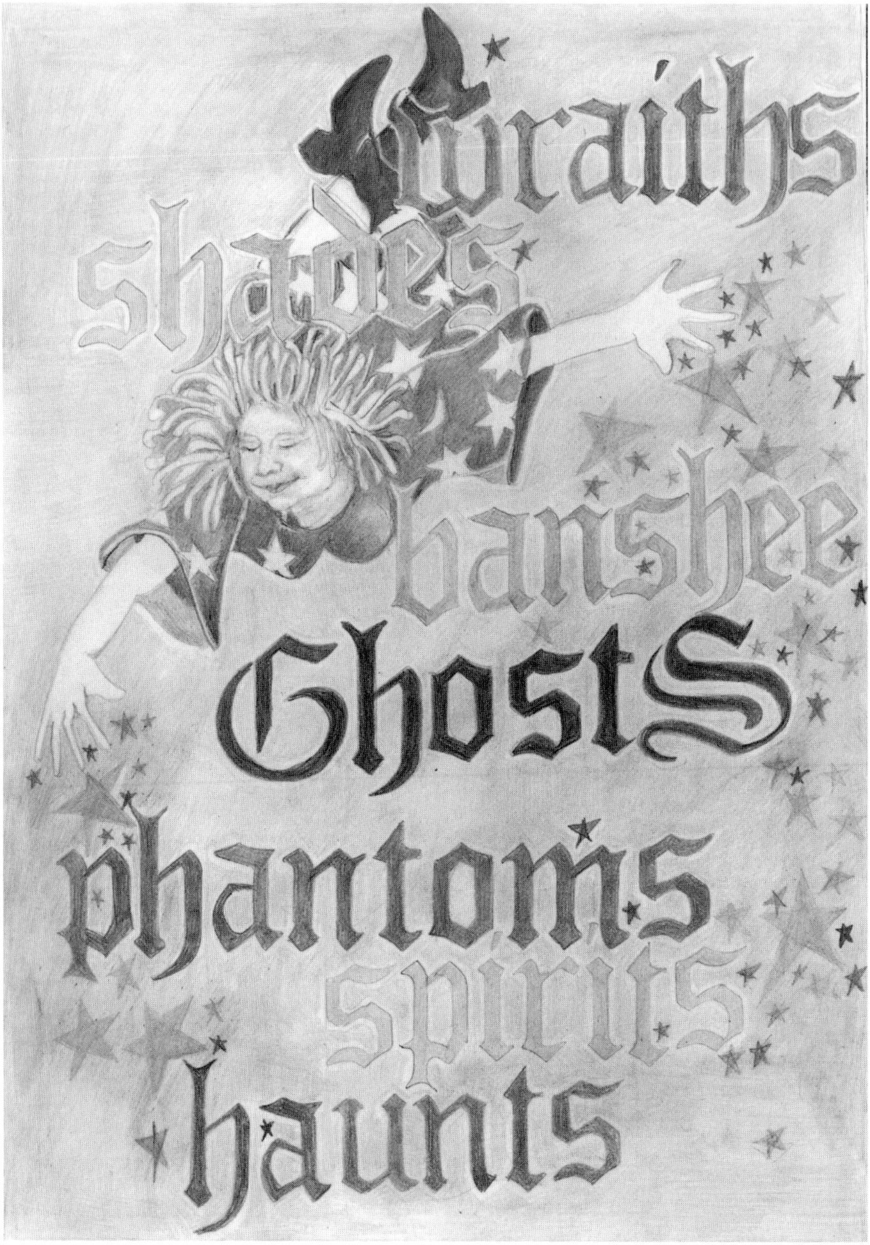
wraiths
shades
banshee
Ghosts
phantoms
spirits
haunts

"Arthur? However did you know about him, Gloriosa?" Mrs. Panita asked with an odd expression on her face.

Thinking quickly, Gloriosa said, "You showed me a picture of him in your apartment."

"Oh, of course, but I'm afraid he died over twelve years ago when he was only ten."

Mrs. Pantia went off to get dressed for a date with Mr. Prince. Gloriosa knew she should have felt pretty proud of what she had helped pull off, but instead her stomach felt queasy. Mr. Raines noticed and offered to get her tea, but she excused herself and tottered off unsteadily down the hall to her apartment. As soon as she got inside, she started to laugh and laugh. She laughed so hard tears ran down her face. She laughed until she accidentally set off a flying spell and found herself hanging from the ceiling, still laughing loudly. It was an hour before she set herself back on the floor. Nobody might believe in fairy godmothers anymore, but maybe fair was fair. Afterall, she had never believed in ghosts.

XI

"Ooooh, that was a good story. Do you think there are really ghosts, Andrew?"

"Probably not, but who knows for sure. Anyway, there is lots of scarier real stuff to worry about."

"I heard a Miner say Mr. Chalder was a ghost of himself," Cindra said.

"That's not what that means, Cindra. That just means he has changed," I explained, "so that he's only a little bit the way he used to be."

"Are you sure he isn't a ghost?"

"Yeah, I'm sure, Cindra." I hoped she wasn't too scared. I hadn't thought about that before I read her the story.

"Hey kids," Dad said coming out onto the porch. "Whatcha doing out here?"

"Go back to bed, Daddy," Cindra said.

"What's going on here that I'm not wanted?"

"Aw, Daddy, if you're awake, Andrew won't read us another story."

"Sorry, come in when you're ready," Dad said, smiling. "And thanks, Andrew."

"Come on, guys, we've got to stop. I'm hungry," I said, grateful for the break.

The girls ran into the house. I stood, stretched and was about to go inside, when the Beetle scuttled up.

"Come, Andrew. Time to go now. Late already."

"If you'd only come a little earlier you could have saved me from my sisters," I said.

"Come now."

"I haven't even gotten dressed. Where are we going?"

"Together," he said.

"Yeah, but where are we going together, Mr. Chalder?"

Typically, the Beetle didn't answer, just scuttled inside in his usual beetle-like way. I followed him and hurried to dress. I didn't want to hang around all morning trying to keep my sisters from fighting.

"Hey, Mom, Dad, can I go with Mr. Chalder?"

"Where?" was the reply from the back room.

I looked at Tomas questioningly.

"To the village?"

His reply was more a question than an answer, but I called back quickly to Mom, "To the village."

"I guess it's okay, but stay with Mr. Chalder, Andrew," Mom instructed.

I ran out after the Beetle, who was already off.

"Where are we really going?" I asked as I caught up to him.

"Town," he replied, surprising me. I had thought he had been kidding. "Errand to stop at."

As far as I could see, nothing in what Tomas called the town had changed. The Water People sat exactly as they had and the houses were still indistinguishable huddles, just as they had been.

The Beetle scuttled to a hovel whose entrance was so low to the ground we both had to squat and waddle through. Inside a Water Person lay lopsidedly on a mat. Its skin was transparent, clearly exposing thick veins that encircled its arms, legs and torso. Its mouth was ringed by a moist, whitened tissue that hung limply over the orifice. Its eye sockets had turned a discolored gray-green and a sickening smell hung in the air.

The Beetle shook his head. "Too young to die it was. Shouldn't be dead, it." His head was turning rapidly in what seemed to be panic.

"Dead?" I repeated, feeling my stomach lurch and putting my hand over my nose and mouth.

"Yes, come. Must inform them," he stuttered.

"Who? Who do you need to tell?" I asked.

The Beetle grabbed my hand and pulled me outside. His face was blanched, but he had straightened out of his crouch to tower over me as his hair tumbled out of a tight net to just below his ears. I hardly recognized him as the Beetle.

He propelled me onto a path. "Go home, Andrew. That way. Safe it is."

He was off at a terrific pace. I hesitated briefly, entertained following him and instead decided to go to the Club. It was closer than the house and I was uneasy about walking home alone as I remembered the sucking sound of the mud.

The Club was dark and cool. At first I thought it was emptied of all the Miners, but then I saw Mrs. Pattison stepping quickly into another room.

"Mrs. Pattison," I called. "Please, can I talk to you?"

"What? Oh my, Andrew. What are you doing here?"

"I was wondering . . ."

"No, no," she cut me off. "You have to wait. Poor Caroline has been attacked."

"Attacked? By whom?" I asked.

"Not now, Andrew," she said, rushing off.

I followed her quickly. She was bent over Caroline whose ashen face was grotesquely accented by swollen purple lips. Between violent spasms, she sobbed and rocked herself. Another spasm and more tears left wet tracks trailing down her cheeks.

"Good grief, Caroline. Drink this and try to tell me who did this to you," Mrs. Pattison urged.

Caroline only sobbed harder, running her hands shakily through her hair, which was tangled and clotted with blood.

"Please, Caroline, answer. Was it one of the Natives?"

The younger woman shook her head no between sobs and finally managed, "A Water Person."

Mrs. Pattison looked up and spied me. "Out, Andrew. This is nothing for a young boy to see."

I turned to leave, and went out the wrong door. Instead of the living room, I was in a small alcove full of chairs. A girl of maybe thirteen was sitting there quite calmly and, despite the sounds of sobbing, obliviously reading with a big smile on her lips. It was strange no one had mentioned there was another kid so near my age on post.

Despite wondering if the girl could be deaf, I experimentally said, "Hello." She looked up immediately. "Do you know what happened to her?" I asked, nodding towards the sobs drifting from the other room, still shaken by what I had seen.

"Sure," she said. "She was attacked."

"By a Water Person? They don't seem to know we exist."

"Righto. All the same, they do attack once in a while."

"Really? There's no mention of it in any of the records my dad was given. You say they sometimes attack women?"

"Both. Men, too, 'specially if you're out about alone."

"Oh," I said lamely. "I'm Andrew Haldran."

"I suppose you must be. New ones are easy to spot."

"We are?"

The girl nodded and went back to her book.

"What's your name?" I asked, trying to extend the conversation.

"Philippa," she said without looking up. She was definitely neither the prettiest nor the friendliest girl I had ever met.

"Well, it's nice to meet you."

Philippa pointed to a door. "That's the way out. You should go home, if you dare."

"Couldn't we get to know each other a little more before I go home?"

"Why?"

"Because there is no one else my age to talk to," I said.

"So, what do you want to talk about?" she almost sneered.

"Why do they attack, Philippa?" I asked quickly, unable to think of what else to talk about with this strange girl.

"Sex, I suppose," she answered nonchalantly.

"That doesn't seem very likely to me," I said. "I have my doubts that the Water People are even sentient."

She looked up. "Do you have to be sentient to want sex?" she laughed and returned to her book, dangling her feet back and forth.

Of course she was right, but I didn't want to look dumb in front of her, so I said, "One of them is dead."

"Dead?" She popped out of her chair. "Oh, let's do go and see."

"I don't think so. I doubt I could find the right hut anyway," I said. The intensity of her interest and sudden warm demeanor was so unexpected it frightened me.

"Oh come, Andrew, you must show me."

I was sorry I had told her. Her eyes were too excited over the death. It made me edgy and I hoped I could end the conversation quickly without being rude.

"No, sorry. No can do. I've got to go home," I said.

"Alone? With one attack already? Show me and I'll walk you home."

Just a moment before she had been eager to send me on my way all by myself.

I felt a hand on my shoulder. It was Mrs. Pattison. "Philippa, leave him be. Mr. Chalder is outside looking for you, Andrew."

"Chalder?" Philippa said. "That little scuzz bug!"

"He's okay," I said. "Thanks, Mrs. Pattison."

As we rejoined Mr. Chalder in the living room, the Club was abruptly hushed. The sobbing had ceased.

"Andrew," Mrs. Pattison whispered, "I advise you not to associate with that young lady. Now, there is Mr. Chalder," she said and gave me a little shove in Tomas' direction.

"Why did not you go home, Andrew?" Tomas asked.

"Because you left me and I was afraid, that's why. Anyway, how'd you know I hadn't gone home?"

"Philippa leaving be," he said, going right past my question.

"Why?" I asked, not expecting any more of an answer than I had just gotten.

"Her father leaves."

"Oh, that actually makes sense. Why is Philippa so weird anyway?"

"Her mother is dead."

"Did she die here?" I asked.

After a long pause, he answered with, "Ask her, not me."

Abruptly, Philippa laughed from the alcove as if she had heard us. Her cackles reverberated and bounced off the walls. The Beetle pushed me out the door. I was relieved to be in the bright air outside. It was too bad about Philippa. I could have used a friend my own age, but even if she was the only other teenager on Miners World, she was too scary. Her twisted laughs echoed with an unwelcome clarity in my mind.

I stopped and faced Mr. Chalder. "Is anything the way it seems here?"

"What mean you?"

"Like Philippa, there's something really strange about her. And then there's you! My sisters think you're under a magic spell. I doubt that, but I know you're not what you pretend."

"What pretend I?" he asked with his head cocked quizzically.

"To be a beetle, all hunched and frail. I've seen different."

"Yes," he said simply.

"So why pretend?"

He cocked his head again and turned into his shoulders just like a bug in a carapace, eyes downcast. "Am what I must be," he said sadly and walked on.

I didn't want to stop talking because I was still trying to block out the haunting whisper of Philippa's witchy cackle, so I asked him, "Where are you from, anyway?"

"This is home," he said, stomping a foot on the dry clay. "Here."

"But before here?" I asked.

He looked at me oddly and answered in a twisted sentence. "Nowhere is there."

Just as we reached the gate to our house, just as Tomas Chalder turned and scuttled off, I noticed the shadowy sound of Philippa's laughter had finally faded out of my mind.

XII

"So what did you find out today, Dad" I asked him over our makeshift kitchen table.

"Humph! I wonder if all this is for nothing? I have no news at all."

"I do," I said, thinking how Dad was going to have to eat his words about his unaugmented son in the next few moments.

"Yes, dear," Mom said absently.

"You know, the Beet . . . I mean, Mr. Chalder took me on a walk. I saw a dead Water Person, Chalder left me and I went to the Club. There's a really whacked out girl there named Philippa. Mr. Chalder came back for me and, oh yeah, Caroline was attacked by a Water Person," I burst out as rapidly as I could.

Mom's mouth was open, her eyes sparking. "Let's just start with Caroline. First, is she okay?"

"I think so, but Mrs. Pattison shooed me away before I could be sure."

"We'll check on that. Do you know how or why she was attacked?"

"No, Mom, but Philippa said it was for sex."

"What?" Dad said and started to chuckle. "Sex? How old is Philippa?"

"I don't know, maybe thirteen."

Dad chuckled again. "So, she thinks it was for sex? With a Water Person? Nobody even knows if they move. Sex?" He chuckled a third time.

"Mr. Chalder says they're useful," I said.

"For what?" Dad asked. "Sign posts?"

"I don't know," I admitted. "Trying to get Mr. Chalder to utter five word sentences is a challenge."

"But, it's true," Mom confirmed, "Tomas Chalder insists both the Water People and the Natives are useful."

"So far I haven't seen the Water People in the villages as much as sneeze," Dad said, "and the Natives in the caves do little more than breathe. I'm telling you, as I sit there and wait and wait and wait for the Natives to even blink, I entertain all kinds of thoughts.

Could they be in hibernation? Could they be in a trance or maybe playing games with us? As to the Water People, I have not a clue."

"I bet they're enchanted," Cindra suggested. "What we need is a fairy godmother to break the spell."

"What a nice idea, Cindra," Dad said, obviously startled by the innocent thought.

"Andrew read us a story about Cinderella's fairy godmother."

"Oh, I see," Dad said diplomatically.

"Just because the Water People are humanoid, doesn't mean they're intelligent. Maybe they're only animals squatting in deserted habitats, like mice and rats do," Mom posited.

"But, mice and rats multiply, and doesn't the population of both races of aliens remain constant, Dad?" I asked.

He nodded. "That's what the satellite heat surveys showed."

"Okay." I cleared my throat. "Here's another question. Who built all these houses? It doesn't seem likely it was either the Water People or the Natives."

"Maybe a race that died long ago?" Dad suggested. "The houses certainly look like ruins."

"Are the Water People dead, Daddy?" Cindra asked.

"That's stupid, Cindra. You are sooo dumb!" Louisa taunted.

"They look dead. They don't move and dead people don't move, either," Cindra said edgily.

"Honey, I promise you, they are alive," Mom reassured Cindra.

"Told you," Louisa said. "I bet they're too stupid to move!"

"You think everybody is dumb, Louisa," Cindra accused.

Dad grimaced at their speculations. "I don't know if the Water People are intelligent, but the Natives had better be," he grumbled.

"How did we get this far off-track?" Mom asked, turning her attention back to me. "Andrew, were the death of the Water Person and the attack related?" Mom asked.

"Got me! I suggest you ask Mr. Chalder. He talks to you."

"Only when he drinks blue tea," she said. "It must have some chemical effect on him. Maybe we should brew some."

"The trouble is, we never know when he is going to show up," Dad noted, "or how much of what he says will make sense."

We ate early, drank blue tea without Tomas Chalder and went outside. Sky-watching had already become a nightly ritual. The air was a dark blue that we peacefully watched spread and fade into a deep blackness studded with stars.

"Gee, it's pretty," Cindra said loudly.

Mom plucked Cindra into her lap. "Do you miss holovision shows?" Mom asked her.

"No," she said sleepily. "I like Andy's stories about Gloriosa Marina Eloise G. Mother and Alvin Peter Pooterbax better."

"Gloriosa Marina Eloise G. Mother? Alvin Peter Pooterbax?" Dad laughed. "I'd like to hear those stories myself."

Dad stroked Louisa's head as she leaned against his chest and he pointed out the star formations above us. It felt good to be together without the distraction of technology laden belongings. I craned my neck to look up at the sky. The air was dry, but light clouds began to drift in front of the stars.

"Rain?" I asked.

"Hal Andrews claims it almost never rains this time of year, even up in the mountains. And I believe it, as cracked as the clay is," Dad said.

"Then where did that mud bath come from?" Mom asked. "I've been puzzling over it a lot."

"Underground streams?" I suggested.

"Maybe," Mom said.

"Another question for Chalder," Dad added.

"Why don't you ask one of the Miners, Dad?"

"I've tried. Most of them have been here between a year and three years, and still they either know nothing, or else are unwilling to tell me anything. They act as if they have never been out of the Club except to go to the caves. But now, Andrew says Caroline was out alone and got attacked by a seemingly catatonic being." He shook his head. "They should have sent a detective here, not a diplomat. None of this makes sense."

Mom looked right at me. "Until we figure this out, no one is to go wandering again, even with Mr. Chalder."

"Aw, Mom," I complained, "I was safer with Mr. Chalder than in the Club with that weirdo girl, Philippa."

"Whose daughter is she?" Dad asked.

"Got me, but she and her Dad are leaving."

"Oh, that must be Brandt's girl. They've been recalled. The scuttlebutt is that he didn't retrieve enough information, but the Miners are so territorial and secretive, I don't know how much of what they tell me I can believe."

"Hey," Louisa said, "I felt rain."

"No way, Louisa. You must have imagined it," I said.

"I did not," she pouted.

"The clouds are thickening," Mom said. "Let's go inside, now."

"That won't do us much good if it rains. The roof is full of holes."

"That's not funny, Stephen. Something is coming and the house is all we have. Now move it!" Mom said in a voice of command.

We scurried inside only an instant before the wind rose up with a roar. Hail and clay swirled violently in through the open doorways and down the holes in the ceilings, filling the house with pulverized clay, coating everything in a fine dust and making us choke, while the ice bounced off the floors, the walls and our bodies in a stinging attack.

"Mom," I yelled over the noise, "we could go into the cold cellar."

She nodded and we started in that direction just as a solidly dust-covered figure sidled through the front door.

"No need," the Beetle said, his face peeping through swarthy wrappings. "Close the roof and door."

"How?" Mom screamed over the wind.

The Beetle climbed onto a box and jabbed the edge of one of the roof holes with a long stick that had been sitting in a corner since our arrival. As he went from hole to hole, a membrane closed at his touch. Lastly he poked at the door frame and the air in the house was suddenly calm. Silence smothered our ears. We wiped at dust, smudging it across our cheeks and backhanding it off of our lips, our eyes standing like blue holes in our clay covered faces.

"There," Tomas said, decloaking, or rather unwrapping mummy-style accouterments.

"How does that work?" Dad asked, reaching up to poke at the membranes which did a jelly-like jiggle.

No answer from the Beetle.

"Those membranes look organic," Dad mused.

"A hybrid, that," Chalder said.

"Is it Native engineering? Is there more in the house?" I asked curiously.

Chalder stared at me before he nodded.

"Will you show all of it to us?" Mom asked.

"Tonight not," he answered noncommittally.

"How do we open the roof when the storm is over?" Mom asked.

"Storm? Not this. A mixing this is, Rebecca."

"Sorry, but how do we open the, uh, windows?"

"Windows, not. Entrances," the Beetle corrected.

"Okay, entrances," Mom agreed. "How?"

"Tap three times in the middle," he said seriously.

"And say, 'Knock, knock, knock, who's there?'" I quipped, unable to resist.

"What?" Chalder looked confused.

"Don't you know, 'Knock, Knock, Who's There' jokes?" I asked dismayed.

"Who is there will depend. On the season," he answered.

XIII

Mr. Chalder was clearly stuck with us until the storm died down. He washed the dust off his face, throwing cold water into his eyes, which when he looked up were briefly and startlingly, predominantly yellow. He actually smiled at Louisa and Cindra and then huddled down into a corner of the room.

Mom handed him a cup of blue tea, which he sipped slowly as he watched the girls at a jacks game.

"Mr. Chalder," Dad said, "I heard someone was attacked."

"The worries," he replied.

"So that's what the worries are," Mom said. "Have other people been attacked?"

The Beetle raised his eyes and looked up at her. "People attacked not."

"Who then?" Dad asked.

Chalder stared at him. "Go mine someone else, Stephen Haldran," he said sharply and clearly.

"I didn't know I was trying to mine anything from you. I just want my family to be safe."

The yellow-flecked eyes dropped. "Of course."

"Did Caroline offend someone? Is that why she was attacked?" Mom asked.

"No, Rebecca Haldran. She was just there."

"Who attacked her?" Mom asked.

"No one," the Beetle insisted.

"Someone attacked her. She claims it was a Water Person," Mom persisted patiently.

"Wrong. Attack it did not on her."

"Then are you saying a human attacked her?" Mom asked.

"Not human. Told you, not an attack. It happened when she was there," the Beetle responded in ever more confusing circles.

"When what happened?" Dad intervened.

Chalder shook his head. "Understand you not," he said. His language reverted to its encircling order.

"Hey, Mr. Chalder," I said quickly, causing his head to twist in that beetle-like way. "Why do you stay here?"

"Waiting," he said.

"Andrew," Mom warned. "Don't intervene, and don't pry into someone else's life."

"Right, Mom. No prying. Shouldn't you and Dad follow your own rules," I remarked.

"Andrew," she said sharply. "You are asking personal questions. Your father and I are trying to get important security information."

"Sure, Mom, but you're going at it all wrong," I burst out.

"Andrew!"

"Right, I'm gone," I said and went into the other room. Nothing made me madder than being put in my place like a child. My parents didn't think I could do anything right. They weren't the only ones who needed information. If I was going to solve this mystery, I had to ask questions, too, and I didn't want to ask the same things they did.

The storm had died and I went outside. I had barely slumped onto the steps when the Beetle came scurrying out. He plunked down next to me and awkwardly patted my shoulder. "It was a mistake, Andrew, not an attack."

"On Caroline?" I asked.

"Yes, no anger, no intent. Please, do not be angry at family yours."

Unwilling to let my anger go yet, unable to think of anything else to say, I asked impulsively, "Were you once 'just there'?"

"Remember clearly nothing I. Please, come inside," he said.

"Naw, I think I should just stay out here. Hey, do you have any suggestions for what my dad should do to get information from the Natives?" I was hoping against hope that he would give me something with which I could show up my parents.

"Mine, of course."

"Yeah, yeah," I said.

To my surprise, Chalder added, "The right questions ask. He is going wrong."

"Huh? Going wrong? In what ways? Can't you help him?" I pleaded, my heart jumping at the chance.

"Wrong questions. He needs imagination," the Beetle said

and ended the conversation when he precipitously departed out the gate. I jumped up right behind him, but he had sped up his scuttle and was gone before I had a chance to stop him.

"Boy, easy come, easy go," I said out loud.

"Who? Mr. Chalder?" Dad asked, coming up behind me.

"Yeah, him and the storm." The stars were back. "Dad, Mr. Chalder just told me that you're asking about the wrong things."

"What's that supposed to mean?"

"Got me. I don't even know what you've asked, but he also said you need to use your imagination."

"Okay, come on back inside and we'll talk about it, Andrew, I promise." It was his form of an apology.

"Dad, I can help if you'll let me. I've got a great imagination," I said. That was one reason I didn't want to be Augmented. I didn't want to lose it.

"I know you want to help," Dad said noncommittally. He put his arm around me and guided me back inside. "Hey kids, I've got a question for you. What would you guys ask the Natives if you had the chance?" Dad asked Louisa and Cindra.

"You want me and Cindra to tell you what to ask, Daddy?" Louisa murmured sleepily.

"We might as well use all our imaginative resources, and we don't have too many to use, so yes," he said, smiling and winking at me at the same time.

"I'd ask how to grow chocolate bars on trees," Cindra said happily.

"Not me," Louisa said, "I would ask how to make little, flying dragons."

"Stupid dragons," Cindra accused. "Chocolate bars."

"Stop, girls. How about you, son?" Dad asked me. "It's your turn."

"I'm not sure, but maybe you should ask about Mr. Chalder."

"I doubt the Natives would bother about him. What else?" Mom said, discarding my idea instantly.

"Well, then I'd ask about the Natives themselves," I answered, still mad at how easily Mom kept dismissing me.

"Interesting. Why?" Dad asked in one of his most diplomatic tones.

"Because, we don't know anything about them, and it would seem that if we knew something about them, we might know what questions they'd actually answer."

"Not a bad approach," Dad mused. "At least a different approach, and at least I'd be asking questions I know they'd have answers for. They couldn't very well pretend ignorance, could they?"

"If they choose to answer," Mom pointed out.

Dad sighed. "I'll have to think about it, now let's get some sleep." He stretched, pulling his arms out to their full length and clenching his fingers into fists.

I lay on my bed and tried to piece what I'd learned together and got nowhere. Instead I wondered again if I'd made the right decision about my future, and I wondered if my mom was treating me this way because of the effects my decision had had on everyone. And, I wondered if things could get more tedious. Then I wondered if wondering had gotten me where I was. I quit wondering and fell into a sleep without dreams.

XIV

Mom woke me in the morning as she opened and closed ceiling membranes.

"Darndest thing," she said. "These membranes let in just as much light closed as open."

"But, what if you want to sleep in, like me? Can you adjust them?"

"I don't know, Andrew. If not, I suppose teenagers on this post will have to switch their sleep schedules. In any case, it's time for you to get up."

"Mom, can I go with Dad today?" I asked, twisting my pajama shirt around to straighten it and me out.

"You slept too long. He's already gone. He wandered out muttering about dragons and chocolate bars and Natives. He was pretty grumpy. I don't think he wanted to go."

"Mom, I don't know how long I can take it here. Most of the day there's hardly anything to do."

"Are you lonely?"

"Sort of," I admitted.

"I feel the same way. Let's hope your father makes a couple of finds quickly so we can go home. Sorry about last night. Listen, Andrew, we never told you, but your Dad is on probation with his company until he proves himself here. It's a lot of pressure."

She kissed me and went into the other room. I could hear Cindra and Louisa chattering as they ate breakfast. I wished Dad hadn't put my suggestions in the same category as a chocolate bar tree. There had to be a way to get him to expand his mind set.

I yawned, stretched and tottered in sleepily for breakfast. It was reconstructed home fries and some pale green, tubular alien fruits.

"Mom, maybe we could help Dad by thinking up some ideas he could explore with the Natives," I suggested.

"It can't hurt. It would give us something to do. Go wash up before breakfast. Mr. Chalder said that the running water in the shower closet was installed by a Miner and that's why it doesn't work all the time."

"Mr. Chalder didn't mention a hidden bookstore anywhere in any of these closets, did he?" I asked.

She laughed. "You're out of luck. I guess you'll have to experience life directly, instead of getting everything from your books," she said unsympathetically as I went to throw water on my face and scrub my teeth.

The fruit proved to be better than the home fries, which tasted bland and papery. By the time I finished eating, Mom was supervising Louisa's and Cindra's language and composition lessons. I kept expecting her to pass the chore on to me, but I guess her own boredom precluded the option. I went outside.

The storm had filled in a lot of the cracks in the yard so that the blue tea flowers no longer sprinkled the dry ground. It made the yard seem even more barren. I wandered about, dragging my shoes in the dust. Anybody surveying our new home would have thought it was ready to fall apart. I walked up close and kicked irritably at a board on the house that looked particularly precarious. It shifted and resettled intact. I looked at the walls more closely. The panels weren't wood. They were softer, almost pliable. I kicked at the first one again, harder. This time it contracted like a muscle and swung open, revealing a deep crawl space beneath the house.

"Mom," I screamed, "come quick." I backed away, half expecting the panel to snap closed or maybe for a native animal to come snarling out at me.

"What, Andrew? What's the matter?" She arrived, poised and ready, battle ready, a long knife in one hand.

"Look," I pointed, feeling my mouth hanging open.

Mom pulled a mini-torch out of her pocket, and beamed it through the newly exposed opening. Dim daylight filtered through what must have been the floor of the house. A sinuous maze of roots sprang from the walls and speared into spiky-pink moss-covered earth. Bean pods sprouted out of orange rootlets and small, pear-shaped fruits dangled from purple rhizomes. Budding off thick yellow roots were wrinkled, maroon balls like the ones Tomas had served us that first morning at the Club.

Mom, drew back. "Wait until your father sees this! How did you find it, Andrew?"

"The panel opened when I kicked it, like the membranes in the windows," I said. "Mom do you think the house could be alive?"

"Alive? How can a house be alive?"

"I don't know. Doesn't it look as if the house is rooted like a plant?"

"It just looks that way because roots are sprouting from the earth of the foundation, Andrew. Fruits don't grow on roots."

"No, but potatoes and carrots and onions are root plants, aren't they?"

"That's true, I suppose," she said, scratching at her head.

"By the way, don't those purple balls look like the fruits Tomas serves?" I asked.

"Maybe so. I wonder who has been caring for this garden?"

"It might not need anyone to tend it," I said out loud before I could stop myself. Mom was going to freak, but I had no choice but to finish my thought. "The Miners think the fruits are bio-engineered. Maybe the house is too."

"I sure hope the garden was put here for the Miners and that those are veggies and fruits humans can eat," she mused, completely ignoring my suggestion.

"Yet another question for Mr. Chalder," I nodded. "How many do you think we have on our list for him by now?"

"Too many," she answered.

"Maybe we can get Dad to ask the Natives this one."

"It might be a wonderful discovery for his company," Mom agreed, "If they could export the fruits for human consumption."

"Mom, what if those roots do mean the house is alive? What if it just keeps growing and growing? I think there are new crannies in our house and I was just thinking some of the old ones look bigger than they did. And that could be why the Miners keep finding new closets and spaces in the Club? It could be growing, too," I said excitedly, as my fertile imagination started leaping about. "Maybe the structures are smaller or bigger depending on if they are younger or older organisms?"

"Andrew, even for you that is farfetched."

"Come on, Mom, stretch your mind. Use your imagination. If the house expands organically, that would explain why the doors don't line up. If they're houses at all," I added at the last minute, deciding to see how far I could lead my mother away from her normal focus.

"What else could they be?" Mom asked.

"Farms? Sure, they could be farms," I said just to prod her. "The holes in the roof let light in all the time, and rain when they're open. The houses could really be organic structures that protect their fruits," I said more excitedly as my mind began to twist onto new pathways and I began to convince myself my imaginings could be leading to the truth.

"And just how does light get to the plants under there?" Mom asked, pointing to the duskiness beneath the house.

"It looks like what light the plants need filters through the floors. Mom, I bet the houses are self-tending farms. Really!" I exclaimed, truly excited.

"Oh, come on, Andrew. Stop. You are way out in left field. Come back to reality."

"Whose reality? Mom, nothing fits together here. This isn't our reality. It's someone else's. Please, use your imagination for once," I begged.

"Okay, okay." She closed her eyes a moment, opened them, blinked and said, "I'm not very good at this, but you seem to be. What else have you dreamed up?"

I laughed. "Wasn't that enough? Do you really want more?"

"No, not really."

"Can't we get Dad to ask about it? What harm could it do?"

"Okay, why not? It gives us an excuse to go find him," Mom said, shaking her head at the same time she agreed.

"Now? Uh, Mom, our last walk wasn't too successful, remember? Just muddy. Maybe we should wait for Dad to come home."

"Your dad and I already argued this through. I can't live here holed up in a hovel. Don't worry, Andrew. I'll be more careful this time. Get the girls ready."

"Mom, I could stay here with the girls, if you like?"

"I'll feel better if we stick together," she said readily. "I don't even like your father going off without a buddy."

"I could go with him," I said jumping at the opportunity.

She just frowned at me and I could only hope I had planted the idea for later resuscitation.

I thought her need for action was outweighing her caution, but she was insistent. She studied the map a long time, suddenly stabbing at it. "There! That is where we went wrong the last time. That spot must be the mud pond. Right there." She stabbed the map again. "Okay, everybody ready?"

The girls didn't skip this time. They walked quietly, looking down at their feet. Mom had on what I called her hunting eyes. With her like that, I figured the safety thing was covered and let bits and pieces of things pull at my mind.

"Andrew, I think we should go to the Club for directions to the mines," Mom called to me.

"Good idea, Mom," I said remembering how easy it was to get lost in the caves. Besides, if Philippa was still at the Club, I had a lot of questions to ask her. I was pretty sure she had some of the answers, if she would reveal them.

Mrs. Pattison greeted us again. "Oh, my, Rebecca! None of you are allowed in the caves, but I'd be happy to take Stephen a message when I go in an hour. You can wait here."

"Why aren't we allowed into the caves?" Mom asked.

"Rules," she answered sternly.

Mom settled into a chair with its back protected by a wall, a puzzled expression on her face.

"I'm truly sorry, my dear," Mrs. Pattison said, "but rules are rules."

"Uh, Mrs. Pattison, whose rules are they?" I asked.

"Why the Natives' rules, of course."

"Really? I'm surprised," I said. "The Natives don't seem to say much at all."

Mrs. Pattison smiled sweetly. "They say enough," she said and walked away.

Louisa and Cindra sat down near Mom's feet as she pulled out a book to read to them. I wandered off to find Philippa.

She was in the little alcove, now piled with boxes and bags. She had enthroned herself atop a medium sized stack of cartons. Despite her precarious balance, she seemed to be sleeping with her head tucked into her shoulders and her hands tucked into her armpits like a little child's imitation of a bird. The way she was perched reminded me of a prominently beaked, redheaded crow. I had never liked crows. There were too many of them and they were raucous and dirty.

I braced myself and said, "Hi."

"Oh, it's you," Philippa answered instantly, without opening her eyes.

"Yeah, me. I heard you're going to leave."

"Oh, yes. Popsi got himself recalled. Of course, it was inevitable in the end."

"Yeah?" I wanted to ask why, but didn't want to spook her. "Bet you're glad to be leaving."

She shifted her wings and her eyes popped open, dark brown pits beneath her feathery red cap of hair.

"Glad? No, not really. I like this place." Her tongue circled her lips, leaving a trace of moisture on them.

"You do? I'm pretty bored."

A sly look crossed her face. "It's not boring if you're a good spy."

"Oh yeah? What's there to spy on?" I asked trying to lead her on while I also tried to ignore how nervous she made me. She belonged in one of my stories, but not in my real life.

"What? Why everything. The best is finding out who's asking what, who's getting what answers. Sometimes there's even an illicit affair or two."

"But, I thought no one talked about their mining," I said skeptically.

"You're awfully naive," Philippa said nastily, her eyes narrowing to slits.

I blinked at the anger she was emitting. "Then maybe you would enlighten me?"

"Why would I do that? I don't even know you. Why would I give up what I've mined to you? And for free? No way!" she hissed.

"Mined? I heard one of the Miners say that mining was made up of A for asking, W for waiting, and R for receiving. I don't think I heard anyone say, S for spying. Did I miss something, Phillippa?"

She grinned. "So A-W-R me, if you want answers. It'll be fun, you against me. Game begins now," she stated.

"Against? Like a match?"

She nodded.

"Okay. Ever spied on the Water People?"

"Why? They're all catatonic."

"How about Chalder, ever spy on him?" I asked hopefully.

"Now there's a challenge. I've tried, but he's one elusive twerp."

"Well, Philippa, I'd say, so far you haven't got anything worth mining for."

"Oh, yeah? Well, you just made a major tactical faux pas." She straightened up and sat rigidly, staring straight ahead at a wall. "You offended your source."

Her face was stony cold and try as I might, I couldn't get her to answer, nor show even a flicker of interest. She was doing an excellent imitation of the Natives. I was going to have to find a question to break her defenses.

"What have you observed about the Natives?"

A smile from Philippa, but no answer.

"Do they actually do anything, ever?"

A shrug and a smirk.

I wasn't making any headway.

"Whatcha doing?" Cindra asked, coming around the corner.

"Uh, playing a game," I answered.

"Can I play, Andrew?"

"Sure. This is Philippa, Cindra. Ask her something and see if she answers."

"Okay. How old are you, Philippa?" she asked.

"Sixteen," Came back quickly. It flustered me that I had mis-judged her age, until I realized she was most probably lying, not just about this, but probably about lots of things.

I was ready to quit the game, but Cindra asked, "How long have you lived here?"

"Three years," came back.

"Wow, that's half as old as me," she said. "Do you like it here?"

"No!" Just before, Philippa had told me she did.

"Why not?" Cindra went on innocently.

No answer.

"What happened to your mother?" I asked, taking a chance.

"None of your business," Philippa snapped.

"No, no, Philippa. Either give information or nothing. That's the game, your own rules."

"She died, here, okay," she snarled. "Died! Dead! Got it?"

"How?" Cindra said softly.

"I don't know. Popsi and I let her walk home alone one night. We found her dead in the road in the morning. Nobody knows exactly who or what killed her," she said in a gush of emotion.

"Gosh!" Cindra said.

"Gosh? Is that all you can say, you dumb, stupid kid? Gosh! My mother's dead and that's it, gosh?"

"Hey," I yelled. "She's only six, leave her alone. Go on, Cindra, go back to Mom." I turned back to Philippa. "It's not her fault your mother died."

"You're right, your sister didn't have a thing to do with it. It was those catatonic creeps, everybody's precious aliens, who slaughtered my mother and she probably wasn't the first."

"Do you know for sure they murdered her?"

"You're just like everybody else. You want proof. Well, I don't have any. I don't know it for absolutely sure. There weren't any wounds. There was nothing except the look on her face! That look! And the smiles on their stupid, silly, catatonic, moronic faces when we asked about it."

"How can the Miners act like nothing has happened?"

She jumped down deftly and shoved past me. "They're all idiots!" she said and vanished into another space.

"Wow," Cindra said from the edge of the doorway where she had apparently stopped.

"Go back to Mom, Cindra. Now!"

I ran after Philippa and bumped into a short man whose hair matched Philippa's in its redness.

"Slow down there," a surprisingly deep voice said.

"Sorry. I think my little sister and I upset Philippa, about her mother. Are you her dad?"

The man's eyes blinked, but he didn't confirm or deny his relationship with Philippa.

Instead he said, "That would do it."

"I'm sorry about upsetting her and about her mother," I said, assuming the man was Mr. Brandt.

"Yes, well, I'll tell her. It's been hard on her. She's so angry."

"Is that why you're leaving?"

"Yes, mainly, but Philippa won't admit she needs to get away from here," the man sighed.

"Philippa mentioned a look on your wife's face?"

The man looked up at me slowly. "You're nosy, aren't you? Yes, a look of surprise, clear, obvious surprise." His eyes focused past me, out of the room as he continued in a barely audible voice. "Thankfully, there was no terror, only surprise. They never found a real physical reason why she died. Her body was stiff. White and stiff and surprised. All they could think to put on the form was she died from shock. She was a wonderful, gentle woman. Wouldn't have hurt a fly. Philippa is just like her."

"Philippa?" slipped out of my mouth in dismay.

"I guess I should say, used to be just like her," her father said sadly, his eyes still elsewhere.

"Did anyone ask Mr. Chalder about your wife's death?"

"Tomas Chalder, that idiot?" he yelped, popping back to the moment, to the present and the room we were in. "No one ever gets anything rational from him. He's as hard to mine as a Native." He brushed past me out of the room, anger now clearly driving him.

I turned to leave, and slipped through a door into the next room, but it wasn't the way out. Musty age filled this room. It was dark, its walls riddled with doorways and cubbies between which foot-wide burls and cankers grew. A thick box rose like a floor to ceiling column. Its sides had been polished to a luster marred only where something had gouged scratches and pry marks along the edges of twelve-centimeter-long bronze hinges. No two sides of the column fit quite properly so that the corners were lined by cracks. I was drawn to the object, standing in its shiny glory amidst the brittle texture of the walls. I circled it, pushed on its sides, tried different patterns of knocks, to see what would happen. I ran my fingers down its edges and around the hinges. It looked like it should open, but I couldn't figure out how to do it.

I gave up and looked for the doorway that would take me back to Mom and the girls, but there were too many choices and I had no idea which was the right one. I played with choosing eeney-meeney-miney-mo-style, and decided it was too risky. Hopefully, Cindra would point out I was missing when I didn't return soon, and someone would come for me. I sat down to wait, sliding to the floor. For just a second, I thought I felt a soft pulse beat beneath my hands, as if I was in the very heart of a living beast.

"Lost are you, Andrew?" the Beetle asked scuttling through one of the narrow entrances. "Rebecca sent me."

"Boy, am I glad to see you! This place is freaky!"

"Smart to wait," he said.

"Yeah? What is this place and what is this thing, anyway?" I asked, tapping the box.

"The place is the center. This, just left there," he answered, tapping the box exactly as I had.

"Why, what's it for and why is it all scratched like that?"

"Miners tried to open it. They couldn't."

"Can you? Open it, I mean?"

"If I can, should not I," he said unhelpfully. "Left for needs of theirs."

"Whose needs?"

He said nothing.

"Oh, come on! For once, couldn't you just tell me. You know more than anyone else about stuff that goes on around here."

"Me? No one agrees, Andrew."

"Yeah, I know, but I still think it. So, can you open it?"

The Beetle smiled. "Andrew, now come with me."

"Mr. Chalder, what killed Philippa's mother?" I asked, not budging.

"A mystery it is. Come now."

"No, I won't come. Answer or I stay here."

He turned back, head cocked, eyes sparkling. "Hungry, not you?"

My stomach grumbled at the reminder, but I said, "Nope, I can wait to eat. Talk or I stay right here."

"Rebecca wants you."

"Nope, that won't work either. Talk, or move I don't."

"Sounds you like me," he smiled, his voice just resisting a laugh.

"Did you always talk this way?"

"No. You come now. You wish to see me when I arrived here? You will see me. Come for you one morning will I. Promise."

I wasn't sure what he meant, but it was the best I was likely to get, and I didn't want to stay there alone, so I followed Chalder.

"Andrew," Mom said. "Where'd you go? Will you please stop disappearing on me."

"I got lost in the inner rooms of the Club. Did you find out how to get a message to Dad?"

"Mr. Chalder is going to deliver it. Mrs. Pattison still insists we aren't allowed into the caverns, but I don't trust her to take him the message without reading it."

"So we can go home?" I asked.

"Yes. Now."

"Mom, what did you put in the message?"

"I told him to go with your newest suggestion, about plants," she said quite clearly.

"Really?" I smiled. I noticed Mrs. Pattison straining to hear what Mom was saying. "Good job, Mom."

XV

Dad came home really happy, a smile spread across his face.

"I have the smartest son in the world!" he exclaimed.

"You do?" I asked.

"Okay, okay, Stephen, what did you learn?" Mom demanded.

"Well now, you guys understand, you can't discuss this with anyone?"

We promised, nodded, promised and prodded, while he paced, scratched his head, shook his head, and paced. Finally he said, "Remember, not a word. Here it is. I asked about the garden you found and they admitted that is where the fruits come from."

"All those fruits from our one garden?" I asked, dismayed.

"No, no, I gather there are lots of them," he said.

"Who harvests them?" I asked. "The Natives or the Water People?"

"I don't know."

"That's the big news, Stephen?" Mom asked, obviously disappointed.

"Rebecca, that is the only thing I have learned in all this time. And, it is apparently not a commonly held piece of knowledge."

"The Miners think Tomas harvests the fruits," she pointed out.

"Maybe he does, Rebecca, but I doubt he could have harvested all those fruits we saw at the market by himself, don't you?"

"I suppose not," she agreed, "but then who does do it?"

"Dad, did Mom mention to you my other speculations about the gardens?"

"No, she didn't."

"That's because they were so wild they were ridiculous!"

"They are not ridiculous. They make a lot of sense."

"To whom, Andrew?" she asked.

"Okay, okay, stop, you two. Andrew, why don't you tell me and I'll see what I think," Dad said, acting as peacemaker.

I counted to five, and tried to calm down before I began. "Here goes. I've been speculating that the houses are organic, living structures," I ventured. "Farms maybe!"

Dad thought it over for a very few seconds before he said, "I'm afraid I have to agree with your mom, Andrew."

"Why couldn't it be, Dad? And think what a real discovery that would be for your company!"

He just shook his head, and made a grouchy noise in his throat.

"Well, I'm going to ask Mr. Chalder."

"You can ask, Andrew, but don't set your heart on being right. It's pretty far fetched," Dad said.

"You'll see, I'm right!" There was an awkward pause.

"I'm sorry if I hurt your feelings, Andrew," Dad said as soothingly as he could.

"Yeah, it's okay." I had to pause again before I was calm enough to broach a different topic while I still had my father's attention. "Dad, Mr. Chalder said he's thirty-seven years old. How long has he been here?"

"Someone said twenty years."

"You mean he came here all by himself when he was only seventeen?"

"It seems unlikely, Andrew, but the man should know his own age."

"Mrs. Pattison doubts he even knows that," Mom said.

"Aw, Mrs. Pattison is just a sour, old, crinkled up grape," Dad laughed. "She hasn't made a discovery in the last two years, but she manages to hang on by stealing tidbits of information from other, careless Miners."

"You seem to have done some spying of your own," Mom noted while I thought of Philippa and her claims.

"Not spying, information gathering. Actually, 'claims', as the Miners call them, are public knowledge," Dad said as if he had heard my thought. "Did you know that Petersenes holds claim on reformable cloth? Caroline found a biodegradable replacement for plastics that can also be used as a fertilizer. But, the best claim ever filed was a very old one made by Tomas Chalder. He can claim the missing piece to a stable, irreversible Augmentation process."

"Wait! Augmentation used to be reversible?" I asked. "When?"

"Well, it wasn't exactly reversible. It just sort of wore off, in some cases, and left the Augment less than whole," Mom explained.

"Who would have chanced that?" I asked, utterly taken aback.

"Lots of people did, most people, in fact. We did. After all, the benefits out weighed the risks. Success! Money! Respect! All assured," Dad pointed out.

"You're kidding! You and Mom could lose your focus?"

"Unlikely, very, very unlikely, especially after all this time. It almost never happened. And, thanks to Tomas Chalder, if you should still decide to be Augmented, it would be permanent and completely safe, Andrew" Dad said.

"I can't believe you took such a chance," I muttered.

"Come on, girls," Dad bellowed and laughed. "Enough grown-up talk. Rough house time." He was quickly barreled over by a tangle of arms and legs, giggles and squeals of delight encircling him.

Mom shooed them outside. Fifteen minutes later he came in breathless and happy. "They're calling for you, Andrew. Something about a Gloriosa G. Mother."

"Oh," I groaned. "I guess I promised, didn't I?" I picked up my little notebook and went outside.

"Andrew, Andrew, another Gloriosa story, okay?" they chimed.

"No, because I haven't written one yet."

"Don't you have some story you could read us?"

"Yes."

"What's it called?" Louisa said.

"*Origins.*"

"Okay, read us that one."

"Wait, I wanna ask something before we begin!" Cindra interjected. "Andy, do you think we could find a way to break the spell on Mr. Chalder, like the prince did when he kissed Snow White?"

"Oh, come on, Cindra. Andrew doesn't know how to break spells. Just let him read."

"Can you break spells, Andy?" Cindra asked.

"I wish I could. Is it okay to read now, Cindra?"

"I guess so."

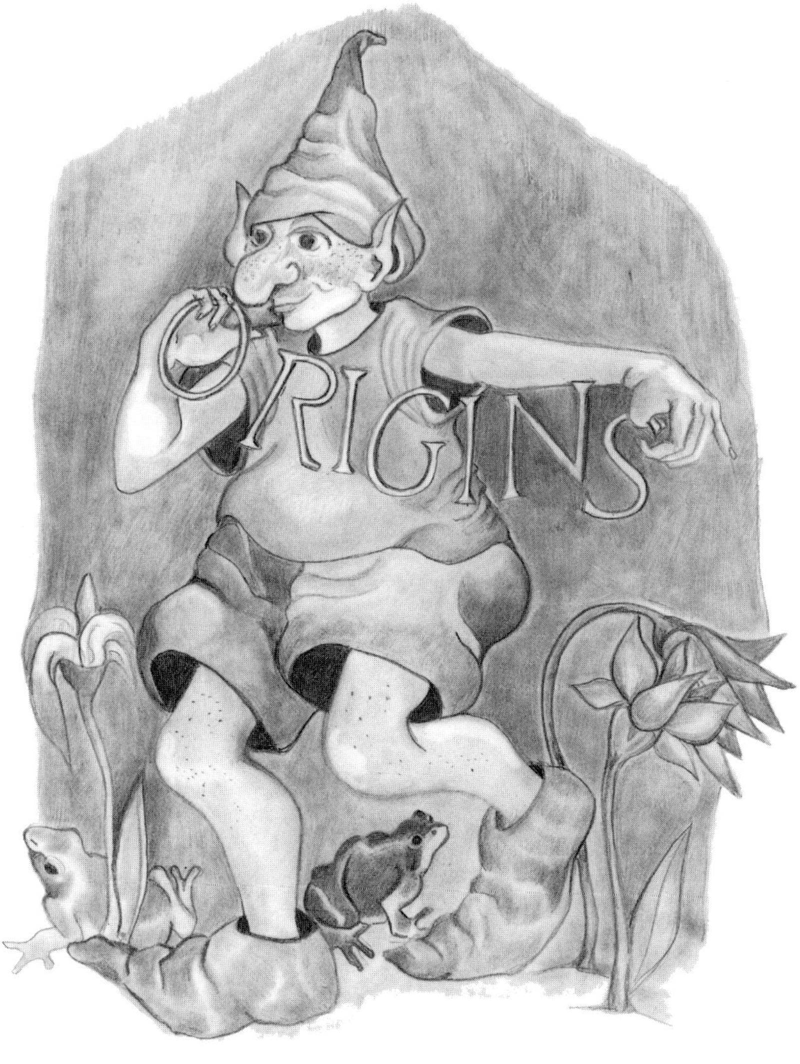
ORIGINS

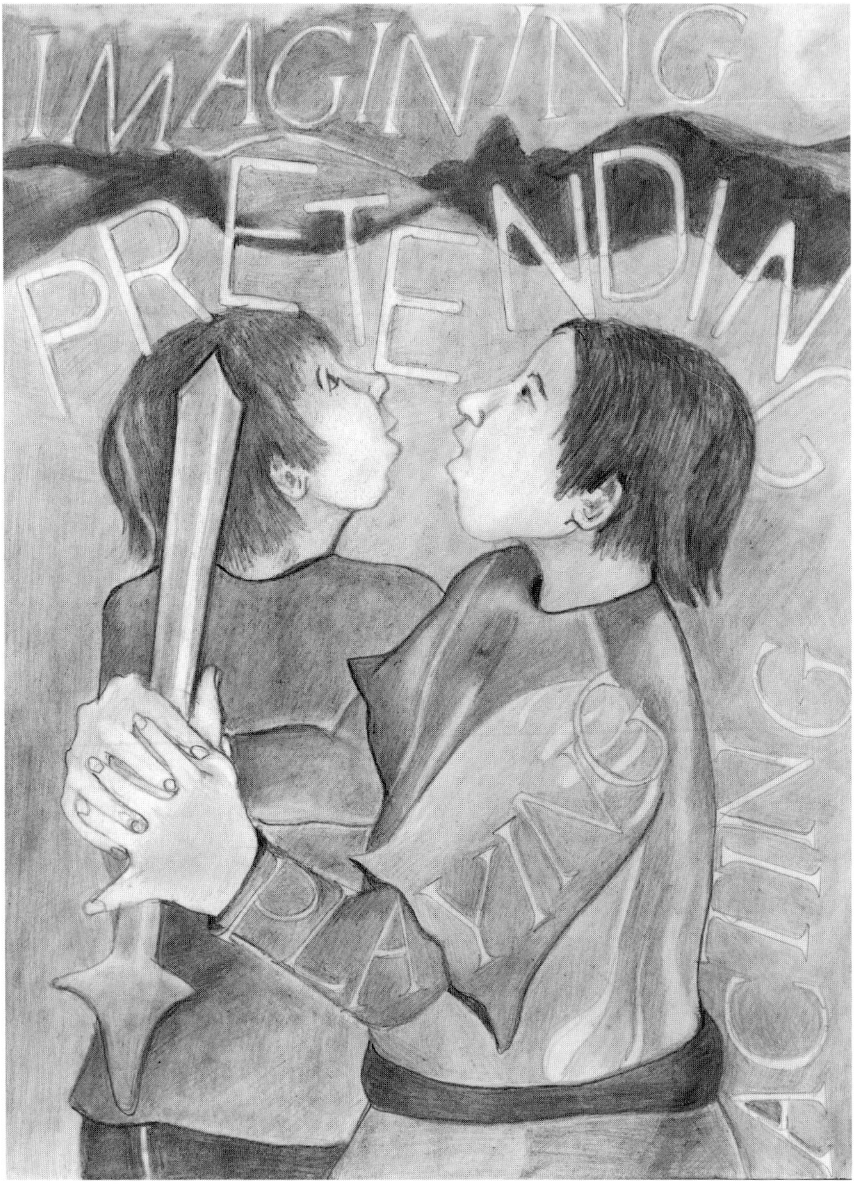
IMAGINING
PRETENDING
PLAYING
ACTING

Sometimes it seemed to the changeling that no matter what he became, it turned out wrong. He had spent an hour perched in the feathery branches of the tree watching the two boys. They called back and forth to each other, pretending to be great warriors.

The one named Prince Timothy drew his wooden sword, which was almost as long as he was tall, and cried, "We shall guard the realm from the dragon, Sir Edmund."

"Yes, Sire, as you wish," young Sir Edmund pledged.

"It has had its wicked way with the kingdom for long enough," Prince Timothy announced. "Its scaly head will grace my father's castle wall by nightfall, and the people shall never fear its fiery breath again."

"To be sure, Sire."

The changeling had never seen a dragon upon the earth, but he waited eagerly for this one to appear. He watched where the boys had pointed, waiting for the beast to tramp over the hump of the hill on the horizon. The boys held themselves at the ready for several moments before they sighed and sat down.

"Ah well, perhaps it isn't coming today, Sire," Sir Edmund said meekly.

"I suppose not. Ah well, we are ready if it does come."

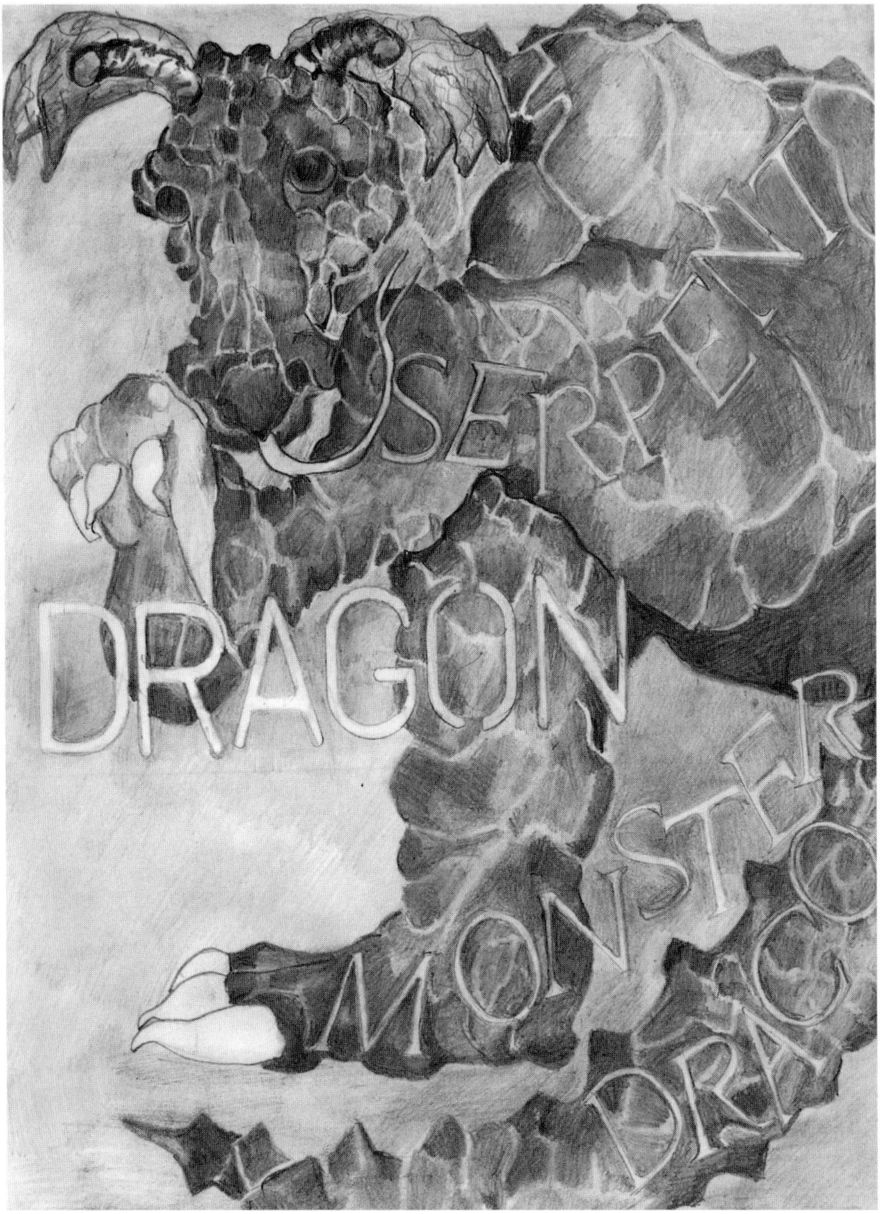
DRAGON
MONSTER

The changeling peered from the tree top towards the hill, but even from his high vantage he could see no dragon approaching. The boys seemed so disappointed. He slid down the tree and slinked off behind the bushes, closed his round red eyes tightly and imagined what he thought a dragon would look like if one existed. Then he stamped, and it was a big dragon foot that came down heavily and made the ground tremble. He stuck out his forked tongue and roared, "I am here to play!" But he was a dragon now and so his words issued forth as a fierce roar.

The boys' mouths fell open and they dropped their swords and ran, pumping their little legs, flapping their short arms and disappeared into the castle huffing and puffing, too out of breath to tell the guards what was chasing them.

The changeling sighed and slid back into himself. He was small, with huge, flat feet, wiry hair and purple, hooked fingernails. His nose was flat and he had an extra eye hidden in the back of his head where it would be least expected. He crawled into a hollow tree stump and pouted. Why couldn't he ever do anything right? He had only been trying to make the boys happy.

A dog padded up and barked. He ignored it. Once he had been a dog for a day, just so humans would pet him. The dogs hadn't minded when he had joined their pack, but it had been boring and he hadn't liked what they ate.

[Yuck!]

[Sorry.]

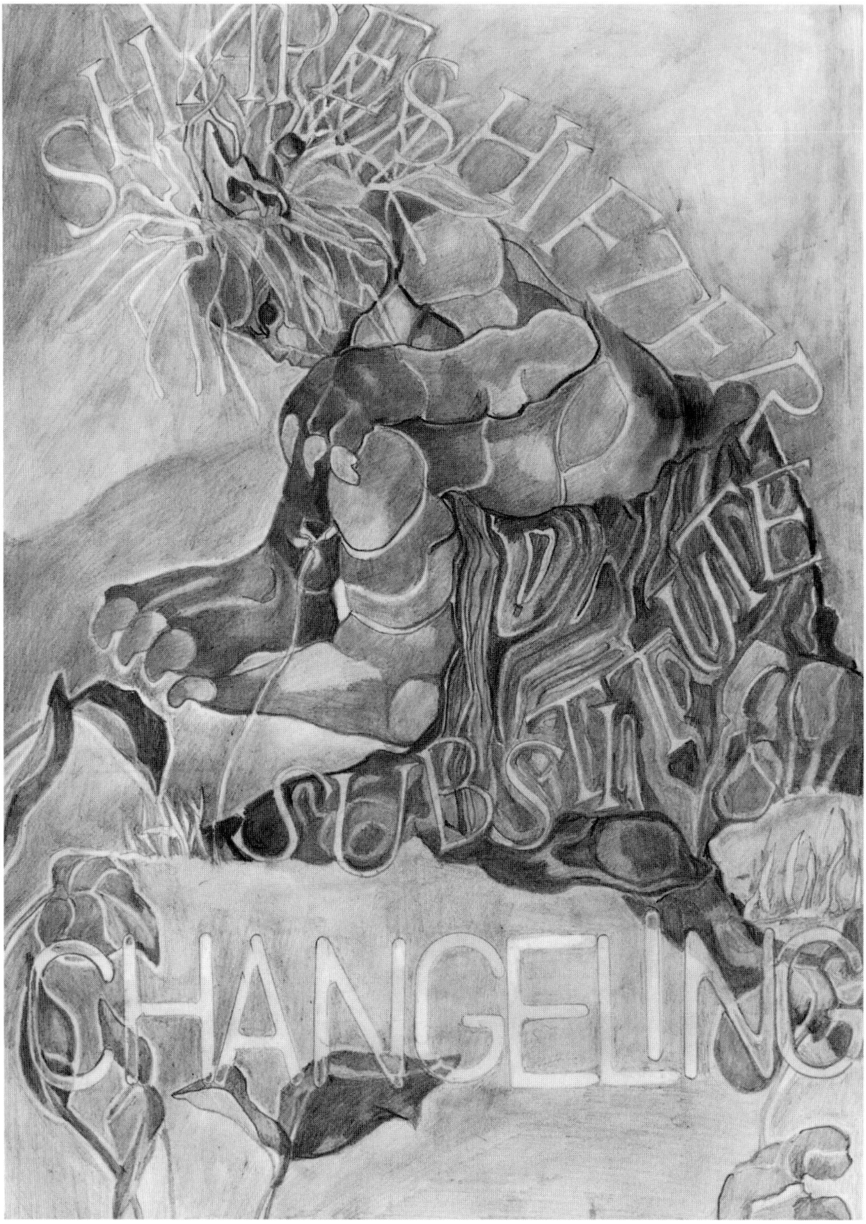
SHAPESHIFTER
SUBSTITUTE
CHANGELING

The changeling sat in the stump until carpenter ants started crawling between his toes. They pinched when they walked on his exoskeleton, so he got up and went home, hanging his head and kicking at little stones and pine cones along the way. He had dug himself a home in the side of a dry creek bed, hidden behind scrub trees. He liked his house. It was snug and comfy, but he was lonely, so lonely. Changelings were particularly in need of being touched and hugged and it had been a long time since anyone had even held this one's hand.

[Where are his mommy and daddy?]

[*Finger to lips.* Just wait.]

When it was dark and he knew all the humans were asleep in the great castle, he changed himself into a golden-winged horse. He had gotten the idea when he had heard someone say that a great stallion the king rode flew like the wind. Now he glided over the ramparts and perched on the roof of a castle tower.

The tower shook from his weight so he changed back into himself and listened. Something had caught his attention. He extended his ears until he could hear that it was crying. He became a raven because it was smaller than the horse and dark like the night. He flew from window to window, searching until the sound got louder. A girl was sitting cross-legged on a fluffy feather mattress, sobbing into a coverlet. Her eyes were as red as his and her hair was as black as his feathers. He wasn't really sure if she was pretty because she was human, and so to the changeling, she mainly looked strange.

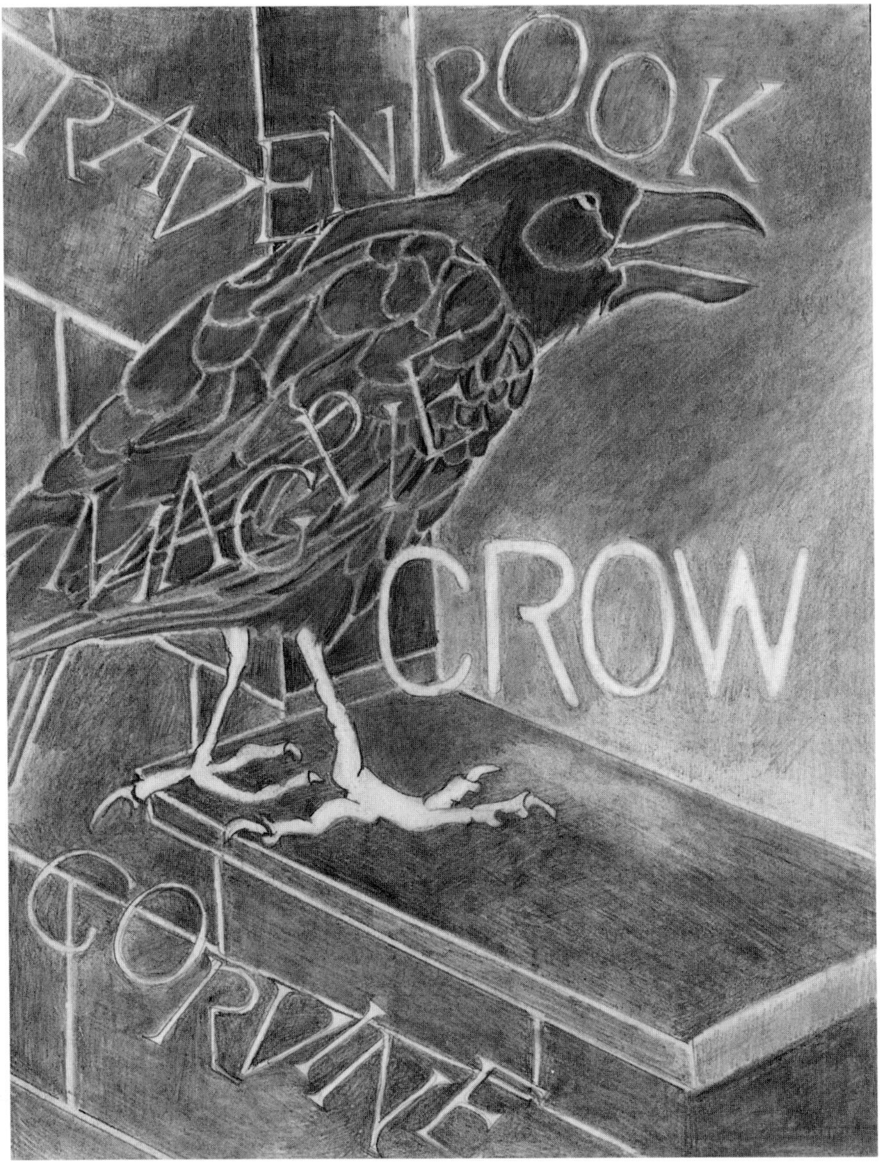
RAVEN
ROOK
MAGPIE
CROW
CORVINE

[Do you think the Water People could look pretty to each other?]

[Could be, Louisa.]

The changeling landed in a window which had no glass in it. Mosquitoes and flies buzzed about him and little moths flew by, drawn to the light of the candle in the room. He flapped his wings and tried to speak, but his voice was the harsh voice of a crow.

"Shoo, go away." The girl flapped her hands at him and cried, "Isn't it enough that I am betrothed to an old man? Surely the fates would not let me be plagued by an ugly bird."

"I only want to be friends," he tried to say, but she threw a pillow at him and knocked him backwards out the window.

The poor changeling flapped back into the night as lonely as ever. When he got home, a tear dripped from his third eye. He wished he could leave earth and go home to Cigam, but his ship had been wrecked, his friends had all died in the crash and he had been stranded on this planet for five of its years.

[You mean he's an alien?]

[I thought this was another story about magic, Andrew.]

[You thought wrong, I guess. Whoops, Dad is calling us. Gotta stop, guys.]

XVI

"Hey, kids, come on in. I have some questions for Andrew."

"No, Daddy, please, Andrew isn't finished yet."

"We'll be in, Dad. Come on, girls, it just makes it more tantalizing when you have to wait to hear the end."

We went inside.

"What is it, Dad?" I asked.

"Okay, Andrew. What should I ask the Natives next?"

"You want my opinion?"

"Absolutely."

"Ask if the houses are alive."

"Not that again, Andrew! What else?"

"Come on, Dad, please."

"No! Something else."

"Then ask them where their children are."

"Yeah, Daddy, we need some friends," Louisa chimed in.

"Okay, I'll ask that when I get a chance, but it isn't high on my list."

"Maybe it should be, Stephen. If they hide their children, maybe they're hiding other things, too," Mom said, unexpectedly supporting me.

"Okay, Rebecca. If you both think it's important, I'll do it."

As I went to sleep that night, I could hear Mom and Dad murmuring to each other. Once in a while I'd catch a word.

"Chalder . . . crazy . . . facts . . . secrets. . ."

I wished I could have heard better, but instead I fell asleep. The sun was barely up when I groggily opened my eyes. Dad was whispering to me, beckoning me quietly into the outer room.

"Andrew," he said softly, "Mr. Chalder is outside asking for you."

"Huh? What time is it?" I asked blearily.

"Early. About five in the morning. He insists on talking to you. He said he is here to keep some promise to you about when he was young. It's awfully hard to make sense out of what he says."

"A promise?" I rubbed my eyes. "Oh yeah, he did promise to

show me something, but I didn't expect him to do it at this hour of the morning. I'll throw on some clothes and go see him. Maybe I can get him to come back later."

Chalder was sitting in the rising sun in a shiny tunic that glistened black and green like a beetle carapace, but he held his head straight and when he looked at me, his eyes were clear and focused.

"Hey, Mr. Chalder, what are you doing here so early?" I asked sleepily.

"Early time is my clear time. Come with me for the promise."

"Could we do it a little later?"

"My only clear time," he said firmly.

I looked up to Dad at the door and he nodded at me and went back inside. I followed Chalder. This was the first time I had seen him when he looked totally human.

"Were you only seventeen when you came here?" I asked, hurrying to walk beside him. His stride was long and rapid and held no resemblance to a beetle.

"Yes, seventeen. Young, full of excitement."

"What happened?"

"That is never clear. Here, come," he said as we trudged up a steep, rocky grade and stepped into a small cave. Except for a series of hooks driven into the walls and a pile of neatly folded tunics, the cave was starkly unadorned. A single garment was spread out side by side with brushes and shallow pots of dyes. Even in the dim cave light, its lushly burnished colors shimmered.

"This is where you live, Mr. Chalder?"

He nodded.

"And you painted all those tunics?" I asked, pointing to the stack of garments.

Again a nod.

He went to an old space-chest and pulled out a scrapbook. "Here," he said, almost shoving it into my face. "Look." He flipped to a page where a young man with a gleaming smile stared at me from a still hologram.

"Me," he said. "Twenty years ago."

Even though I could see the resemblance through the elapsed

years, something basic had changed in Tomas Chalder from the young hologram.

Tomas looked at the picture a moment himself and said, "Quite a bit changed."

"Some," I agreed gently.

"A lot," he insisted to me.

I turned the page. It was a clipping, hand typed and labeled *Miners' Notes*. It read:

"Tomas Chalder was found wandering vacantly on the old mud road. There was no apparent physical damage, yet he was disoriented and his speech was almost incoherent. Dr. Pease says he has perhaps suffered a small stroke."

"Was it a stroke?" I asked.

"Dr. Pease said yes. I was twenty-five. What do you think, Andrew?"

"I don't know. That seems awfully young. What do strokes do to a person?"

"Left me what I am. Maria left me. Dr. Pease went home."

"Who's Maria?"

"My wife. She was."

"I didn't know you were married. Why'd she leave?" I asked.

"She said I wasn't me anymore. She said I was more like a . . . I cannot remember. She said at night I went away. Trances. She took the baby and left."

"Baby?" I said.

Tomas ignored me. "She begged me to come home. Get help."

"Why didn't you?"

"I don't know. No one could help?"

"But . . ."

"And," he added without hesitating, "need to be here do I."

He stopped and took the book and closed it.

"Mr. Chalder, what happened to Philippa's mother?" I asked, pushing for more information.

"I was not there. Home you go now."

While we walked home his feet began to scuttle and he slid his head down into his shoulders. Tomas Chalder had vanished. The Beetle had returned.

XVII

"Mom, do we have any medical books?"

"I have a general reference. What do you want to look up, Andrew?"

"The effects of strokes on people."

"Really? What's it for this time? I know you aren't considering becoming a doctor."

"Naw, I'm not, Mom. It's just they thought Tomas had a stroke when he was twenty-five."

"A stroke? That young?"

"Yeah. They found him all confused, wandering on a road. It wasn't long until his wife took their baby and left, but he chose to stay."

"He should have gone home for treatment."

"Well, that's why I want to look up strokes. He claims it wouldn't have helped."

"Of course they could have helped him. He would have known that."

"He seems absolutely sure it wouldn't have helped."

"Okay, I'll get the book, but it's very general."

She gave me a thick, blue volume she always carried around, post to post. About fifty years ago, a way to affect cures for strokes had been found. Aftereffects, such as aphasia, paralysis and others were wiped out. People could even have parts of their brains re-tooled, sort of jump-started by medication. So, if Tomas had gone home, he could have been cured. If he had had a stroke.

"Mom," I called. "Do you think there are any official records of individual Miners anywhere?"

"When we go to the Club today, I'll ask for you. How's your research going?"

"It's weird. Do you think, Tomas, goes in and out of phase?"

"What do you mean exactly, Andrew?"

"It's as if he changes, as if he has different phases during the day."

"I have noticed that a little bit, but he may just tire easily."

"I'm glad it wasn't my imagination. Mom, you should have

seen his picture at seventeen. I mean, he was like a holovision star. Really handsome. Blonde, sturdy jaw, shoulders like a bull. Girls must have swamped him."

"Mr. Chalder? Is that who you're talking about, Andrew?"

"Yeah. Unbelievable, huh? And this morning, he was straighter, more, I guess, human."

Mom frowned. "Andrew, just because someone suffers a deformity, it doesn't take away their humanity."

"I didn't mean he's a monster or anything. I like him, Mom, but you have to admit there is something awfully strange about Mr. Chalder."

"Okay, when we go to the Club later, we'll ask for the records, but until then there isn't much we can do. Go clean up your area of the bedroom."

When we got to the Club it proved to be in an uproar. Philippa was missing and her father was towering over Tomas Chalder, who squatted in a corner with his arms over his head as Mr. Brandt screamed at him.

"You filthy misfit, where's my daughter? Get up, you gruesome excuse for a human, and tell me," he yelled as he jerked Tomas up by his shiny tunic front.

Brandt pulled his fist back. Wrapped in his fingers was a roll of coins which he held just above Tomas' head. Mrs. Pattison screeched for him to stop, while Hal Andrews egged him on. Cindra and Louisa whimpered. Just as he prepared to strike, he found his wrist trapped in my mother's iron grip.

"Stop it, Mr. Brandt, or I'll break your arm," Mom ordered. "Just put it down, now."

It took a moment of testing, but Philippa's father let the coins drop and rubbed at his hand.

"Now," Mom took over. "What makes you think Philippa's disappearance is related to Mr. Chalder?"

"He knows everything. He just pretends he's crazy so he doesn't have to share his secrets, but he knows."

"No, he doesn't! Leave him be!" I said, helping Tomas up.

He was shaking and retracted into a ball, with no resemblance to the tall, straight man of the morning.

Caroline rose from a chair shoved into a corner and walked slowly over to us. She bent down to Tomas, gingerly patting his back, but he only cringed at the contact. Avoiding the light, she turned with a jerk to Mr. Brandt. In a voice that was barely audible, she uttered, "Bully," and scooted back to the dark corner where no one could see her clearly.

"You'd be better off looking for Philippa, Mr. Brandt," Mom said calmly, "than terrorizing Tomas. We'll split up and search the Club. Andrew, you come with Tomas and me. Mrs. Pattison, brew some blue tea for everyone and watch my girls. The rest of you look around outside."

"Nobody is going to find her," Hal Andrews said. "Chalder has made sure of that."

Mom stuck her face right up to his face and hissed, "Well, you surely won't if you don't try."

She set Tomas on his feet and he slowly, unsteadily started off, stabilized by her hand on his back. He wasn't scuttling and he gradually straightened out some, but he kept his head lowered. He led us straight to the room with the column. He began to pace around it, shaking off Mom's support.

"What is that?" Mom asked, as she followed in Tomas' trail.

"She found the way into it," Tomas said, speaking hoarsely for the first time.

"What makes you think that?" Mom asked.

"There is nowhere else to look."

"Come on, Tomas, the Club is full of hiding places!" Mom exclaimed.

He shook his head. "Looked have they. Looked I, too. Here she went." He ran his hand down the edges of the column. "The scratches match not anymore. See?" he pointed.

"If Philippa found a way in, we can get in, too. She's not that smart," I said.

"Doubt I, she will come out as she went in," Tomas said.

"There's another way out?" Mom asked.

"Always in alien things, not as she went in," Tomas repeated.

"Does he mean something may happen to Philippa and she might come out changed, or does he mean she's coming out a different entrance?" Mom asked me.

"Got me."

"What might have happened to her?" Mom asked Tomas.

He ignored her altogether and just paced around and around the column.

"I can't believe Philippa found a way in and you can't, Tomas," Mom said.

"Mom," I whispered into her ear, "Tomas may be able to open it, but I don't think he will."

"You're surprised that Philippa is smarter than the moron there?" Mr. Brandt growled from the doorway, startling us. Obviously, he hadn't heard my comments.

Mom whirled around and said acridly, "If you and your daughter are so smart, then you clearly don't need a moron's help. Mr. Chalder, my family, and I are going to have tea. Figure out your daughter's whereabouts by yourself."

"Tea?" Mr. Chalder said and scuttled off.

Mrs. Pattison's blue tea was a deeper color than ours and Mr. Chalder wouldn't let us drink it until he had watered it down. "Too strong, too much calming." We relaxed and sat sipping our diluted tea, until Tomas looked up and announced, "I'll look on the road."

Before we could stop him, he was up in an amazingly graceful movement, and had scuttled out the door.

"Oh my, he's off again," Mrs. Pattison said, tssking between her teeth. I wondered how anyone could be such a perfect stereotype of a little old lady. Did she practice?

"Mrs. Pattison, did a Dr. Pease leave any papers?" I asked her.

"Medical records? Why I suppose. As I recall, Dr. Pease recorded everything, all very neatly. Whose did you have in mind?"

"Anyone who was here at the beginning," I said as obtusely as I could.

"Oh my, Andrew, you do need a bit of training in subtlety, but yes, Mr. Chalder's records are here. I'll get them for you. In fact, I'm interested as well. I don't know why I never thought to examine them before. Good thinking, Andrew."

"If you weren't interested before, why are you now?" Mom asked the old lady as she led us to a small, file-filled room.

"Why, because you are, dear. It's I who should ask why Andrew is interested?"

"I'm taking a correspondence course and I'm doing an essay on interesting people."

"Oh," Mrs. Pattison said, winking at me. "Well, here you are. His file is quite thick, don't you think? Tomas Chalder should make an interesting paper."

"Yes," Mom said. "Mind if we borrow that for a few days. We'll return it so you can read it as well."

"I suppose, though truly, I doubt there's anything of value in it," she said, returning to her previous disinterest. Still, she peevishly held the file just out of reach for a few seconds before she finally handed it to me. "Why don't you just let me know if it would be worth my time to read this?" she added.

Mrs. Pattison vanished and I hefted the file happily.

"That lady is lazy to the end," Mom noted.

"You said it! Will you help me?" I asked.

"Sure thing, Andrew. It'll give me something to do, and who knows, maybe you're onto something."

XVIII

Tomas Alexander Chalder had had an Intelligence Quotient well above the genius range when he had arrived to be a Miner, fresh from Augmentation and apparently eager to succeed. He had stood 6'4" in stocking feet, had been brown eyed, blonde and competitively athletic. There was a pre-arrival medical form that had all that information and all his vaccinations listed.

"Look here," Mom said. "His medical record indicates only a .005% diagnostic probability of stroke by age seventy-six. That's about as little chance as possible at age twenty-five."

"Mom, it says he was single when he came. He married Anna Maria Valta about seven years later. She was a twenty-five year old Miner who worked for a robotics firm and had been on Miners World eighteen months at the time they married. He was twenty-four and was working for a bio-tech firm. Here's a photo of her."

The snapshot was an old fashion still, not even a hologram. Her hair was jet black, her eyes cold blue, her mouth a soft line. She was attractive, but not a knock out.

"Let's keep going," Mom said. "Apparently Dr. Pease combined their files when they married."

I skipped forward to the time of Chalder's apparent stroke. He had been a day or two under twenty-five. He had vanished from his home one night and not been found for three days. When he was found, Dr. Pease described him as vacant, his eyes unfocused, his body retracted and stiff. His speech had been garbled, his reflexes slow or delayed. The doctor had run blood work, but not found any chemistry out of the ordinary.

"Wait," Mom said, skipping to her medical reference. "It says here stroke victims almost always have elevated levels of certain hormones in their blood chemistry for a number of days after."

"So he didn't have a stroke?" I asked excitedly.

"Slow down, Andrew. That's a big jump. Maybe Dr. Pease didn't have the equipment to run the tests."

The girls' chatter filtered to us. We raised our heads and listened. They were having a wonderful time playing one of the many old fashioned board games we had collected at each of our postings.

Mom usually collected one from every culture we visited, but I thought she was unlikely to find an addition to our collection on Miners World. So far, except for the houses, we had seen no artifacts, art, or crafts at all. The culture was surprisingly sterile.

We resumed our search. Tomas had never really recovered, although shortly after he was found he kept mumbling about "the mistake," how they had made a "mistake." Apparently Maria was frantic. She kept coming to Dr. Pease about Tomas. They finally tried retro-drugs. The result of the hypnosis they induced was transcribed:

They're moving this way! I've never seen them up close before. What are they doing?

Thank goodness. There's a Native from the caves coming towards me. Wait!

Please! No . . . no . . . you don't . . . no (screaming)

They had ended the session.

The next time Maria came it was about herself. She had gotten pregnant. Dr. Pease wrote that she was hysterical. Something about Tomas not being himself since he had been found, and how she couldn't be pregnant now, not with him like this. Dr. Pease had told her she was just stressed from all the shocks and anxiety, and that everything would work out.

She had tried to hit him and he had given her a mild sedative. Finally she had told Dr. Pease that at unpredictable moments, Tomas would press up against her as close as he could, until she felt as if something was seeping its way through her skin. She said it burned, but there was no sign of any irritation or any substance on her skin. Dr. Pease had said that she was understandably distraught, and he was sure Tomas was just seeking comfort, a hug and closeness. Maria shook her head emphatically, but either couldn't or wouldn't explain further. She said Dr. Pease would think her crazy. He hadn't, but he had noted she was on the verge of a nervous breakdown.

"Mommy," Louisa said, crawling into her lap. "What are you guys doing?"

"Trying to solve a mystery," I said.

"Really? What mystery?"

"One about Mr. Chalder, Louisa," Mom said.

"Oh, him. He's nice," Louisa said.

"Is he?" Mom asked.

Louisa nodded and jumped down. "Cindra thinks he's under a spell because of Andrew's story."

"Andrew!" Mom said to me warningly.

"It's not my fault. Cindra's only six. She still believes in stuff like that, and Mr. Chalder is mysterious."

"Well, I like him," Louisa said. "He likes to do kid-stuff, like jump rope."

"Yes," Mom acknowledged, giving Louisa a hug.

"Can we have lunch?" Cindra asked.

"Sure," Mom said. "Keep reading, Andrew."

"Listen to this, Mom," I called to her as she began chopping vegetables. "When the baby was born it wasn't normal. Dr. Pease claimed the prenatal gene screening didn't match with the outcome. What's that mean?"

"They screen to make sure a couple won't produce children who are genetically abnormal. If they might, they can prevent it by neonatal gene manipulation. Pease must have missed it. Not surprising on this post."

"Well maybe, but he writes here he did a comparison of the parents' recorded gene scans and that neither parent carried a genetic makeup that could have accounted for the baby's. He wondered if the baby had suffered from a late stage, gene mutation?"

"I have never heard of such a thing," Mom said, coming to the table to peer over my shoulder. She skimmed the report. "Hey, look at this. Dr. Pease rechecked Maria's and Tomas' gene scans, and Tomas' didn't precisely match his previous scan."

"Greek to me," I said.

"That's because you haven't gone through pre-pregnancy counseling. It finally came in good for something. Dr. Pease wonders here if it was a result of the stroke. That's really reaching. He must have been desperate for an explanation. Even I know that strokes don't cause genetic scan changes."

"Mom, Tomas told me his focus had changed. I suppose that's possible because he was an early Augment, but do you think it could have been because of whatever happened to him?"

"Who knows," she said. "They say Augmentation loss has only happened in about 2% of the early Augments. That means there's a 98% possibility that it was something else. Then again, if his Augmentation faded, maybe that changed his scan."

"Okay, that's a no win train of thought," I noted. "Do you get the impression, Mom, that Dr. Pease had no idea what happened to Mr. Chalder?"

"I do get that impression, Andrew, but you can't discard his assumptions yet because we don't have anything with which to replace them."

The baby was normal looking, but its reproductive genetic scan was messed up. Dr. Pease had never seen anything quite like it. When he told Maria, she had sobbed something about Tomas being responsible. Dr. Pease had assured her that wasn't possible. She stayed eight months, during which time the baby grew normally, except for an overly transparent skin. At the end of eight months, she left with the baby.

After that Dr. Pease had noted that Tomas had seemed depressed, then moved out of his home. He wasn't seen for several months except in passing. He stopped mining, even though he had been the most successful of anyone at gathering information. When he began to come into the Club again, his appearance had changed greatly. His hair had gone from blonde to completely silver, his eyes were constantly dilated and his posture had deteriorated into a hunched state. He allowed Dr. Pease to examine him, but the doctor found no further physical anomalies to account for the change and chalked it up to depression.

The only further note was that Maria sent Dr. Pease the death notice of the child. He had lived three-and-a-half years and died of unidentifiable causes. The notice was in the file along with a picture of the baby. Something about him looked familiar to Mom and me, but neither of us thought he looked like Tomas. He had his mother's eyes and hair, but his skin was so pale, the veins beneath were distinctly delineated shadows.

"Yew," Louisa said, "that baby looks like a Water Person."

Mom and I looked at each other in surprise.

"He does, sort of, doesn't he?" Mom said.

"What does that mean?" I asked.

"Maybe coincidence. Maybe a native infection or parasite? This is turning into a real mystery. The question is, is any of it significant?"

"Let's talk to Dad tonight," I suggested.

"Absolutely, Andrew," Mom agreed.

Tomas came by before Dad got home. As usual he walked to the door and stopped, standing silently until one of us noticed him.

"Come in," Mom invited him.

"They found Philippa," he offered, as soon as he stepped over the threshold.

"Is she okay?" Mom asked.

"Quiet, very quiet, she is."

"Where was she?"

"She will tell not. She is very pale, very quiet. Calm she is, her anger gone? Or maybe only hidden."

"Did anyone find out if she actually opened the column?" I asked Tomas.

"She knows not, has only vague memory, she says."

"Is she faking it, Tomas?" I asked. "I don't think she tells the truth very often."

"Who is to know?" Tomas said, shrugging. "With Philippa, always careful be. Angry still? Maybe, maybe not."

"Let's hope not," Mom said. "Maybe she'll be able to tell us what happened later."

Even if Philippa remembered what had happened to her, I doubted she would tell anyone. She might caw and tease about it, but I didn't think she was likely to tell, unless her anger really was gone. But if so, how had she finally found peace? Where? What had happened to her?

"Would you like tea, Tomas?" Mom suggested.

He shook his head. "Freighter here, early schedule. Belongings yours at the landing mark."

"Great!" Mom exclaimed. "Will you help us? I'm afraid it's quite a bit of stuff."

"Take you now I will. A cart there will be. Best we go."

The cart proved to be motorized so once it was loaded, we just walked beside it, guiding it with gentle nudges. The day was nice with a breeze wafting about. Endless sky spread unmarked to the edge of Miners World. The air was clean and fuzzy animals cavorted playfully, jumping between the shade of rocks and feathery bushes. The girls chattered happily to Tomas, who smiled shyly back. I thought about the smiling hologram of the young Tomas. It was hard to imagine what could have changed him into this hunched, inarticulate creature that accompanied us.

"Tomas," Mom said. "Andrew told me about Maria and your child. I'm sorry."

"I tried for her. Could never be what had been." He always seemed to speak with grammar that provided more than one possible meaning.

"Life changes us," Mom agreed.

"The change was not complete," he said restlessly.

"Did you ever hear from Maria?" Mom asked, pushing her hair back from her face.

"No, no," he said. "She left absolutely. The change, it was an accident."

Mom spoke gently. "I'm sure you didn't do it on purpose."

"Not me, it was the accident."

Mom shook her head as if to clear it, and swiped at her hair once more.

"Dr. Pease said baby gone," he said very quietly, in hardly more than a whisper.

"Yes, Tomas, long ago."

"He was so small. Wrong, so wrong," he said shaking his head.

"It's never wrong to have a child," Mom said. He just lowered his eyes and quit speaking.

Cindra came up and walked beside him until I saw him take her hand squeeze it.

When we got home, Dad was there waiting for us. He greeted us with a grin. "I see the freighter came in. How about if you ladies fix a feast, while the three guys unload the cart."

"Okay, girls. Come on inside," Mom said.

"But, Mommy, you havn't ever made a feast!"

"Are you saying, I'm not a great cook?" she laughed.

"You always put weird stuff together when you cook," Louisa complained.

"Okay, I'll unload and Daddy can cook!" Mom offered happily.

"No, no, that's okay. Daddy always burns everything," Louisa said quickly.

"Get in there, you two, and quit insulting my cooking," Mom instructed, pushing them inside.

Dad and Tomas and I began unloading boxes and cases. The light was fading as we dumped the last case into the house and stretched. Even Tomas raised his arms and arched his back. For just a moment he held the posture and then sank again.

"Come on, guys. We deserve a good meal," Dad said. "Tomas sit there, near Cindra. Now, my fair wife, whatcha got for us?"

The girls must have picked the menu because it was a pretty traditional for one of Mom's meals. Freeze-dried fried chicken, native fruit salad, mash potato flakes and vanilla, freeze-dried ice cream.

"I miss chocolate," Cindra moped. "I like chocolate on my ice cream."

"I'm sorry I forgot to bring any, darling," Dad apologized for what seemed like the one-hundredth time since we had arrived.

Mr. Chalder munched quietly and sipped his tea. "You have the nicest family," he told Dad.

"Not bad, not bad. How about you, Tomas?"

"No," he said, his eyes sinking.

"Well, you're welcome here any time," Dad added.

Tomas nodded and surprised us by asking, "Did you learn much today?"

"No. Wish I was better at this," Dad sighed.

"I will help you," Tomas Chalder offered.

"Isn't that against the code? I mean, you being a Miner and all," Dad reminded Tomas.

Now it was Mr. Chalder's turn to laugh, a loud clear laugh. "Me, Miner? Me? Not for ever so long. Was I good."

"So I heard. Why did you quit?" Dad asked, apparently interpreting the Beetle correctly for once.

"I got lost," the Beetle said. "Early tomorrow, before anyone. Meet me. At the caves." He got up and left abruptly.

"Stephen," Mom said, immediately, "people have been attacked. You will not go alone to the caves. Either Andrew or I will go with you, but you won't go alone."

"Rebecca, don't be silly. I'm more than big enough to take care of myself."

"You're a puppy. No, that's official," she said.

Dad sighed. "All right. Andrew can accompany me. I suppose Chalder and I can drop him off at the Club before we go to the caves."

"Get some sleep, Andrew," Mom said. "You've got an early morning."

XIX

It was only dimly daylight as we left for the caves. Dad flashed a torch ahead of us that cut a narrow swatch out of the Cimmerian hour. Every once in a while an Earth-side imported cat would slink across the road, its eyes two glowing spots. Once something bigger skittered in front of us and we froze for a minute or two, watching and waiting, but never saw what it was.

It might have been smarter for Mom to have come. She was the quickest and the fiercest of us. Still, she had trained us well. I thought I wouldn't be too shabby in a fight, and Dad's size was bound to be a big advantage in a skirmish.

We were almost there when a figure emerged and blocked the road. I thought it was an alien until it moved slightly, and a straighter and thinner Tomas Chalder stepped forward to greet us.

"Sorry if I startled you," he said.

Dad glanced at me. "I almost didn't recognize you, Tomas."

"Yes, it is a different time for me. Quickly now," he said.

"What about Andrew? Don't we need to take him to the Club?"

"He comes," Tomas said.

"But the rules," Dad protested.

Chalder ignored him and started towards the caves.

"I've never been this way," Dad mused.

Tomas Chalder smiled and guided us to a cave entrance where the clay was blushed with a pink glow. We followed him down a short tunnel and emerged into a large cavern. Its ceilings supported an assortment of carved stalactites, and its walls were deeply etched with pictographs depicting a plethora of wild life and a sprinkling of humanoid life-forms tending them.

"Have you ever seen any of those animals?" I whispered to Dad.

"No, and I haven't seen any art work before either. This is breathtaking!"

"Look over there, Dad," I pointed

Near the edges of the cavern were five large Natives, sitting with their legs tucked under them. They were close to the rusty color of the cave itself, each with thin, shiny lines of paint wrapped around broad bellies and bald heads.

"Query now," Chalder whispered.

Dad hesitated, which gave me the chance to ask, "Where are your children?"

Dad bit his lip and glared at me, his face turning a bright shade of rosy anger.

"Come on, Dad, just let it answer this one question."

"I can't believe you wasted a question on that," he said from between clenched teeth.

The smallest of the five creatures raised its eyes, clear and golden, not so different from a cat's eyes except for the silver that encircled them like a mask.

"It is as it is," was the enigmatic answer.

"Do you have a question for us?" Tomas asked the Natives clearly.

I could see Dad's expression of surprise. Surprise that there was more than one Native, surprise that Tomas thought they might ask us something. He kept a straight eye on the Native, who finally said in a singsong clip, "Tomas Chalder is back."

"No," Tomas answered quickly. "The I is not here, has not returned."

I barely had time to think that his answer made no sense when Tomas said to Dad, "It is your turn, Stephen."

Dad surprised me with what he chose to ask. "What happened to this man, Tomas Chalder?"

"We regret the loss," a particularly wide-bellied Native spoke.

"Whose loss?" Dad asked, but now the Natives were immobile, frozen, the moment gone for some unknown reason.

"Sorry, Tomas," Dad said. "I guess I blew it."

Tomas shook his head and motioned for us to follow. He led us silently through a maze of tunnels into another cavern.

"Isn't this Lady Pattison's territory?" Dad whispered to Tomas.

"Who made such rules?" Tomas asked, leading us right through the good lady's territory and deeper into the caves. He stopped in an unlit space. Slowly glow-spots came up on the walls.

"It is I, Chalder, no longer am I Tomas," he said addressing a silent Native, sitting with rounded posture. "Remember you, me?" Tomas asked.

The Native's eyes flickered open into two, huge, yellow-green-fire-balls.

Tomas nudged me. "Ask."

"Me, not Dad?" I said, disbelievingly.

Tomas nodded. "You, Andrew."

I managed to stammer, "Uh, what happened to Tomas Chalder sixteen or seventeen years ago?"

"Ask him," came the reply.

"He doesn't know," I answered back.

The Native's eyes darted, narrowed and reopened. It stared right at me, but said nothing.

Out of the corner of my eye I saw Dad reach out to stop me and Tomas reach out to stop Dad.

"I don't care much about mining for a profit, but something happened to Tomas and I'd like to know what caused it. Tomas is our friend."

The Native still stared at me, its eyes beginning to close down when Tomas stepped in and said, "Attacks, why? What are they?"

Its eyes stopped, just at the slitted stage and it said like a warning, "Now, stay away." Its eyes closed.

"Quickly now, before I can no longer be here." Tomas gently pushed me and Dad off in another direction, without giving us a chance to ask what he meant.

"Whose chamber is this one?" Dad asked as we entered a small, smooth-walled room.

"No one owns a chamber," Chalder answered.

The Native here was shorter and slighter of build than any of the others we had seen. It had several striped, silver panels along its head as well as some broader ones down its arms and across its stomach. Even its fingers-tips were decorated.

"Chalder, Andrew, Stephen, who should speak?" Tomas asked it respectfully.

Its finger pointed straight at me.

"Uh, what are those stripes?" I asked impulsively.

"Signs of age," it replied.

"But if you're older, why are the others bigger?"

Its eyes opened a bit more. They were yellow-green, going towards crystalline.

"You wish an answer," it said, not asking a question not giving an answer, just making a statement.

The Native was still staring at me and I realized it was waiting for a response.

"Yeah, I want an answer. Maybe if we understand you guys better, we'll have a better chance to help Tomas Chalder."

"You cannot change him," it said, its eyes beginning to close.

"Perhaps not, but he could understand," Dad offered, following my lead.

The eyes reopened fully and stared at Dad, then closed in a single, final motion.

Tomas led us out quickly, collapsing as he did, his body posture compressing back to the Beetle.

"Did not help you, I?" he asked.

"I am amazed, Tomas. I had no idea! I had heard you had gotten more than anyone, but they actually know you, like you even, I believe," Dad reassured our friend.

"Like me? No way to know. Owe they me."

"They owe you or you owe them?" I asked.

He blinked, much like the Natives. "Must go now. See soon you," he said as if he, too, was closing down.

Dad and I watched him scuttle off.

"Do you think the Natives walk like that?" I asked Dad.

"Who knows. Maybe we'll find out someday, if we ever see them move."

"Was that helpful, Dad, or just confusing?"

"You know, Andrew," Dad said, putting his arm around me, "I think you're right. Understanding the Natives is very important. I'm going to ask something about it every time I mine. Thank you, Andrew."

"That's okay, Dad, but will your company approve?"

"We'll see," he smiled, "but if not, I may appeal to someone who definitely will."

"Who?" I asked.

"Andrew, do you know how I got this job? The Technical

Advancement Company, Inc. wanted to see what would happen if a diplomat instead of a scientist tried negotiating with the Natives. So far, no results, so maybe it doesn't matter what I do as far as the company is concerned, but the Corps has been wondering about this place for a long time. They just never had a reason to put any manpower on it, nothing amiss, no real danger, no one to negotiate with. If my company isn't interested, I know the Space Corps Bureau of Diplomacy will be. When I think about it, they had a reason all along. They should have seen that no one can garner anything valuable from a society without knowing who they are dealing with."

"Dad, I thought this was a safe posting, and that's part of why you took this job."

"True enough, Andrew, but it looks as if we were mislead. There's been a death, and at least one attack. For all we know, safety was compromised on this planet nearly fifteen years ago when Tomas had his accident, and I want to know why."

"Me, how, I want to know," I said trying to sound like Tomas.

"Very good, Andrew!"

"Dad, did you notice how Tomas' speech degraded over the time we were with him?"

"Yes, I did. Any ideas about it?"

"Not yet, Dad, but I'm thinking on it."

"Good, good. Now, let's go home, Andrew

XX

We passed Brandt, Andrews, Petersenes and Mrs. Pattison heading to the caves.

"Going the wrong way, aren't you, Stephen?" Mr. Andrews called.

Dad just said, "I've got to take Andrew home."

"I guess that wasn't a total untruth, Dad," I pointed out.

We weren't halfway back when an alien rose up from the edge of the road. It was a shanty-town Water Person, tall, thin-skinned, more gruesome in motion than when catatonic.

"Don't move, Andrew," Dad said.

"Don't worry," I whispered.

The Water Person focused on Dad, sidling closer. It seemed to be leaching liquid from its pores, almost melting.

"Dad, don't let it touch you, please, please!"

"I'm not sure what to do! Any ideas? Think fast, Andrew," Dad said. It scared me that he sounded so panicky.

The Water Person's skin and veins throbbed as it edged closer, ever closer to Dad. I felt my blood thumping to the pulse of the throbbing veins. The Water Person moved nearer and nearer. My heart beat more frantically until I screamed, "No!" The creature didn't pause. It came on, its arms out now, clear thick gel dripping from its fingertips, oozing from its face, its orifice, its eyes, its feet! I needed a weapon, any weapon. Closer, closer. Unthinkingly, desperately, I grabbed a flat stone from the ground and heaved it. It made contact just above the streaming eyes and vanished, absorbed as easily as a sponge absorbs water. The creature reached towards where the rock had hit and stopped moving.

I just stood there, staring. I turned to Dad and it felt as if I was moving in morph-mode where time and space stretched and pulled at everything until it created impossible versions of reality. I saw Dad reach out his hand, his eyes stretched in his big face, propped wide by surprise. Slowly, oh so slowly, his eyes blinked. As the lids touched, they shifted back into normal time. He grabbed my hand and yelled, "Let's go! Now!"

He jerked me into motion, and dragged me stumbling along

until my feet started moving by themselves. For a big man, Dad could really run and I had to pump my legs to keep up. I glanced backward, but all I saw was a shiny reflection on the road.

"I think it's gone, Dad," I rasped and despite the mad dash we had just made, felt my heart begin to slow.

"Good, because I'm not much of a long distance runner," Dad said and bent over, panting heavily from the sprint.

"Where'd it come from, Dad?"

"I'd like to know what it wanted. It reminded me of a very old horror flick called *The Blob*." He took a deep breath. "The Blob was an alien organism that landed on Earth and absorbed everyone in its path." He took another gulp of air. "It was all I could think of back there. And to think, I always made fun of those old movies." He finally began to breathe normally.

"Wait until Mom hears about this!" I said.

"Uh, Andrew, promise you'll let me tell her. We don't want her to think we were scared."

"Okay, Dad, but I've got to tell you, I was terrified."

"Me, too," he admitted.

I sighed in relief when we walked through our gate until I saw that the membrane over the door was closed.

"Knock, knock, knock," Dad boomed, because knocking didn't make a noise. He punched the membrane open.

Mom stood on the other side of the door with a pan of boiling water in one hand, a stun gun in the other, her eyes hawk steady and steeled.

"Thank goodness," she said. "Come in quickly!"

"What's wrong, Rebecca?" Dad asked.

"What's wrong is catatonic Water People are activated and oozing," she announced like some tabloid report. I had the feeling she was a little too in control, even for Mom.

"We know," Dad said, taking the water from her and setting it on the stove before he took her in his arms. "We had our own little run in with one."

"What? Where? What happened?" Mom burst out, pushing away from him.

"On the road. Not too much to worry about."

"Really?" Mom said, a look of disbelief on her face. "You're not a very good liar, Stephen. The girls were near the door playing dolls when the thing walked right in. I didn't have time to think. I just grabbed the first thing I could find, a pan of hot oil, and threw it. The oil didn't even splatter. The thing absorbed it, completely absorbed it, and then turned and walked out."

"Sounds familiar," Dad said with a slight shudder.

"Oh really! Then I promise you, it was something to worry over," she said.

"They sure move fast for creatures that are usually stationary," Dad noted, still not directly admitting to any danger.

"Mom, Dad, what's going on here?" I asked.

"I don't know, Andrew, but Cindra and Louisa are terrified. Could you go check on them?" Mom asked.

They were huddled in the back room. Louisa was hugging her elephant and trying to read, but kept looking up towards the other room. Cindra just lay there clutching Bernie the Bear.

"Come on guys. It's time for our story."

"Andrew, it was scary," Cindra said quietly.

"Yeah, well, don't worry. Mom and Dad will figure it out," I said, hoping I was right. "Let's read now, okay?"

"Wait, Andrew. Is the changeling the hero?" Louisa asked, climbing into my lap.

"Why?"

"Because, if he's the hero, he should be handsome."

"Mr. Chalder isn't handsome," Cindra said, swiping at her curls with her little fist.

"But he isn't a hero," Louisa protested.

"I think he's a hero," Cindra replied

"Right, and he's just under a spell like the Beast," Louisa said. "You're too little to know a hero if you saw one, Cindra."

"Quit you two. Louisa, wait and see what happens, and, Cindra, you're right, not everybody who is a hero is handsome. Now can we start?"

"Sure," they said, nodding their heads.

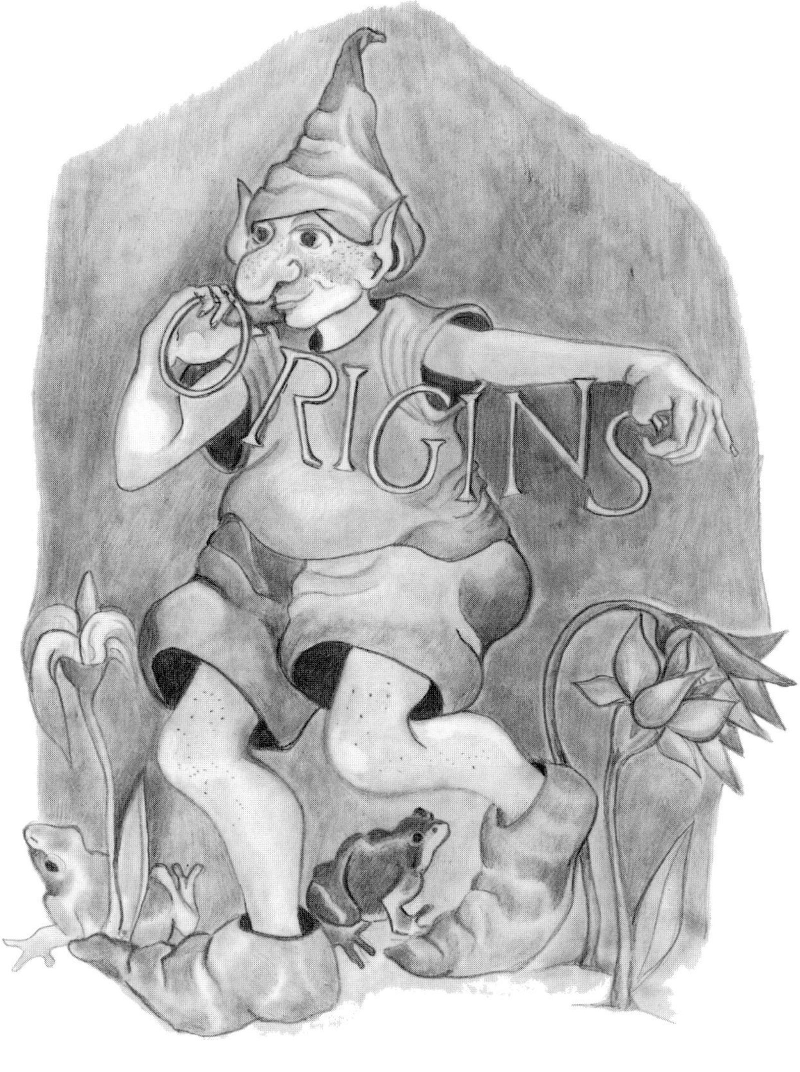
ORIGINS

The changeling tried to sleep, but all he could think about was the sad face of the girl on the bed She had seemed sadder than he was. He tossed and turned all night. At last his eyes closed, except for his third eye which always kept watch. He dreamed about his childhood sweetheart, she of the beautiful spotted skin and yellow teeth. She had died in the crash and when he dreamed of her, his third eye cried.

At dawn he was awake again. He changed back into the crow and flew off to the castle. It was bustling with activity. Carts rolled in and out of its gates, children ran about screaming and yelling to each other. Prince Timothy was trying to stand up in a new suit of mail, but kept falling down, despite Sir Edmund's best efforts to support him. The Changeling ignored it all and flew to the window of the crying girl. There she was, brushing her long hair, her eyes big and solemn.

"I promise you my dear," a large, white-haired man said, "you will be happy. Sir Hillary can offer you many luxuries. Please, do not be so melancholy."

"But Father, I do not wish to marry an old man. I am only fourteen and I dream of a handsome prince who will take me traveling to distant lands."

"My child, my child, you must look at the world through realistic eyes. So many young men died in the war. This is the best you can expect. Get ready my child, Sir Hillary will arrive later this afternoon."

"Please, Father, don't make me do this. Sir Hillary has no hair, his stomach is pouchy, his eyes are small and mean!"

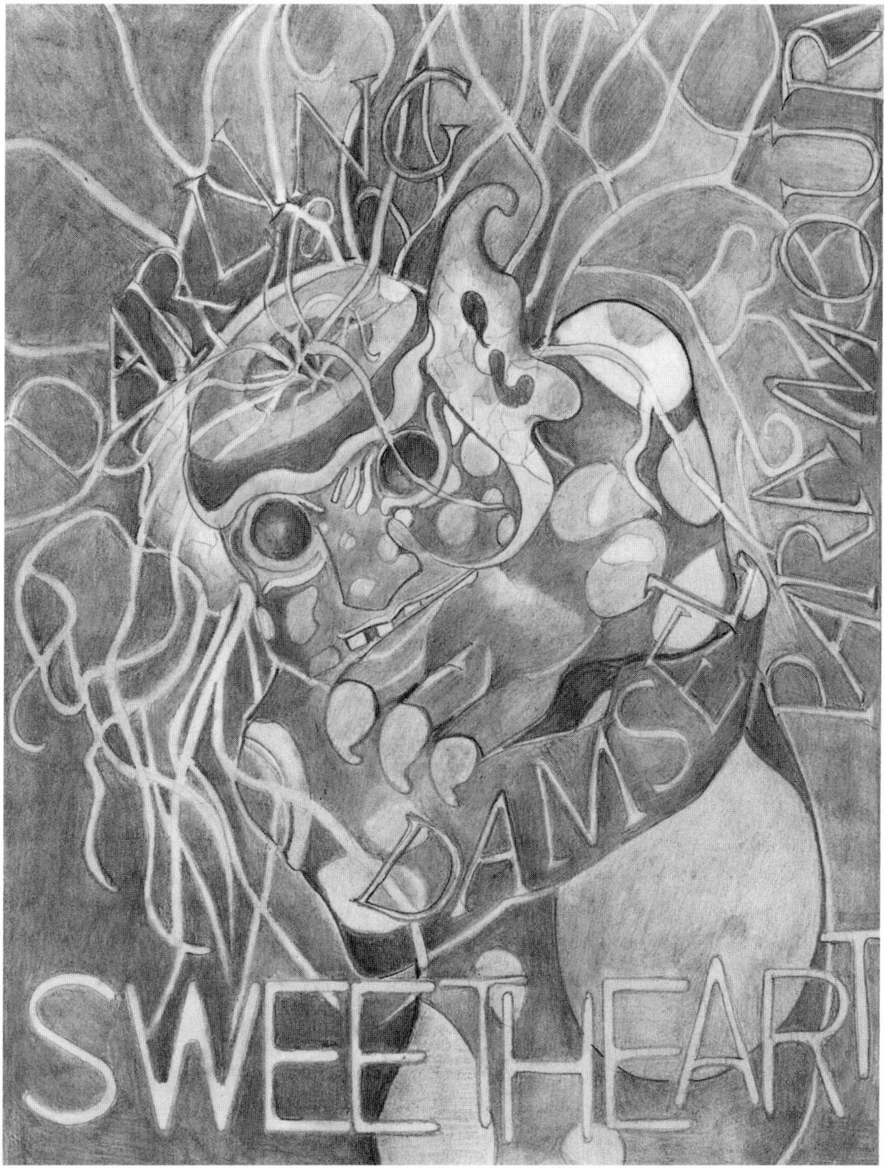
DARLING
PARAMOUR
DAMSEL
SWEETHEART

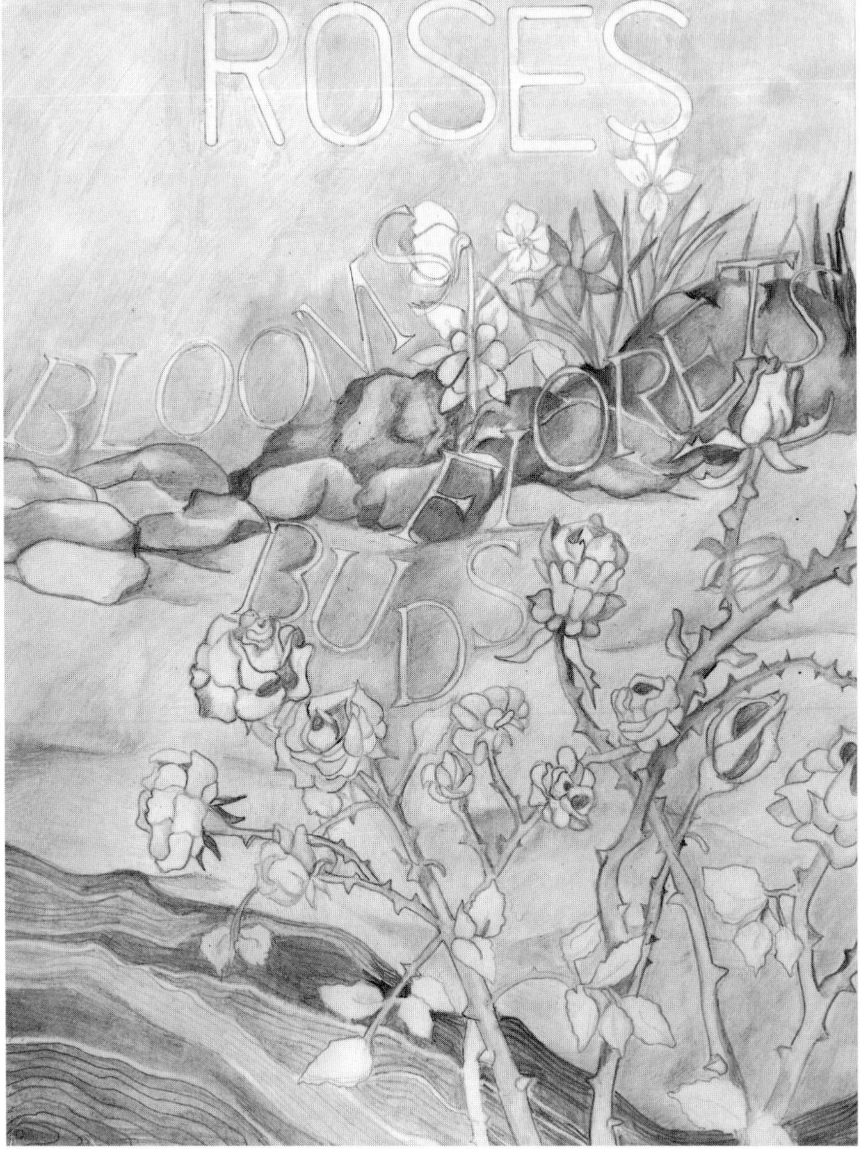
ROSES
BLOOMS
FLORETS
BUDS

"Oh, my sweet child, I wish it could be different. If you could find an appropriate young man, I would not deny you, but it is hopeless. Now ready yourself."

He patted his daughter gently and left her there. As soon as he was gone, a tear rolled down her cheek. A chamber maid came in and the girl said, "Please come back later, Gennevieve."

"Yes, my lady Alice."

Alice slipped into a plain shift and soft slippers and went to the window. She climbed out onto the ledge and down the trellis. The changeling followed her. She wound her way around the edge of the castle wall to a hole where the stones had fallen out, and crawled through. The changeling flew above her, watching her with his two front eyes, and watching behing him with his third eye, but no one followed them.

[Where is she going?]

[You'll find out.]

Alice picked her way along a stony trail between briars and brambles and down a rocky bank. She worked her way through a thicket of vines, stopping at last by a small pond. All around it pink and yellow roses gave off a sweet perfume. She tossed a small polished stone into the water and little frogs jumped from lily pads. The sun came through the trees and cast bright patterns of light across the vale. The crow landed high abouve her and shifted back into an alien changeling. The girl began to sing.

"Oh, little toads and baby frogs,
Sitting quietly on floating logs,
Singing your songs in voices sweet
I wish that I could bring you treats."

The Changeling shook his head. Even though the girl's voice was pleasant, it was a terrible song. He watched her pick a rose, smell it, and then throw the petals into the water.

"This may be my last day here with you little frogs, but try not to be sad," she said.

She gathered some leaves and rose petals into a pile and put her head down on them, closed her eyes and slept.

[Which is what you girls should do. Why don't you take a nap?]

[Aw, Andrew, read some more please!]

[Please, Andy, please.]

[I can't right now. You two get some rest.]

[Andy, do you think Mr. Chalder could be a changeling?]

[Oh, Cindra, you think that Tomas is whatever Andrew's stories are about. He's not a changeling. He's just a person.]

[How do you know, Louisa? I could be right, couldn't I, Andy? He might not be what he seems to be.]

[You could be right, Cindra. You just might be right about that.]

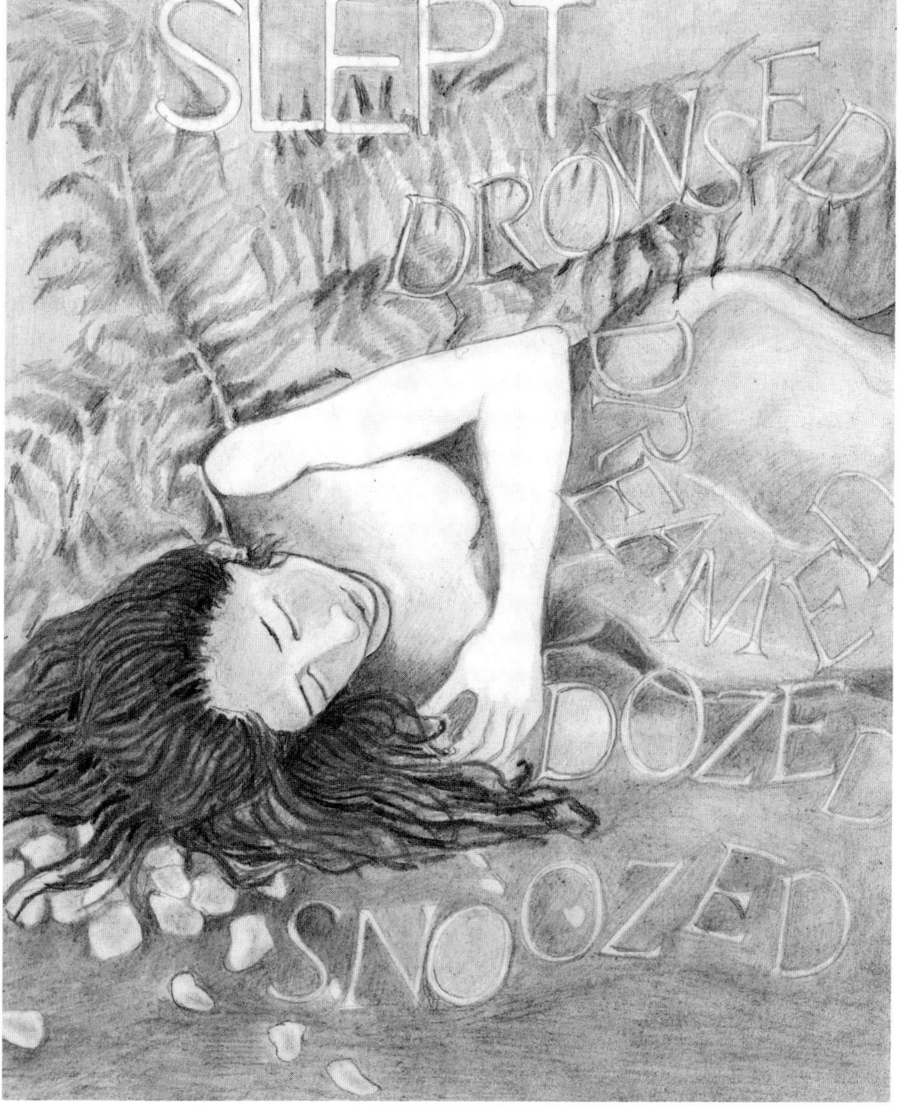
SLEPT
DROWSED
DREAMED
DOZED
SNOOZED

XXI

The girls cuddled up with their animals and I sat with them, rubbing their backs until their eyes got droopy. I left them with their animals and rejoined Mom and Dad in the outer room.

"Mom, do you think the Water People were actually attacking us?" I asked.

"What else could it be, Andrew?"

"I don't know. It seemed as if they might have just been wandering. Ours seemed sort of unfocused, except that it wanted to touch Dad."

"I admit it frightened me to think what might have happened if it had," Dad said.

"The Blob, right?" I laughed.

"Who knows," he said seriously.

"I don't want to find out," Mom said emphatically. "What I want to know is why normally immobile creatures are suddenly walking zombies. And, why hasn't anyone ever mentioned the potential danger to us?" A certain tone in her voice told me she had turned bodyguard, and she was mad, too.

"Maybe no one was aware of the danger," Dad said, trying to calm her temper.

"Stephen, don't be naive. They at least knew about Philippa's mother before we arrived and never mentioned it, probably never reported it to anyone."

"Maybe they didn't know who to report it to," I suggested. "I'm certainly a little confused about who's in charge here."

"Okay, let's go," Mom said. "I want to get to the bottom of this."

"Go where?" Dad asked.

"To the Club, now, all of us. Pack a few extra clothes. We might have to stay there the night. Get the kids ready."

"They're napping, Mom," I said.

"Wake them. We're going now. Go, Andrew."

"But no one will be there. Dad and I saw them all on their way to the caves."

"Fine. We'll go through the records while they're gone. And,

Andrew, hang onto to Tomas' file for a while. If these people have been hiding something, I may officially confiscate all the records anyway."

Mom could do that, I thought as I went to get the girls. She was an official, actually a high muckety-muck, in what I jokingly called the Guard of the Realm and Dad referred to as the Knights of the Universe. Mom was a modicum of sweetness and decorum when she wanted to be, but when she was mad, well, I was always glad when she wasn't mad at me.

We got to the Club in record time because Mom moved us along at a such a pace that the girls were practically running to keep up. She had tucked a small stun-gun and even some mace into her belt, but we didn't see a single alien. They probably would have absorbed a stun-gun discharge anyway. When we passed the village, the Water People there were as catatonic as ever. When we got to the Club, it was far from empty. Everyone was there. Everyone was mumbling and grumbling.

"Why aren't you guys at the caves?" I blurted out.

Matina Borsus looked up sullenly, as did Petersenes and Andrews.

"You'll never, ever follow in your father's footsteps, young Andrew," Petersenes grouched.

"I don't know about that," Dad said.

"The rules do not allow exchanges about why we're back," Hal Andrews reminded us tersely.

"Well now," Dad said, "it was pointed out to me today by a friend of mine that no one owns any one cavern. By the same ken, it seems that what keeps you from sharing information is your greed, not rules."

"Quite right," Mrs. Pattison said proudly.

"Well, Mrs. Pattison, Mr. Andrews," Mom said, "when it comes to security, secrecy is about to be disrupted. What happened today? Spill it."

"You know we can't say!" Andrews insisted.

"As an invested and ranked member of the Space Security Administration, I am officially initiating an inquiry into any and all attacks since the first Miner arrived," Mom announced.

A hush descended on the group.

"And, you will answer my questions, or I will begin official prosecution of those of you who don't cooperate. Now then, what happened," Mom continued undeterred.

Hal Andrews took a deep breath. "Okay, okay, it's not much of a secret anyway. My Native wasn't in his cavern."

"Nor mine."

"Nor mine," went around the room over and over.

Only Caroline, crouched in a corner chair nervously twisting a napkin back and forth, said nothing.

"Do you know why they weren't there?" Mom asked.

"Never happened before. How would we know why, even if it had?" Mrs. Pattison said.

"You Miners don't know much after all the years you've put in here," I pointed out.

"What's the longest anyone has been here?" Mom asked.

"Five years and a bit."

"That's not true," I said. "Tomas Chalder has been here twenty."

"Yeah, and he's a lunatic," Brandt accused. "Gone Native, years ago. Even looks like them."

I thought on that for a while, but Mom went on.

"Aside from Mr. Chalder, five years then. Okay, where are the records?" Mom demanded.

"You have no authority over our personal records," Mrs. Pattison hissed.

"For the moment, the Club's records."

"Except for medical, I doubt there are any. We're all privately and discretely funded," Mr. Andrews snorted.

"Oh, great!" Mom said.

Dad stepped in. "We'll start with medical then. Hal, Mrs. Pattison, you two will help me gather and sort them."

"While they're doing that, I want to talk to each of you individually," Mom said. "Andrew will record our conversations. Let me warn you, this is not a time for secrecy. I'll start with Caroline. Come on, we'll do this in one of the back rooms."

Caroline followed us passively. We each carried a chair, but instead of using one, Caroline sank to the floor, sitting with her back against a wall where she could keep her face in the shadows.

"Caroline," Mom began gently, "tell me about the attack on you. You seem to be the only one who has survived an attack whole."

"Is that what I am? I don't feel whole, don't even feel like myself anymore."

"Try to tell me what happened," Mom prompted.

"It wasn't exactly an attack," Caroline whispered hoarsely. "I was alone on the road. I like to take walks to get away from the other Miners. I've taken walks several times a week for over six months, and never had a problem. But this time, one of the Water People appeared, kind of slid into view. It was oozing something thick and slimy. I tried to walk around it, but it blocked me. I tried to stay calm. I really did try, but it reached out anyway, and rather gently touched my face. Did I say gently? It was like a blow when its hand actually met my flesh." She turned her face directly to us, which until then she had hidden against her shoulder.

"I'd say it was a blow," Mom said, glancing at me. Caroline's face was covered in patterns of yellowing bruises.

"It never hit me. There was no physical force behind it. It was more like a caress. Anyway, I screamed. I have always had a piercing scream." She smiled slightly. "Things got fuzzy as if something was covering my eyes, and I screamed again and then Mr. Chalder was holding me, oh so gently. Only he didn't look like himself. He wasn't so hunched up. 'It's gone,' he said. 'I chased it. Am I too late?' I had no idea what he meant? Too late for what? I was bleeding and bruised, but my eyes had cleared and he helped me get back to the Club."

"So, you wouldn't actually call it an attack?" I asked.

She shrugged. "I don't think so, but it wasn't friendly either."

"Okay, did you think it meant you violence?" Mom asked.

"I don't know what it wanted. Can I go now?" Caroline asked nervously.

"Sure," Mom said. "I'll walk you out."

Mom came back with Mr. Andrews trailing reluctantly behind her.

"This is an outrage," he protested.

"Let's hope it stops a real outrage," Mom said undeterred. "Now, how long have you been posted here?"

"Almost four years."

"And during that time, how many attacks have there been?"

"Nary a one until Mrs. Brandt, if that's what happened to her," he said.

"All right," Mom said, "in those four years, how much information have you actually collected?"

"I average three to four items every six months," he said proudly, tossing his head back.

"Is any of it applicable to anything?" I asked, truly curious. Dad had either gotten no answers or completely useless ones so far, and I wondered how much of what the Miners collected was of interest to their own companies. Of course, maybe Dad's lack of success was because he was a newcomer, in which case, Mr. Andrew's answer might give him hope that he would eventually make some useful finds.

"I'm not answering questions from your kid, lady," he said snippily to Mom.

"It's a good question. Answer it. Has your employer found any practical use for what you've unearthed every few months?" Mom asked, repeating my question.

"Sure," he answered.

"How many applications?" I asked.

This time he didn't argue. Instead he held up one finger.

"One?" Mom asked, dismay saturating her voice. "It must have been a doozey if you're still here. But, how many did Tomas Chalder get in his first three years?" she continued, changing the discussion before I got to ask what Mr. Andrews had discovered.

"Twenty-three, Mrs. Haldran. How an idiot like that came up with twenty-three usable discoveries, I'll never know."

"But he did, and he set the standard, didn't he?" I asked.

"I suppose so. By the time I arrived he was legendary. Some Miners think the Natives prefer youngsters, and Chalder was only seventeen when he came here, not much older than you, kid."

"Was Tomas attacked?" Mom asked.

"How would I know? I've only been here four years."

"Okay, you can go, but I'm going to want to talk to you again."

"So I shouldn't try to leave town?" he quipped with a sarcastic sneer.

"Righto, partner," Mom replied.

He left as Mrs. Pattison pattered through one of the doors.

"I thought you were helping Dad," I said to her.

"I am. Your husband wants you, Rebecca."

"Mrs. Pattison, how come there's no doctor here anymore?" I asked as we walked out to the sitting room.

"Why ask me? Ask your father's former employer. They're the ones who used to send the doctors."

"Well, do you know what happened to the last one?" I asked again.

"It was before my time, so all this is gossip. Someone told me he was doing some sort of biological study and not bothering with the Miners' health, but who knows? Maybe it was just boring. No need for him."

"So he was recalled? Why didn't they replace him?"

"How should I know?"

"Do you realize, Mrs. Pattison," Mom said, "that your ignorant 'code' of secrecy may have put every one of us in danger. People are getting killed. People are getting hurt, and you haven't even requested medical staff to remain here! Why that's it, isn't it? You didn't ask for a doctor to replace the last one."

"We never needed one before. It wasn't dangerous, and doctors keep records and they are nosy. Too nosy," she hissed.

"Well, Caroline could have used a doctor," I pointed out.

"That's true, but who could have known?" Mrs. Pattison said almost regretfully.

"But that is precisely the point. You never know when you might need a doctor," Mom said with what I knew was frustration.

"There you are," Dad said when he saw us. "Look at this. The whole set of medical records ends seven years ago. Skimming the first five years, we uncovered no mention of attacks, but there were three cases of mild disorientation and confusion. Tomas seems to have been the most extreme case recorded."

"The latest victim is still slightly confused," Mom said, speaking of Caroline, "but I think she was more frightened than damaged. At least, I hope so. Without a doctor, it's hard to tell. Then again, if Tomas was a victim of an earlier and more violent attack, a doctor didn't help much."

"That's a big 'if'," Dad said.

"Dad, Mom, Tomas calls whatever happened to him an accident, not an attack," I reminded them.

"That could be a euphemism that this Dr. Pease used for want of a better choice," Dad pointed out. "And clearly, Tomas' memory of the incident is blurred."

"So, you think we've been under attack almost from the start and we were too dumb to realize it? Is that your premise?" Mrs. Pattison sounded peeved.

I thought the Miners were probably too greedy to acknowledge any danger for fear of Corps interference, but Dad said, "Not necessarily. The pattern is extremely random, which certainly doesn't imply a plot or directed action. On the other hand, it might just be a ruse to make it difficult to identify what's going on."

Who needed a ruse if your opponent was too focused on one thing to notice and match up clues, I thought. Then again, I wasn't focused at all and I didn't have much of an answer either. Not yet. I needed more time, that was all.

Most of the Miners were wandering over to join the conversation. Even though it was a small group, the nature of their jobs had prevented them from bonding or even knowing each other well. Most of our postings had drawn us into close and long lasting friendships. Everybody took care of everybody else. Not here. Here everyone lived in a communal building, and there ended all closeness. These people were incapable of understanding each other, yet were supposed to understand aliens. I wondered if anyone here had been Augmented as a cultural anthropologist, or even a bio-anthropologist. Probably not, because their companies wanted information about technical products, not understanding of another race. My mind clicked along this path until something new came to me.

"Mom," I said to her where she stood watching what was rapidly turning into a verbal melee. "Mom, listen, I've got an idea. What if the attacks have nothing to do with us directly? What if the Miners who have been attacked were just in the wrong place at the wrong time, period, the end? An accident, just like Mr. Chalder keeps saying."

"What? What are you talking about, Andrew? People don't attack other people because they accidentally meet them on the street."

"That's the point, Mom, not people! The Natives and the Water People are not people."

"What? Andrew, can't this wait?"

"No, I don't think so. Mom, we've only been here a few weeks and we've walked by Water People a zillion times. No response! They ignore us. They're in Catatonic Heaven."

"So? Hurry this up."

"So, what activates them? That's what you asked, Mom, and that's exactly what we need to know."

"Andrew, this is going to have to wait. Right now we have other problems," she said curtly, and stepped into the group of now shouting and gesturing Miners, dismissing my idea simultaneously.

"Enough," she barked. "Everybody be quiet. I think we should all stay here in the Club for a while."

I wished Mom would listen to me. I wished she would stop viewing everything as a security issue. I was sure there was something else, something more complex going on.

"Why are the Natives gone from the caves?" Louisa asked me.

"I don't know. What do you think?" I asked, suddenly realizing that Louisa, Cindra, Philippa and I were the only unaugmented humans on the planet and I needed their help.

"Maybe they're looking for the Water People out on the paths," she suggested.

"Maybe," I said. It actually wasn't a stupid idea. "Why do you think that, Louisa? Do you think they're trying to stop the Water People from hurting us?"

"Maybe, maybe not," she said, lifting her shoulders in an imitation of Mom.

"Dad," I said as he sidled up to us. "Do we have to stay here in the Club, too?"

"For now, Andrew. I wish I knew what was going on!"

"Dad, try to think like an alien," I said. "Maybe that would help."

"Andrew, how can I do that? I'm human."

"Use your imagination," I suggested for the second time to one of my parents.

"This is serious, not a game and not one of your stories," he said, and turned his head towards the petulant Miners. "Where is Tomas, anyway?"

"I don't know."

"I hope he has the sense to stay away. Some of these idiots are trying to blame him for all this. Let's find some quarters and get some sleep," Dad said, rounding up the girls.

XXII

Cindra woke me when it was barely light. She and Louisa had been up for a while, and finally with an unusual show of discretion, decided to wake me instead of Mom and Dad. Cindra shook me until I quit moaning.

"What do you want?" I groaned.

"The bathroom."

"Well, go find it. You don't need me," I complained.

"Yes, we do. Remember, Philippa got lost, really lost in the Club. We're scared."

"Okay, okay, I'm coming."

We wandered back into the central room and discovered Tomas Chalder sitting straight-backed in an over-stuffed, flowered chair.

Cindra bounded into his lap. "Louisa and me were worried about you," she declared.

"Not to worry," Tomas said.

"But people is getting attacked and stuff," she said.

"Won't hurt me," he reassured her.

"Why not?" I asked.

"No hurting intended," he replied.

"But they do hurt," I pointed out. This should have been his good time of the day and I was hoping for answers.

"Accidents only. Why are humans there?" he asked back.

"Where?" Cindra asked.

"When they are there," Tomas said.

"Where?" she repeated.

"When they are ready," came back.

"Ready for what, Tomas?" I asked.

"To do it," he replied.

"Do what?" I asked, getting more and more frustrated. His speech was clear, his sentences simple, his meaning obtuse. Tomas looked straight and in control of himself, except for the brief flickers of yellow in his eyes, yet my hopes for answers were being dashed by an ambiguous, incoherent Chalder conversation.

He replied simply, "Anything."

I had never seen him seated before, but he fit perfectly in this chair. "Do you sit there often?" I asked, thinking how absurd the idea was.

"Every morning," he said, taking me off guard.

"Really?" Cindra said. "Then this is your chair."

He nodded. "I brought this chair when I came. My thinking chair. I sat here always before the caves. Sat, thought, tried to answer the questions."

"What questions?" I asked, as my hopes rose again despite the fact that he was unlikely to give me a cogent answer.

I almost jumped when he said precisely, "About their life cycle."

"What's that?" Louisa asked in the silence I left gaping.

"How they procreate." His voice, his grammar, his shoulders and posture held firm and steady. He was a real Jekyll and Hyde.

I held my breath, as I asked, "Why was that important, Tomas?"

He smiled, the yellow in his eyes flickering faster and faster. Cindra and Louisa were as transfixed as I was watching the light show. Abruptly, the yellow stabilized into tiny dots, and Tomas Chalder slumped into his Beetle shape.

"Poor Tomas," Cindra said, stroking his stooped shoulders.

"Thank you," he struggled to say.

I was dumbfounded. What had just happened?

"Sorry am I, Andrew Haldran. Forgive me?"

"There is nothing to forgive."

"I could not finish," he sighed.

"Did you find the answer to your question?"

"The accident I found," he said obliquely. It was as if everything about Tomas was off-centered and unfinished. His research, his speech, his life were all struggling to be consummated, were waiting to be completed. He rose and scuttled for the door.

"No you don't, you bug," Hal Andrews snarled, blocking his departure. "Not until you explain all this."

"He can't" I said.

"Oh, really now? Watch this, kid." Andrews picked Tomas up under the arm pits. "Stretch out, right now, and talk," he said, trying to shake out the Beetle.

All that happened was that Tomas retreated, his eyes filling with terror at each jolt of his body.

"Stop it," I said loudly.

"He knows," Andrews growled. "He's already half Native."

"Stop saying that," I yelled. "He's human, one of us."

Andrews turned his head and laughed. "Human, this? What a joke." He dropped Tomas to the floor. "Are you an idiot, kid?" he asked turning angrily on me. "This, human? I think the Water People ate him and left this replacement. Just left a tiny piece of his brain to fool us. Want him? He's yours," he spit and stomped off, but not before he kicked Tomas like a piece of refuse.

Louisa bent down to Tomas. "He's crying," she said sadly. "Tomas, are you hurt?"

His chest heaved and tears ran down his face, his eyes squeezed shut.

"He meant harm to me. Humans it is who attack," he finally gasped, his eyes still lidded.

"And the aliens, don't they attack?" I asked.

He looked confused for a moment. "No, no, no. Touch," he stammered.

"Did the Water People touch you?" Cindra asked, patting his head.

"Touch," he repeated. Or was it an answer? I couldn't tell.

"Tomas, the accident that left you like this? Was it caused by the Water People touching you?"

"Touch. Can't remember who be I."

"Tomas, please, I'm confused," I said, trying to focus him.

Cindra wiped at his tears with her little hands and for an instant, the half-lidded eyes opened fully before they closed as tears swept him again. The eyes in that instant had been dull brown, unsparked by any yellow.

"Andrew," Mom said, still in her nightgown, rubbing sleep from her eyes as she entered the room. "Why is Tomas crying?"

"Mr. Andrews attacked him," I said, "and it wasn't an accident."

"Is Tomas hurt?"

"I don't know, Mom. I know he's scared," I said.

"Where is Hal Andrews?" Mom asked.

I shrugged, but Louisa said, "He went outside."

"Ah, yes, a work day, the idiot," Mom sighed. "Tomas, are you hurt?"

"Cracked," he mumbled.

"How about standing up?" Mom suggested.

He didn't budge.

"Hal has gone to the caves, Tomas. No one else is going to hurt you, I promise," she said.

"Caves? Not return," Tomas answered.

"No, he's not coming back to hurt you," Mom repeated.

"Agreed," he said.

"What are we agreeing to?" I asked him.

He didn't answer.

"Mom," I whispered. "This really is like mining a Native."

"Andrew," she reprimanded me, "Tomas is a human being!"

"I know, Mom. He's our friend, but . . ."

"No buts," she said turning back to Tomas. "Can you stand?"

I wished she had let me explain. No matter how much I hated it, the evidence was pointing to some physical transformation of Tomas into something at least partially alien. How could she not see it?

Mom put her hand on Tomas' shoulder to help him up and he screamed. Thrashing out, he shoved her and sent her flying like a rag doll into a soft chair. She landed in the seat with a loud plop and a surprised look on her face.

"I think you hurt him, Mom," I said. "It was a reflex action."

"If he's that strong, why didn't he protect himself from Andrews?" she asked, standing slowly and starting back to him.

"Sorry," Tomas said softly.

Mom smiled at him kindly. "Can I look at your shoulder?"

"No," he said frantically, pulling his head down as if retreating into a shell.

"Tomas," she protested, "let me help you."

He looked at her and pulled back further.

"Please, Tomas. We are your friends. Let me help you."

"Friends? Help me?" he repeated and shakily reached with his other hand to undo two small, hidden snaps. The tunic slid off his shoulder. Beneath was a band of shimmering silver.

"A Native band!" I half whispered, half gasped. I had thought the stripes were decorative body paint, but this one was an eggshell-thin leafing of silver skin growing from beneath his tunic, over his shoulder and down his back. It was split and blood oozed from the open wound.

"What is that?" Mom asked bewilderedly.

"Broken," Tomas answered, his eyes closing down again.

"Mom," I whispered, "if the Miners see that, they're going to freak."

"Why, Andrew? What is it?"

Before I could answer her, I heard more voices.

"Quick, Mom, trust me, cover it. Tomas, you have to get up. Can you at least sit in a chair?"

"Wrong shape," he mumbled.

"Andrew, Cindra, Louisa, come here. Pretend you're playing jacks with him," Mom said, handing me the ball and stars from the table where we had left them. "No matter how angry they get, stay cool. Andrew, you do the talking. I'm going to get your father! I'll be back quickly."

"Mom," I began, but she had already disappeared, leaving us alone with a wounded person who was no longer totally human. I sat on the floor next to Tomas and tried to calm down.

"Psst, Tomas, keep your eyes open if you can," I said.

"Well, well, isn't that cute," Mrs. Pattison said condescendingly. "Mr. Chalder has finally found his level. Jacks!"

Cindra looked up at her, oh so sweetly, and threw the stars.

Mrs. Pattison took a seat in a chair. After a bit she said, "Where is Mr. Andrews, children?"

"Gone," Tomas piped up.

"Gone? Where has he gone?" she shrilled.

"Caves," came back before I could stop Tomas.

"The caves! I thought we had all agreed not to go, or should I say, we were all ordered not to go, and now he has been allowed out," she cried, popping up like a jack-in-a-box. "That dishonest so and so. He has gotten the jump on us all!"

"No, not he," Tomas said, stopping her.

"If he's at the caves, he is mining, or don't you remember

that, Mr. Chalder? Are you too far gone Native to remember why we are all here?"

Chalder looked down and said, "No."

"No what, you idiot? No, you don't remember or no, he's not there?"

No answer came back and Mrs. Pattison dropped back into the chair with a little huffing sound. "You have associated yourself with a perfect partner, Andrew. Both of you are useless."

"Mrs. Pattison, let's take one thing at a time," Dad said, coming into the room. He bent and breathed hard into her face. "If I'm not mistaken, your code is never to share and if that's true, Tomas owes you zip. Next, my son is far from useless."

"Your son is impertinent and clearly takes after his father," Brandt said from where he stood.

"Then I thank you, for I'm right proud of Andrew," Dad said smoothly as he swooped down on Tomas and scooped him up into his arms.

"We're leaving for a bit," Mom informed Mrs. Pattison, "but we'll be back soon. I advise you all to stay in the Club. If on the off chance you care more about the possibility of a tidbit of useful information than your safety, go ahead, risk your lives, but at least don't go out alone."

"So you want us to stay here, while your hubby and Chalder run off to mine without competition? Fat chance of that, dearie," Mrs. Pattison sniped.

"First you say Mr. Chalder is a moron, then you think he's a devious cheat? Which is it, Mrs. Pattison?" Dad asked.

Mom just shook her head. "Don't bother, Stephen. It's her life. Do whatever you want," Mom said to the old lady.

Dad walked rapidly, as if Tomas weighed nothing. I'd never realized how strong he was. Mom brought the rear up with Cindra, Louisa and me enclosed in the middle.

"Eyes alert," she told us. "This could be dangerous."

"No choice, Rebecca," Dad called back to her. "Which way to your cave, Tomas?"

I couldn't hear the answer, but Dad turned to our left and we began to climb. At the first plateau, the sky opened before us in a burst of lavendar streaked with aqua.

"Tomas says it's a rain sky," Dad called and started forward.

The land tilted more steeply and the climb got rocky, but Dad and Mom herded us on as rapidly as they could. Louisa pulled Cindra along by the hand doggedly until Dad finally paused, stopped again by the sight of the sky as the lavender darkened to royal purple and diffused yellow-green light flickered wildly across the horizon.

We watched wordlessly until Mom shook her head and tapped Dad. "Let's go."

We climbed the last few feet and hurried into the cave just in time to escape a soaking. I stood at the mouth of the cave and watched the rain roll and rush down the hill. Usually the smell and rhythm of rain calmed me, but tonight it didn't help.

"Okay kids, try and occupy yourselves," Mom announced, pulling my attention away from the storm.

She turned on her torch and set it upright, its beam spraying yellow light outward around the cave and overwhelming the glow of the membranes embedded in the walls. The change stunned me.

"Mom, can I ask Tomas something before you look at his wound?" I said blinking and rubbing at my eyes.

"If you're quick, Andrew."

"Tomas, did you ever figure out the Natives' life cycle?"

"No."

"Did you figure out any of it?"

"Yes."

"Did that part explain the attacks?"

He didn't answer.

"Did you keep a record or a journal of what you found out?"

He nodded, wincing, obviously in pain now, his face wet with sweat.

"Could I read it?"

He paused and I thought he wouldn't answer.

"Yes," he gasped at last and pointed vaguely to his collection of tunics.

"That's it, enough, Andrew!" Dad said.

"Okay, Dad. I'm going to look around for the journals."

"Fine, fine," he said as he opened Tomas' tunic again. Mom pulled out her ever handy first aid kit from one of the many pockets in her security vest.

I turned away. "Come on, Cindra, Louisa, help me look, okay?"

Cindra peered curiously into corners and Louisa pawed through a heap of tunics. I noticed that there was more out of place than when I had been here before. Had Tomas cleaned up for my previous visit the way Mom did when we were expecting company?

"He's sure got a lot of these," Cindra said. "Hey, look, hooks on the walls. Let's hang the tunics on the hooks."

"Okay, maybe it'll be easier to find the records of his experiments if we straighten up in here," I agreed.

The hooks proved to be rammed all the way around the cave walls in patterns that were perfectly spaced to hang the tunics on so that they were stretched out like panels.

"What order?" Louisa asked.

"What difference?" I said.

"Let's do it like we do crayons," Cindra proposed. "All the reds together, all the blues, like that."

"Sure, why not," I said. We hung the first two and went all the way around. Altogether there were nineteen tunics. We stood back to view the garbled color.

Cindra shook her head. "Yucky!"

"They don't match up," Louisa said.

"Why should they?" I asked. Who would have thought Tomas would have had so many clothes?

"Maybe it's a puzzle. We should match the tunics edge to edge," Louisa insisted.

"Why bother?"

"To make them pretty for Tomas," Cindra said.

Why not if it would entertain the girls? We certainly had the time. We scrambled and unscrambled the tunics and thirty-five minutes later, we had, much to my amazement, matched the edges. We stepped back.

"Dad," I said, "Can you come here for a moment, please?"

"Will you look at that?" Dad said as he stood next to me.

Across the walls hung a unified landscape that rivaled the beauty of the one outside. Hues of green ran to shadow. Orange-tinged sky radiated over blackened mountains. Dusty clay spread above deep caverns filled with aliens. The landscapes moved around the walls, blending into scenes progressing from clear skies to misty fields to ice bound mountains in a fever of seasonal changes

"Who made the picture?" Louisa asked.

"Mr. Chalder," Cindra said assuredly. And I was sure, too. The Beetle, Tomas Chalder, was some kind of artistic genius.

"Andrew," Cindra said, "what's the story?"

"Huh?" I said.

"The story Tomas is telling with his pictures?" she insisted.

"It's not a book, honey," Dad said.

"Uh, Dad, look at it again. Maybe it is some kind of story or record."

We looked at the mural again, but if it held some deeper message, it was veiled and hidden from us, just like Tomas' mind.

Tomas slept. The girls begged me to finish the changeling story, but I hesitated in front of Mom and Dad.

"Please," they begged over and over and over until I gave in. We went into a corner and I began, keeping my voice as soft as possible.

"Is this the end of the story?" Cindra asked.

"Yes, we'll finish this time."

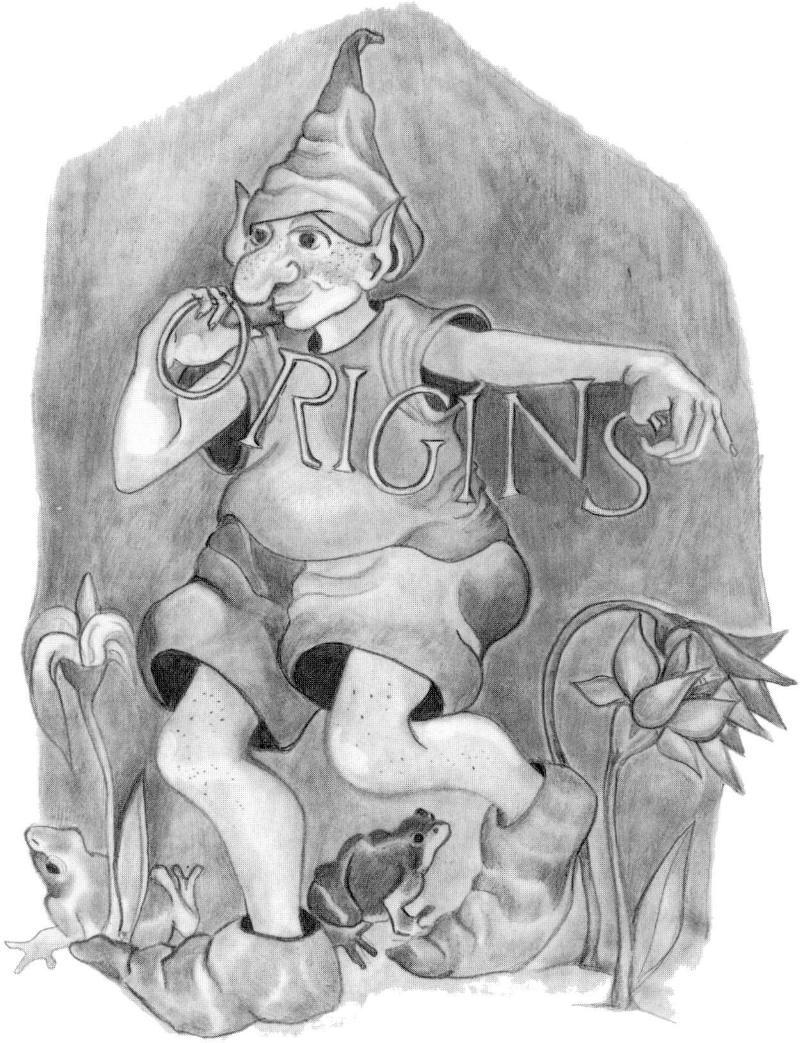
ORIGINS

The changeling watched the girl sleep. She wanted a young prince so much, and he needed someone to love. He could easily be a prince, maybe even the prince of her dreams, but every time he had tried to be with humans he had made a mistake. He was afraid if he tried, he would scare her and send her screaming back to her betrothal.

The breeze got a little stronger and stirred the branches and the twisted vines and made the flowers nod. The sound of the wind whispered to him. The girl cried out in her sleep. The changeling climbed down to the ground and peered into the girl's face. She stirred and her eyes began to open. He jumped back and fell in the pond with a loud splash.

[Uh oh! Can he swim?]

[Is he gonna drown, Andy?]

[Don't worry, girls.]

The changeling sank immediately. He saw the little fish and frogs swimming by him. He gagged and thought he was going to drown. His frantic floundering in the muddy bottom of the pond turned the water slimy and dark. In a desperate panic, he transformed himself into a frog and hopped out quickly onto the bank of the pond. Alice stared at him with wide eyes.

"Oh my, you are the most beautiful bullfrog I have ever seen. Are you my prince in disguise?

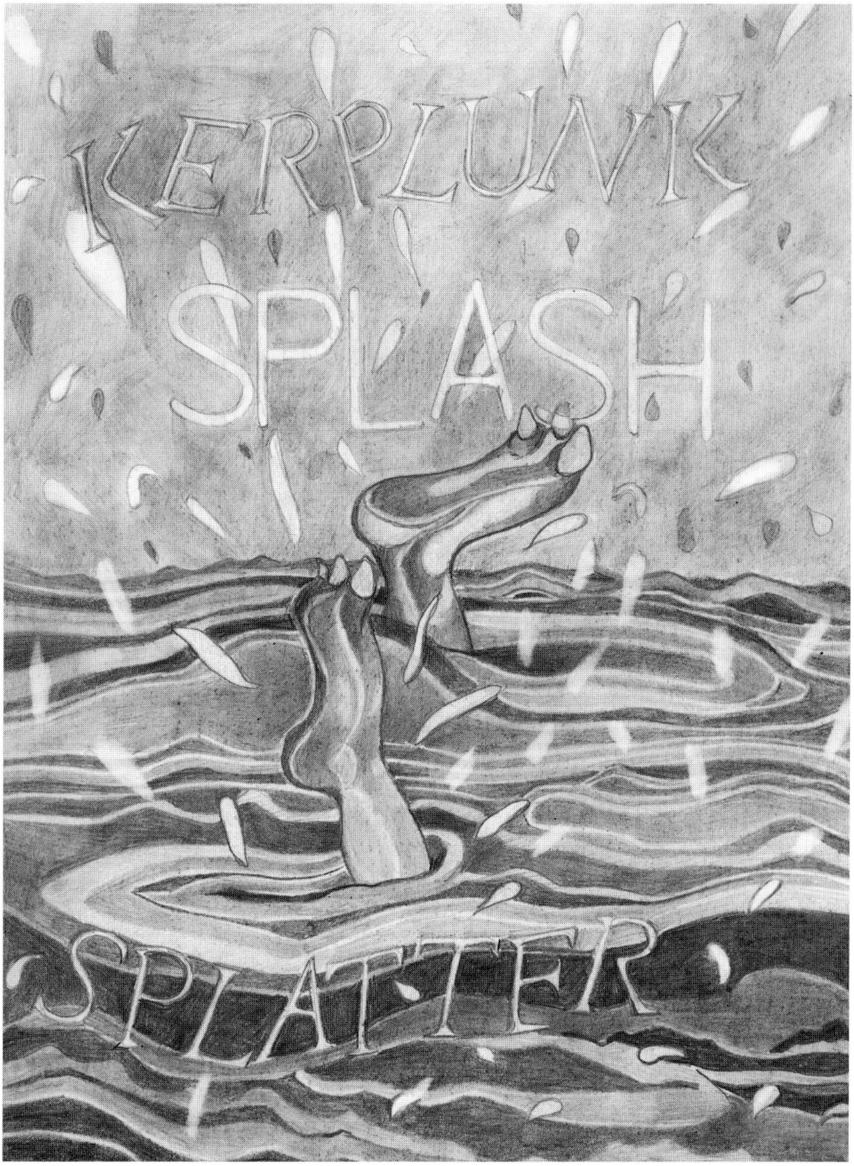
KERPLUNK
SPLASH
SPLATTER

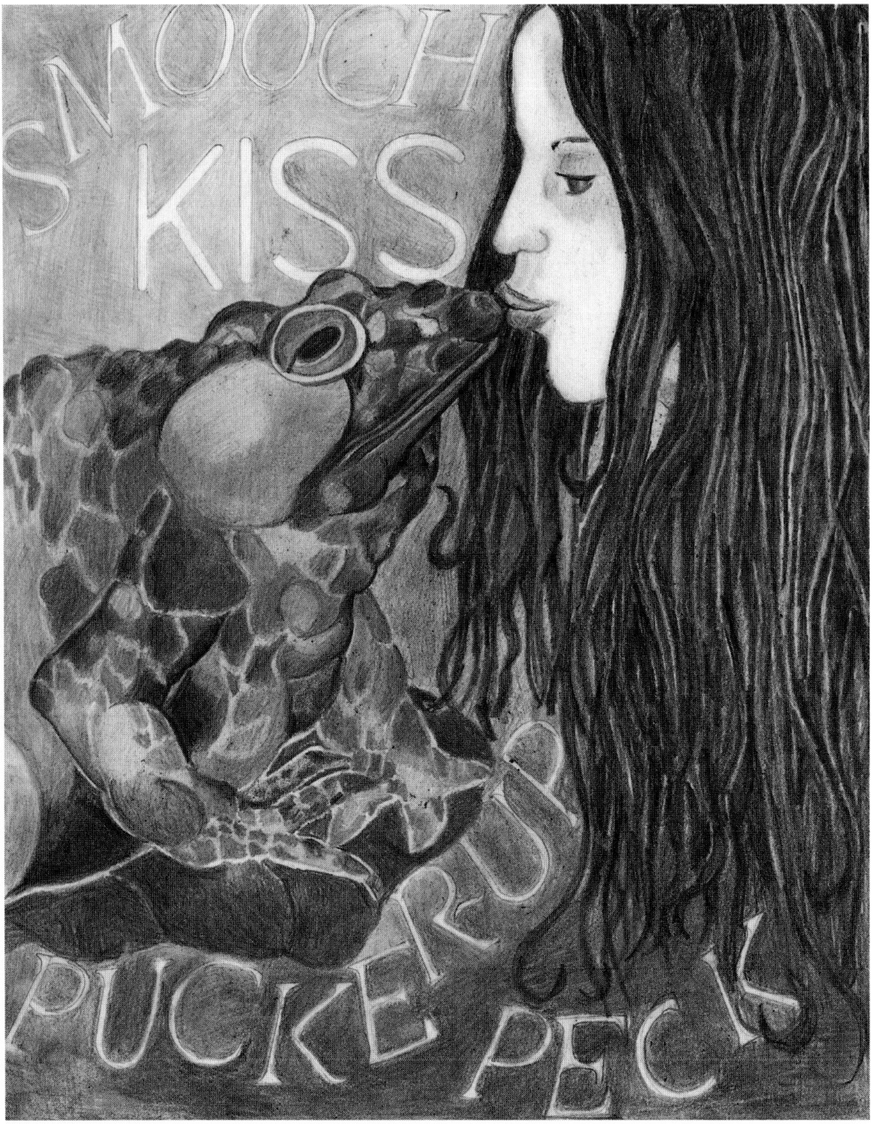
SMOOCH
KISS
PUCKER UP
PECK

The changeling croaked trying to say yes, but of course it was only a croak. Alice smiled and reached down very slowly to stroke his back with one finger. The changeling felt a thrill. It had been a long time since anyone had touched him.

"Croak, croak," he sang, his throat blowing up and deflating with a deep froggy sound.

"Oh, you are so special. Do you think I could kiss you?" Without waiting for further permission, she leaned down and lightly kissed his head. In that instant he made a decision. He changed into a handsome young man. His hair was coal black and silky, his eyes were deep blue and his lips were a lush red.

[Was he handsome?]

[He hoped so, but he wasn't sure what a human would think was handsome.]

The girl stared at him, mesmerized, and finally in a faltering voice asked, "Who are you?"

"I am a prince. An evil witch turned me into a frog. Only the kiss of a beautiful girl named Alice, and the promise that she will marry me can undo the enchantment permanently." The changeling, cum frog, cum prince crossed his toes, and hoped that he wouldn't scare the lovely girl away.

"My name is Alice," she exclaimed, "but I am to be married to someone else."

"Oh no! Is there nothing I can do to get you to marry me instead?" the changeling begged.

The girl sat down, scattering rose petals which went whirling off in the breeze.

"What can we do?" she moaned.

"Don't you think true love like ours will win out," the changeling asked, "if we tell your father the truth?" He lifted her out of the petals and stroked her face. He felt such happiness as he had not known since he had crashed on this world.

"But how would that help? No one believes in magic. It doesn't exist. My father will never believe us."

"I will prove magic exists to your father, for if you cannot promise at once to marry me, I will be trapped again in the body of a bullfrog under the enchantment of the witch."

"How will that prove to my father that there is magic?"

"Wait just a bit, and after I turn back into the frog, take me to the castle and tell your father your story. He won't believe you, but make him promise that if your kiss can turn me into a prince, we can be married."

The changeling slid back into the body of the bullfrog, making himself just a little bit bigger this time, and jumped into Alice's outstretched and waiting hands. She carried him carefully back to the castle and went straight to her father with their story.

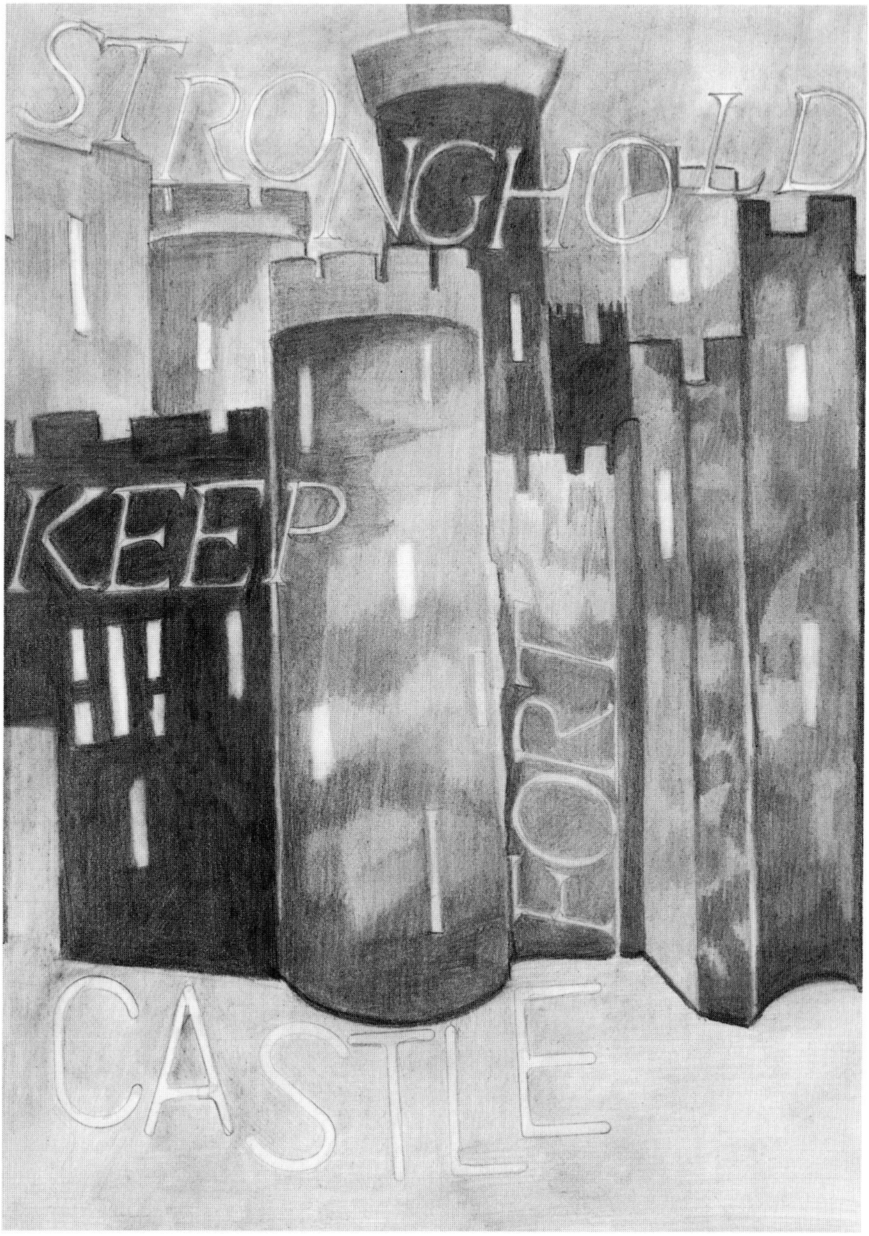
STRONGHOLD
KEEP
FORT
CASTLE

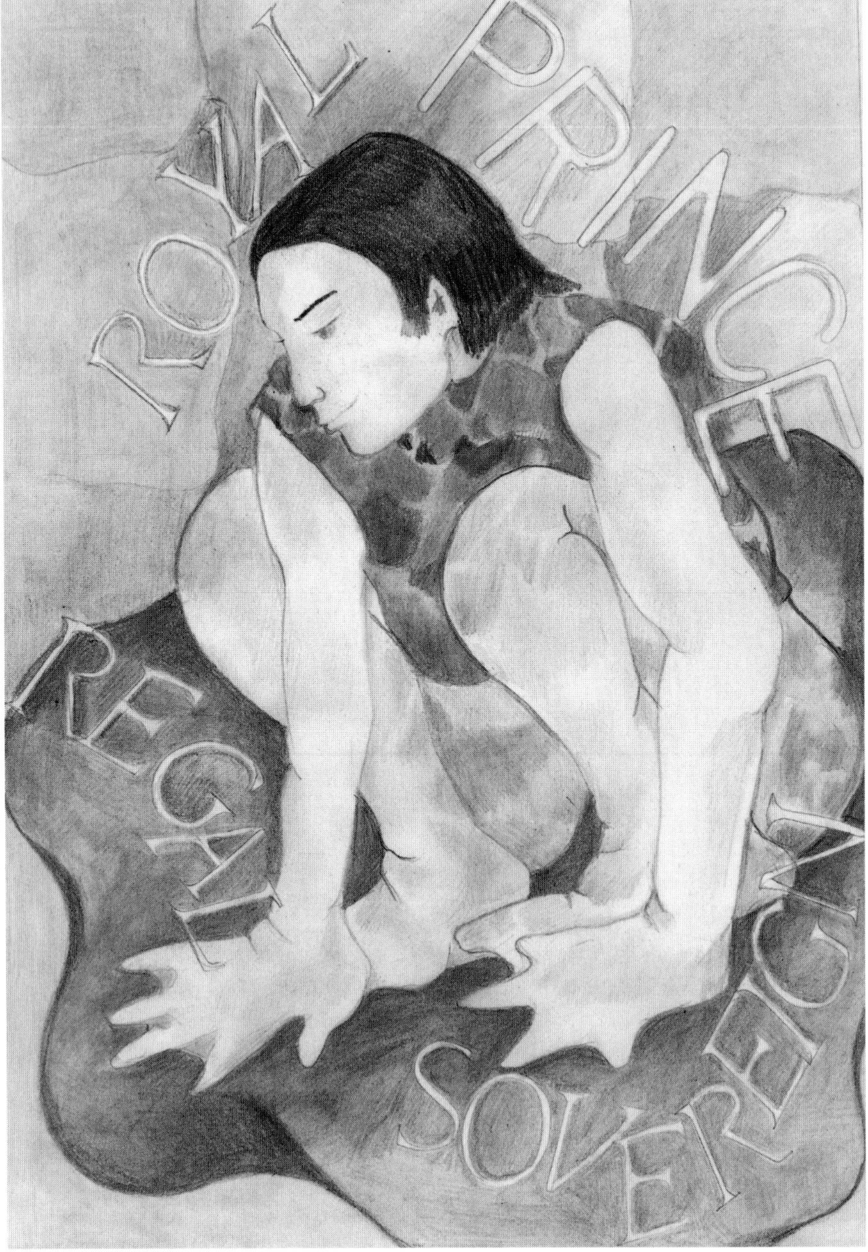
ROYAL
PRINCE
REGAL
SOVEREIGN

Of course, Alice's father, who was also the King, laughed loudly when Alice told him about the frog prince and held out the beautiful bullfrog for him to see. He stopped laughing when he saw how serious her face looked and because he loved her, he let her kiss the frog, who was really a changeling, but transformed himself into a tall and stately prince instead of the big-footed, three-eyed alien from the planet Cigam that he really was.

Even so, her father, the King, fainted from the shock. Alice and the Prince knelt down and fanned him with a lily pad until he awoke. He grumbled and mumbled, but kept his promise and gave permission for Alice to marry the changeling.

[Oh goody! Is that the end?]

[I think you guys always have to ask that. No, it isn't the end.]

The Prince, whose name was Nilrem, and Alice had a beautiful wedding in the castle garden, and Prince Timothy and Sir Edmund tossed rose petals at the bride and groom and then ran to the pond to hunt for tadpoles.

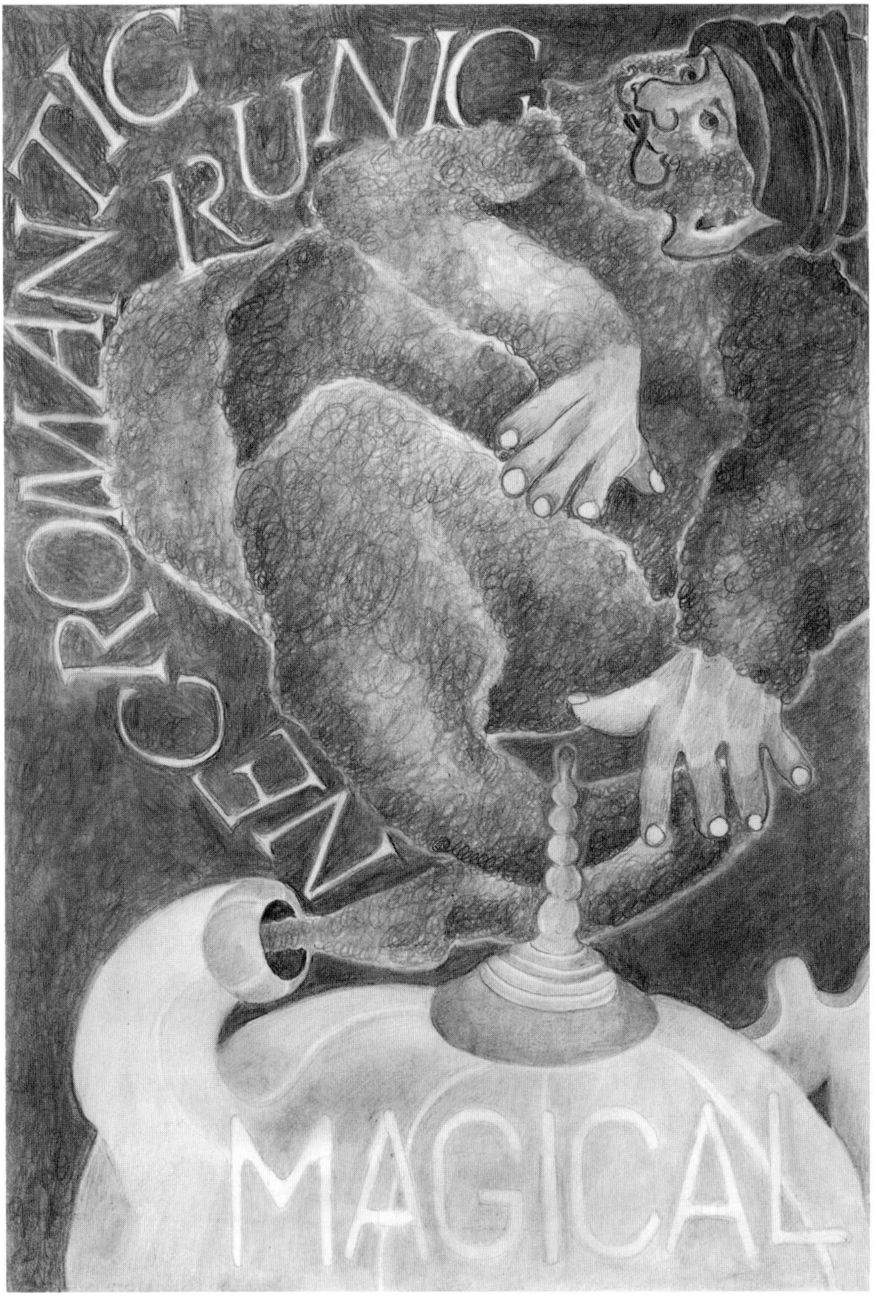
ROMANTIC
RUNIC
NECROMANTIC
MAGICAL

Now you might be expecting me to say that everyone lived happily ever after, but that isn't quite what happened. You see, the King was sure the whole thing was a trick and that the Prince was a charlatan, and so he hired spies and had them watch the Prince night and day. He was positive they would report something to him, but they never caught Nilrem at anything, because of course, even when he closed his eyes, his third eye always stayed open and warned him of intruders.

As the years passed, many magical creatures were reported in the kingdom, particularly by the King's spies who seemed to see an abnormal number of such events whenever they weren't watching the Prince. Many reputable people made these reports, but no one ever convinced the King, for he himself never saw a single dragon, pixie, genie or witch. Not a unicorn, nor flying horse. No fairy godmothers or wizards or anything magical at all.

The King tried decreeing that there was no magic, but the rumors could not be put to bed. He tried offering rewards to anyone who captured a unicorn, but although many people saw Alice hugging one, no one could catch it. He tried punishing people if they claimed to have gotten riches from a genie because he was sure they had stolen them. He even locked up all their lamps, but the only thing that changed was that people lived in dark houses. There was nothing he could do to stop people from believing in what they claimed to have seen.

More years passed and the King grew old and his beard turned white and he became frail and sickly. At last, he lay on his death bed with his children, grandchildren, nieces and nephews gathered around him. Each one kissed him, said their good-byes and left the room until finally, only Nilrem was left." My King, is their anything I can do for you?" he asked.

"I must admit, you have been a good and true husband to my daughter, but I still do not believe you were enchanted. Before I die, I would like to know the truth. Who are you?"

Nilrem looked at the old man, anxious and pale on his death bed. It was a dying wish, so Nilrem slid into his true form and stood humbly before the King.

"Sire, I am Nilrem, a changeling from the planet Cigam, who crashed on Earth many years ago. I did not mean to trick you, but I was very lonely and needed hugs. Hence, the disguise," Nilrem explained and slid back into the princely form he and the King knew so well.

The King turned very pale and gasped, his eyes full of wonder. "Oh my! All these years I have been wrong. You were enchanted!" The old man took one last breath and died believing in magic.

So you see, sometimes, seeing is believing, but other times, believing is not seeing.

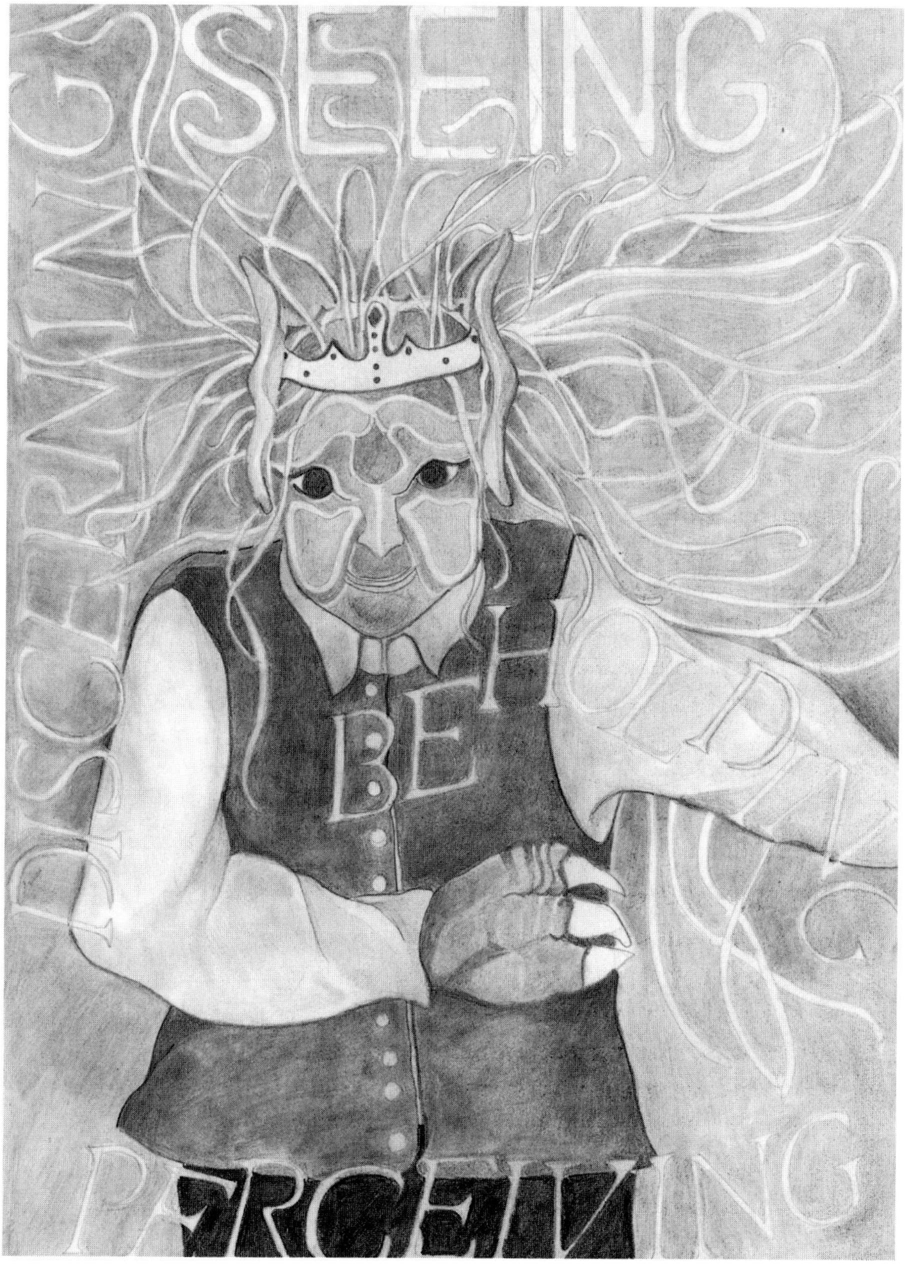
SEEING

XXIII

Louisa went straight to Mom, but Cindra stayed in my lap.

"Andrew," she whispered. "Do you think Mr. Chalder has a fairy godmother?"

"I don't know, Cindra. Didn't you just say you thought he was a changeling?" I whispered back conspiratorially.

"Maybe, but even if he is, he seems so sad. I thought if he had a fairy godmother, she might be able to make him happy."

I patted her head. "Then I hope he has one. Oh, look, here comes Dad."

"Well kids, I think we're here for the night," he sighed as the drumming rain thudded on clay. It was only three in the afternoon, but outside the day had been consumed by coal-black clouds.

Mom turned the torch down. "Let's get some sleep."

Cindra and Louisa cuddled up to Dad's bulk and within a few moments were softly snoring. Mom paced a while and finally sat on the ground by the cave entrance to keep watch.

I wanted to sleep, but the torch light lit the lower half of the tunics and I found myself staring at aliens. The first panels showed them as we knew them: the Water People, wafer thin in their hovels; the Natives in the caves, eyes half-lidded or closed. Not a human was visible, and yet the Natives sat as if waiting for a question, waiting to be mined. Somewhere in the sixth panel the aliens changed. The Water People were now standing, but static, and the Natives' eyes were wide open. By the eighth panel the Water People were on the move, filtering closer and closer to the mouths of the caves. In the tenth panel, the caves were emptied holes, round and foreboding, staring out from where the Natives had been. Under the hovels, roots were heavy with fruits and flowers. Tomas did know about the gardens. By the fourteenth the Natives and Water People were crawling out of a labyrinth of tunnels that fed the caves. By the seventeenth, the Natives were back sitting silently, and by the nineteenth, all was returned to its original state, down to the number of aliens represented in the first and last panels. Complete balance had returned.

"What are you staring at?" Mom asked. "You should be asleep."

"Mom," I said rolling over, "do you think the tunics could really be a story or illustrations of something Tomas discovered?"

"Who knows. They're certainly exquisite and Tomas is certainly an amazing artist!"

"Yeah. Strange though, in his medical survey and psych profile they didn't mention artistic talent."

"Those things are sometimes wrong."

"How often?"

"I think three percent of the time, or some such."

"Not very likely is it, that they could have missed such an obvious gift?" I said quietly.

"No, not very," Mom agreed.

"Mom, look at the fourteenth panel. Where do you think all those tunnels go?"

She stared closely at it, getting her face almost next to the fabric. "I don't know. Maybe just to the other caves."

"Or, maybe to something or someplace hidden?"

"Maybe, maybe not. I wish there was more light," she said. "These are really amazingly detailed."

She picked up the torch and beamed it right at the panels.

"How beautiful, how very beautiful!" she said "There are even stripes of shiny paint on the Natives. Some are covered in them."

It was true, Tomas had almost totally covered some of the Natives in miniaturized, glowing stripes.

Mom ran the torch around the panels, catching tiny silver lines in its spray, then did it again, once, twice more after that.

"Hey," I whispered. "Do it again. Look at the last panel. The Native there doesn't have as many stripes as the one that sat there in the earlier tunics."

She slowly moved the light again, stopping at each panel, finally exhaling. "So?"

"I don't know yet. Maybe those aren't the same Natives in the last panel as the first. I can't wait to look at these in better light."

"Right now, get some sleep, Andrew," Mom said wearily. She had dark shadows around her eyes, and her face was drawn.

"You should sleep, too, Mom."

"I'll try," she said.

I may have slept an hour, maybe two, when I heard Tomas breathe into my ear, "I must go. I will return, will I."

"What? Why?" I asked, instinctively knowing he was in his good time, in his taller, straighter shape.

"Andrew, find the answers."

Had he been asking for my help or saying he was going now to get the answers for us?

"Tomas, please don't go," I whispered to him.

"No, I must," he answered ambiguously.

"Tomas, where do all the tunnels you painted on the tunics lead?" I asked, hoping I could delay him.

"No knowing," he said glumly. "If only I knew."

I heard him slide out of the cave and sat up. In that instant I decided to follow him. I stepped out as quietly and as quickly as I could. Tomas' tunic lay discarded on the ground. The air was heavy with moisture, but it was no longer raining. I caught a glimpse of silver gleam and hurried after him, trying to keep him in sight without being seen, hoping he'd rescue me if I was attacked, praying I wouldn't be, sending a spray of mud and gravel rolling under my hurried feet.

Tomas didn't seem to notice. Whenever I caught sight of him, he seemed lanky and graceful, except for his wounded arm which he held stiffly against himself. Somewhere as the moon got higher in the sky, I realized we were headed for the caverns. I wanted to stop him, to get him to lead us back to safety, but he was too far ahead. He loped along with the speed and grace of some unearthly night vampire, even less human than when he was the Beetle. I ran now, not caring if Tomas heard me, hoping he would stop, would turn, shift downwards and scuttle towards me with a smile, but he didn't. The distance between us stretched out. I rounded a hillock just in time to see him reach a cave. In a burst of energy I raced to the entrance, but he had already disappeared into the blue-black maw of a tunnel. Breathless and suddenly frightened, I crouched behind a rock to wait. I watched vague sprays of stars gather in the sky, trying to see if their positions changed so I could tell how much time was passing. Nothing, I thought and awoke from an unexpected sleep in confusion. Something had screamed in my dream, but the night was silent and empty except for the shrill drone of alien insects.

Sunrise brought me little comfort and no sight of Tomas. I gulped a big chest full of air and stood. I started back to the cave when I saw something move. It was pale in the early mist and seemed to be leaning in a tree. I crept toward it and stopped. A body was half-sitting, half-hanging over a branch, there against the tree, silent and in some way un-whole. I waited for the Water Person to move, but it didn't. I walked past, trying to look at it out of the corner of my eye.

It wasn't an alien. It was Hal Andrews, white as ice. I felt a scream rolling up over my stomach, out of my mouth, when a soft hand clamped over my lips.

"Ssssh," someone said. The hand was wet and smelled of salt and something else. "Quiet be, young Andrew." With his hand still over my mouth, Tomas pulled me away from the dead man, just as a Native and a Water Person wandered by absently in their half-formed way, ignoring us.

The new day was quiet. Something had passed in the night.

XXIV

Tomas pushed me along, keeping me directly in front of him so I couldn't see him.

"You should not come here," he said softly into my ear.

"I followed you, but lost you in the caves. What were you doing in there?" I demanded, my discretion suppressed by my fear and shock.

"They are there," he answered.

"I thought the Natives were missing."

"They are there," he repeated.

"So you went to find them?"

"No," he said simply. "I was, I went."

"Yeah? I know that! Why did you go?" I insisted.

"To finish it, but it is not over. Wait now," he finally said. "We are back."

His cave faced us, morning light just touching its entrance. His hands let go and he turned me to face him. He was standing in a pool of first sunlight. His pale body was covered in at least ten wide silvery stripes and his eyes were less brown than yellow.

"Tomas?" I asked. "What's going on? What's happening to you?"

"I am a ruined human."

"No, no, you're not. You're a great talent, a great artist. You painted those tunics. They are incredible!"

He laughed. "Once, I was incredible? Now what am I truly?"

"I don't know," I said honestly. "Did you find out what has happened to you?"

"Maybe," he said. "Go to your parents."

I started forward climbing slowly up the slope. When I glanced over my shoulder, he was gone.

"Mom, Dad," I called softly.

"Andrew, what are you doing out there? Where have you been? If your mother knew you were out all night, can you imagine your punishment?" Dad whispered to me as he jerked me into the cave. "Where were you? You had me worried sick!"

"Dad, Hal Andrews is dead, I think, hanging in a tree, icy white."

"What? Where is Tomas?"

"I don't know."

"Now listen to me, Andrew. Take all the tunics down, fold them up and see if you can find something to put them in. Then look and see what else we should take home for safe keeping."

"Shouldn't we leave this stuff for Tomas?" I asked.

"Once the Miners find out about Hal Andrews, they'll come looking for him."

"What will they do to him? He didn't kill Mr. Andrews."

"Maybe not, but the Miners need to blame someone and they are afraid of the aliens, so that leaves Tomas and maybe us."

"Dad, why haven't the Miners tried to figure out what's been happening? They've had years to work on it."

Dad sighed. "There isn't time for this discussion, Andrew. Besides, it's too late. People are being murdered. Now, get busy."

I carefully pulled the tunics down. Silky and delicate against my fingers, they shimmered with color as they rippled in my hands.

"Whatcha doing?" Cindra asked me.

"Folding them up so we can take them home and hide them for Tomas."

"Why?"

"Cause Dad thinks the Miners are going to destroy anything we leave here."

"Even Tomas' picture books?" she asked.

"What books, Cindra?" I asked urgently.

She pointed to a dark, convoluted corner of the cave. Dad was talking with Mom, and Louisa was splashing water on her face as I pulled the first small book from a jumbled pile.

"Come on, hurry now, kids," Dad called.

I searched for a box or a bag and finally settled for wrapping everything in a blanket with the four corners tied together.

"Ready?" Dad asked.

The cave looked forlorn stripped of its color. We stumbled down the hill and had barely gotten onto level ground when we saw the Miners. They were all there, all working together, headed by the tiny and furious Mrs. Pattison.

"Go home with Mom, quickly," Dad said.

"But, Dad, you'll have to come home alone," I protested.

"Go," he said again.

I heard Mrs. Pattison say, "Hal Andrews is missing."

"He's dead," I heard Dad say.

"So, your pet has killed someone," Mr. Petersenes said, and then we were out of earshot.

Mom hurried us along.

"Mom, I don't care what the Miners say, Tomas didn't kill anybody."

She smiled. "I doubt if he did either, but we can't prove that. We don't even know when Hal Andrews died."

She was right. I thought I had heard someone or something scream, but it could have been a dream, or it could have been an animal or even one of the aliens. Even if it had been Mr. Andrews, I had no way of proving where Tomas had been or what he had been doing out in the black night like an interloper.

We made it home and Mom took a post at the gate. Cindra and Louisa crawled onto a bed as I dumped my load. First thing I did was to put the tunics into plastic storage bags, seal them and hide them in the cold cellar. Next I opened a little book. Perfect handwriting, in pale orange ink, greeted me.

The first storm howled in on us today. Although the others thought it was unbearable, it sounded like a calling to me. I wondered what the Natives were calling for? I wondered whom they were calling to? Of course, I asked in the caves. The other Miners said it was a useless, irrelevant question. They proved to be right because I got no answer. It is very lonely here. I am having a problem viewing the Natives as creatures only to be milked and mined for information. Yet they give no sign of personality or feelings.

The change from entry to entry was marked only by the skipping of a single line.

Months have passed, and I am convinced that it is wrong to approach the Natives as if they are computers. They are not machines, programmed to meet our needs. I have stopped asking questions the company would approve of. Other Miners are frustrated, but I think the greatest secret here is what the Natives are actually like. I have begun to phrase my questions so as to ask about their lives. Yesterday a Native's eyes popped open, yellow, clear, lucid. It did not answer my question. Instead it gave me a technical tidbit that the company will love.

A second howling. The new Miners came prepared. They drugged themselves. Almost everyone who had been here from the beginning joined them in the sleep of the damned. Only Maria and I stayed awake. She is a very nice woman, quite lovely really. The howlings were very loud, but she began to dance, as if she could hear an orchestra behind the noise. She drew me in, and I could just hear what she must have heard so clearly and so completely. When it was over, the silence was unbearable. I found I almost wanted the howlings to recommence. That night I went out to watch flocks of comets crossing the skies and saw not only that incredible sight, but also my first aliens in motion. Amazingly, not one of them looked up to the performance above them, but moved onward in a flowing, liquid-like way. Yes, that was it. They flowed like water, one rain puddle meeting another. Water People.

Maria and I found ourselves caught in a rain storm the other day. The downpour was flooding the road, so we climbed a hill. Soaked and cold we found a cave to wait it out in. We were lucky, as it was empty of alien life. There are lots of small animals here. My favorite is a bit of a thing with soft fur and a silvery nose like velvet. I call it a Velveta, but Maria says one of the Natives calls it a Raosta. How she got that tidbit I'll never know, but she obviously didn't consider it pertinent as she shared it with me. The Miners are becoming more and more secretive since Marty Isinweitz made his fourth big find! I almost wish he hadn't. Maria feels the same. She's a biologist by Augmentation, and is fascinated with the animal life here. She's had a few small successes. No one but me would consider my best finds important, but they are leading me on and I know it is to something auspicious. Luckily for me, the Natives have given me several more good pieces of info, so I have been able to satisfy the Company.

XXV

"Dad's back," Mom announced.

"What happened?" I said, closing the book and dropping it back into the pile.

"They were very angry. Frequently people are angry rather than admitting to fear. I got them calmed down until they saw Andrews' body. That shook us all!"

"Us?" Mom asked.

Dad nodded and took a deep breath. "At first I thought it looked drained of all blood, it was so white. All kinds of vampire legends bubbled out of my childhood. I even backed away, expecting his eyes to suddenly roll from side to side and his teeth to slide out of his mouth alongside some hideous scream. It was startling, but when we got close, it was something else altogether. Hal was coated in a hard shell and the shell was icy white. Only his eyes were free of it. Green, startled eyes," Dad sighed.

"Like Philippa's mother," I said. "Surprised!"

"Yes, surprised," Dad confirmed. "It was very quiet for a few minutes, and then, still silently, the Miners left and went home. Just left the body hanging there. I came home for the decontamination suit and gloves. I'm at least going to bury the poor man."

"I'll help," Mom said.

"No, Rebecca, I think Andrew should come. I'd rather not leave the girls without an adult right now. If we're not back in a couple of hours, come looking for us. Oh, and if Tomas comes by, keep him here."

"Dad, you don't think Tomas did this, do you?"

"No, Andrew, I don't. I doubt seriously any human could have caused this."

"Did the Miners say whether Philippa's mom was all chalky like that?" I asked.

Dad shook his head.

"Dad, do you think Tomas is still human?"

"What do you mean, Andrew?"

"I followed him. He vanished into the caves and when he came out he had a lot more of those shiny stripes on him."

"Andrew, I have no idea what is happening to Tomas, or what is causing it. All of this is past me. We would need a whole team of Augments in fields not represented here to solve this one. Get the second suit and let's go."

We walked warily along the road. All the exposed clay was dark, like it had been rinsed in chocolate. I noticed a creeping, yellow vine crawling among the rocks, putting out twisted shoots tipped with sprays of rubicund spines.

It wasn't far to where Andrews hung. Tiny diaphanous fliers already buzzed about the corpse, especially around its wide, green eyes. I didn't remember him having green eyes. We dug the grave first. The dirt proved to be brittle, though I had assumed it would cut like pudding after the rain.

It took a long time to make a hole the size of a man. I dug and thought. Looking back, it seemed Tomas had known while we were still at the Club that Andrews wouldn't return. Looking back, it also seemed as if Tomas knew lots of things, but on the surface of it at least, didn't remember how he knew. I decided not to point any of that out. Dad might think Tomas was hiding something, and my instincts told me we had to trust him.

We donned out suits to move the body. I thought the chalky shell and rigor mortis would make Mr. Andrews rigid, but instead the body crumpled on itself as we tried to move it. We jumped back and it fell flat, face down, causing a shower of slimy white droplets from the body to splatter our faceplates. We bent over, each took an end and, as fast as we could, plunked him into the hole just as he had fallen, face down, afraid he would disintegrate completely if we turned him over. As we straightened, I looked back at the tree. Directly behind where Hal Andrews had hung was the oozing body of a dead Water Person, green-eyed, its position perfectly matched with where the human had hung in the tree.

"Dad," I called into the phone of the suit and pointed.

"What the devil?" Dad stammered.

I glanced back down at the corpse in the hole. Along its back was a body-like imprint in the remaining shell that coated it. Dad knelt by the grave and poked at the body.

"Let's turn him over," he said.

We reached in and our fingers went through the shell as if it was softening. I felt like I was going to throw up into the suit. I swallowed something acrid and tried to calm myself and my stomach. We flipped Andrews over and more of the shell melted away. Hal Andrews' sky blue eyes stared at us. Dad closed the dead eyes and stood silently, stunned.

He finally stuttered, "What a mess. Let's cover it up!" I could see through the faceplate of his suit that his face was white.

When we had finished, we turned back to the alien corpse where it hung. Dad prodded it gingerly. It immediately lost its form, melting into a gelatinous sheathing devoid of humanoid shape. It was too much for me. I ran, tearing off my hood, doubled over and threw up. I straightened and wiped my mouth on my sleeve.

"You all right?" Dad asked me.

"I guess so. Can we go home now?"

"Absolutely! I've got a lot of questions for a lot of people. I'll lay odds the Miners have seen this before. Nobody seeing this for the first time could have walked away as calmly as they did."

Me, I wanted to run away as fast as I could. I wanted to wipe the images of the crumbling man and the dissolving alien shell out of my mind. I wanted to forget them, erase them, but I doubted I was ever going to be able to.

We headed home. The light was getting edgy, blinking around threatening clouds. I noticed there was an eerie calm to the air.

"Let's hurry it up," Dad said. "The sky doesn't look very welcoming."

We hadn't gotten far when a streak of lightning flung itself into our path nearly sizzling us. Dad looked for cover, but we were on an open stretch and it didn't look good.

"What now, Dad?" I asked.

"We run, again," he said. This was getting tiring, running all the time.

We were almost home, when I saw Tomas, standing naked, head back, mouth open, arms outstretched.

"Tomas," Dad boomed, running at him. "Good grief, man, let's go!"

He faced Dad, his eyes deep yellow, hair and stripes shimmering in the electric light. "Go on, Stephen," he said. "Hurry."

"I'm not leaving you here," Dad said, planting his big, stubborn body in Tomas' way. "If the Miners find you . . . " He let the sentence trail off.

"They went back to the Club," Tomas said. I noticed his speech was clear.

"Tomas," Dad said, "when we buried Hal Andrews, we found a dead Water Person behind his body. When we touched it, it disintegrated. Rebecca and I need to know what's going on."

"Go home, Andrew and Stephen. The dark rains will last for weeks. Stay in the house. Eat from the garden. Be safe. When it's over, you can return to the caverns."

He slipped past Dad with a long stride, and ran off towards the hills. Another streak of lightning cursed the sky, and I pushed Dad to start him moving. Night-like light was falling fast as the storm ate the rest of the day and expelled it in frightening explosions.

By the time we got home, Mom and the girls were pacing frantically. Mom threw her arms around Dad in an embrace that almost knocked the big man over, and made me and my sisters laugh until the next boom brought us to sudden silence.

XXVI

The next day, our watches told us morning had come, but it was pitch black. Despite the wind outside and the heavy smell of rain, the house was silent. Even our footsteps seemed muffled by the dark.

The girls and Mom used supplies from home to make thin doughnuts by torch light, and we fried them in hot oil and dunked them in sweet ground sugar. Mom brewed pale, blue tea, and we gorged on the doughnuts. When we finished the girls got out their dolls and began to play, giving each doll a pretend voice. I heard one doll say squeakily, "I'm Alvin Peter Pooterbax."

Dad and Mom began an outline of all the events, trying to piece everything that had happened together. I sat down on the floor with a wall behind my back and one of my notebooks in my lap and tried to concentrate on a story. I closed my eyes to think and froze. The familiar rhythm that always accompanied rain on the roof at home wasn't there. I leaned back to listen for the missing sound and jerked away. The wall had given under my weight. I poked it with a finger. The soft slosh of liquid moved under my hand. The walls were engorged with rain water.

My parents were still talking. I peered over their shoulders at the lists they were making. They weren't having much success connecting the disparate events they had written down. Tomas was at the top of the list, then Mrs. Brandt, Caroline and Hal Andrews. Next they had the Water People. The howlings and the lack of a doctor, the lack of records and of a local government were lined down the paper. Missing from their list were the gardens, no visible alien children, the dirth of crafts, and the disparity between the Miners' discoveries and the way the aliens appeared to live. I wanted to point out what they were overlooking, but I knew they would resent it if I did. I left them to it without speaking and went to investigate my own discovery.

I took a torch, slid the crate away from the steps to the cold room and went down. The walls were bulging with water, which was slowly dripping into thin channels that ran through the floor to where the gardens grew below. The rain was feeding the gardens. I went upstairs to tell my parents, but they were arguing.

"I'm telling you, that can't be, Stephen! How could you think that?"

"You don't know what you're talking about, Rebecca!"

"Dad, Mom, can I talk to you?"

"No, Andrew," they said at the same time. "Don't you dare say a word."

I put my own notebook away and went back to the journals.

Maria and I have decided to wed, only there is no legal service here. Still the Miners are actually preparing a celebration and doing it cooperatively. When we go home we can sign legal papers. She is making a gown with Alice Tamairia's help, but of course I am forbidden to see it, so I am occupying myself with developing a theory I have. For several weeks, I went about tagging the catatonic Water People by marking them with a small, painless tattoo. Already I have found that although the same number of them are always sitting about, over time they are not always the same individuals.

Bingo, I thought.

I have marked the new ones in different colors. They seem to change every few months or more, especially after howlings, but where the new additions come from and where they go to I have no idea. I do not even know why they switch places or what triggers it. As for the Natives in the caverns, I have no way to track them. The caverns are riddled with tunnels and caves, and I am afraid to enter them too deeply. I've requested equipment from my company, but so far it does not seem to think it a worthwhile expenditure.

Today the Native that I mine in my cave laughed at me, I swear. Then it would not converse at all. The days seem to be growing shorter at this season, although my records last year at this time do not note such a phenomenon. Perhaps their year or seasons differ from ours, although I would think we would have determined this already. Or maybe it's an atmospheric phenomenon.

In three days we will wed, Maria and I. She had written her parents months ago, and only now have they sent a response. I don't think they're thrilled. I wish I could have met them before. Last night we watched shooting stars. It is so peaceful here. We hope to move into one of the deserted houses with windows in the ceilings so we can watch the stars all the time. The Club Miners are more and more secretive and paranoid. My studies continue and I have realized it will take years of observations to figure out the rotating population, much less the weather patterns. I started marking caves in hidden places and taking holograms of the Natives we mine while labeling which caves they occupy. I found each Native seemed to remain in the same cave at least while we are mining it. I don't know if they ever leave.

Today was our day. We had the ceremony outside, but no stars were visible. Everyone came and on the surface it was celebratory. Old Mr. Patts, he played the harmonica and everyone danced. He's a sharp old buzzard, Mr. Patts, and what a tune he can blow. In a moment, Maria and I will share our first night together.

We had just awakened this morning, not planning to work, when a horrible ruckus occurred. The Miners came screaming and storming into our room. There we were, huddled under our wedding sheets, and they barged in and jerked me, stark naked, from my bed.

—*Who the hell do you think you are, marking up our caves? We don't care what you do with the Water People, but leave our mines alone!*

Appleton slammed me back onto the bed.

—*I didn't know anyone owned a cave. I thought we could mine where we wished,* I said angrily.

—*Really, well you're wrong. You come in my cave again and I'll break your neck. You're not gonna steal my secrets!*

—*That isn't what I was doing.* They wouldn't let me explain.

Maria wouldn't either. She asked me how I could have done such a thing? It was our first fight.

"Hey, Andrew," Dad said, sitting down next to me. "What are those?"

"Tomas' journals! I'm still on the first one, but he was studying the Natives until the other Miners found out."

"I hope it's okay with him that you're reading those."

"He said I could, remember?"

"I guess he did. I hope he remembers. What was he studying?" Dad asked absently, picking up a journal.

"I'm not sure yet, but he discovered the Water People switched around a lot, even though the numbers of their population remained the same."

"Really? Where did they go? Did he say?"

"He didn't know? Maybe they just switched places, maybe they left to go somewhere else."

"Somewhere else?" he asked, getting more interested. "Did he find out where?"

"He didn't. The Miners went nuts and forbade him to continue his studies."

"Too bad," Dad said, flipping open a book.

It was all pictures. I had assumed they were all written. The drawings were obviously portraits, some of Miners, some of aliens, each distinctly drawn in beautiful detail and line that matched the precision of the script I had been reading.

"Well, I guess we were wrong. He always had talent," I said.

Dad flipped through some more notebooks. They were divided between drawings and writing.

"Wait, that's not Tomas' hand," I cried.

Dad flipped back to the front of the book and read:

I know Tomas would want me to make entries for him in written form. This is the second day he's been missing. I have such a sense of dread. Where could Tomas be? The weather was vile when he went out this morning. He was just going around the house to the garden. I don't think he planned to go to the caves, but some of the Miners say they saw him there. I've tried and tried to think back to anything, but he was just gone, poof!

I don't have time to write much! They just came with word. He's been found. Dr. Pease thinks he may have had a stroke. I haven't seen him yet. I'm going now to the Club. It's been three-and-a-half days. Where was he all that time?

We're back. Tomas is not doing well. He is very confused and cries in the night, sobbing into the pillow. I found his first drawings today. He never drew before, and now, no words, not since they found him. He is very bruised and I know it hurts him if I touch him, yet he presses against me constantly, hugging me, I guess for comfort. I hate to push him away, but he oozes something when he hugs me. His hair is turning snow white. His speech is garbled part of the time, but in the wee hours, he talks, as if during sleep everything is clear. Yesterday he spoke lucidly: *"This cannot be. Don't try. It will end us both."* I had no idea whom he was addressing.

There were five or six unused pages. Dad flipped over them until the writing resumed. Months had apparently passed. Dad began to read out loud again.

I miss the old Tomas. The baby is due soon and he seems excited, as if a small boy himself. He still warbles out of syntax, his grammar odd and elusive. I take him to the Club every morning where he sits in the same flowered chair, waits for an hour before his posture slumps and he gets up and seems to adopt an odd gait. At those times he seems to be more and more hunched. At night he sometimes draws and paints. Before he always said he was a visual nincompoop. The images he paints now are perplexing, very alien. When I asked where he has seen them he says, *"Somewhere once, someone saw."* I'm afraid, very afraid.

The baby finally came, three weeks late. I named him Tommy. Tomas watches him silently for hours. I found drawings of the baby. They show his deformity so clearly, even though it isn't actually very visible. I have feelings of panic that it is my fault, but Dr. Pease denies it. I can't stand much more of this. Tomas seems to know. He begs me not to take Tommy from him. He said clearly the other early morning, *"Tommy must stay here. The change will help him, save him."*

I can't stand it here anymore. I hate myself for not being able to stick it out with Tomas, but I can't. I'm going home. I've begged him to come, but he says he can't. He says he has to wait for it to be over, whatever that means. For me it's over now! Good-bye to these stupid journals, to mining and Miners. Good-bye to some maybe-sometime-recompense. I'll go crazy if I stay. Tommy and I are going home.

"Too bad," Mom said as she listened to Dad finish Maria's last entry. "Do you think the baby might have survived if Maria hadn't taken him away?"

"Who knows," Dad said. "There are so many mysteries here, I'm beginning to wonder if any of them fit together. They don't seem to."

They did fit. I could feel it, but not prove it, not quite yet.

XXVII

Ten days into what we decided to call the Black Storm, Mr. Harlin burst into our home. His eyes were wild and he could barely speak at first. After a little blue tea, he said, "Where is that creep? I'm going to kill him."

"Who?" Mom said calmly.

"Chalder, that insane half-man. Where is he?"

"We haven't seen him in a long while. What's happened?" she asked, her voice level and commanding.

"The Natives are wandering. Lots of them, all of them maybe. We had gone to the caves to start work again and they weren't there and, and then . . ."

"Who told you fools to go to the caves in the middle of this storm?" Mom asked.

"We have to earn livings, you know?"

"So? Are your livings worth your lives?" Dad interjected.

"How many came back?" I whispered, but no one heard me over the shouting.

Mr. Harlin's eyes seemed to lose focus and he mumbled his words.

"I was still outside, almost to the entrance when they came, softly padding out. They seemed much smaller standing up, but their eyes were burning, green flames. One of them carried Arnold in his arms and set him down where he twitched and twitched. Arnold has epilepsy, but it'd never been active. Now he twitched in seizure after seizure."

"Mom," I said as quietly as I could, "which one is Arnold?"

"I think he means Arnold Torguey, the short, chubby Miner with the sideburns."

Mr. Harlin stared at us, silencing us instantly. His eyes were wild and distant. "I hid from them. I had to. I didn't want to end up like Arnold. They didn't even look sideways, just walked right past me, but I didn't take any chances. I hid. Their eyes glowed so brightly, I was sure they would see me. I hid. I waited and when no one else came out, I went to Arnold. His eyes were open, but dull and glassy and I couldn't rouse him. I think he was in shock. I, I came looking for . . ." His voice trailed off.

"You left him there? And now you want to blame Tomas? Did you try to find the others?" Dad asked.

Harlin clamped his lips tightly.

"Tomas wouldn't have left him there," I said.

"He was with the aliens. He is an alien," Harlin hissed and then spat.

"Nonsense," Dad said cool-headedly, "now, let's all go to the Club and see if anyone has returned."

"No," Allen Harlin said. "I'm not leaving. I'm not going out into that blackness again."

"Fine," Mom sliced into the conversation. "Stay here alone. We're going."

"Rebecca, do you think we should take the kids?" Dad asked.

"I'm not leaving them here with that shivering coward, Stephen. Not with the Natives on the move. They are a lot safer out there with us than in here with him."

"Are you that sure of your ability to protect them?" Dad asked.

"No, but I'm that sure that Harlin won't even try," she said. "Let's go!"

Mom and Dad's torches cut a skinny path of light through the rain and dense fog, but only for a few yards before the black mist reflected it back at us like an opaque mirror. Cindra and Louisa grabbed my hands in the dark.

"Andrew," Louisa said, "can you see anything?"

"Course he can," Cindra said.

"Uh, sure," I said, choosing to lie rather than scare them. "Just follow Mom's and Dad's lights."

"What if we walk into mud in the dark?" Louisa whispered.

"We won't," I promised. I hoped I sounded more confident than I felt.

"Mommy," Louisa called. "How much further?"

"We should almost be there now," she called back.

We weren't of course, and Mom probably had no idea how close we were. Ten minutes later I began to worry.

"What be you doing out, Stephen?" we heard a familiar voice say.

"Tomas?" Dad asked, and I could hear his relief as he spoke.

"Yes, me."

"We're trying to get to the Club. Allen Harlin is holed up at our place, claiming the Natives did something horrible to the Miners. Did they?"

"Yes?" Tomas chuckled. "The Natives walked away from the Miners! That was the something terrible which was done to the humans."

"That's all?" Dad chuckled, too. "Where are the Miners now?" he asked when he finished his laugh.

"All returned. All mad, especially at Chalder."

"That I believe. How about Arnold. Is he okay?" I called out.

"Mr. Arnold! Left by his friends, but we returned him."

"We?" Dad asked, just as his torch swept the porch of the Club. "Tomas?" Dad said into the dark. There was no answer.

The Club's small earth bound generator buzzed dully like a swarm of tiny bees at the end of a long summer. "Been running that thing too long," Mom commented.

The lights were dull and at first I was sure everyone would be asleep, but as soon as we stepped through the doorway, we heard conversation.

"Hello," Dad boomed into the Club, for we saw no one. "Hello, hello," he called twice more.

Mrs. Pattison stuck her head out. "Oh my, you have come at last. We wondered if you had been swallowed up by the storm. Come, come."

Mom and Dad glanced at each other and followed Mrs. Pattison's hurried scurry.

"What's going on?" I asked as we came into a room of Miners, all spread out around drawing paper on the floor. It looked like a kindergarten classroom with a first assignment in progress.

"What's going on?" Dad repeated my question.

"We're drawing a map of the caves," Mrs. Pattison said.

"Why?" Mom asked.

"We're going to find Chalder," she answered sweetly.

"Why?" Cindra asked.

"Why? Why, to make him get our answers. We've suffered enough because of him."

"You told us he was a simpleton," Dad reminded her.

"He may be, but we are pretty nigh sure it's all an act."

"An act, I doubt," Dad said, shaking his head.

"You do, do you? Well if you'd seen him today, you wouldn't think that. Strutting with the aliens, head up, eyes flashing."

"Slow down," Dad said. "Exactly what did you see?"

"The aliens is what we saw." Philippa looked up with calm eyes and said, "The Natives walked right out of the caves in a procession with some Water People."

Those eyes were disarming, but it was her voice that caught my attention. It was soft, the acid edge missing. It made me nervous. Somehow she was more disconcerting this way.

"What else?" Mom asked.

"What else?"

"Yes. Did they threaten you? What details did you observe?"

"Did they threaten us? They're killing us, aren't they?" Mr. Brandt said angrily. "Or have you forgotten my wife and Hal?"

"Stop it," Dad said. "All you saw were the native peoples of this world walking around together. The only thing they did was to do something unexpected. That is not a crime."

"Just tell us exactly what you actually saw," Mom prompted.

"We saw what we saw," Philippa answered, her face awash in paleness.

"Yeah, but did anyone hurt you or try to?" I asked, thinking that now that the anger was gone Philippa was almost pretty. Almost, if she hadn't looked so disconcertingly ghostlike.

"Hurt," Philippa repeated. "Hurt, no. Accidents only," she added in a feathery whisper.

"Uh, Dad, did you hear that?" I asked, really shaken now.

"No, what Andrew?"

"Never mind." I was sure Philippa had found the Aliens when she had vanished. I looked at her grey eyes, but nothing flickered there yet. I sighed quietly. Maybe she was just in shock. Maybe.

"The Natives have always looked squat and wide when they were sitting, but standing straight-up, these were almost wiry," Caroline said from the corner where she sat in isolation away from the others.

Like the two Chalders. Beetle and human, I thought.

"Caroline is right," Mrs. Pattison agreed. "And they were herding the Water People along like cattle.

"And these thinner Natives," Mom persisted, ignoring the significance of the Water People and the Natives being together, "was there anything else odd about them?"

"They didn't have stripes," Petersenes said. "They were completely covered in that silver stuff."

"Right," Mrs. Pattison agreed again. "Even in this black soup, they had a low sheen to them."

"Yes," Caroline said, "but a few like Mr. Chalder still had stripes, not exactly broad stripes, just not quite connected yet."

"And Chalder was as naked as a jaybird," Philippa laughed, "marching around like some cheap imitation of the Natives."

"Maybe," Caroline started and stopped.

"What?" Mom asked.

"Never mind. I'm not sure," she said so quietly she might have only been talking to herself. "It was too hard to see much detail in the darkness and the rain."

I nodded, but before I could say anything, Mrs. Pattison hissed, "That low-life. He could have made things easy for us all this time. He's found some way to get whatever he wants from them and he never told us, never shared."

There was a general wash of anger as they went back to work. Mom and Dad motioned us back and tiptoed into the front room.

Before I followed, I tapped Philippa on her shoulder. "Are you okay?" I asked. She was still birdlike, but no longer had the strength I associated with the big black bird of Poe's old poem.

"Sure, Andrew," she said. "Why wouldn't I be?"

"Oh, I don't know? Maybe you met the aliens and had an accident?"

"Go on, Andrew. I'm fine, really." She squeezed my hand and left a white residue on it. "Oh, I'm sorry. It's chalk from the maps," she said. She began to sketch again. She had drawn the column and begun on what looked like a passage beneath it that appeared to connect to other passages. She was meticulously drawing under all the caves, as if the passages were everywhere.

"Phillippa, what is that?" I pointed.

"A way in," she said.

"In? To what? What did you get into?"

"Into the Club, of course."

I shook my head and it took me a moment to try a new approach. "Get into the Club from where?" I pushed on.

"From beneath, from the roots, from the caves," she whispered hoarsely.

I tapped the drawing. "That's where you were, isn't it?"

She looked at me blankly and said, "When?"

"When you met one of the aliens," I said gently. I hoped she would remember.

She didn't answer, but I saw her hands were shaking. I tapped the drawing again and accidentally smudged it.

"Look, look what you did," she screeched. "Now it's lost, lost, lost. Like me!" She was shaking and everyone was staring at us.

"It's okay, Phillippa," I said, trying to calm her down.

"Lost," she screamed and tried to hit me. "Lost."

"Let me help you," I said, grabbing her hands.

"Help me," she whispered and then like a banshee came at me, scratching and clawing.

I backed out of the room fast, as she cawed over and over, "Lost, lost, lost, lost!"

"They are crazy," I burst out as soon as I joined Mom, Dad and the girls, rubbing at a claw mark on my arm and another that ran down my cheek. Mom put her fingers to her lips.

"You may be right, but have a little discretion and use a little judgment, Andrew. Remember, we're stuck here with them, and they are definitely at a breaking point. Who did that to you?" she asked, pointing to my scratches.

"Philippa. I think she may be in big trouble," I said, trying to wipe the white powder off on my pants.

"They're all in trouble," Dad said.

"Maybe, but either Phillippa is an incredible actress or she is really over the edge," I insisted.

"Sorry, I couldn't help overhearing," Caroline said, joining our conference without warning or invitation. "I can understand why you're put off by us, but you're new here. You don't understand yet. This place has a way of taking a toll on people."

I glanced at Dad and saw him give a brief grimace at the comment.

"I know, I know, we can't claim the to be the nicest people in the world," Caroline said to him, "but don't be too harsh on us."

"You're nice, Caroline," Cindra said. "You aren't all grumpy like the others."

"Thanks, Cindra, that means a lot to me. Until you came here, I was wondering if I was just like the rest of them. Every one of us sacrificed something to come here in the hopes of winning the jackpot, and it looks more and more as if we have lost the gamble we took. Sometimes the only thing everyone seems to have in common is that we all try to make someone else responsible for the bad things that are happening. In this case, Tomas is the perfect scapegoat."

"What about Philippa? Why's she so nuts," I asked.

"Andrew, think how you would feel if you found your mother dead on an empty road, on an alien world, with no way to explain it. It might turn you a little strange, too, don't you think?" Caroline suggested.

"Yeah, maybe," I admitted. Maybe.

"And you?" Dad asked Caroline. "Are you a gambler, too?"

"Me? No, not really, but I still came here for the wrong reasons," she sighed. "Of course, I guess ultimately we all may have come for the wrong reasons."

"What do you mean?" Mom asked.

"Money. We all got caught up in the money we could earn here, didn't we? Isn't that why you came?"

"Originally, partly, I suppose so. But, we're smart enough to know that money isn't worth our lives," Mom pointed out.

"I agree. Still, I have to admit, I came hoping to make a big discovery so I could go home rich. But, this place is more than I bargained for. The people here barely speak to one another except to try and wheedle information out of each other. The only person who looks after anybody else is Tomas. He brings us our food, cooks for us, runs our errands, watches over us and never asks for anything. When Philippa's mother died, I saw him comforting the child."

"But, she hates him."

"I know. Everybody blames him for everything that goes wrong. It's easy that way. It's even easier because he got rich here, so they're jealous as well as a little scared of him. Despite his discoveries, the Miners treat him badly, and excuse it by saying he's crazy. But he isn't. He's kind and gentle. Knowing Tomas has kept me human. All the others care about is feathering their own nests. I think they would die to protect their precious finds from each other."

"It sounds like you're fond of Tomas," Mom commented.

"Does it?" Caroline frowned. "I suppose I am." She frowned again and rubbed her eyes. "I can't live like this anymore."

"And?" Dad asked.

"And, I'm scared. People are dying." She stopped then began again. "I've been thinking about Tomas. He was attacked, wasn't he? Like me? That's what's wrong with him."

"We think so, but no one, including Tomas, is sure," I said.

"Could what's wrong with him, happen to me?"

"We wish we knew. Tomas won't say," Mom said.

"Or can't," I corrected.

"I can see why. I'm not even sure I was attacked. It just didn't seem violent like that."

"Then what did it seem like?" Mom asked.

Caroline took a deep breath. "The Alien seemed to want to, I don't know, maybe hug me? Oh, it does sound so stupid, every time I think about it!"

The word "hug" made me think of Maria and Tomas, but before I could figure out why, Dad said, "The way the aliens absorb things still reminds me of *The Blob* or *The Invasion of the Body Snatchers*."

"Maybe the aliens really are trying to absorb us," I suggested as seriously as I could without laughing.

"Don't be ridiculous, Andrew! Blobs are only horror flick nonsense," he said. "I was only kidding."

"But, Dad!" I began again. This time Mom cut me off.

"Enough, Andrew!" She rolled her eyes toward Cindra and Louisa, and I clamped my mouth shut. They looked terrified.

There was an empty pause, so I asked Caroline, "Did you know that before his accident, Tomas tried to figure out the alien life cycle?"

"Really? What did he discover?" Caroline asked curiously.

"We're not sure. We don't know how much he remembers from before his accident," Mom said.

"That's odd. I remember it all, oh so clearly, so terribly clearly. I just can't describe it."

"Lucky for you, Miss Caroline, you remember," Tomas said quietly.

Our heads all turned in surprise. Tomas stood in the doorway, a light sheen glimmering over him.

"Tomas," Cindra giggled, "you're all shiny!"

He didn't come any closer, but even in the shadows I could catch glimmers of green and yellow in his eyes. He stood there shyly with a look I equated with embarrassment. His tunic hung lopsidedly and his hair hung in wild tangles.

I started towards him, but Dad put a restraining hand on me. Several minutes passed, I looked at Mom and Dad questioningly.

"Miss Caroline," Tomas finally said, plaintively, "help me?"

"Of course, if I can, Mr. Chalder," she said.

"You are a biochemist?"

She nodded.

"Good," he said, stopping and taking a deep breath, stopping again. "Can humans," he resumed with obvious difficulty, "exchange DNA through cell membranes?" The air whooshed out of his mouth as he finished in a strange whistle that I realized I had heard many times while we had been out in the black storm.

"Not people. Some very primitive organisms like bacteria can exchange DNA through cell membranes which are semipermeable. Why do you want to know?"

"Not people?"

"No."

His breath came in wheezes as he looked around frantically

and collapsed on the floor in a pile of arms and legs. Dad and Mom carefully helped him into a chair, where he fell asleep instantly.

"Why did he want to know that?" Caroline asked. She walked over to the chair and brushed his hair off of his face rather tenderly. "What goes on in that head, do you think? Why did he stay here all these years?"

Dad shrugged. "I have no idea."

"Caroline, I hate to ask, but have you noticed any changes in your interests since you were attacked?" I said.

"Not really, except, well, I've been humming and longing for music. I think maybe I'm looking for solace. I've never been very musical, but it's always comforted me."

"Well, Tomas, as far as we can determine, wasn't artistic before his accident, and now he is." I said. "In fact, now he is a great artist! You should see the tunics he has painted."

"What tunics?" Caroline asked.

"The ones he wears. When you hang them up side by side they make a mural. I think he got artistic after he was attacked."

"If he was attacked," Mom corrected. "Any other changes, Caroline?"

"None, except some sudden white in my hair from stress. Not unexpected since my mother was gray by twenty-one," she said.

"Not a very scientific survey, is it? We only have two survivors, no controls, very little data," I commented, remembering my recent school science labs.

"True," Caroline said, biting her finger, "but we can make lists of common traits and see what we get. It's primitive, but it's about all we have. Let's start with some background."

The lists took shape quickly. Both Caroline and Tomas had begun in research fields, with intense hobbies in the arts. In Tomas' case he had liked to write, and in Caroline's she had liked to act. They were unusual for Augments in that each of them had kept their hobby and each had been good at it. They weren't raised in similar environments; they weren't similar physical types. Caroline was brown haired, blue eyed, shortish and, although slender of bone type, a sturdy build. Tomas had been blonde, brown eyed, lanky and exceedingly tall. Neither had been very musical. That was the before. No one was absolutely sure that Tomas had been attacked, but assuming he had been, the attack had done more damage to him than Caroline.

His speech was impaired, hers intact. His crippled body was inexplicably blessed with temporary relief in the early morning hours. His lack of speech made him appear to have lost intelligence, but the truth of that was unclear. Physically a number of obvious changes had occurred. His hair, and sometimes his eye color, had changed; he could not maintain an upright posture; he was increasingly covered by a silvery, chitinous substance.

Caroline's initial confusion and speech stammer had vanished, but her hair was rapidly whitening. The bruises on her face and arm were turning to an odd coloration, perhaps slightly silvered. Of course, she had not been attacked thirteen years ago, so maybe it was too early to tell yet.

The last change was that both Caroline and Tomas seemed either to have, or to be developing, new means of creative expression in areas in which they had shown no previous talent.

"Well," Dad said, "what do you think, everyone? Any hypotheses or conclusions?"

"Yes, I'm scared stiff," Caroline said.

"Are you, Miss Caroline?" Tomas asked, rejoining us.

"Weren't you? Aren't you? And please, just call me Caroline. No Miss, okay?"

"Sure," he said, "just Caroline."

I heard a sound and caught a brief flash of Philippa at the doorway.

"Oh no," Caroline said. "Tomas, go, leave before the Miners come."

He sprinted out the door as the Miners arrived in a pack. Their silence was more frightening than their previous angry prattle.

"He's gone," Mom said. "Go back to what you were doing."

"Please, this isn't the answer," Caroline added. "We need to work together, don't you see?"

"Oh my, dear Caroline, your good natured personality has finally overwhelmed your common sense!" Mrs. Pattison said in a sugary voice that quickly turned nasty. "Stuff it, dearie, it isn't going to wash with anyone."

Caroline's eyes narrowed. "Mrs. Pattison, you are missing something. We are alone on an alien world, and all we do is blame the only person who might be able to guide us out of this mess."

"Hogwash, my dear," she said. "You have lost your senses since you were attacked. You seem to have developed a perverse attachment to the most dangerous person on this planet."

"He isn't dangerous," Caroline snapped, her cheeks turning pink.

I watched tensely, my eyes glued to everyone's furious and reddened faces.

"Enough," Mom commanded. "Everybody back off. Go on, go back to what you were doing."

They turned, perhaps a little too easily, to leave. Mr. Brandt looked over his shoulder and sneered acrimoniously, "I'd advise you Haldrans not to overstay your welcome. You either, Caroline."

"Mom," I said when they were gone, "I can't believe they just left."

A smile played across her lips. "I guess they didn't like my smile, or maybe it was my weapon." The cuff or her blouse flipped up as she waved her hand blithely. Twisted around her wrist was a famous and deadly Spaceman's Viper gun.

XXVIII

Mom and Dad woke us in the wee hours of the morning before the Miners stirred. They herded us home through the rain, with Caroline tagging along at the end of our parade. Each of us looked over our shoulders nervously at staggered moments, perhaps expecting to see an angry mob behind us. We arrived at the gate soggy and weary to find Tomas waiting on the porch steps, anxiously tapping one of his feet.

"Good, unharmed are you all," he said when he saw us.

"Let's get out of this rain," Mom said, hustling us inside. She had stood guard all night to insure our safety and looked exhausted.

It was cold and damp inside and out. The house had a funny smell to it, like freshly mulched gardens back home. The grey light that filtered through the ceiling holes cast an uneasiness that I couldn't put aside.

"I'm going to brew blue tea," Mom said. "Stephen, turn on some of our torches. It's gloomy in here."

Tomas scuttled back and forth across the room in a semblance of pacing. His edginess increased my own nervousness. I couldn't settle my stomach until Mom put a steaming cup of tea into my hands. The warmth traveled up my arms and I finally felt calmer, but Cindra and Louisa were huddled together, their faces painfully frightened. They were so little. What were they making of all this?

Tomas straightened his body and held his head high. He waved his hand around the room, and then beckoned Cindra and Louisa to him. "For little girls, something hidden here is. Something yummy. For it look. Search down low."

"Really?" Cindra asked. "What is it?"

"Really, yes. Look."

Giggling they dropped to their hands and knees and crawled about like two little puppies, sniffing in the cubbies and at the boxes scattered about.

"Is it chocolate? I smell chocolate," Louisa exclaimed, a smile spreading across her face.

"Search must you, then will you see," Tomas told her.

"Speaking of searches, we need your help with one, Tomas." Caroline said as she shook her hair out until it hung below her waist. I watched the whitening waves bob up and down.

"Help will I if I can."

Caroline cleared her throat and asked with just an edge of nervousness to her voice, "Do you have any idea what happened to you when you vanished?"

"Water People and the Natives were fitting together then," he said. It was the first time I heard him answer with more than "accident only" or "I was there".

"What? What does that mean?" Caroline asked very nervously.

He sighed and stared at her.

"Fitting into what, Tomas?" I asked.

"Fitting? Into the wholes they become."

"Wait, wait, I don't understand!" Caroline cried out.

"If only I still could speak."

"I'm sorry," Caroline said. "Let's try again."

"Look, look," Cindra interrupted, holding up what resembled three malformed chocolate bars.

"Where on earth did you find those?" Dad exclaimed.

"On Earth not," Tomas answered solemnly.

"What did you do, grow them on trees?" Dad asked him without thinking.

"Yes! See, see, see, Louisa, Daddy, Mommy! See, chocolate trees!" Cindra shouted.

"No, no, Cindra, it's only an expression, sweetie," Dad said.

"Sure, Daddy, sure." She winked right at him and bit another piece off the chocolate. "Told you, you shoulda asked about it." She licked her lips.

Everyone laughed.

"Okay, Cindra, Maybe I should have asked. I've learned my lesson. I should listen to my children."

"Uh huh," she said.

"So, Louisa, following up on that, what do you think Tomas means about the Aliens?" Dad asked.

Dad was humoring the girls, but Louisa took him seriously. She licked her fingers and said, "Maybe if they touch each other, they stick together, like chewing gum sticks to your shoes."

"Yeah!" I agreed giddily, relieved to participate in a little silliness. "Or they absorb each other, like the Blob absorbed people!"

"Yes!" Tomas actually yelled, making us all jump. He was so excited that as he nodded his head rapidly up and down, it made a distinct clicking sound.

"The Blob!" Dad said. "See Rebecca, the Blob! I was right to be scared of it when I was seven." He laughed until he had to take a breath to stop and then said, "But come on, Tomas, that's just a story."

Tomas looked downcast. "No, no."

"No? See, it isn't a fairy tale," I said, ribbing Dad some more.

"Could Tomas be serious?" Dad pondered dramatically, scratching behind his ear.

"All of you, stop this! This is a dangerous situation," Mom said, frowning at our momentary hilarity. "Andrew, be quiet. Stephen, I can't believe you would waste our time on this. Just let Caroline continue."

"This doesn't make sense, Rebecca. I have no idea what to ask next." Caroline paused. "Tomas, I don't understand."

It seemed we rarely understood Tomas. Neither he nor his words lined up quite right. Everything about him was a little out of alignment, like the doors of the houses. How many times had one of us thought or said, "I don't understand." Understanding Tomas always came back to understanding the aliens of this world.

"Try again to explain, okay, Tomas," I said gently.

"The Natives, the Water People joined, apart, joined, apart, joined," he chanted until even though I felt as if I should clap my hands in time and accompaniment, I still wasn't sure what he meant.

"Tomas, I've been here two years and I have never seen the Water People and the Natives together until a day ago," Caroline said.

"Well, so much for the Blob Syndrome," Dad said.

"Wait, don't discard it yet," I said.

"Andrew, the Blob ate people, but it never spit them back out. Let's just let it drop."

"No! Tomas, please, explain why they join?" I insisted, trying to understand without even knowing what joining meant.

The other three adults sighed in one simultaneous breath, but Tomas patted my arm and said quickly, "For the change."

"What change?" Caroline asked, her voice suddenly edged with what sounded like panic. She had to be scared. We all knew she was changing and that Tomas had already changed.

"To wholeness," Tomas answered.

"Wholeness?" she asked. "What does that mean?"

He shrugged and sighed. His body began to shake, but he didn't collapse yet into Beetle form. "Too late today for more," he said, finally giving up. His eyes faded to a yellowish brown instead of green, and his body seemed to curve inward on itself. A tear fell from one eye.

"Tomas, please," Caroline said, begging for a little more information, "can't you tell me more? What does it mean to join?"

"Memory gone. Random accidents only." His voice seemed to beg understanding that was past our ability.

"It's okay, Tomas. We'll talk when you feel better," Dad said as comfortingly as possible. "We'll find a way to figure it out."

Tomas scuttled into a corner. Cindra and Louisa looked up with chocolate covered mouths.

"That was yummy," they said happily.

"Are you done?" Mom asked with obvious amusement in her voice.

They bobbed their heads up and down.

"Then wash your hands and faces, and go play."

They bickered about what to play for a little before they found their jacks and invited Tomas to play with them, but he wouldn't. He looked sad to me. I noticed Caroline was also watching him.

"It's such a waste," she said. "How did such a brilliant man come to this? I wish I knew what has happened to him."

"Me, too," I said. "Me, too."

Mom broke into our conversation from the doorway where she stood watching the sky. "Well, if we don't figure this out soon, I'm afraid for everybody here. The storm is starting to lift and when it does, the Miners are probably going to erupt."

Dad nodded. While they talked I went and sat with Tomas.

"It must have been lonely for you here," I said. "I'm lonely and I have my family."

"Sadness, Andrew," he muttered.

"I bet. But you know, Mom and Dad won't desert you."

"Yes," he said and patted my hand. I couldn't tell if he meant he knew or they would.

"Really, we won't leave you!"

I thought I heard him mumble something, but his language was worse, as if the effort was draining him. His eyes drooped and he seemed to sleep.

Mom called me over to eat a sandwich. The food tasted good even though the bread in the sandwich was stale. I reached for a piece of fruit that lay on a plate. It was pale blue and tasted vaguely like oranges, but with the aftertaste of strong plums.

"Did you guys ever notice how Tomas' eyes close down when he falls asleep, sort of the way the Natives' eyes close when they quit answering our questions?" I asked as I nibbled at the fruit.

"Virtually all animals sleep with their eyes closed," Caroline pointed out.

"But when both Tomas and the Natives sleep, it's more like they turn off. It doesn't look natural."

"Andrew, Tomas is not a Native. He's a human being." Dad said.

"Yeah? Are you still sure about that?" I said back as calmly as I could. "What about the Native bands? How do you explain them?"

"None of this makes any sense," Mom said.

"To us it doesn't, Mom, but it will. Eventually, it has to!"

"And just how do you propose to figure it out, Andrew?" Mom asked me.

"Maybe we should start with what Tomas has already told us. Let's just say that some way the Natives and Water People do stick together for a while," I suggested.

"What would the purpose be?" Caroline asked.

"I don't know yet. We're stumbling about in the dark, but isn't that how a lot of scientific discoveries used to be made, by tripping over them?" I said stubbornly.

"That was before Augmentation. We've made great progress since then," Caroline said.

"Yeah? Were you Augmented to understand aliens?" I asked her.

"That's absolutely enough!" Dad said sternly.

"Everybody, calm down. Andrew could be on to something," Mom said more sympathetically than I had expected.

"I'm sorry, but please, Mom, Dad, humor me. That's how I found out about the houses being alive, by tripping over it."

"Not that again," Mom moaned.

"Give me a little credit, guys," I begged.

"All right, Andrew, but you be polite. You are only a boy," Dad said. I could almost hear the word "unagumented" in his tone. I went into a corner, and rested against the water-bloated walls, and sulked. They were never going to take me seriously. Nobody even looked in my direction. I gave up on being part of the conversation for the moment and just listened to my parents and Caroline.

"Do you realize we didn't even know about the howlings until we got here, yet the Miners are so scared of them, they drug themselves to get through the storms? How come they didn't report that?" Mom asked.

"What I want to know is why the Natives and Water People are moving about in the middle of this weather. I'm so confused," Caroline added.

"I guess we're going to have to ask Tomas," Dad said.

"Do you think Tomas will answer? Do you think he can?" I called from where I sat.

XXIX

The clouds parted, disclosing the stars and soon insect-like songs filtered back into the moisture laden air.

"How much time do you think we have before the Miners explode out of the Club?" I asked Mom after she tucked in the girls.

"Andrew, let's hope we have years."

"You think it'll blow over?" I asked.

"If not, I'm afraid they'll truly attack the aliens."

"I wonder if the aliens will know they have to protect themselves?" I said.

"That's absurd. They couldn't survive without self-protective instincts."

"You mean, no one and nothing we've run into before could survive that way," I corrected her. "Mom, Tomas didn't protect himself when the Miners beat him up, and the Water People and Natives normally don't even respond to us at all. They're sitting ducks."

"I doubt they are defenseless, Andrew, but I guess we have to consider all possible scenarios."

For no reason, my mind suddenly focused back on the tunnels in Philippa's map and Tomas' tunics. "Mom, do you remember the caves in Tomas' mural? Where do you think all those tunnels he drew went?"

"Honey, it was just a picture. I don't know how you could tell," she said.

"Yeah, but what if it's a picture of something real? Then what? The tunnels must lead somewhere, to something."

"Andrew, you sound like you're writing the script for a bad movie. It might just be a depiction of a natural geological formation." She shook her head and wandered over to Dad, who was napping in a corner of the room. I turned around to follow her and swallowed a yell as I bumped into Tomas.

"You're up!

He nodded. "So much to answer while I can."

"Yes, and before the Miners go off half-cocked," Mom added.

"This is a fear. Where is Caroline?"

"Hey, everybody, Tomas is awake," I called out.

We gathered over blue tea and sipped quietly for a few minutes before attacking our problems and mysteries again.

"Tomas, are you able to answer some questions now?" Caroline asked.

He nodded calmly. "Try I will."

I watched him as he sipped his tea. Even his face now had a sheen on it that foretold a full silvering. His eyes were no longer brown, but a yellow-green. His features were more like the holo-photo he had shown me than I had noticed before. It was as if he was both coming closer to and getting further from his old self at the same time. Moving into what?

Caroline began. "Stop me whenever you want to, Tomas. You said that the beings of this world spend a lot of time apart."

"Unjoined," he added.

"Okay, unjoined," she acknowledged.

Caroline didn't seem to see any significance in the word, but I did. Apart and unjoined had different connotations. Apart could mean at a distance, but unjoined seemed to mean disconnected, taken apart.

Caroline had already moved past the new word and was saying, "Let's try something different. Andrew thinks that both you and the Natives switch off, sort of turn off when you sleep."

Tomas repeated ambiguously, "Sleep. Dormant. Good. Go on, on, on."

Caroline glanced at me before she said hesitantly, "Andrew also thinks you are a warped version of the Natives."

He drew his head into his shoulders and smacked his lips like the Beetle, but his eyes at that moment were very human and very sad.

Caroline paused with tears welling up in her own eyes. "I can't go on," she said too softly for comfort.

I jumped in quickly and picked up the conversation. "My turn. During the Blob syndrome, when the aliens are together, where do they go, Tomas?"

I saw Mom grimace and shake her head at my question. I could see her lips form the unpronounced words, "Stubborn kid."

I persisted despite her. "Do they retreat underground into the tunnels?"

"Except for I, who remains unjoined, truly a half a life, neither Water Person nor Native nor Human. I stay here always."

"See, you guys," I said.

"Andrew, you're putting too much significance on Tomas' answer. It could mean several things," Dad intervened.

Of course, Tomas' answers could always mean several things. It was hard to argue about that.

"Do you know exactly where the joined individuals go?" Dad asked Tomas, rephrasing my question.

"I cannot remain with the joined ones. Afraid for me, afraid of me, be they." The sadness in Tomas' eyes deepened.

"So, you don't know for sure if they go anywhere, do you?" Dad said.

A smile twitched at the corner of Tomas' mouth. "For sure, beyond the surface."

I smiled to myself at the possible double meaning, wondering if it was intentional or not. Maybe Tomas hadn't followed any aliens below ground, but I was positive that he knew the truth. I wished he could just answer more clearly.

"This is pointless, Stephen. There is too much at stake here to decide what to do based on wild guesses and speculations," Mom said skeptically.

"But, Rebecca, what if the Water People are actually trying to join together with the Natives, and not trying to attack anybody?" Caroline asked unexpectedly.

"But why would they try to join with humans?" Mom insisted. "Wouldn't that be unnatural."

"Case of mistaken identity maybe?" Caroline suggested.

"Yeah," I said, "maybe they can't tell us from them."

"That is ridiculous!" Mom practically yelled. "We're humans. We don't look anything like them. We don't even smell like them."

"Is Andrew right," Tomas said in one of his sentences that was neither question nor answer.

Snapping her fingers as if accompanying herself with a musical rhythm, Caroline asked timidly, "Tomas, if the two species of Aliens do join and separate in order to change through some sort of symbiotic relationship, and if your accident was a joining, is that what changed you?"

"To change?" he asked simply.

"Are you still changing?" she asked again with bulldog insistence.

"It is vague, lost in a fog."

"But you think so?"

"I feel it, seek it, fear it. Do it, I do not know?"

Caroline half sobbed. She had to be terrified. It was a nightmare, a horror movie coming true, and she might be the character about to mutate into a monster.

"Tomas, are you frightened when you go out in the storms?"

"Yes, Caroline. Alone and frightened."

Dad had begun pacing. He stopped by the front door and froze.

"Uh oh! We're out of time. Look outside!"

Miners stood there, light torches in hand reflecting on twisted faces. They knotted closer together as the whole human population of Miners World pushed through our gate, clearly much bolder and far more dangerous than that single alien who had crossed the same threshold a few days before.

"Where is Chalder?" they demanded in what seemed like one, big voice.

Mom was trying to shoo Tomas into the back room, but he stood his ground.

Dad stepped out onto the porch to address them. He straightened up to his full height, chest out, increasing his size. "Tomas is not the issue here," he said calmly.

"Like heck he isn't," someone yelled. "If it weren't for him, none of this would have happened."

"You should stop talking such nonsense. Tomas is the biggest victim of all. His life is irretrievably destroyed. He lost his wife, his child, his career, his ability to communicate. In fact, if you stop and think about it, this is not an issue of blame. Something is happening on this world that we do not comprehend. If it is premeditated, we need to negotiate. If not, we need to be able to take precautions so we can all get back to mining."

"Yeah? Like what precautions?" a voice asked.

"When we understand it all, we'll let you know. Until then, go home and stay there if it's storming," Mom said.

"Oh no, we're not likely to give you an advantage like that. What did Chalder do, discover the key to life or time travel and get you guys to go into cahoots with him for the money?"

"Go home," Dad repeated, a little anger showing in the tone of his voice. "I don't want an advantage. At this point, I just want everyone to survive. Go home."

They muttered and their voices began to rise. No one moved. The tension was overwhelming. Finally, I saw an arm flash, beckoning everyone back through the gate.

"Come on," I recognized Mrs. Pattison's voice. "Let's go talk in private."

Some more muttering reached us, but the Miners retreated out of view. When we checked, they were nowhere to be seen.

"Rebecca," Dad whispered, "this is your call. Where will we all be safest?"

"The caves, I think, but even there it's a bit if-y. These people are terrified. They've been isolated from other people, even each other, far too long. The most frightening thing is to see them trying to work together. They're on the verge of being very dangerous."

"How much time do we have before it all blows?" Dad asked.

"Not much, I'd guess," Mom answered. "Let's pack what we need and get out of here. Tomas," she said, turning to him, "will you take us, and can we get there without being noticed?"

"Yes, Rebecca."

"Good," she answered and I heard her mutter under her breath, "and let's cross our fingers."

XXX

Tomas and Caroline stood watch by the gates while we tried to gather a few things of ours and those of Tomas' we thought important. We didn't have much expectation that the Miners would leave the house intact. Mom pulled out a carefully crafted silver and aluminum box.

"What's that?" Louisa asked.

"Insurance," Mom said. "Go on now, Louisa, we're almost ready. Andrew, go tell Caroline and Tomas, another twenty minutes."

I popped out the front door and looked around for them. "Mom, Dad," I called, "where are they?"

I walked around the house. Nobody. I peeked outside the gate and pulled back quickly. Tomas and Caroline stood in the starlight pressed hard against each other, not with passion, but hard, as if they needed to get closer than was humanly possible. They stared past each other vapidly, their bodies locked and wooden.

"Caroline, Tomas," I called softly. They remained in the trance. I moved closer. "Caroline, Tomas," I said again more loudly. I poked them with a finger. Nothing happened. I pushed my nose close to them, trying to be sure they were alive, and something grabbed my wrist. I screeched.

"Shssh," Caroline whispered hoarsely, her fingers squeezing gently. "What's going on?"

"You tell me," I said, pushing away. "You guys were locked in stone like a sculpture. I couldn't get a flicker from you."

She started shaking as if she had the chills and looked at Tomas, who seemed dazed as he shook his head from side to side.

"Tomas?" she said. His face was blank. "The last thing I remember we were standing back to back to prevent anyone from sneaking up on us. We accidentally backed into each other, and that's it. That's all I remember."

"I think you guys shouldn't have guard duty together anymore," I said, suddenly wondering if they had been trying to meld. "We're ready to go. Are you guys okay?" No answer. I gave them each a little push to get them moving. Tomas still hadn't said a word and Caroline kept glancing at him surreptitiously and then looking away quickly.

"Andrew, did you find them?" I heard Mom call.

"Yeah, are we ready?"

"Yes, come on and help carry things."

Tomas guided us along at a clip despite the thick, slippery mud under our feet and the steady, cold rain that pummeled us. The rain grew harder and I hoped it would keep the Miners in the Club as we sloshed by their abode. Where were they? Maybe it was too dark out for me to see them, maybe they were all around us and I couldn't tell it. I kept twisting my head nervously, expecting to see them prowling in the shadows, running from tree to tree or boulder to boulder, stalking us, hidden by the downpour.

Finally we were climbing to the caves. The path was slick and Dad and Mom carried the girls which left me with extra luggage. Caroline gave me a hand, but Tomas didn't offer.

"Caroline," I said, "were you two trying to join?"

She frowned. "Got me, but I promise you that version won't work with our physiology."

"Yeah, I'm happy to agree."

"How much longer do you think?" she asked. "I'm getting tired. It never seemed this far before."

"Maybe it's just because it's night and we're running," I said.

Abruptly, Tomas ducked under an overhang and vanished into its shadow. Each of us followed suit, squeezing through a narrow tunnel and coming out into a chamber that looked vaguely familiar. It was empty, except for the perpetual pale, alien glow-lights.

"This was my cave," Tomas said. "Here sat I, Alien and questions. See there are the tunnels of the tunics."

"I'll be!" Mom said. "So they are. Where are the aliens?"

"There was the accident. I never returned. It has been many years. Safe here be we. To safety I brought you."

"Seems that way," Mom acknowledged.

I was cold and wet, and as far as I was concerned none of this looked too promising. I had the persistent, nervous notion we'd been followed, and hardly felt safe.

"Mom." Even whispering the word sent an echo around the emptiness of the cave. "I have a bad feeling that we're not going to be alone for long."

"Why?" she asked.

"I felt like we were being followed all the way here. Don't you think the Miners gave up awfully easily?"

"You are probably being paranoid, Andrew. It's raining and the Miners are cowards, but I'll stand guard."

I sat down at the edge of the cave, my knees drawn up against my chest realizing, that in this case, Mom's Augmentation as a superior warrior didn't really reassure me. Dad turned on a battery-driven warmer torch and everyone except me and Tomas huddled close to it. I was nodding off when I heard the soft hum of Tomas' voice.

"This place once was full of aliens. Now gone, left, and I also, was gone, but now have returned. Empty, fear, longing."

"Tomas," I whispered.

"Yes, Andrew. Sorry. Fear is strong this night."

"Yeah, but at least you aren't alone anymore."

"Always, I will be apart."

"Maybe not. We're trying to understand."

He reached out and patted my arm with silky skinned fingers just as all hell exploded. Mom screamed a warning from the cave entrance at the top of what I called her warrior yell. Dad crashed towards her like an enraged bull elephant. I grabbed Louisa and Cindra. Mom and Dad tore back inside and Mom grabbed the silver box as we all scooped up what we could. The Miners charged into the cave, light lances in hand, armed, blinking blue-green, high stun stage, which in some cases had been known to kill.

Tomas whispered clearly in my ear, "Third tunnel from the right. Take everyone."

He turned and calmly stepped forward. One of the Miners sent a stun-spear flying which Tomas neatly sidestepped.

"Now, Andrew," Tomas said loudly and clearly. He turned like a bolt, grabbed the nearest Miner and flung him like a rag doll into the group. The Miners fell, flailing and floundering. Then we were all dashing into the tunnel. It was pitch black and I was in the lead, feeling with my hands down dry, raspy walls. I stumbled on a hump of something sticky, and heard Caroline say into my ear, "Stay calm. Everyone is here. Keep going, Andrew."

I could barely catch the sound of the screams and yells of the Miners, and my mother's voice was reduced to a whisper.

"Is Tomas with us?" I tried to turn and ask, but felt a hand push me gently forward. "Is he?" I called back, but now I couldn't even hear my own voice. The tunnel was swallowing the sounds and signs of our existence.

Mom and Dad should have turned on a torch, but maybe no one had managed to grab one in the confusion. I rammed a wall with my toes just before I came slam up against it. Someone ran into me from the back and my breath left me in a huff at the same moment something slimy slithered over my left foot. I wanted to scream, I opened my mouth and tried to scream, but didn't have enough air in my lungs. Tears slid down my cheeks as I tried to listen for the Miners. If they were coming, I couldn't hear them. We would have no warning. I punched the wall in frustration, and something soft gave under my hand. This time I managed a small yelp, before I realized it was a glow light. It hummed on, bringing a ghostly illumination to the stone walls. The narrow channel we were passing through ended in a wall as the tunnel did a dog-leg turn. Just beyond was the passageway, but in the dark I might never have found it.

My eyes adjusted slowly and although I was still virtually deaf, it was good not to be blind. Everybody was there. I looked back at Tomas, whose eyes were glowing now. How much longer could he maintain his posture and what was it costing him? He met my glance and it was like sinking into a yellow haze. He worked his way up to me by squeezing past the others and mouthed something right into my ear, but the tunnel absorbed every one of his words and all I heard was a muffled mumble. I wiped at my wet face with my knuckles. Tomas reached out and gently raised my chin as he gave me a thumbs up sign. He slipped by me and took the lead, remaining upright, but clearly struggling not to collapse. His hand shook as he briefly reached back and motioned us on. He set a rapid pace. In the heavy silence and the dim light the tunnel seemed interminable. The walls were covered in what looked like flaking bark. The floor was an uneven patterning of stones like the ones in the roads. The roof was curved and roots grew over the remains of paintings and mosaics. We popped out into a cave and into sound that numbed us just as if it had been an explosion.

"Thank goodness," Dad sighed. "It was like walking in glue. What do you think, Tomas? Did we lose them?" He looked back at the tunnel we had just escaped.

Tomas sank down onto the floor, head in hands. "Someplace safe." His eyes were puffy, but glowed even more brightly now. The skin on his face was drawn over his cheekbones until it looked thinned.

I saw Caroline talking quietly to Mom. She gazed at Tomas and then went and sat beside him. He took her hand and she left it resting in his.

"Okay, kids, let's try to rest for a few moments," Mom said. "You too, Tomas, Caroline." She opened the tin box, laid it in her lap and closed her eyes, her back against a cave wall. Pretty soon, I could hear everyone's gentle breathing as sleep ensued, but somewhere in the midst of one of my dreams I lost some sound and heard a new one. I groggily opened my eyes and blinked. In front of me were two statue-like figures. Frozen against each other were Tomas and Caroline, and even in the dim light I could see their clothes in a heap by their feet. They were not alone. Pressed tightly against the two of them, were a Native and one of the Water People. The Native was almost completely silvered in fine scales that looked something like snakeskin. Its eyes were wide and green, but opaque, not glowing. Its nails were yellowed-lime, and its mouth ringed by a deep purple membrane. Like an echo of the Native, Tomas, too, was silvery.

"What?" I started to say and felt Mom's hand on my shoulder. She put a finger to her lips.

I watched, fascinated and repelled. If two people got any closer than Caroline and Tomas, they would truly have melted together. The Water Person pressed against the Native. It seemed to flatten and spread as it adjusted itself to fit perfectly against the shapes of the Native, Caroline and Tomas. Its skin started to flow, forming and reforming until it bled into the other three and was only a thin shadow against them.

It lasted maybe ten minutes before a single Alien pulled away. The Native and Water Person were nowhere to be seen. Tomas and Caroline sighed, then slowly released each other.

The Alien noticed us for the first time. It's mouth opened and it hooted briefly before it swiftly vanished around a corner.

Mom rushed to Caroline, Dad to Tomas. Caroline was shaky and confused. She slapped at Mom's hands and tried to push away with unseeing eyes rolled halfway back into her head as Mom draped Dad's copious rain coat around her. Tomas was covered in a fine, slick film and his breathing was shallow and rasping.

"Is he going to be okay?" I asked.

"I don't know, Andrew."

"How'd this happen, Dad? Why?"

"I don't know. I don't even know exactly what happened, and my guess is Tomas and Caroline don't either."

"Caroline is really terrified," Mom whispered to us. "She is hysterical, keeps crying. I don't know what to say to her."

"Tomas almost seems comatose. I can't get any response from him. I don't think he'll be able to move on for a while," Dad said.

"What if the Miners find us right now?" I asked, watching Tomas where he sat, hunched into himself, a pale, wet glimmer of silver.

"I don't know," Dad said, not too reassuringly.

I looked over at Caroline. Cindra had crawled into her lap and was hugging her.

"Mom," I said, watching Caroline as I spoke, "why didn't you stop whatever just happened?" I was breathing heavily and trying hard not to be frightened.

Mom frowned at me and pointed. Caught in the shadows of what I now realized were multiple exits or entrances to the cavern we were in, stood alien figures. Silent guards or guardians, their burning eyes lit the dusky air where they stood, increasing the shadows around them. Every once in a while one of their heads would swivel and a low pitched whistle would pass between them.

One scuttled forward into the light. Despite its odd gait, muscle and sinew glided under its lustrous snakeskin. Moist, lemony tissues hung like a turkey's wattle from its orifice.

"What do you want?" Mom asked, her fingers twitching around the silver box she had picked up once again.

It raised its whole arm and gestured back and forth between Caroline and Tomas. "To help," whistled airily from its mouth, making its wattle waver.

"Help Tomas and Caroline? How? By violating them?" Mom asked. Her voice was even, but her words were angry ones.

"We did not intentionally harm," and again it waved its arm between them, "Tomas or Caroline."

It watched Mom intently. I thought it was waiting for her answer, but as she opened her mouth, an alien whistled breathily. I couldn't identify which one it was before the single note was followed by a series that converged into a long, held signal.

"Your Miners are in the tunnels," the alien in front of us said, each word released in a slow huff of air.

"Great! Okay, listen, we need answers now!" Mom commanded.

The alien scuttled backwards, as if physically pushed by the force of her words.

Dad stopped Mom from speaking again by gently putting his hand on her shoulder and squeezing slightly.

"Rebecca, let me try. Please help us. We have to know what to do before this culminates in more tragedy," he said to the alien in his best diplomatic posture, although I had my doubts it would help in this circumstance. It seemed as if we still didn't know enough to make a decision and it didn't look like we had much time.

"Tragedy." The alien interjected the word in a hiss of air as its eyes flickered in dashes and dots of color. "Death," it added to the conversation.

"For you or us?" Dad asked anxiously.

"For both," it said, watching us closely with its white-less, pupil-less, yellow eyes.

"Why?" I asked. "Why death and why for all of us?"

It swiveled its head towards me, but Dad imperiously interrupted before it could answer.

"Why did you just attack Caroline and Tomas if you wanted to help them?"

It's head swiveled back around to Dad. "Attack?" The word hung motionless and heavy in the air. Though more complete, this conversation was reminiscent of our ambiguous Tomas Chalder conversations. "Hardly an attack!" It spit the words out in a shrill whistle. "A joining," it added at the end of the sound, "with hope of completion." It took a breathy pause. "For Tomas."

There was a hole in the conversation, a wide hole that gaped at us silently. We were missing something.

"What happened to Tomas?" I whispered into that emptiness more to myself than to anyone else, but it fell into that hole like a rock hitting the bottom of a dry well.

Dad glared at me as if I had deliberately interrupted sensitive negotiations, even though he was as in the dark as I was.

"I joined. I was joined," Tomas' voice came out of nowhere to save me.

"Tomas, you're okay!" I said loudly.

"Perhaps," he said. He didn't try to stand or move from where he had collapsed.

"What is joining?" I asked quickly, trying hard to avoid looking at Dad so I didn't have to deal with his bubbling anger at me. Tomas' eyes mirrored the alien's, yellow and white-less, with only pin-prick black centers to mark them as human eyes. The wetness that had covered him had hardened into a solid film of uninterrupted, chitinous silver. His stripes were filled in, as if someone had completed the coloring of a picture. Completed?

I watched Mom, still avoiding eye contact with my dad. She was surveying the perimeter of the cave. There were fewer aliens now, but a soft whistling was purring at the edges of my hearing.

I turned back to Tomas. His eyes were opening and closing, opening and closing. Finally he took in a deep breath and blew it out in a whistle of his own that melted into his human voice.

"Joining is a physical melding of the Water People and the Natives," he answered in an amazingly complete sentence.

"How?" Dad asked, shaking his head. "They aren't even the same species."

Tomas's answer was a laugh that drew itself out into a whistle which was joined by other whistles.

"Is that funny to everyone?" Dad asked.

Tomas smiled and said, "It was the mistake we all made. All the Miners. They are the same species, just separated." He stopped and gestured towards the alien who took up the explanation.

"A joining is a random, physical merger of our two halves that occurs when the Water Person meets a Native with sufficient body heat," the alien recited quickly, as if it was a speech memorized for a class presentation. It seemed to be able to speak our language in short bursts only.

"Okay, assuming that, why would the Water People try to join with humans?" Mom asked skeptically.

"You have approximately the same body heat as the Natives," Tomas answered. He pulled the sentence out into a long sigh. I wondered if anyone else noticed he hadn't included himself as human. "It is an accident."

"Why didn't they warn us?" Caroline asked, speaking for the first time from the corner where she had retreated with Louisa and Cindra.

"We could not," the alien said, hunching into its shoulders a bit. "We are sorry."

Another alien standing in the shadows clicked and whistled briefly.

"The Miners have turned onto a false course," the first alien announced.

"A reprieve then," Mom noted. I saw her stance relax ever so slightly. "Let's keep going with this. Please answer Caroline's question. Why couldn't you warn us?"

The alien's eyes opened and closed but it said nothing. I wondered if it had closed down from the stress of the contact with us.

"They couldn't," Tomas answered instead of the alien. "They do not know when it will happen nor are they actually conscious during the act. If one of you is there at a joining, then it will happen." Now Tomas had separated himself from the humans and the aliens. He was neither and both. "There is no time for warnings, Rebecca. Only the howlings."

"Couldn't you have at least helped Tomas?" Caroline asked, her voice shaded by panic.

The alien twisted its head towards her, its eyes half covered by green-dotted lids. "We have tried, but as you can see," it swept its arm at Tomas, "little success."

I wished we understood their body language better. Did the position of their eyes mean something? Did arm gestures indicate a state of mind? Inclusion or exclusion? What? What chance did we have of finding a solution to all this in the little time we had before the inevitable confrontation with the Miners?

Dad brought my attention back to the cave as he said, "Let's stick to the point. Can't you just avoid wandering at your joining times so you don't encounter us?"

"No," the alien answered simply and firmly.

Dad looked nonplused by the nonnegotiable tone of that answer. I could see he was considering what to ask next.

"How come you separate?" I asked quickly in that pause.

Dad struck out icily at my interference. "Andrew, please stay out of this."

I opened my mouth to protest and he actually hissed at me. I backed up until I hit a wall and had to stop.

Mom tapped him and Dad said to the alien, "Give me a few minutes to consult with my wife." The two of them retreated into a huddle and whispered exchanges.

I sat down next to Tomas. "Geez, why doesn't my dad listen to me?"

"He is frightened."

"Yeah? Me, too. Tomas, how come the aliens separate and then join back together?'

"They do it many times."

"Huh? Not just once?"

His head nodded jerkily. I could see he was still unsteady, maybe in shock from his own, last joining. "They spend their childhood united. When their parents die, they begin the changes."

"Yeah?"

"After their first separation, the novice Water People are escorted by joined aliens out of the caves to faraway farms."

He stopped and his eyes started to close again, but before he could I startled him when I excitedly cried out, "Faraway farms?"

"Yes. You guessed correctly."

I felt a fleeting ecstasy and then came the unnerving message that the Miners had split into three groups to expand their search. Mom and Dad looked up briefly at the news and then went back to their discussion.

"Why faraway farms? Why not the ones nearby?" I asked turning back to Tomas as quickly as I could. It was too late. He had fallen asleep again, his skin glistening faintly.

I stood and walked as casually as I could over to the alien. Mom and Dad were absorbed in a conversation that looked like it was rapidly turning into an argument. They weren't paying any attention to me or anyone else, but the alien was fixated on them.

"Hi," I said to it.

It swiveled its head swiftly from them to me, so that its eyes were only inches from mine. I stepped quickly back about a foot.

"Uh, look, uh, why do you take the Water People away?"

"They may not meet their birth half until the end." Its breath blew in my face as the words came out. It smelled of fruit and something akin to garlic. I stepped a little further away.

"The end of what?" I said, feeling even more confused.

"Changes," it huffed. "Until the completion."

"Of what?" I asked again.

It never answered. Instead it joined into what I was sure was a series of conversant whistles and toots.

Dad and Mom looked around. "What now?"

"The Miners are arguing loudly. Don't you hear it?" Tomas asked with eyes just slitted.

I strained to hear, but no human voices greeted my ears.

"I hear it," Caroline said, moving her head up and down. "I hear it."

"Why are the humans so angry?" the alien asked us as we strained our ears into the silence.

"They thought you were attacking them," Mom said.

"When?" it asked.

"When you were moving about the other night. They had never seen you in motion and all of a sudden, you were moving and someone else was dead. Does that explain it?"

"There are no attacks," it said, then clicked its tongue.

"Humans are dead," Dad pointed out again.

"Water People are dead, too, Dad," I reminded him.

"Andrew!" Dad warned me with a frown.

"Stephen, Rebecca, there are no attacks," Tomas said, standing unsteadily, leaning against the clay wall. "Accidental meetings only while they wander, as they wait to encounter partners."

"But we can't partner with them," Mom said, frustration infusing her voice at the circular nature of the conversation.

"Only rarely," the alien said.

Was he referring to the joinings with Tomas and Caroline?

"Joining is part of their natural cycle. It's not something they can control," Tomas said reasonably. He was still trembling where he stood, his arms wrapped around himself as if he was cold.

"What happens when they join that is so important?" Mom asked. "Is that how they reproduce?"

Tomas shook his head no.

"They do it more than once, you know?" I interjected.

"They do?" Caroline asked, her curiosity apparently peaked enough that she broke her silent retreat once again.

"Yeah, lots of times," I said.

"And they never know when it will happen, so they can never warn us? How convenient," Mom said disbelievingly.

"It wouldn't matter if they did give us notice," I pointed out quickly, intervening before she could actually accuse the alien of lying. "You know the Miners would still mine. They're too greedy to listen to reason."

The angry red blush which had appeared at the edge of her forehead retreated as she exhaled loudly. "I hate to admit it, but I think you might be right, Andrew." She turned back on the alien and said, "You still should have tried to warn us."

"We cannot," it hissed. Did the hiss indicate anger or frustration or something else altogether?

"Tomas," I begged, "can't you explain what's going on?"

He bit his lip and once again his eyes opened and closed until he finally said, "Separation brings an instant loss of awareness. I should know," he added in a whisper. He cleared his throat and continued. "After separation the Natives exist in a semi-conscious state while they process and store the new information they received when they were paired. The Water People, on the other hand, are the vessels of creativity. After separating, they perch in the farms, virtually dormant while they create new neural pathways. Neither Natives nor Water People are in control until they rejoin. So, how can they warn you?"

Now it was Dad who protested. "The Natives must be conscious. They give us information when we're in the mines!"

"Meaningless tidbits which spill out without thought. I knew that before the accident," Tomas said calmly.

Dad stared at him, caught off guard, and then insistently repeated, "But, they aren't meaningless. The knowledge the Miners have gathered here has helped humans immensely."

"It's only luck if what is said in the caves is helpful," Tomas repeated, his tongue clicking on the roof of his mouth. Even with all the odd clicks and hisses and whistles in his speech, he was making complete sense for the first time since I had met him.

"I can't accept that. What about when we went to the caves with you? The Natives answered us then. What about that?" Dad asked indignantly.

"We were surprised," the alien answered instead of Tomas. "No explanation."

"Well, that won't do," Mom said.

"Morning is always the best time," Tomas offered. "Always the good time."

"I would like the truth," Mom said firmly.

"Come on guys, why would they lie to us? What would the point be?" I asked.

"Andrew, you are out of your league. Now be quiet, please."

"Oh, come on, Dad. You're just upset because it didn't matter what you asked the Natives since they never really understood you anyway," I said almost gleefully.

"Andrew, I asked you not to interrupt." He turned to the alien. "How could you trick us like that? It wasn't right!"

"It wasn't done on purpose, Stephen," Tomas answered. He was standing now without support and his posture was straighter than I had ever seen. I noticed that he and the alien answered for each other interchangeably, except that Tomas' answers were longer and more complex.

"You know something else," I said, "it's ironic, but your company could have hired any U-A, for almost nothing to come here and mine. And they would have gotten the same results as they did by paying big money to the Miners."

Dad was frowning deeply. "Great," he groaned, "we've been duped by semiconscious beings!" He was truly distressed and I was sorry I had just been so glib about it.

"Do not be too sad. The Miners' words may have triggered some small response on occasion," Tomas said, obviously trying to comfort him.

"Completely duped, misled! The greatest negotiators and specialists in their fields!" Dad groaned again, utterly dismayed, and sat down next to Tomas, dropping his head and covering his face in his huge hands.

Even though Dad got mad at me sometimes, I had never seen him show his emotions so clearly during a negotiation.

Caroline suddenly began to laugh. "What a great joke on us," she said.

"Yes, wasn't it though," Dad agreed, listlessly.

Tomas reached down and patted Dad's arm, but he was watching Caroline, the corner of his silvery lips turning up slightly. She looked up and gave him a smile back.

"It was not in the Natives' abilities," the alien said in a high, pure whistle, "to have corrected your misconceptions."

"But, you could have," Dad pointed out accusingly. "Did you get a kick out of embarrassing us?"

He was really mad. He had, after all given up something he loved to come here, only to find that what he had forfeited so much for was out of reach. His undisguised anger was so out of character it made my stomach flip nervously.

"I'm waiting for an answer," Dad said in an unexpectedly undiplomatic voice.

"Why should the aliens have risked the Miners' violence?" Tomas asked simply.

Dad's face was a solid, deep crimson. He looked like he was going to burst. Mom reached out and put one arm around his waist. She leaned up and whispered something into his ear and patted his arm with her other hand. Then she said, "Just to recap all this, you separate and rejoin once, then again and again, and either you couldn't or chose not to warn us of the danger during these events?"

The alien whistled.

"So, what's the point to it all. Does it ever end?" Dad asked a bit petulantly, I thought. He wasn't used to being made a fool.

"It ends when their birth halves reunite with each other," Tomas said. I wondered what that meant for Tomas who had no birth half. Was that why a Water Person and a Native had shared their joining with Tomas and Caroline? Had it been to try for completion for Tomas? Had it worked? Could it work for a human?

"And after that, then what?" Dad asked.

Now Tomas swept his arm at the aliens around us and said, "Completion, like them."

His arm fell just as another alien glided into the center of the cave. It was huffing and hissing small whistles. Tomas cocked his head, obviously listening to what must have been a message.

"Soon, they come," Tomas announced, and I knew he meant the Miners.

"To hurry now," the first alien said. It inhaled deeply and expelled another recitation. "When we are complete we are covered in a thin silver, outer skin. Our bodies are no longer porous and we can no longer accept a joining. We cease to separate. When complete, we are conscious at all times until we die. We are complete." It gestured around it to all the aliens in the cave. "We are useful." It gasped and a shrill tooting escaped its mouth.

"What about children?" I asked quickly.

"For goodness sake, Andrew," Mom said. "Not now!"

The alien ignored her protest and answered me, although it was obviously an effort for it. "In the deep caverns where it is safe. We mate once after completion. Two offspring result. Once it was more children, but now all is balanced." It repeatedly whistled in and out in short bursts as if it was out of breath.

Tomas took up the explanation. "And when the parents die, they are each replaced by one of the two offspring in the litter."

"And that's when the children start separating?" Caroline asked. "When the parents die?"

"Yes," the alien mumbled the one word.

"So that's why the population never changes," Dad said.

"It all fits," Caroline said.

"Just as I suspected so long ago," Tomas stated simply.

"Yeah, I get it now," I agreed.

"Yes, but there is still a problem," Mom said. "People are dying."

"Human people and Water People," Tomas corrected. "The accidents cause their deaths as well as yours." There it was again. I wondered how Tomas defined himself now. It wasn't as a human, it wasn't as an alien. "When one of their creative halves dies from contact with you, its birth partner has no one with whom to make a final joining. In the end, it too dies an agonizing death and no child is left to replace the individual."

"How could we have been so blind?" Caroline asked.

Just too focused, I thought, but I said, "I guess the aliens are as afraid of us as the Miners are of them."

"I can see it now," Dad said. His trademark poise was returning. "I hope we can remedy this."

"With so many genetic recombinations, the potential for new knowledge must be endless. No wonder even your leavings are so valuable to us," Caroline said to the alien, amazement and revelation suffusing her voice.

The alien's head swiveled rapidly towards her. "You do not recombine to expand your minds?" it asked, its eyes beginning to flash.

"Nope, we focus," I said without even thinking.

Now it made a gesture that was almost laughably like human

head shaking, except the alien's head could turn so much further than ours.

"Let's get on with this. What can we do now?" Dad persisted nervously, obviously not too happy with the newest turn of the conversation.

Our time was running out. I could hear human shouts now, still distant, but clearly human and there was still one huge question left unanswered. I had been waiting for Dad or Mom to ask, but I couldn't wait any longer. "Could you be more specific about what you do when you're complete?" I blurted out.

"Why?" the alien asked.

"For understanding," I said, carefully not looking at Dad or Mom who would be sure I was wasting time.

Neither Tomas nor the alien answered. Several seconds passed and I wondered if they had shut down. Finally it was the alien who said, "A time of passion, a time of joy." It seemed to almost sing as it spoke.

This time it was me who asked, "Why?"

"Because," Tomas took up the conversation, "they are creating what humans call the arts. You should see the caverns, you should hear their music and listen to their stories."

I sighed enviously. "Any chance of a tour of those caverns?"

"None."

"That's what I figured."

"But that can't be all they do at their height. They must undertake scientific investigations, or create machinery, or new technology," Caroline objected. "They couldn't just throw all that information away and only make art!" She was standing now, one hand resting on Louisa's shoulder, the other gripping Cindra's hand.

Tomas came to her and wrapped his arm around her waist tenderly. "They leave those things to the aliens in interim connections before completion," he whispered. It was as if the things humans sought here were of almost no import to the aliens.

Nobody got to ask any more because whistles began blowing about in a flurry and more aliens appeared. Their orifices were stretched wide, expanding their wattles into frills and revealing rows and rows of thin, spiky teeth in their cheeks.

Mom cleared her throat. "It's time to move on. I take it the Miners are very close now," she said looking at the frilled aliens. "We need a solution so we can coexist, and we need it now. Tomas, do the howlings trigger the joinings?"

"The howlings mark both partings and joinings. It is an homage to their anguish and their joy."

I thought of the howls that covered the songs we had danced to in the storm. Anguish and joy. That had been exactly it.

"Then that could be the signal we need," Mom said excitedly.

"No," Tomas said. "They wait for the first orange sky after the joinings and the partings to howl, even if it comes months later. By the time they howl, it is too late to warn you."

"Then what do we do?" Caroline asked.

Everybody, alien and human, sighed in a composite, loud aspiration. When the sigh ended, a new sound began. It was rapid-fire sets of clicks and rushes of air that ended in different tones and notes of whistles. There was no mistaking it. A fast and massive conversation was passing from alien to alien all around us. Caroline huddled against a wall and Cindra and Louisa watched wide-eyed, holding tightly to my hands. Mom and Dad kept their eyes roving while they tried to talk to each other over the din. Only Tomas was included in it. His whistles were slow, his clicks punctuated by pauses, a newcomer, but part of the arena.

It ended. Just stopped. For long seconds, Tomas was frozen in the silence. When he finally moved, he walked over to Caroline and lifted her up protectively.

"The aliens have an important question for you." He spoke to all of us, but never took his eyes off Caroline.

"We will try to answer, if it will help," Dad said.

"It is something they need to know to make a decision, and there isn't much time left now." Tomas stopped. "They say they must know, what is the goal of human lives?"

We all looked at each other.

"Tomas you have to know there isn't a simple or single answer to that," Dad pointed out.

He shrugged and then whistled what I presumed was Dad's answer. "You must answer," he said insistently, maybe urgently.

Caroline stared at her hands and suddenly burst out hysterically. "Look at me!" She held her hands up. The backs of them were crisscrossed with small stripes of silver that were branching up her arms. "Look at me! Look, look! I'm changing already, so quickly." Her head jerked up and she pinned Tomas with her eyes. "Ask them, no tell them, I have to know what they are going to do to help us. You and me," she said, her voice breaking up as she spoke, her face crumpling.

Tomas reached out to her. Gingerly he took her hands and then gently pulled her into his embrace. "Don't worry, it isn't so bad." He kissed the top or her head affectionately. "I promise, I'll be with you, no matter what. I promise, always."

She burst into tears and even as she sobbed into his chest he said again, "What is the goal of human lives?"

None of us moved except for the aliens who were closing the gap between us and them, moving closer and closer. Caroline pushed back from Tomas and wiped at her eyes. She cleared her throat and said, "Tell them, everyone sets their own, individual goals. Why do they care?"

"I told them, humans want to own things, want money," Tomas said sadly. "That's why I came originally."

"They want power, too," I said.

"True?" an alien asked, looking right at Dad.

"Frequently, but not always," Dad answered honestly.

A whistle slid into the air and four or five aliens glided off into the tunnels. Now what?

"Is there something else they want to know?" Dad asked.

Clicks, whistles, exchanges of notes and tempos blew about.

"They say there is no extended meaning to your goals," Tomas translated.

"Why not, Tomas?" Caroline asked, her eyes red and swollen, but dry. "It makes a lot of people feel good."

"Are humans so blind?" an alien shrilled, its eyes flickering wildly. It began to scuttle threateningly towards Caroline. Tomas stepped between them and whistled into its face. It backed up, but alien eyes around the cave were flickering wildly.

"What's wrong?" I asked. "What just happened?"

Before Tomas could reply, three aliens answered, each taking a phrase as if to relieve the burden of our form of speech.

"Wealth is lost, gained, easily lost again."

"Knowledge is frequently found to be wrong."

"Power is vanquished by death."

"Then what does that leave?" Mom asked, truly perplexed.

"Creativity," Tomas said with absolute surety, as if he was a fourth alien in the line of voices.

"Yes!" I said. "Creativity for its own sake. That makes sense." It was also what was important to me, what I desperately wanted to hold onto, what had brought us all to this moment. My passion, my own need for creativity.

A darkly shaded, almost pewter alien swiveled its head towards me. "Andrew," it said, making my own head jerk around. "A great work of art is never surpassed. It lives forever."

"I'll remember that, I promise," I pledged, thinking about the truth in its simple statement, but also slightly scared that it had singled me out and addressed me directly.

"Will your focus let you remember?" it asked.

I flashed Mom and Dad a smile, as if to say, see, but my father grabbed my arm and growled, "There isn't any time for this kind of nonsense. In a few minutes the Miners are going to find us and as far as I can see the aliens have no defense and we are caught between two hostile groups." He turned his head and said to Tomas, "Ask your new found friends what they have planned?"

Tomas twisted his head slowly in Dad's direction. "Stephen, they want me and Caroline to go with them, now."

"What would that accomplish?" Dad asked.

"You don't understand. They won't let us stay with you."

"No way," Mom said. "Caroline needs to go home so she can get help before it's too late."

"Like it is for me?" Tomas asked. "Come, Caroline." He held out his hand to her.

"I said, no," Mom insisted at the same time that she opened the silver box and removed an evil looking weapon.

The reaction was immediate. The aliens' frills turned scarlet at the edges, with green veins winding through them, pulsing in a way that reminded me all too much of our encounter with the walking Water People.

"Mom," I tried to say, to warn her, but it was too late.

The aliens swarmed between us and Tomas and Caroline. They encircled them and in an undulating wave of bodies, swept them towards the cave exits.

Tomas looked over his shoulder and called back crazily, "Andrew, the answer, remember, forever!"

"No!" Mom shouted as they pushed him down the tunnel. She raised the weapon, but an alien caught her from behind, twisted it easily from her grip and threw it against the wall.

Whistles and clicks combined with snarling and were followed quickly by streams of spit. We stepped back instinctively to avoid the saliva and found ourselves flat against the cave walls, blocked from action by a furious crowd of aliens.

"Tomas! Caroline!" Mom called, but they had already disappeared into the tunnels.

"Mom, Dad," I begged them, "do something!"

The aliens were backing away now and suddenly we heard a horrible, piercing set of screams, screams that were clearly human.

One alien turned and said clearly, "They could not return with you. They could not come with us."

"So, what?" Dad asked. "What are you saying?"

"It is over now. It is completed."

"You killed them?" I asked stunned. "Why, why? What harm did they do you?"

"Leave this world. Take the Miners with you. It is over."

I felt sick. Tears streamed down my cheeks. Dead? Gone? It had been so quick, so sudden. Dully I heard human shouts all too close.

The last alien scuttled to a tunnel and melted into the darkness within it. Inside of a few seconds, the tunnels were empty and silent as if no one had ever been there but us. Cindra was crying inconsolably, and Louisa was silently wiping her nose with the back of her hand. Dad was stunned and wordless.

"I don't understand. What did we say to make them kill them? What, what?" I asked as I banged the cave wall over and over with my fists.

"Stop it, Andrew," Dad said. He grabbed my fists and held them inside his big hands. I saw my blood dripping out between his fingers. "Listen to me. I dont' think we are are ever going to understand why the aliens did what they did. It's frustrating, it isn't fair, but it won't help Tomas or Caroline for you to pound your hands into a bloody pulp."

He let go of my hands.

"Quiet, everyone." Mom held her palm up as her training kicked in.

I heard it then. Tiptoeing feet, the scratch of cloth, the whisper of human language, a pause and with a war cry they burst into the cavern and stopped. Their heads turned, they swirled about, their stun guns at the ready, but all they saw were the five of us. Cindra was in Dad's arms, her big eyes staring at them, and Louisa clung to Mom's legs, her face buried against her waist.

"Where are they?" Mrs. Pattison screeched.

"Gone. The aliens are gone, and Caroline and Tomas are dead," Dad said. He looked down at his feet and I saw him rub at his own eye.

As if someone had pricked a balloon with a needle, the air went out of the Miners. Their guns hung loosely from their hands, the anger faded from their eyes and I saw that they were just as dirty and dejected as we were.

"Let's get out of here," Dad said. "Does anyone know the way out?"

There was a moment of silence and then of all people, Philippa said, "I do. I marked the walls with chalk as we came." She held up chalky hands, clapped them and sent the white dust flying into the air.

XXXI

We all exited bleakly from the caves into bright sunlight without any idea of how long had passed. A day, three, a week? Time had suspended itself, left us disoriented, confused and exhausted. No one spoke. Everyone walked walled off in their own thoughts. Finally the Miners mutely peeled away from us, and wearily dragged themselves up the hill to the Club. Mom watched them keenly until they had all vanished into its depths.

"They'll have to be supervised closely for a while, especially when they find out we're leaving," Mom said, her eyes narrowed. She pushed her hair back from her forehead and motioned us on.

"Are we? Going home?" Louisa asked. "I wanna go home," she said and sobbed.

"When the Miners find out what we're proposing, they will be very upset," Dad said as we turned away from the den of humans.

"Then you agree?" Mom asked.

"Under the circumstances, I don't think we have any choice. The aliens made it very clear we are no longer welcome. Too many people have died already, anyway."

"The Miners won't care. They'd gamble their lives for the money any day," I said bitterly.

"It isn't their choice any longer, Andrew." Dad turned to Mom. "I'll contact the Space Corps and you will have to invoke a security order, Rebecca."

Exhausted, we trudged home. It was dry again. The clay seemed closer to blood red since the rains than the sienna it had been. I was so tired I could hardly lift my feet to drag myself through the gate to our house.

We all collapsed onto our beds and slept the sleep of the dead. I had no idea how long it had been when I awoke soaked in a cold sweat. I couldn't remember what dream had frightened me so, but the fear was deep and I was still shaking as I crawled out of bed and crept out onto the porch. I stared into the desert. I couldn't believe they were dead, gone. It had been so fast. One moment we had been conversing almost civilly with the aliens, the next they had barbarously hustled Caroline and Tomas off to their deaths. I wondered if Tomas had known in those last moments with us what lay just ahead. Had he traded his and Caroline's lives for ours and the rest of the Miners'? I shivered uncontrollably as I thought of it. Dad was waiting for me when I finally went back inside.

"Hi," he said.

"Yeah, hi, Dad."

"I'm surprised you're up." He waited for me to say something.

"Bad dream. I think it was about Caroline and Tomas."

He waited again.

"This isn't how it was supposed to be, Dad."

"I know, I know."

He opened his big arms and took me into them the way he used to when I was little.

"Dad, what am I going to do when we get home?"

"I wish I could answer that, but you are the only one who can decide. There will still be a small window of time for Augmentation, if you change your mind." He released me and left me standing by the doorway.

I looked back out as the sun came up and cast its light on the plains of clay.

"Andy," Cindra said, and tugged on my arm. "Whatsa matter?"

"Uh, nothing."

"Good, cause Louisa and me want a new story."

"You do? Well, I might not have any more stories."

She giggled. "You're always gonna have stories for us." She looked up at me. "Aren't you?" she asked.

"I don't know," I said. "Go get Louisa, and meet me out on the porch."

I didn't really want to read to them. Everything was too painful, but I didn't want to disappoint them, either.

Cindra returned with Louisa and took my hand in her little one. "Are you sad, Andrew?"

"A little bit."

"Don't worry. It'll be okay."

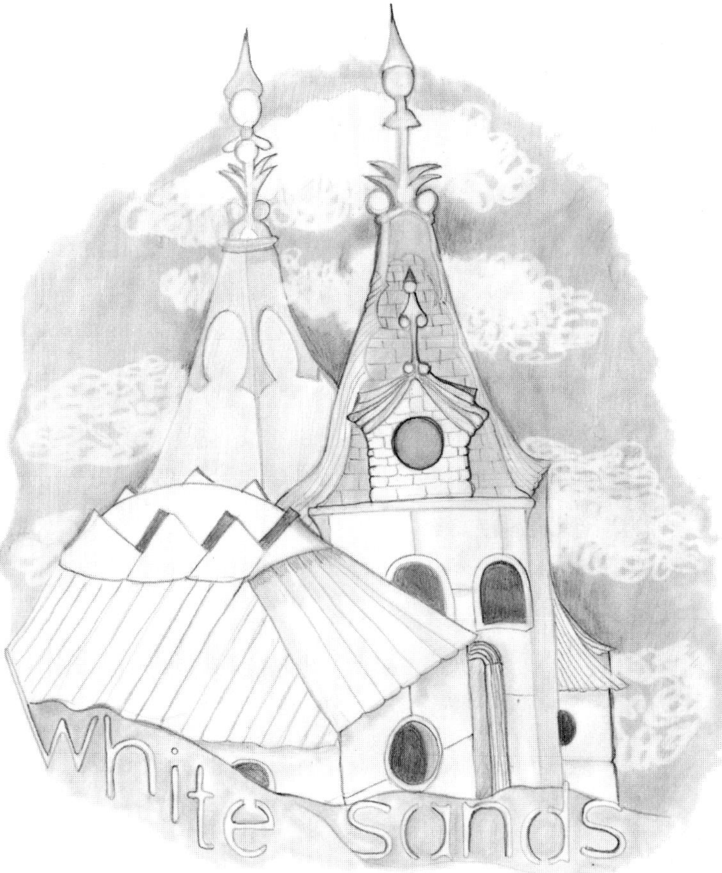
White sands

THERE ONCE WAS A BOY NAMED JAMIESON WHO WAS A PRINCE OF A DESERT KINGDOM. THE DESERT WAS WHITE SAND, PURE, BEAUTIFUL WHITE SAND, ROLLING ACROSS DUNES LIKE POWDERY DRY SNOW. JAMIESON'S FATHER WAS A GOOD AND KIND KING AND THE KINGDOM WAS PEACEFUL. TOO PEACEFUL, IN JAMIESON'S OPINION. HE WAS BORED AND HE WANTED TO MAKE A DIFFERENCE, BUT THERE WAS NOTHING HIS FATHER NEEDED HELP WITH, AND NOTHING THAT THE PEOPLE OF THE KINGDOM SEEMED TO WANT THAT THEY DIDN'T ALREADY HAVE.

[What do you think so far?]

[Cool. *Both heads nodding, both faces smiling.*]

[I'm glad.]

HE BEGAN TO COMPLAIN AND COMPLAIN ABOUT HOW BORED HE WAS, SO HIS FATHER GAVE HIM AN ULTIMATUM. "FIND SOMETHING TO DO UNTIL YOU BECOME KING, JAMEISON."

SO JAMEISON DECIDED TO SEEK OUT AN OLD LOCAL WOMAN WHO WAS RUMORED TO BE A WITCH NAMED TAMERELLIA. HE WALKED FROM HIS PALACE INTO THE DESERT AND TURNED LEFT AT THE FIRST SANDSTONE TOWER AND THEN LEFT AGAIN AT THE FIFTEENTH CACTUS. FINALLY HE CAME TO A CAVE IN THE SIDE OF A SALT DEPOSIT WHICH WAS EVEN WHITER THAN THE SANDS.

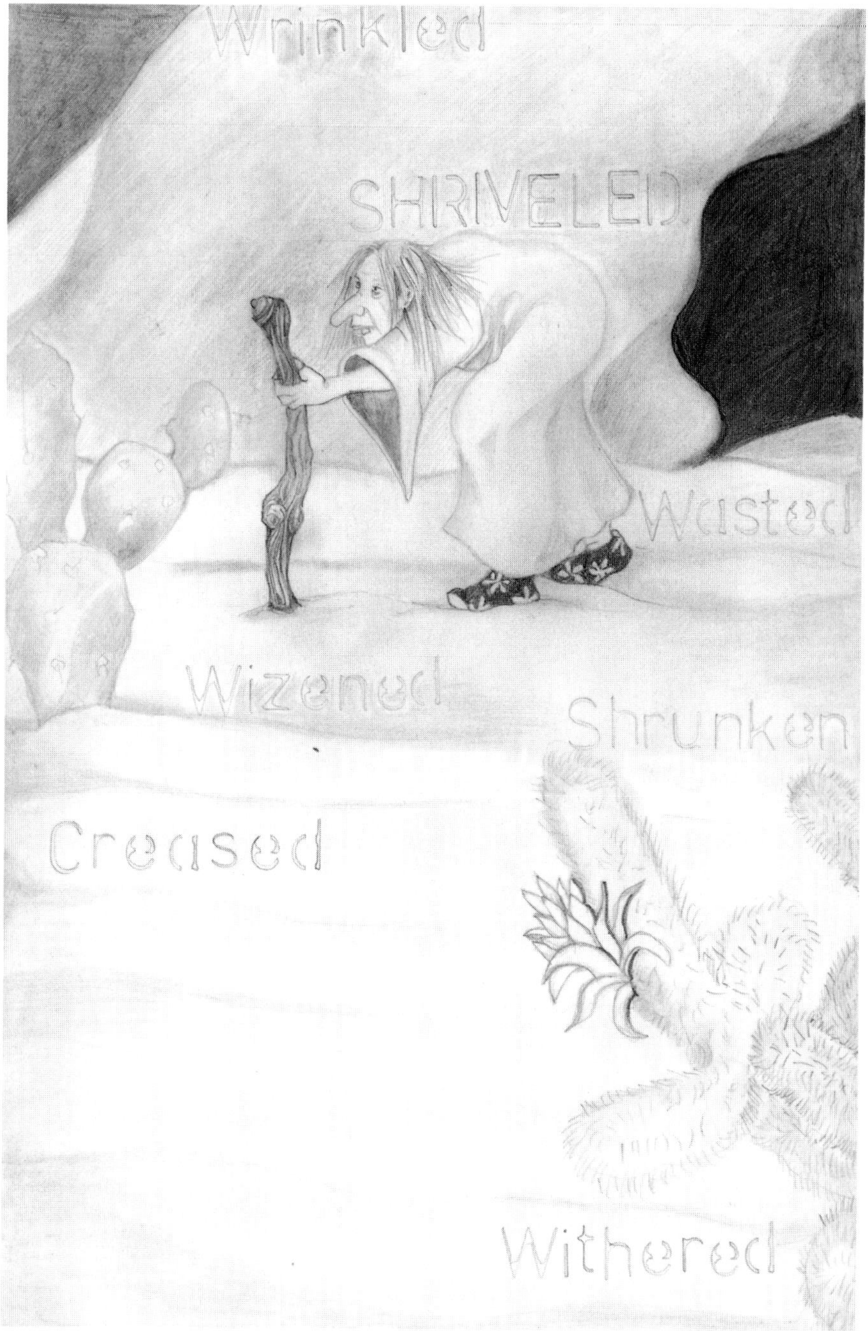
Wrinkled
SHRIVELED
Wasted
Wizened
Shrunken
Creased
Withered

THERE STOOD TAMERELLIA, BENT AND SHRIVELED. TAMERELLIA WAS NINETY-NINE-AND-ONE-THIRD YEARS OLD, AND EACH YEAR OF HER LIFE HER NOSE HAD GOTTEN A LITTLE BIGGER, UNTIL IT HAD WEIGHED HER NECK DOWN SO MUCH THAT SHE WAS ALMOST BENT IN HALF. JAMIESON WANTED TO TURN AND RUN AWAY, BUT TAMERELLIA LIFTED HER FACE UP TO HIM JUST AS HE NOTICED SHE HAD ON DEEP-BLUE, FLOWERED SHOES, A COLOR HE HAD NEVER SEEN BEFORE. SO HE SMILED AT HER INSTEAD OF FLEEING.

[Why would he stay because of her shoes?]

[Shsssh. *Finger to lips.*]

WHEN SHE SAW JAMEISON COME GLIDING UP IN HIS SHINY WHITE SKIN, DRESSED IN HIS CREAMY WHITE PANTS AND SNOW WHITE SHIRT, SHE CACKLED.

"WHAT CAN I DO FOR YOU, YOUNG SIR?" SHE ASKED.

"LIFE HAS GOTTEN BORING. MY FATHER THE KING GOT SO TIRED OF HEARING ME COMPLAIN THAT HE SAID I HAD TO CHOOSE A PROFESSION TO PRACTICE UNTIL I BECOME KING."

"INDEED? AND YOU WISH ME TO CAST A SPELL SO YOU CAN BE WHAT YOU WANT TO BE?"

"NO," HE SAID.

[What does he want, Andrew?]

[I have a couple of ideas, but I haven't decided yet.]

[*Frowns.* Well, go write some more, right now.]

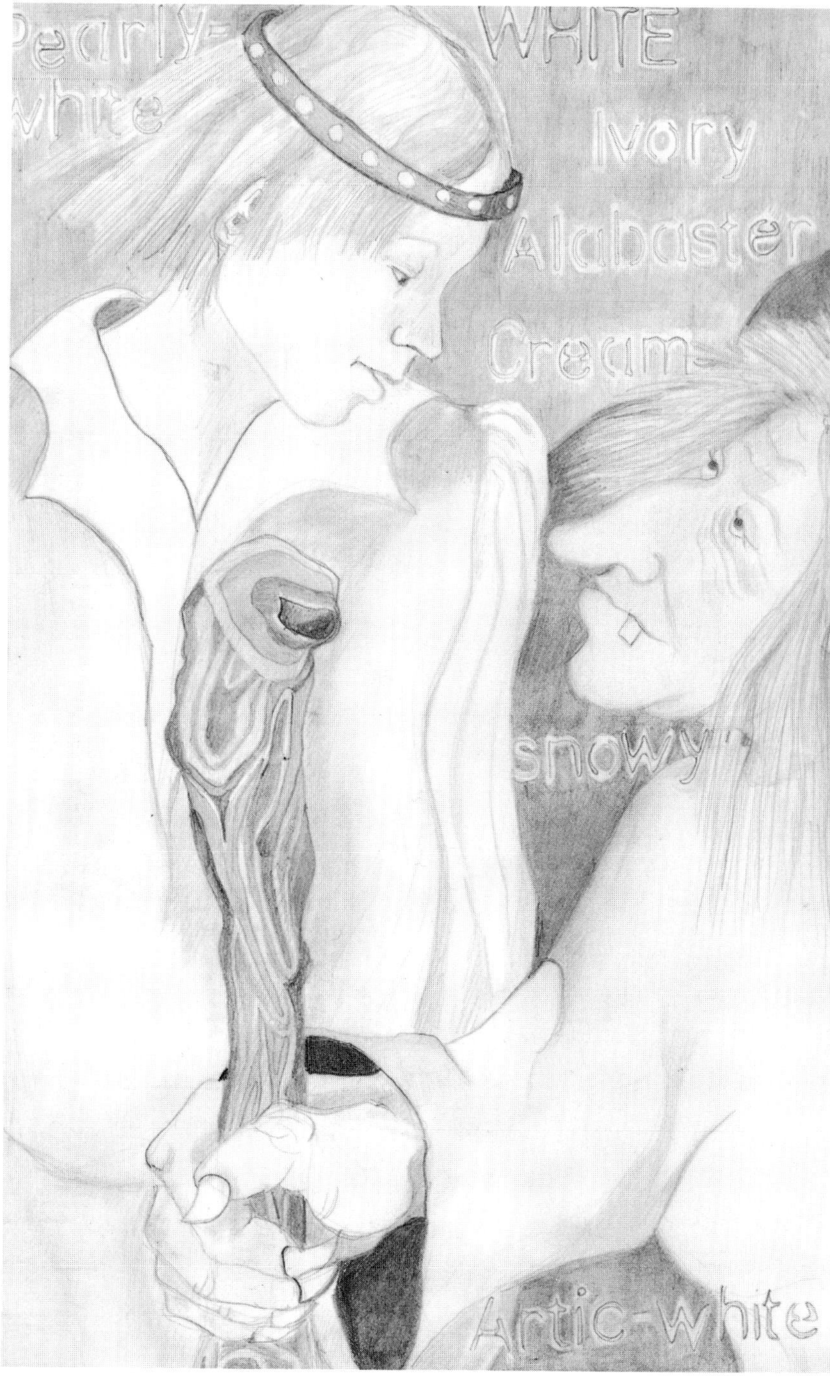
Pearly-white
WHITE
Ivory
Alabaster
Cream
snowy
Artic-white

XXXII

When we came back in, Dad was cooking breakfast and Mom was dressed and armed.

"I'm going to the Club to inform them of our decision," she said. "Do you want to come, Andrew?"

I rushed to dress and brush my teeth, grabbed a piece of fruit off the table and left with Mom. We walked in silence from that moment until we got to the Club. It hung darkly on the cliff above us. Mom checked her pockets and started up the hill. We poked our heads through the door and called out. They came as we called, dressed and obviously ready to go to the caves.

"What do you think you're doing?" Mom asked.

"Why are you here?" Mrs. Pattison asked back.

Mom ignored her question. "You can't go to the caves."

"Of course we can. It's our job," Mr. Petersenes said.

"Not anymore," Mom said firmly. "We're all going home."

"What are you talking about?" Mrs. Pattison asked.

"I'm not here to argue with you," Mom said. "A quarantine has been imposed. This is an official sanction." An angry buzz erupted.

Mr. Harlin shoved his way to the front of the group and glared down at Mom. "You've no right to interfere, and besides we aren't going to listen to anyone who was Tomas Chalder's friend." With unexpected speed his hand came up and shoved Mom.

"Hey," I said angrily and stepped between them. "Don't even think about touching my mother again," I growled without raising my voice.

"So, the cub has grown fangs," I heard Mr. Petersenes drawl nasally.

I glared at his silly, pretentious face. "I'm sick to death of all of you ninnies," I said.

Philippa's unmistakable cackle broke out when I used the word ninnies. The next instant Mom was shoving her sleeves up. A Spaceman's Viper was twisted around each of her wrists, both of which she raised and aimed at the Miners.

Mom began her speech again. "An official quarantine has been placed on the human population of Miners World." She rattled off the legal notification and stopped. Someone snarled like a cornered animal. Only the guns she held at the ready kept them from rushing us so they could go on, business as usual, just as if Tomas, Caroline and Hal Andrews were still alive. Mom shook her head and tried to explain that it was pointless to mine anyway and that their successes had all been random. The more she talked, the angrier and more sullen they became. She sighed and announced, "Anticipating your response, we have asked the Space Corps to prevent any further payments for finds you report from this date forward."

They flopped into their chairs, scowling, arms crossed, feet tapping, and refused to do more than hiss at us.

Finally Mom threw up her hands and said, "Okay, sit, sulk like five-year-olds, but it's over! Accept it."

"Ha!" Mrs. Pattison exclaimed. "We shall just see."

I pulled Mom into a corner. "They don't even care that people they know have died. What's wrong with them?"

"Money, fame," she said.

It made me think of the aliens. Wealth and fame didn't have much meaning if you were dead. Mom and Dad were going to have to trade off baby-sitting the Miners if they expected to keep them in check.

"How long before we'll be evacuated, Mom?"

"At least four months. Did you all hear that?" she said turning back to the Miners. "We have four months. If you insist, I'll put you under house arrest, but I would rather have your word that you will abide by the quarantine Stephen and I have imposed."

Mrs. Pattison pursed her mouth into a real pout. "And how do you intend to enforce that, dearie?"

"Well, firstly, right now, Andrew and I are confiscating your weapons. Get started," she said to me. "And secondly, if we have to, we'll drug you until we leave, but we would prefer to have your cooperation. Think about it for a few minutes."

"Mom, you're bluffing, right?" I whispered.

She gave me a shove. "Hardly. Go, do what I told you." She had never taken her eyes off the Miners.

I started through the first doorway, got through the second room, found the key to the weapons closet and was heading in that direction when I bumped into Philippa. She smiled if you could call it that. Her upper teeth barely overlapped her lower lip and her tongue darted out and whipped back. She brought her mouth close to my ear, and in a hushed voice said, "Andrew, oh, Andrew!" It was all I could do to keep from turning and running.

"I like your parents. Now everyone has to leave, not just Popsi and me," she snickered and drew her face away from mine. "What fun I am going to have teasing the Miners. I should be able to make their lives miserable."

It seemed to make her truly happy that she had a chance to work mischief. In fact, she appeared to have reverted to the old Philippa. I watched her eyes carefully, but they weren't sparking and her hair was as red as ever, untouched by a single white strand.

"There isn't any chance that you might restrain yourself, is there, Philippa?"

She grinned broadly and said again, "Andrew, oh, Andrew!"

I hugged the weapons in front of me like a protective wall.

"Right, okay, I don't know why I'd expect anything else from you," I said and went back towards Mom with the confiscated weapons.

"Mom, what are we going to do with all these?" I asked.

She walked over to me and said, "Do you think you could find the mud pond again?"

"Uh, I don't know, but Tomas showed me a swimming hole. Would that do?"

"Perfect. Go dump them in it."

"By myself?"

"This time you're going to have to, and then go home and get your father to come to the Club as soon as he can. Can you do it or do you want to stay here while I go?'

I saw Philippa watching me. Her tongue was licking at the edge of her lip. "No, I'll do it."

"Want some company?" Philippa asked.

"No." I whirled around and left. I waited until I was at the pond to look over my shoulder and take in a deep breath of relief that I had left Philippa with the unfortunate Miners. I watched thin yellow vines snake out and wrap around the stun guns as they sank into the pond. Shimmering aqua bugs skimmed the surface of the water and then flittered off into the sky. It seemed impossible that a place so beautiful could conceal so much danger.

I got back to the house late, so Dad decided to wait and leave for the Club as soon as the sun came up. He woke me to give me instructions, and to tell me Mom and he would take turns staying at the Club so that we would only be alone while they were switching places. I watched from the porch as he walked out into the desert just as dawn broke. I sat down sadly as the sky brightened and the air filled with the whistles and hoots of the awakening life of Miners World.

"Andrew," the morning chatter seemed to call. "Andrew," it sang to me as if I belonged to this world.

"Andrew," the bugs buzzed to me. I closed my eyes and listened.

"Andrew!"

I jerked my head up. Philippa was standing in front of me, her eyes bright and a smile on her face I had never seen there before. Maybe it was the early light that made her look pretty.

"What are you doing here?" I asked, unable to think of anything else to say.

"I came to see you."

"Me? Why?" I asked cautiously, all too aware I was virtually alone with her.

"We're really leaving?" she asked.

"You know that already. What is this all about, Philippa?"

"Thank goodness," she exhaled and without being invited, sat down close to me on the step.

I moved away. "What do you want?" I repeated.

"I can't pretend anymore." She sounded almost desperate as the sun came up quickly, suddenly casting shadows on her face. The smile that was pasted on her lips began to look out of place.

"Philippa, why did your parents bring you here?" I asked trying to take the offensive away from her.

She answered readily, completely unflustered by my change of tactic. "It all started because I kept making up stories and pretend stuff. Mama wanted to get me away from the schools. They claimed I was psychotic, but she insisted the teachers didn't understand me. I was just creative."

"You like to write?" I asked, completely taken aback by the idea.

She laughed at me. "Write? Me? No, oh, no! I like to make things up. It's fun to make things more exciting than they really are."

"You mean you lie?"

"That's what the school called it, but I just like to make things more interesting, so I exaggerate a little. It's more fun that way, getting everybody all twisted about and curious. Keeps all those Augmented ninnies on their toes. Poor Mama, she couldn't accept that I was," she laughed, "wicked."

"Yeah?" Just hearing her confess it with such delight made me anxious.

"I enjoyed tying Mama and Popsi up in knots, but I didn't want Mama to die." She shut her eyes for a moment.

"I don't get you, Philippa."

Her eyes popped open. "Oh, come now, Andrew. You of all people should understand."

"What do you really want from me?" I asked, furious now at her comparing us, seeing how she was trying to manipulate me.

"Ask, wait and receive. A-W-R me, Andrew," she said.

"No, I won't. You either tell me or you don't, but I am not playing your games anymore!"

"What do you want to me to tell you?" she asked very calmly as she looked right at me with her sharp, little eyes.

I jumped at the invitation even though I knew she was probably toying with me. "What happened to you? Was it a hoax?"

I needed to know if she had been in the tunnels. I had to know what was down there, to know if it had been worth Tomas' and Caroline's lives to protect whatever it was.

"Hoax?" She smiled and reached out to touch my arm with damp fingers.

"I have to know what you found when you went missing!"

"Promise, you'll write to me, okay, Andrew?"

"And if I say no?" I asked, bracing for a tantrum.

"Then you'll never know for sure," she said simply. "I just want to be friends. Won't you write me?"

"Why now? Why do you want to be my friend now?"

She shrugged. "It isn't fun to be alone anymore. I don't want to go home without any friends."

"You'll make friends," I assured her even though I couldn't imagine her with other kids.

"Me? Friends? Come on, Andrew. I never had friends before. You and I, we'll never be like anyone else, so I'll let you be my first friend."

"You might not want me for long. I might get Augmented," I said angrily.

"Yeah? Not me! But, even if you succumb, you'll always know what you missed, won't you? If you write to me, it'll help."

"Okay, okay, I'll write you," I capitulated, unable to deny what she was saying.

"Good," she said and stood up abruptly. "And if you A-W-R me, I promise to play by the rules and give you real answers."

"Philippa, give me a hint before you go. What did you find in the tunnels?"

She didn't answer me, just skipped out to the gate. At the last minute she turned and said, "I'll send you holographs. I took lots. They'll knock you out. I'll send them one at a time so you'll keep writing to me longer. Maybe we'll get to be friends before it's over, and then I could even visit you. Oh, and thank your dad for me," she said. "Here, catch." Dad's missing holocorder came flying through the air and landed in my outstretched hands.

She waved and then laughed. Her laughter mixed with the hisses and whistles of Miners World and then faded as some animal, or maybe Philippa, cackled. Her bright hair glistened in the sun as she walked out onto the red clay. All I could do was let the goose bumps run up and down my arms and shake my head.

After her visit, I tried to decide what to do when I got back to Earth, but my mind kept skipping to Caroline and Tomas. The days passed slowly. I filled the pages of my writing journals with descriptions of the planet and of every detail I could remember about Tomas and Caroline. I put off finishing *White Sands* until I couldn't stand Louisa's and Cindra's constant begging for me to read the rest of it to them. I settled down on the porch and tried to begin, but even as I scribbled the story, I kept seeing what had happened to Caroline and Tomas, as if my mind was stuck on instant replay. I had to keep reminding myself to finish the story before me. At last, I folded the pages, still unfinished, and inserted them into one of my writing books. That night, I cried, sobbing silently into my pillow so no one would hear me. I fell asleep with my face buried in the wet pillowcase only to be awakened by another dream. This time I remembered it clearly. Tomas had been in it. His eyes no longer had any black in the centers. His hair had become a starched, silver frill that stood up when he spoke. He was standing in a white desert, dressed in a tunic covered in white on white snowflakes. He had waved a finger at me as he had spoken. "The answer you know," he said in his old, ambiguous syntax. "On the List, is it." I wrote the message down carefully and tried to go back to sleep, but the words kept repeating themselves: "On the List, List, List, List." I slept on the edge of consciousness trying to decipher what the dream-Tomas had meant until finally I got up and padded into the other room so I wouldn't bother the rest of my family. I sat down on the floor, turned on my mini-comp and called up the Augmentation Choice List. I scrolled past occupation choice after choice, searching for the meaning of my dream. The variety was astounding when it was seen all together. So many focuses, so many opportunities, but every one of them was too narrow, too limited to satisfy me. Maybe it had only been a dream, nothing more significant. I hurried down, noting a few asterisked professions, casually wondering what those stars meant. Finally, at the very bottom was an asterisked notation labeled *disclaimer*. I clicked on the star out of curiosity. The little computer program blinked and a message came up:

"*The following notation is a disclaimer in regard to artistic occupational choices. Although it is possible for Augmentation to increase a person's technical proficiency in of one of these areas of endeavor, it has not been possible to increase the imagination of those who choose Augmentation in the arts. Success or failure is determined by the Augment's own expressive abilities, breath of vision and knowledge. Therefore, success in these fields cannot be guaranteed and the Augmentation Corporation cannot be held responsible for the results. In general we advise against making one of these choices."*

I skimmed back up the list, looking again at the asterisk-marked professions and then turned off the computer. There in the night-darkened room, where home was no more than a blur in my mind, I found what I had been looking for. The only thing that kept me from laughing was my sleeping family. I tried to calm down, but I could barely sit still. Finally in desperation, I pulled out my note-book and concentrated on *White Sands*. I didn't put one word onto the paper, but the story wrote itself in my head. Light was filtering in through the holes in the ceiling when I finally sneaked back to bed. I dreamed again of Tomas and this time, I thanked him.

The day before we were to leave, I was scribbling as fast as I could, describing the sunrises, the odd deformities of the clay that grew up unexpectedly from the flat desert, the trailing vines of yellow that now engulfed the rocks and climbed the trees near the Club. I was concentrating so hard that it startled me when Mom called.

"Andrew, you still have things to pack. Come on in. Dad wants you to pack up Tomas' things."

I spent a couple of hours carefully wrapping the tunics and journals in plastic, fitting them into foam packaging for shipping. I flipped open a purple covered journal and stared at a beautifully delineated drawing of an alien. The next page folded out and out and out, until the plan for the mural of tunics was lying exposed on the floor. I folded it back up and turned to the next page. It was empty. I closed the journal and picked up another. This one was full of drawings of Maria and the baby. Endless pictures of Tommy, his little face lit up with a smile, his lips turned into a cry. Maria holding the child, her eyes full of tears. A self-portrait of Tomas holding both of them tightly, embracing them and then the pages were empty.

I closed the book and wrapped it tenderly in plastic and laid it with the others. I opened another. This one was full of drawings of Caroline. It must have been really recent. I closed it quickly. It hurt to think of them. They were gone and all that was left of them was here, in these notebooks. They deserved more than that.

It was already dark when I finally finished packing them and wandered out to the gates. The sky was brilliant with stars. The tea flowers were withering for a winter we would never see. I stared at the shadows cast by the moon and the starlight onto the plain.

"Andrew." A familiar voice seemed to whistle my name on the wind. "Andrew," it called. I knew it was in my mind, but I whirled about, my heart pounding. "Caroline?" I whispered wishfully into the darkness.

She stepped from the shadows. I reached out to touch the image, even though I knew my hand would go through it, that it would melt away and leave me foolishly reaching for something that had never been there. Hairs on my neck rose and I jumped back as fast as I could when my hand met solid, silky flesh.

"Don't be frightened, Andrew. It's me, really," she whispered in a voice no louder than a breath of wind.

"You're a ghost! You have to be," I mumbled dumbly, unable to think of anything else to say.

She laughed lightly, but there, with the silver gleam of her body shining in the dark, I was still sure it was a wishful delusion, a trick of my vivid imagination.

"You're dead!" I cried, denying my innermost desire that she be alive.

She laughed again. "No."

"How? What happened? Where have you been? Where is Tomas?"

She ignored my questions. "I had to say good-bye and tell you, we're okay, but you can't tell a soul. The companies would never agree to abandon the planet if they thought we were alive.

"But, Mom and Dad should know."

She shook her head. "Your parents are good people, but they wouldn't have quarantined the planet if they thought we were still alive and there might be some hope of reasoning or negotiating with the aliens. There is no such hope. None. The aliens thought that they could allow a few humans here, allow them to use their droppings of information, but it cost everyone too much. It is over. Do not tell your parents. Promise. As long as no one knows Tomas and I are alive, we are all safe."

She was right. I couldn't take a chance on endangering Tomas and Caroline, my parents or the aliens. I had no choice. "I promise. Caroline, does it hurt? The changes?"

"It's not so bad. I know what's coming and Tomas is always with me. I'm not alone the way he was. When it's over, I think I'll compose music." She pulled her head down into her shoulders slightly. "Tomas is methodically lining the cavern walls and even the ceilings with paintings. It isn't exactly human imagery, or native," she said, "but it's so beautiful! I go and sit and watch him. He is amazing and I think he is happy now."

"Aren't you scared?"

"Sometimes, but what can I do?"

"Where is Tomas?" I asked.

"He's keeping watch while I talk to you. He can hear and sense so much more than I can."

"This isn't what you thought you'd get from life, is it?" I said.

"I'd say not, but at least Tomas and I have each other. I never expected that either. I never expected to have a family. What are you going to do now, Andrew?"

It was my turn to smile. "I'm going to get Augmented."

"What? I don't believe it! Oh, Andrew are you sure?"

"Yes, I am. I'm going to be Augmented."

"I was hoping you would find another way out."

"I had hoped so too, but it's okay." I patted her arm. "Really. As soon as we get home, I am going to opt for Augmentation Choice Number 885: Writer. "

"I don't understand!"

"See, I love writing, but I always thought that Augmentation would keep me from knowing about enough things to be able to write. And to finish it off, I thought Augmentation would limit my imagination to one way of looking at things."

"So?"

"So, the Augmentation Corporation has a disclaimer about the arts. They won't promise success if you choose one of them.

"Why?" she asked, rotating her head with a click.

"Because you can't create an art work without imagination and wisdom and knowledge and the Corporation can't Augment you for that. You get that stuff by living. That's why they put in the disclaimer. The Augment is on his or her own, more or less unchanged. Don't you see, Caroline? It's both the way in and the way out for me!"

She stared, open-mouthed. Then her eyes sparkled and she laughed. Her laugh was joined by a whistle that turned into a sound of delight. I saw Tomas around the corner. He waved. Caroline kissed me and stepped away. As she turned sideways, I saw a soft swelling of her belly. She rubbed it gently and nodded to me. Then they slid off together, their silvery hides reflecting the starlight.

"I promise, you won't be forgotten. You'll find yourselves in my stories," I said under my breath.

I heard more whistles and knew the aliens had been out in the desert waiting for them, watching over them still.

"Andrew, where are you?" Mom called. "Come in. It's late."

"I'm coming, Mom."

"Where are you going, Mommy?" Louisa asked as I came in.

"To help Daddy herd the Miners to the ship. They aren't very happy or cooperative," she said. "We want them packed up and to the shuttle site tonight. You okay with baby-sitting, Andrew?"

"Sure, that's fine. We'll finish reading our story while you're gone."

"So, it's okay if I go, kids?" Mom asked again.

"Sure, but be careful, Mommy," Cindra said. "The sky is getting orange. A storm might be coming."

"Howlings on the way," I corrected.

Mom patted Cindra on the head, kissed us all and left.

"Now, now, now! What happens in *White Sands*," Louisa said.

"Let's sit outside on the porch where we can watch the sky," I suggested, pulling out a small torch to read by.

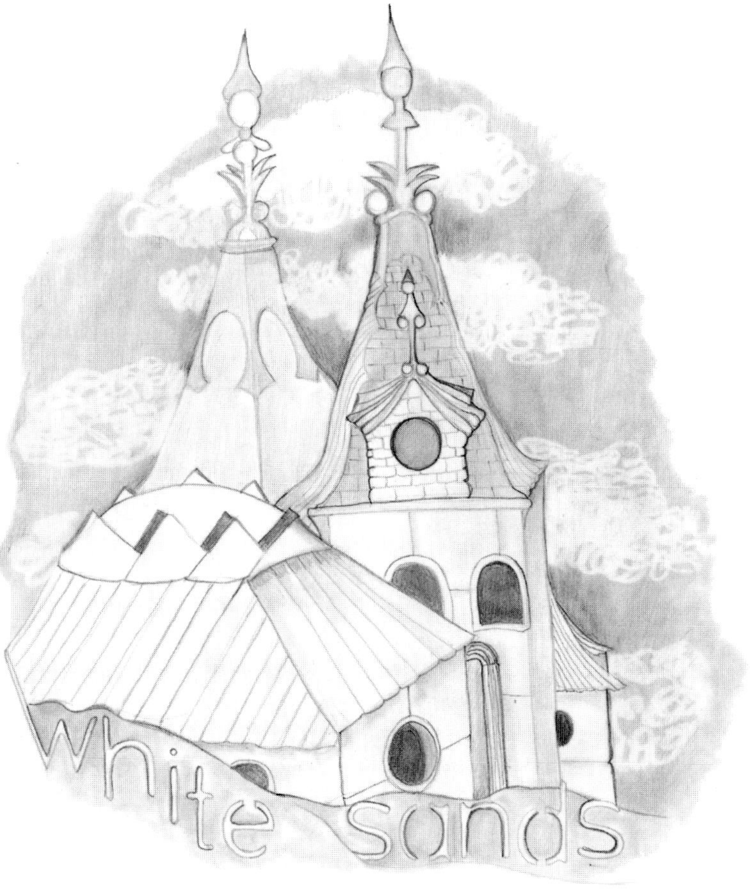
White sands

"I want you to help me figure out what to do," Jameison said to Tamerellia.

"Me? I only know how to cast spells and brew potions. How can I help you?"

"I heard that when you were a young witch with a short nose, you traveled the world and saw many places. What did people do outside our Kingdom?"

"Oh my, it has been so long since I ventured into the outside world. Let me think," Tamerellia said. She sat down in the sands and leaned her heavy-nosed head onto her hands, for it was hard for her to stand up for long. "My, my! I remember that one man put iron shoes on camels so they could walk long distances on hard grounds. And one woman looked at stars through black tubes so they would look bigger, and a young boy harvested wild seeds and sold them to farmers and gardeners."

"But, nobody in the White Kingdom needs any of those things. What else?"

"You are asking a lot of an old woman," Tamerellia pointed out.

"I want to do something important," Jameison said firmly. "I am your Prince and I command you to remember more."

The witch laughed at him and stretched her legs out straight in front of her. "What do you think would be important? Your father is already rich and powerful. Your mother is already brilliant. We already know about the stars, and nobody is hungry or needs clothing. The Kingdom is happy."

One-humped CAMEL

Dromedary

Bactrian

Cameloid

"There has to be something that is missing," Jameison insisted. "I command you to think!"

"Oh my dear boy, that is not something you can make somebody else do. You must think of this for yourself. Come sit here in the sand by me and rest your feet while you think."

So Jameison sat in the sand with his legs stuck out in front of him, side by side with the old, heavy-nosed witch. He stared at their two pairs of feet, his in white satin slippers with pointy toes and hers in deep-blue flowered sneakers.

"Where did you get those shoes?" he asked sleepily, for the sun was warm and the breeze was soft and it made him drowsy.

"Long ago on one of my trips. I had never seen such a color. Fortunately, although my nose has grown and grown, my feet have stayed the same size so I can at least still wear my wonderful shoes."

Jameison liked that color of blue. He had never known before that there were any colors of blue other than that of the clear blue sky.

[*Giggles.* Silly witch! Silly Prince!]

"Are there more colors in the world?"

"Oh, so many, many colors. The blues alone make up a myriad of shades and hues. You should see the pinks and yellows, but my favorite are the purples and the lovely lavenders," the witch said wistfully.

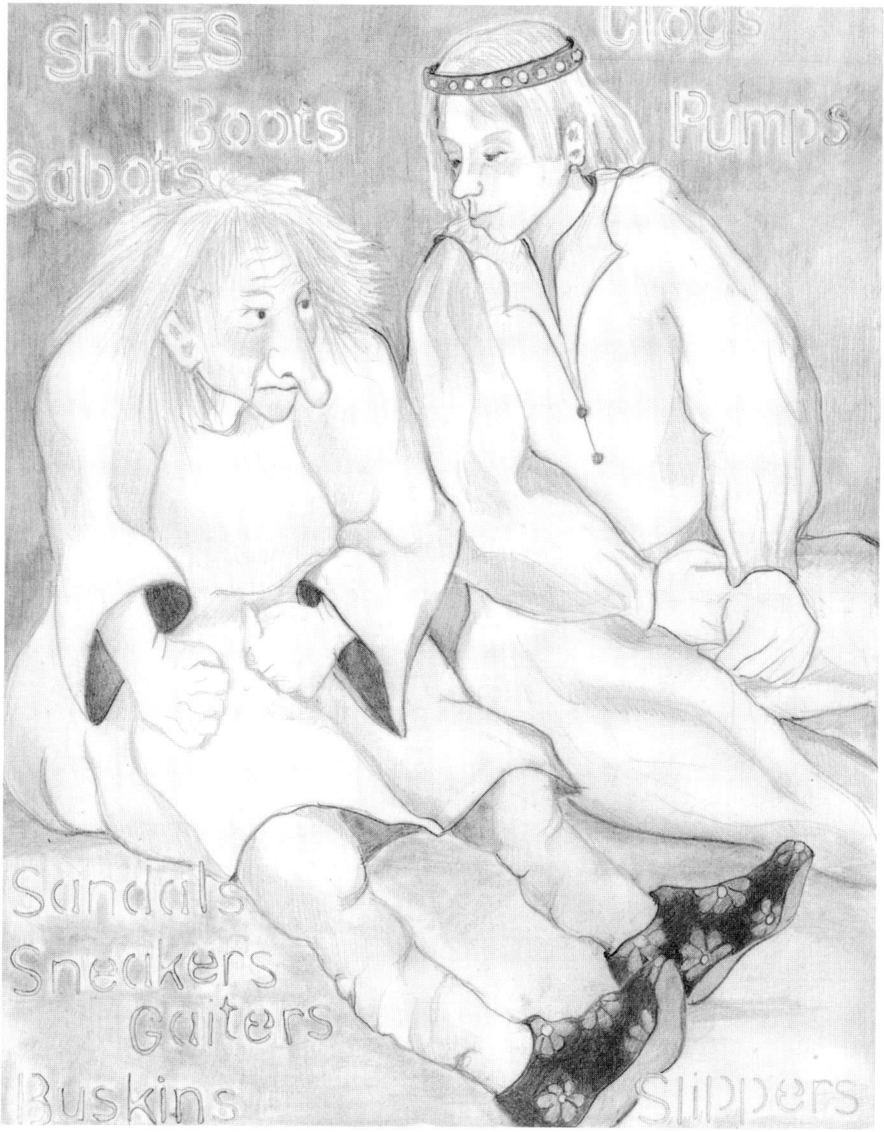
SHOES
Boots
Sabots
Clogs
Pumps
Sandals
Sneakers
Gaiters
Buskins
Slippers

"That's it," Jameison cried out. "That's what I will do. I will bring colors to the White Kingdom."

"And how will you do that? I have heard your father will not let you travel out of the desert."

"That's true, but you could help me."

She grinned now, her crooked teeth sticking out beneath the sides of her huge nose. She put her hands onto the ground and pushed herself to her feet. "Hmmm, perhaps. What are you thinking of?"

"You have seen the colors. You could help me make them."

"And what would you do with them?" the witch asked curiously.

Now Jameison smiled. "I would paint beautiful pictures into the sands. Pictures that would last forever and make the world more beautiful. That is something that the White Kingdom needs."

Tamerellia scratched her wrinkled chin and laughed loudly. "The sand would cover your silly pictures, foolish Prince."

"Couldn't you cast a spell to protect the paintings?" he asked hopefully.

"Yes, I could help you, but why should I?" she asked.

"For the Kingdom," he said happily.

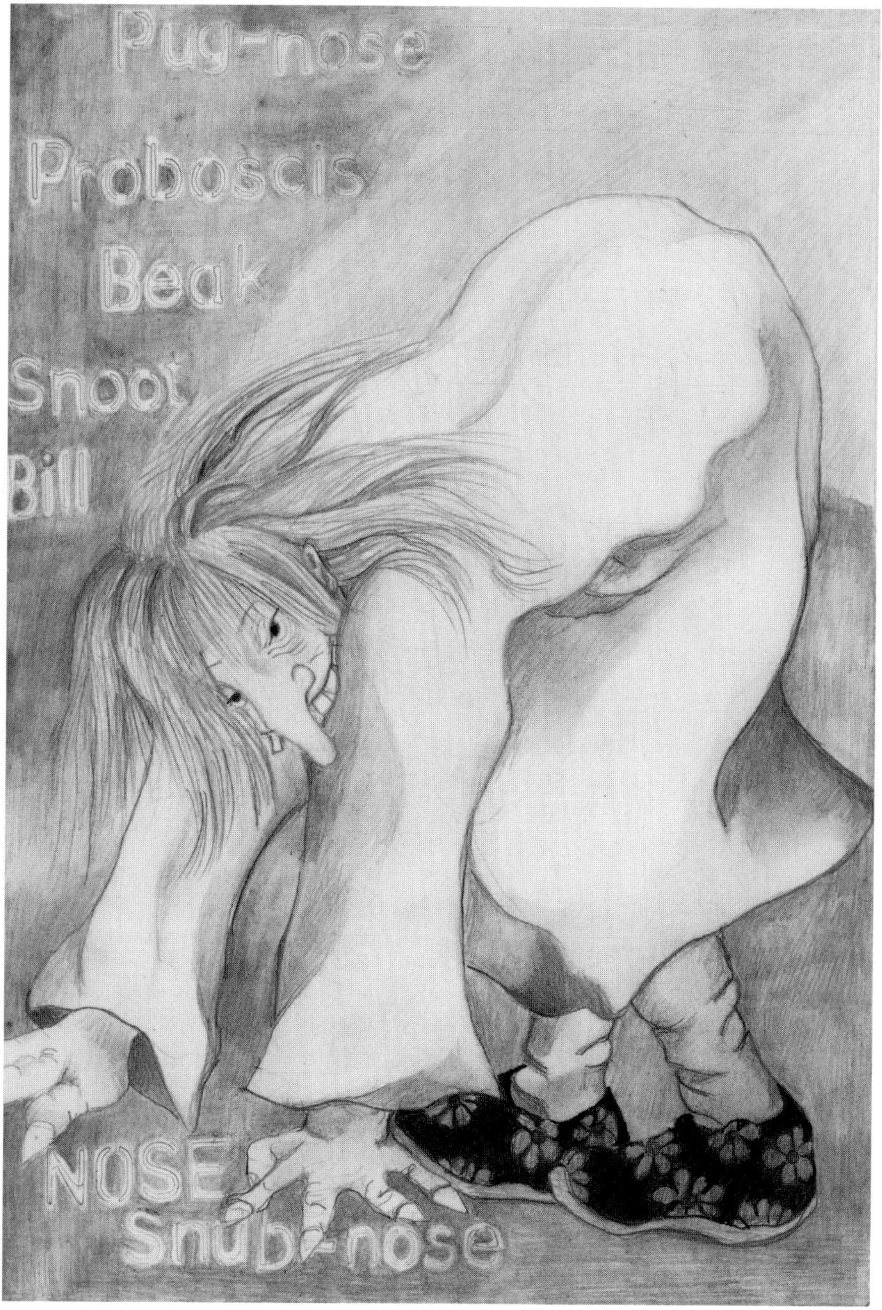
Pug-nose
Proboscis
Beak
Snoot
Bill
NOSE
Snub-nose

"THE KINGDOM? AND WHAT HAS THE KINGDOM DONE FOR ME? DID THE KINGDOM HELP ME WHEN MY NOSE GOT TOO BIG FOR ME TO WALK TO THE MARKET? NO, I HAD TO CONJURE UP A CAMEL TO SEND TO GET WHAT I NEEDED AND PAY A BOY TO LOAD IT AND UNLOAD IT. DID THE KINGDOM BRING ME A COMFORTABLE CHAIR AND A FOOT STOOL FOR MY WEARY FEET AND POOR SORE BACK, SO SORE FROM CARRYING AROUND MY BIG NOSE? NO, I HAD TO CAST A SPELL TO GET THEM. WHY SHOULD I HELP YOU TO MAKE THE KINGDOM MORE BEAUTIFUL?"

JAMEISON SCRATCHED HIS YOUNG, HANDSOME FACE AND RAN HIS FINGERS THROUGH HIS ALMOST WHITE, TOWHEADED HAIR. "WHAT DO YOU WANT?"

"WHAT DO I WANT? WHAT? SOMETHING YOU CAN'T GIVE ME, SO FORGET IT, YOUNG PRINCE JAMEISON." BENT OVER BY THE WEIGHT OF HER NOSE, SHE HOBBLED INTO HER DARK CAVE IN THE SIDE OF THE WHITE SALT DEPOSIT.

JAMEISON STOOD OUTSIDE AND STARED INTO THE DARK ENTRANCE. "TAMERELLIA, TAMERELLIA, PLEASE COME OUT."

SHE IGNORED HIM.

"COME OUT, PLEASE. THERE MUST BE SOMETHING I CAN DO THAT WILL CONVINCE YOU TO HELP ME."

"LIKE WHAT? GO HOME, YOUNG PRINCE AND THINK ABOUT IT, AND IF YOU CAN FIGURE IT OUT, COME BACK."

[Okay, guys, it's your turn. What do you think he could do that would make Tamerellia help him?]

[Uh, buy her a fancy scarf and a pretty necklace.]

[Okay, Cindra, that sounds good.]

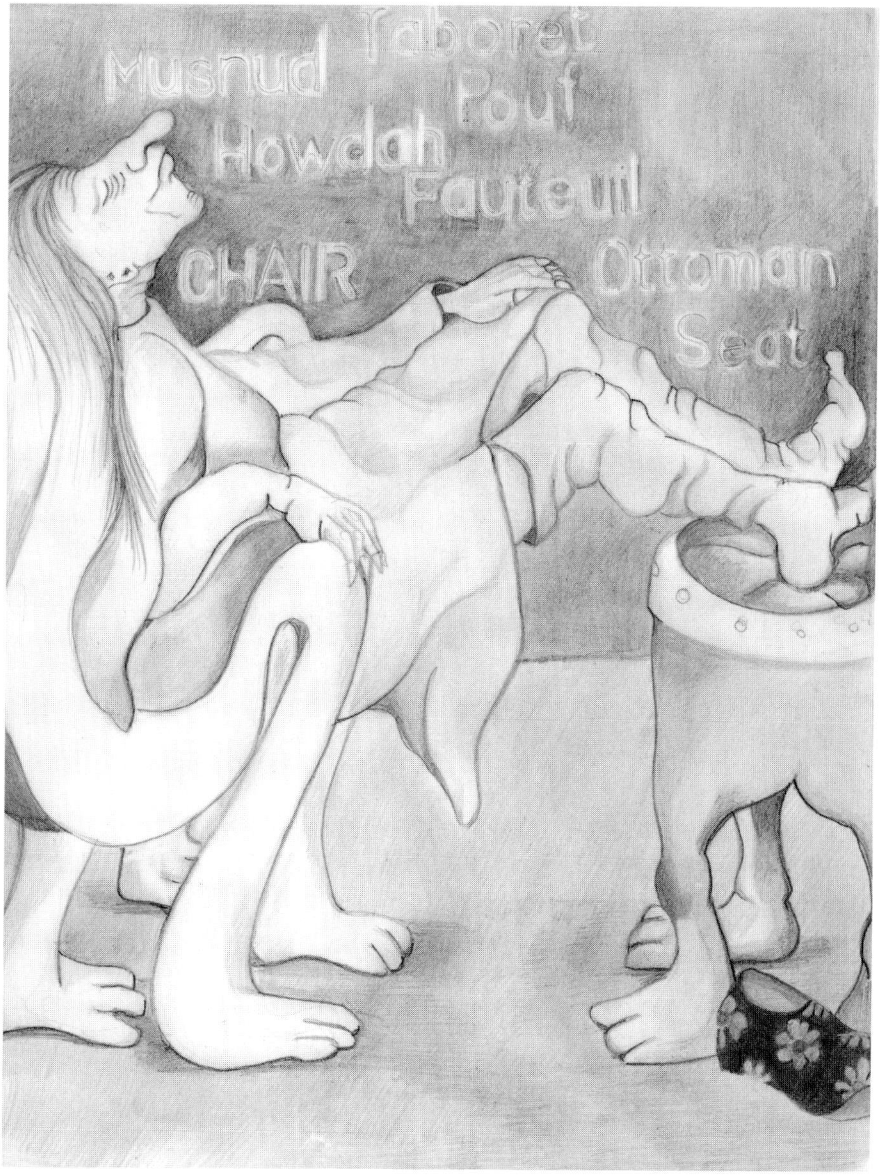
Taboret
Musnud
Pouf
Howdah
Fauteuil
CHAIR
Ottoman
Seat

SHIMMERED Gleamed Sparkled Glittered

JAMEISON WALKED BACK TO THE PALACE AND WENT TO HIS MOTHER AND SAID, "I NEED A GIFT FOR A FRIEND."

"GIRL OR BOY?" THE QUEEN ASKED.

"GIRL," HE SAID. "I DON'T KNOW MUCH ABOUT GIRLS. WHAT DO YOU THINK WOULD MAKE ONE FEEL PRETTY?"

"LET'S SEE? A FILMY SCARF OR MAYBE A PRETTY NECKLACE."

SO JAMEISON WENT TO THE MARKET AND BOUGHT A LONG WHITE SCARF WITH SILKY WHITE TASSELS AND A BEAUTIFUL WHITE, OPAL NECKLACE, AND WRAPPED THEM IN LACY WHITE TISSUE PAPER WITH A BOW OF SILVERY WHITE RIBBON AND TOOK IT BACK TO THE CAVE OF SALT.

"TAMERELLIA," JAMEISON CALLED INTO THE DARK OPENING. "I HAVE A PRESENT FOR YOU."

THE WITCH CAME HOBBLING OUT AND LOOKED AT THE BEAUTIFUL PACKAGE. SHE PULLED AT THE BOW UNTIL IT COLLAPSED AND CAREFULLY PUT HER LONG NAIL UNDER THE TAPE AND PRIED IT UP. SHE SHOOK OUT THE SCARF AND HELD THE LOVELY NECKLACE UP TO THE SUNLIGHT SO THAT IT SHIMMERED AND GLITTERED.

"NICE. WHY DID YOU GIVE THESE TO ME?"

"I THOUGH YOU MIGHT LIKE THEM," JAMEISON SAID.

"GO HOME, YOUNG PRINCE. YOU WILL NEVER THINK OF WHAT I WANT." AND SHE VANISHED BACK INTO THE CAVE WITH THE WRAPPING, SCARF AND OPALS STILL HANGING FROM HER TALONS.

[She shoulda given the present back if she didn't want it, or else she shoulda helped him.]

[Probably, but she's a witch and witches aren't very nice. I need a drink of water, girls. My throat is dry. Let's go inside. We'll finish the story in a little while.]

XXXIII

I gulped some water, letting it wash down my throat. The dust had risen on a night wind as I read. The cool, clean interior was welcome, even though the house felt naked and empty without our belongings. I pulled out the sandwiches and fruit Mom had left for us and gave the girls their supper.

"Can we eat it on the porch?" Louisa asked.

"Sure, but it's dark out there."

"I know, Andrew, but it is so sad in here."

"What do you mean, Louisa?"

"We're leaving and when we go, there won't be anything to say we were ever here."

I looked around the house. "Louisa, I don't think we were ever meant to be here," I said.

"But we were, and I don't want the aliens to forget us. Couldn't we leave something for them?"

"Like what?" I asked.

"I don't know," she said.

"I could draw them a picture," Cindra said, "except Mommy packed all our crayons."

"I don't think there is much we could leave that the aliens would care about anyway. Go eat your dinners."

I ate my own meal alone, perched on a crate while I read one of the classics I had brought along. It was a gripping story with great imagery and I wanted to read it straight through, but I never had time. I sank into the story as I munched. I could hardly wait to finish it during the trip home.

"Andy, come on and read more of *White Sands*," Cindra called.

I stood and stretched with my finger in the pages to mark my place. I paused a moment as Louisa's words flitted across my mind. I closed the book and searched about for a piece of plastic. Despite a sense of regret, I wrapped the novel in it and stuffed the book quickly into a cubby. I tore a piece of paper out of one of my notebooks and printed neatly, *Great works of art are never surpassed -- Andrew,* and slid it into the cubby with the book.

"I'm coming," I called to the girls and went back outside.

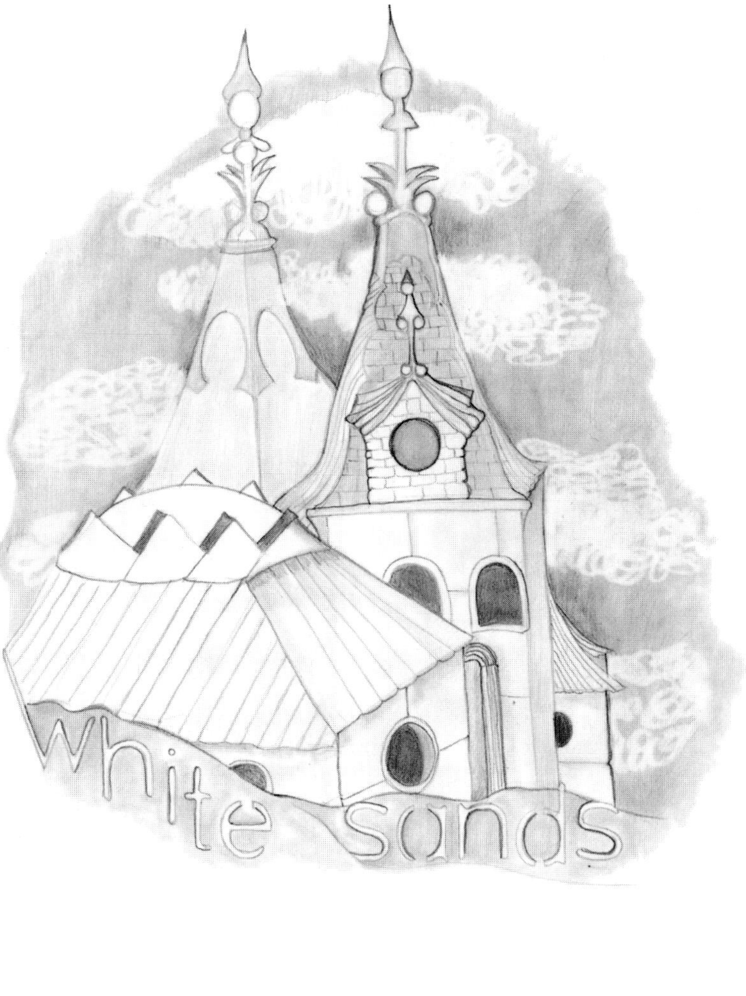
White sands

[Okay, Louisa, your turn. What do you say would make Tamerellia help Jameison?]

[Hmmm. How about a nose job?]

[I doubt they had nose jobs in the White Kingdom, but see if you like this idea.]

Jameison went back to the Palace and went to his father. "Father, how do you get people to do something for you?"

"Why that's easy. I decree it."

"Yes, because you are King, but what could I do?"

"Offer them gold," his father said and smiled. "Do you need some gold?"

"I guess I do," Jameison said.

He loaded the gold onto a camel and pulled the stubborn beast across the white sands to the cave of salt.

"Tamerellia, I have brought you riches," he called and added, "and a beast of burden so you can travel more easily."

She stuck her head out around the edge of the cave and grinned widely with her crooked, yellow-white teeth clacking together. "You think I want riches? What could they buy me that I can't conjure up for myself? And how would I ever hoist myself onto the camel with this load of a nose on my face? Go home, young Prince. You have nothing I want. If you didn't need something from me, you wouldn't even remember I was here. Soon I will die, and then no one will ever think of me again. Go way and leave me alone.

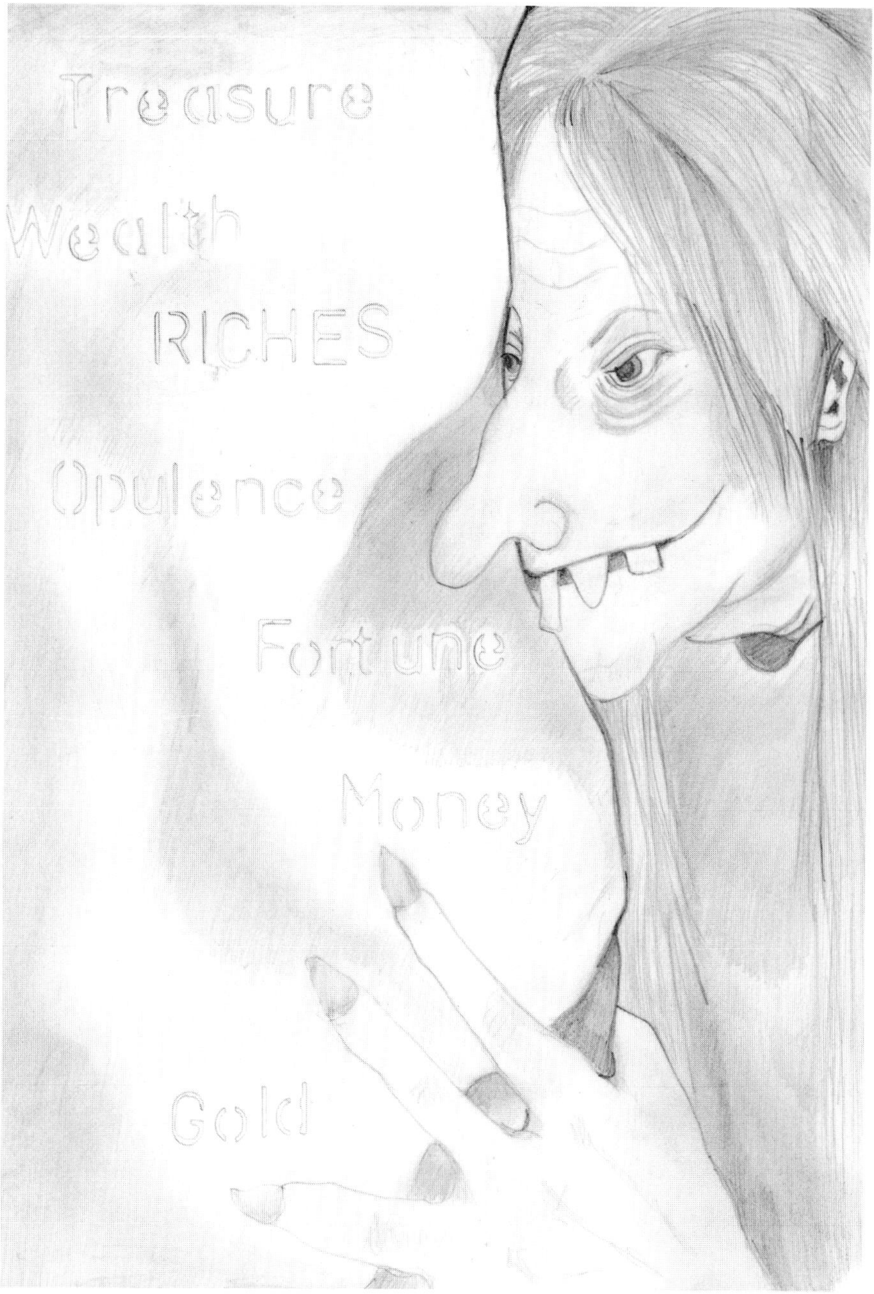
Treasure
Wealth
RICHES
Opulence
Fortune
Money
Gold

Jameison left the camel by the cave and trekked home, lifting his feet high to get through newly drifting sand. He took a drink from his water bottle while he stopped to think under the hot sun. Tamerelllia didn't want pretty things, and she didn't want gold or a camel. What would she want that he could give her? He scratched his head and thought and thought until he was almost at the palace gates. Suddenly he turned around and started back to the cave. He didn't get there until it was almost dark.

He stood at the cave entrance and called, "Tamerellia!"

"Go away," the old, cracked voice called out.

"No, no. I know what I can do for you."

"Oh, surely, yound Prince, you have given up. There is nothing you can offer me that I can't get without your help.

"Yes, there is."

Her face appeared once again at the edge of the cave, her eyes glowing like spots of red fire from the darkness.

[You got that idea from the aliens' eyes when we were in the cave.]

[Writers get a lot of their ideas from life.]

[Uh huh. So, what happens to Jameison? Hurry up, Andrew, before Daddy comes back. We wanna finish the whole story this time.]

[Okay.]

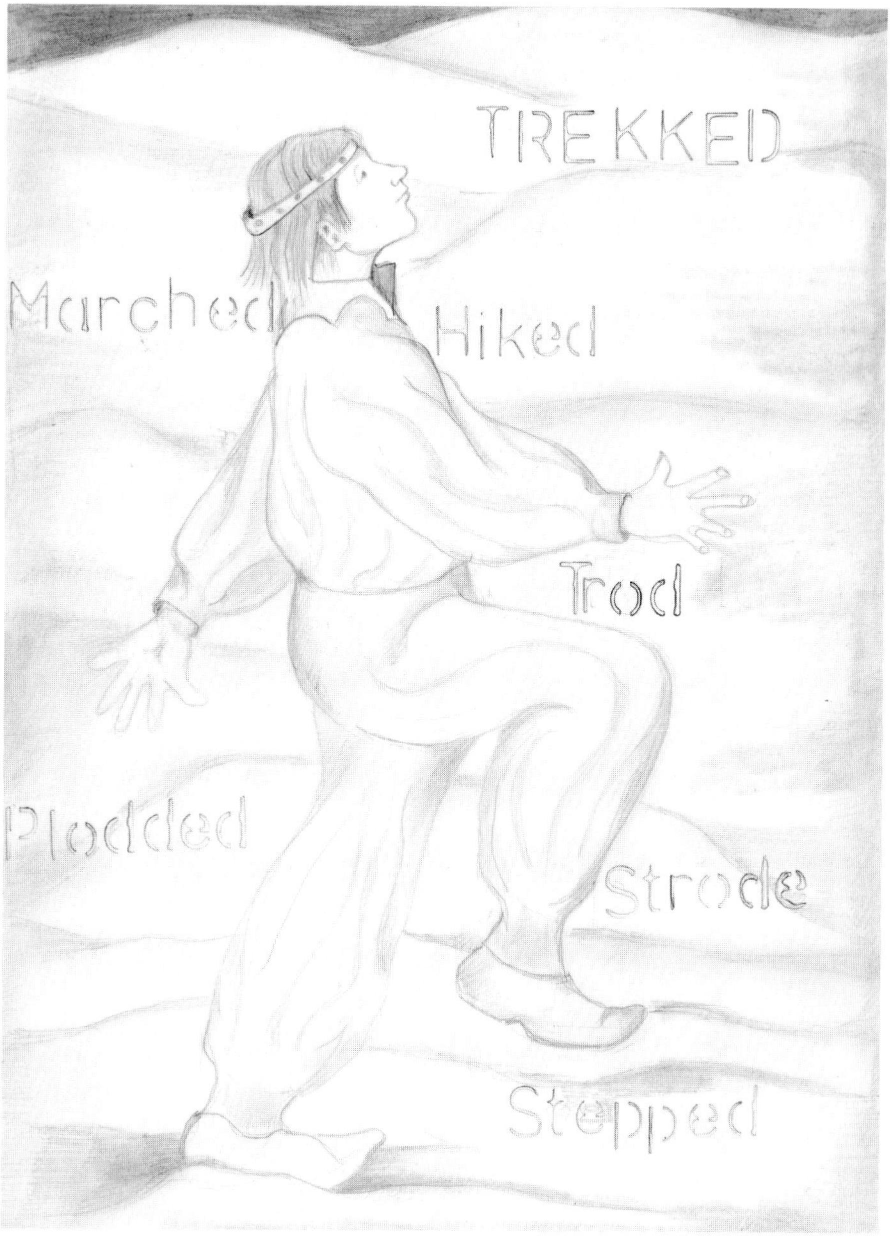
TREKKED
Marched
Hiked
Trod
Plodded
Strode
Stepped

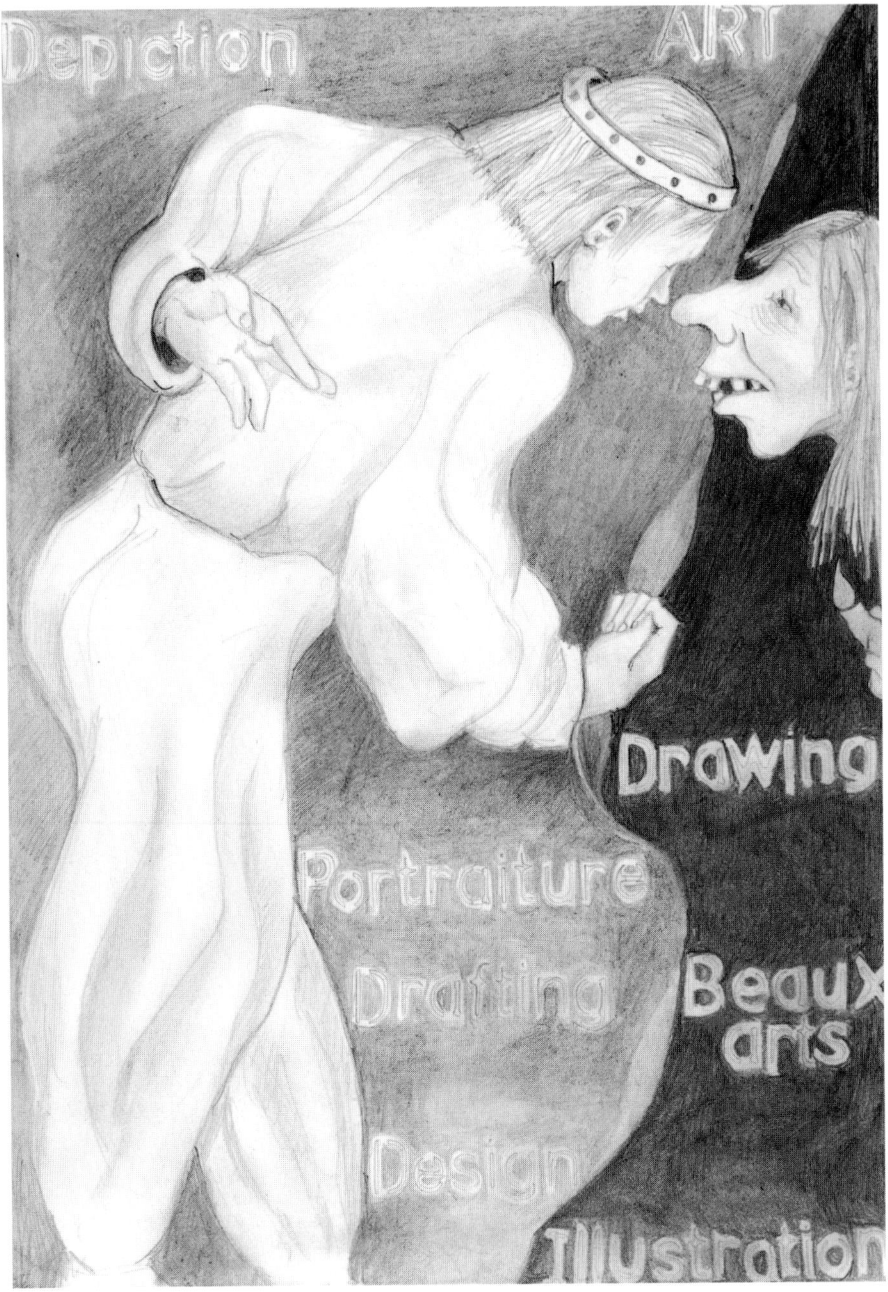
Depiction
ART
Drawing
Portraiture
Drafting
Beaux arts
Design
Illustration

The Prince crossed his fingers and began, "I will put you in the art I make."

She laughed or rather she cackled like a crow. "And why would I care about that?"

"Well, I can't make your nose smaller on your real face, but I can paint you any way I want to."

"And why would I care if you made me pretty in pictures. People would still know I was an ugly, old witch."

Now Jameison smiled. "You know, that's true. But after everyone who knows you dies, no one will remember that you were ugly."

She hissed at him. "You stupid boy. Do you think you can get what you want by insulting me?"

[He is kinda dumb, isn't he?]

[Looks that way, but he might surprise you?]

She started to go back in the cave, but he grabbed her and said, "You know, you don't want gold or a camel or pretty things, so I asked myself what would you want? You'll never have a small nose in this life, and you're so grumpy, nobody wants to be your friend. I was stumped, but I kept thinking, and then I knew."

"OH YES? WHAT DID YOU FIGURE OUT?" SHE SNARLED, BUT SHE DIDN'T TRY TO PULL AWAY THIS TIME.

"ART WORKS LIVE FOREVER, DON'T THEY?" HE DIDN'T WAIT FOR HER ANSWER BECAUSE HE KNEW IT WAS TRUE ALREADY. "AND I CAN MAKE A PICTURE OF YOU IN THE SANDS WITH A SMALL NOSE, THE WAY YOU WERE WHEN YOU WERE YOUNG. AND YOU WILL LIVE FOREVER, JUST LIKE THAT, WITH A LITTLE NOSE."

"AND PEOPLE WILL LIKE LOOKING AT ME?" SHE ASKED.

"YES, I PROMISE."

"FOREVER?"

HE SMILED AND NODDED. "NOW ALL YOU HAVE TO DO IS MIX AND BREW THE COLORS OF THE WORLD SO THAT UNTIL I BECOME KING, I CAN PAINT THE SANDS ALL AROUND THE WHITE KING-DOM. AND DON'T FORGET THE LAVENDERS OR THE LASTING-SPELL TO PRESERVE THE PICTURES."

THE WITCH TAMARELLIA LOOKED AT THE YOUNG PRINCE JAMEISON AND HER FACE BROKE INTO A SMILE, ONLY IT WASN'T A CRAGGY, WITCHY SMILE. IT WAS A BEATIFIC SMILE THAT LIT UP HER FACE MAKING HER BEAUTIFUL. WELL, AS BEAUTIFUL, AS AN OLD, CRAGGY, BIG-NOSED WITCH CAN BE.

[She's gonna help him. That's a nice ending.]

[But it isn't quite the end, Cindra. There's a little bit more.]